Devil's Seed

LOUISE FURLEY

Devil's Seed

ISBN- 978-1-7363452-2-1 (Paperback)
ISBN- 978-1-7363452-1-4 (eBook)

Cover design by Pixel Mischief Design

DEVIL'S
SEED

Dedicated always to my biggest supporter, Bob.

Chapter One

On the heels of the fleeing kidnapper, Kesindra Jasmari's stomach clenched in mortal fear that she'd lose him and the victim would die.

The suspect's shoes clacking furiously over stone and blacktop diminished as he moved further from her, out of sight into deeper darkness.

She could still hear him splashing in puddles, kicking and stomping on garbage as he raced down the alley. Alarm that she was losing him clogged in her throat, drawing a deep breath past her pounding heart was impossible.

A brand-spanking-new agent in the city of Ships Bay, near Boston, her confidence flagged, she wasn't sure what to do. The Glock 19 heavy and awkward in her small hand, it was not the subcompact she had trained with. Even then, she'd only had a few days of target practice.

"Just buck up, Kesi," she scolded herself, trying to peer through the dimness.

No longer able to hear his footsteps, her pace faltered.

Other than rusty pipes dripping plop-plops on the scummy broken-up blacktop and her panting, it was bone dead silent.

Slowing to a cautious walk, her head tilted listening for any sound to indicate where he went. *Where the heck was the rest of her team?*

Carswell was to stay back, and Richard, Jersey and Chris were to close off the exit to the alley. They had been instructed to only keep furtive eyes on the kidnapper, but Jersey had stared at him too long and the kidnapper made them as agents and fled.

Creeping to the end of the alley, she stood beside the dumpster, her held breath whooshed out. Darn, the alley didn't end as Richard had thought. He had read the map wrong, there were more corridors, more dark squalid corners for the kidnapper to-

She never heard him as he dropped from the dumpster on top of her, slamming her down flat onto the asphalt.

The wind snapped out of Kesi as she crashed on her stomach- the gun flew out of her hand and she was suddenly in a fight for her life. Skin scraping and gouging, she scrambled on her belly for her weapon, but his weight held her back.

"Oh no you don't, bitch," he snarled in her ear, "you're done." Heaving bear grunts and vile curses ground from him as he wrestled her to keep her down. Yet small and slender, Kesi was able to squirm out from under him.

Spotting the Glock, she tried to make for it. He grabbed her around her knees, jerked hard, and she crashed again on the hard jagged blacktop.

"Bitch, you ain't goin' nowhere!" he yelled.

Before she could put her hands up in defense, the man started pounding on her. He punched her in the side, in her head, ruthlessly pummeled his big fists like sledgehammers all over her body.

Literally hearing the crack of her bones breaking Kesi screamed for help. Darkness rapidly enveloped her, pulling her under from the vicious beating, the agonizing pain blinding, then she caught sight of her gun again.

With her last bit of strength, she kneed him in the balls and when he cried out and folded double, she scrabbled forward on her belly. Her destroyed arms too fractured to hold her up, she still went for the gun.

But, gagging and groaning, he limped over, jumped on her again and grabbed her arm to hold her from reaching the gun.

Jerking her arm back, he broke her shoulder and snatched the gun himself, her scream of agony withered to a pained hoarse gasp.

A voice nearby yelled, "Don't move or I'll shoot!"

Kesi fought to stay conscious. Thank God, Carswell Cartwright was in the alley with his gun drawn.

Unfortunately, Carswell was as green and inexperienced as Kesi. His gun wavered all over the place, his boyish face sweaty and strained with fear.

"Okay, all right, I give up," the perp huffed. Straddling Kesi, he raised one hand in surrender.

Carswell commanded, "Uh, okay, don't try anything funny, get on your feet dirtbag with your hands in the-"

Bang!

The perp rolled while shooting Kesi's gun. A red dot exploded between Carswell's stunned eyes, then he crumpled to the gritty ground.

"*Nooo*," Kesi cried, her shattered arms flailing uselessly at the killer.

He staggered to his feet with a sneering smirk. "You think to capture me you dumb bitch? Last mistake you will ever make," and he fired at her as she rolled trying to elude the bullet.

Feeling the hot steel slam into her, Kesi heard more gunfire. The kidnapper screamed.

Kesi thought, *good, got him*, then she felt the hot lick of fire as she went under, crashing into the black.

Chapter Two

A hand from the grave, the kidnap victim's fingers burrowed up through the cracked pavement.

Skeleton of splintered bone, grey shreds of skin and tissue and ligaments clinging to it, blood dripped from the ghastly hand as it reached to grab her leg.

"No!" she screamed thrashing, trying to get away from it. But it clutched at her, scraping gnarled cadaver fingernails over her already skinned flesh.

"Wake up, Jasmari! Wake up, Agent!"

The voice kept shouting until Kesi managed to crack her sore lids open.

It wasn't the poor victim, mother of two tiny children; it was her FBI senior agent in charge, SAC Keith Dukes.

"Ah, ah, Jasmari, back from the dead." Sounding more annoyed than concerned, the agent sniffed with mild condescension.

She struggled to sit up but couldn't make her limbs move. The pain knifing everywhere through her body, unbearable agony, tears sprung.

The dry words barely a whisper in her parched throat, she asked, "Sir, what…happened?"

The fortyish agent plopped down in a chair beside the bed. "What happened? I'll tell you what happened. I sent the most green, useless, sorriest excuses for agents I've ever had the misfortune to be in charge of, to be a tiny part of a vital mission. Simple. So fucking simple."

He shifted in his seat and glared at her.

"You observe the kidnapper until senior agents come and follow him, he leads us to the victim, and," he snapped his fingers, "voila. We rescue said victim and lock up the sick perp for the rest of his miserable stinking life."

Trying to gather moisture in her scratchy throat, Kesi uttered, "But, I remember, uh," her mind blanked. Then, "Carswell, is he-"

The look on Dukes' grim face told her. She really had seen the agent die in front of her eyes.

"Yeah." The senior agent nodded regretfully. "Carswell didn't make it. You barely did." He dragged his fingers through short trimmed dark hair, then pulled at his rigid lips.

His long face all sharp angles and hollows under his cheekbones, his nose strong but not as jagged as the rest of his features, it evened out the elongated jaw.

With a sniff, eyes like brown pebbles regarded her with mild dispassion.

"But, I don't understand," Kesi mumbled, her brain beat against her skull, the pain struck with grinding jabs, her head vibrated from the ceaseless pounding.

In full sarcastic mode, he replied, "Again, what happened was, when we located the kidnapper, you fucking inept agents were sent in to only watch him, not arrest, not chase, not kill him, just fucking watch him, keep him in sight." He glared at her as she lay immobile from her numerous, life-threatening injuries.

Hawking out an aggravated breath, he went on with his rebuke, "Let the seasoned team come in and take him down after we find where he stashed the victim. But no, you comedy gang of misfits decide to chase him down, against orders."

Blurry pictures straggled through her bruised brain. Sucking in a dry breath, she responded weakly, "But, we, he made Jersey and ran. Chris, our team leader said we needed follow him. I…" she took another gasping breath, licked her dry lips, her forehead winced in creases with the pain.

Coughing through the agony, she went on, "I stayed after him. Richard said they would block the exit, that we would, catch him, and…" her wheezing breath scraped at her lungs inflamed with thick fluid.

Sitting back, Dukes crossed an ankle over a knee and regarded her with unveiled contempt. Running fingers down his tie to straighten it, he said, "And, you idiots, Richard read the map wrong, there was no end of that wing of that alley corridor."

Her eyes clenched with physical pain, the mental pain was only just beginning. "I…remember, branches, there were other corridors."

"Yeah. To make matters worse, Chris led the rest of your bumbling team over to a passageway to wait in ambush. But stupid dolts, they weren't at the correct alley you were in. Carswell followed your screams. Apparently, when he tried to arrest the kidnapper, he waffled and the suspect shot and killed him."

7

Rubbing his angled jaw with a few knobby fingers, his voice softened slightly, he said, "Then, after he had already almost beat you to death, the suspect shot you. His first shot missed." He paused, shifted with some awkwardness.

Clearing his throat noisily he went on, "His second bullet caught you in the head. Ah," he cleared his throat again. "There was a can of spilled kerosene in the alley, the first bullet set off a fire, you were, ah, burned somewhat before the others could get to you."

His expression showed some sympathy. "Fortunately the docs were able to extricate the bullet from your noggin and they claim it hadn't hit anything dire, you should expect a full recovery. One shining thing at least. Eh?"

But Carswell was dead. He had family. Oh God. Her mind was swimming with stinging agony, dread and loss. Licking her dehydrated lips, she whispered, "The- the victim, did we save-"

He shook his head. "No. The rest of the bumbling team raced in with reckless abandon and shot the kidnapper dead. He'd had his hands up in surrender but they panicked. We found Mia Collins a week later in the trunk of the car he had stolen."

"Oh my heavens," she cried, tears of sorrow falling. Voice a wounded rasp, she questioned, "A week? How long have I been here?"

He got up and paced to the window, combed the tips of his fingers in irritation through his hair.

Turning back to her with a frown, he replied, "You were critically injured. It was touch and go for a few weeks. We looked for family to call, but couldn't find any on record."

Tears eked out the corners of her scrunched eyes. "I have no one."

"Yeah, we found that out. Anyway, you've been here in mostly a coma for about six weeks."

Her lids flew up so fast it hurt. "Six weeks? Oh…" Her head spun, her apartment, what happened when she hadn't paid the rent?

Gaze flitting to him, her voice weak, strained, barely a raspy whisper, she asked, "Have I been on medical leave? Have I been drawing pay?"

"Really, Jasmari, after all this, that's all you have to ask, for fuck's sake?" Boomerang-shaped brows drew down. "No, you moron, you are too new. Hadn't even halfway completed the academy when we put you on this mission. You and the other misfits are only probationary agents."

His voice softened again at her look of despair, "We pulled you from the academy because we needed a person the perp wouldn't notice, a young-"

"Nondescript, plain female," she interjected with a sad sarcastic snort.

"Ah, well," sounding abashed, his long face colored somewhat. "I wouldn't go that far, but, yeah, pretty much. Hair always in a tight bun under a scarf, big bug-eyed glasses, baggy clothes, no one would look twice at you, you'd blend into the crowd."

It barely hurt her anymore. She'd always been told she was plain. "Plain as a wooden post," her mother used to say.

Her father would add, "Let's hope she has brains. She's too small and delicate boned to be any use physically, no sports scholarships for you, girlie."

Kesi had grown up home-schooled in an isolated farming commune. Both parents were killed in a flash flood. They had tried to cross a swollen river with cattle and all were swept away. She had no siblings and no other relatives.

Her parents hadn't owned the house they'd lived in, they only had the shirts off their backs. Mr. Thompson, the commune's appointed leader had told Kesi she was too small to do the hard work her parents did.

He had slyly advised her that she could work off her rent in another way, and he was very clear about her spreading her legs for him, or she could leave.

She had no job, no money for college, and therefore was unable to rent an apartment with no funds or credit to her name. She had tried to leave a few times, to get regular employment when her folks were alive, but they had begged her to stay with them.

Kesi could relieve them of the burden of taking care of the household, cooking, cleaning, maintaining the home and doing menial tasks for them, thereby leaving them free to do the farming heavy lifting.

With no options, after her parents died Kesi went straight into the FBI. She was a hardship case, they took her in without a college degree but with a contract that she would obtain her degree while working for them.

"Well," bending over her, Dukes said, "look on the bright side, you can't miss what you never had. You've never experienced the life of a beautiful woman, so," one shoulder rose in a 'so what' kind of a shrug, "it can't hurt as much now that you're disfig- uh-" he broke off awkwardly with a small cough.

"What? I have permanent damage?" The tears welled and ran over down her cheeks. She tried to raise a hand to touch her face but the pain was too intense just trying to raise her arm. All four limbs were in casts.

"Uh, well, the doctors have, uh, hope that, I mean they said the bones in your face would heal, but you would never look the same. At least all of your hair didn't burn off, since you have at least that one pretty, uh, element. Now that I've seen it loose. Uh..."

He stuck a finger under the knot of his tie and tugged at it, went on, "And of course, thank God, your eyes weren't damaged, the heat, they were afraid, I mean your glasses burnt over your eyes. They thought, you know, there was a chance of blindness..." he trailed off.

Then smiling, he said cheerfully, "They are a nice actually, um, an extraordinary color, kind of, uh, you know, amazingly sexy like, anyway," he rushed on, "now that they aren't hidden behind those ugly dark glasses you wear."

As her painful lids lowered, Kesi thought it was unusual everything wasn't a big blur like it normally was when she didn't wear her glasses. Must be the medication.

"So," she started, licking her lips, she was dying for a glass of water but she would never ask this stick-up-his-ass boss for anything. You would think he would see her distress and offer to help her.

Flopping back down on the chair, he crossed his legs and said coolly, "So, then, this is what happens next."

He waited until her lids rose slightly and her eyes slanted up at him. "The entire mission was one big clusterfuck. It gave the agency a big black eye. So, you, and the rest of the bungling team, are being sent to Původně."

"What?" Her mouth dropped with the question. "Where is that? I've never even heard of it?"

"Um, it's kind of a really tiny, third world country, it's pretty, uh, rural. Like jungle rural. The village is quite rustic, called," he pulled out his cell phone and leafed through his notes. "Brutální."

Blinking at him in bewilderment, she stuttered, "B- but, I don't understand. Why are we to be exiled to a foreign land, will we even understand the language?"

He looked slightly uncomfortable. "I think they speak English."

The senior agent leaned over her, frowning. "Like I said, you guys fucked the thing up so bad we need to get you out of the picture, way out of the picture. Maybe you can somehow redeem yourselves. If not, out of sight, out of mind, right?"

Confused and unnerved at his words, she made no response.

"Ah," he sighed. "Think of it as an extended vacation, well, a working vacation. You won't have to worry about the hustle and bustle of the busy dangerous streets here. Except, there have been alien sightings there. But," he shrugged, "that's to be expected out in the primordial jungle."

"Aliens? Are you serious?" Kesi drew a shallow wheezing breath. "I've only heard the occasional news report of them."

She closed her eyes trying to recall the information the authorities had given out regarding the intruders from outer space.

The reports indicated there was a truce of sorts between Earth and the extra-terrestrials. The aliens stating they were staying temporarily for observation.

To Kesi it sounded like they were visiting the zoo. When their curiosity was sated they would return to their own planet, or whatever they were from.

Hopefully they wouldn't desire to take any 'pets' home with them for entertainment or...further study. Like dissecting.

Darn, she was letting her crazy imagination get carried away. She has enough on her plate without worrying about aliens coming to abduct her and experiment on her.

The reports had also indicated the aliens were from the far future and considered earthlings to be quite rudimentary and backward.

They might even consider snatching a few humans to force them to do dangerous or dreadful, wearisome work for them.

Okay, Kesi thrust the frightening thoughts away. Her brain already hurt so much. She asked, "But- but, what would we do there?"

"Well, you would actually be acting sort of like police officers. You know, checking out petit thefts and shoplifting, stuff like that. However, there is some oddity going on out there, there've been vague reports of, well," his eyes flicked away from hers as he said, "entire towns disappearing."

"What? How can-"

"Anyway, you agents are really being sent out there to keep an eye out to look for anything suspicious. Might be some of those aliens fucking around. There have been two different species sighted. They may have some involvement in the disappearances. You and the rest of your misfit team, Christopher Carpenter, Richard Valsaint and Jersey Gerard, will go."

Kesi's anxious voice rose stridently. "But we aren't police officers, we are FBI agents-"

"Listen here, Jasmari, calm down." He leaned forward, glaring at her. "You fucked up, you guys need experience and need to get the hell out of the public eye, and the Bureau's. You just keep your eyes and ears open, take notes, do not, I repeat, do not engage and create another catastrophe."

Never knowing where to settle his hands, he smoothed his palms over his slacks, then forked the knobby fingers through his short dark hair. "It's for the best. All the way around. You'll see." He patted her arm not noticing her face crease in pain from his touch.

"At least you're alive, can't say as much for poor Carswell. You're lucky, you missed the funeral. Hell, it was long and boring and his young wife crying and carrying on, you-"

Speaking of pain, the intensity was creeping up, her entire body burned as if on fire. Kesi cried through the excruciating suffering, "Agent Dukes, please, God I can't bear it." She shrieked hoarsely, "Get the nurse!"

Quickly hopping to his feet, thankful to get out of there, he said with awkwardly cheerful reassurance, "Yeah, sure, you'll see, it will all be for the-"

The torment roared out of her throat into racking hoarse screams.

He scurried out as fast as he could.

Chapter Three

Eight months later

Stopping home for lunch, Kesi chewed a tasteless sandwich while standing in front of the yellowed, cracked mirror wondering why she never covered it. She seldom bothered to look into it and it only made her cringe when she did.

Before the incident, all she had seen were eyes too big like a cartoon character, hair so light blonde it was too light, almost white, and skin so fair it was boring. Her lips were plump but too tiny.

Her one friend had teased her calling her a philodendron because her face was so heart-shaped with wide high cheeks and a tiny chin.

It didn't matter, she told herself; she would just continue to hide her plainness under a hat, tinted glasses and loose clothes. The FBI wanted her because she was plain, nondescript and unnoticeable, she would keep that image the same.

Everything was still the same, but different. The local doctor had told her that her facial bones were almost completely healed. The burns were about healed too, but they hurt, her bones hurt, the gunshot hurt.

Her reflection was an ugly horrid blur to her. She couldn't see past the horror of what had happened. The deaths, the blood that was on her hands, her disfigurement. Kesi only saw the damage that had been done, she didn't see the healing.

She hadn't had much of an appetite since the mission had gone wrong and the months spent in the hospital. And now, her stomach churned at the endless guilt-ridden memories.

Losing what was left of her inclination to eat, she set the barely eaten sandwich down and picked up her bottle of pain meds off the old dresser. Shaking one out into her hand she swallowed it without water. It got easier after eight months of taking them.

She pushed the long curly hair back. Three quarters of it had burnt off around her face and partially down her back. The nurses had cut it raggedy below her shoulders, and she hadn't bothered with it since.

The back was long, the sides shorter because of what had burned, the locks twirled in a curly V down her back.

Her gaze lowered with an expelled sad sigh, she still hadn't gained back the weight she'd lost. She looked down in irritation at her breasts.

Her body was so thin it made her breasts look ridiculously bigger. Like they were swollen. She had to hide them with big loose clothes, making her even plainer, uglier, no man had given her a second look, which, she sighed, was fine, she had zero desire to be with anyone.

Kesi didn't deserve happiness when other innocent people were dead because of her.

Piling her hair up under a fedora she wore to hide the damage she imagined was still there, she slipped her cell and badge into her pocket, finished buttoning her khaki blouse leaving it loose over brown chinos, and slipped on worn ankle boots.

Her cell rang, she pulled it back out. It was spotty, but they did have some cell reception out there.

Picking up the heavily tinted, nonprescription glasses, she slid them on to hide her damaged face and said, "Kesi here."

"There's been a murder in this one-hock fucking town," Richard advised her. "Me and Chris and Jersey are busy, you need to check it out."

"A murder? I thought we were to only handle misdemeanors and stuff like that."

"Whatever. There isn't any other law out here but that fat lazy Dempsey. The other cops are out of town so that leaves us. You going or what?" he snapped impatiently.

"All right. Where is it?" Kesi was well aware the three male agents were *busy* playing poker.

She heard him tap on his phone to get the information. He said, "At, wait a sec."

He was quiet as he reviewed his notes, then said, "10 Palm Ave. That's, uh, down far end of Bernard Boulevard over by the grove-"

Somewhat testy she cut off Richard Valsaint, one of the co-agents exiled with her. "I know where it is, Richard, it's a small village."

"Kesi," he groused, "you don't have to be so fucking snippy, none of us wants to be here. Fucking hiring women for fuck's sake in the FBI. Shit," snarling his complaint, "you know, if you hadn't been so careless-"

Great. Still bombarded with her coworkers' sexist and misogynist attitudes and comments. And blame.

"It's 1:45, I'm leaving now." She clicked the phone off. Her fellow agents banished along with her all blamed her for the disaster the kidnapping mission had blown up into.

Ad nauseam, they told her if she had moved more cautiously, waited until the others realized their error of being at the wrong alley then none of the horror would have happened.

No one blamed their handler, Agent Dukes, who had sent them, a handful of dreadfully inexperienced agents after a murdering kidnapper.

Or Richard, who had read the map wrong, or Chris who was the one who said to chase the perp after Jersey had been made, instead of making a wide net to still keep him under observation.

Or Chris again who had led the men to the wrong alley, or Chris and Jersey and Richard who shot the felon without trying to capture him so the victim could be found and saved.

In their debriefing they had all stated the suspect had tried to fire the gun at them but it had jammed, and they had freaked out and shot him.

No, everyone, including the victim's family and Carswell's wife blamed her. But no one blamed her more than Kesi herself. She sighed wearily.

Grabbing the pill bottle, she shook out another one, popped it in her mouth and headed for the door.

She was happy actually to get out of the dreary little shack the landlord had called a house. It was a dilapidated box containing a tiny living room, kitchen, bathroom and tinier bedroom.

Dark and dingy, she had painted it pastel yellow to try to brighten it, put ruffled curtains over the dank windows, and scattered a bunch of plants around to green up the place.

It would take a lot more to make this cow's ear into a silk purse. Dukes had said they would be there indefinitely, she didn't know how much more work she should put into the place.

There were few vehicles to rent in the village. Her co-agents had arrived two weeks before Kesi was given medical release, and the three men had commandeered the only remaining jeeps for rent.

And, although they resided in a large house and were usually all together most of the time, none of the men would part with their vehicle and give one to Kesi.

Hence, Kesi was walking to the murder site.

The village was miniscule and rural. The majority of the residents worked the mines, farms, or the vegetable fields; the others serviced the few shops, small restaurants, the numerous seedy bars and a couple of grocery stores.

The ambulance techs and firefighters were all part timers. The only two doctors in town bickered more with each other than they provided any medical care.

The indigenous people were humble, simple, plain people with skin of dark olive, they worked hard for pretty

19

much nothing. The minute a child graduated from the rural school they ran off as fast as they could to the next nearest town, Milčent, 150 miles away and ten times bigger than Brutální.

Kesi could identify with the plain and humble aspects of the residents. She and the grumbling team had been there for two plus months.

Due to the Bureau's contempt of the agents, the men did not want to hang around and wait for her to heal so they could all be sent over together. They resented her for that, too. The most they got was a two-week head jump on her.

Because a week after they arrived they were bored to tears with the lack of real entertainment. The villagers worked long, hard days and had little left over for frivolities and fun.

As Kesi arrived at the murder scene the body was being hauled away. She went up to the paramedics who were wearing old jeans and T-shirts and held her hand up.

"Hold off," she flashed her badge. "Tim, Joey, you know me of course, Agent Jasmari. I'd like to look at the body before you take him."

"Sure, he's in no hurry," Tim joked. "Oswald Francks is only going to the coroner from here then to the interment deposit, so take your time. But remember, he will be smelling rank soon."

The other paramedic, Joey blatantly checked Kesi out. "Ya know, Jasmari, you need to wear clothes that can show a guy your shape, that loose crap you wear is for old fat ladies. Those glasses and hat are bad enough, whadya think?"

Kesi didn't respond. Tipping her glasses up, she lifted the sheet and peered down at the dead man. His skin was colorless, eyes closed. Blood had seeped through his white shirt right over his heart.

Laying the sheet back down over the deceased, she said to Joey, "Tell Gwanas as soon as she knows the make of gun to let me know." Of the two doctors in the town, Gwanas Pagano was the one who performed the rare autopsies needed.

"Sure thing," Joey replied with a jaunty salute and a wink. The two men pushed the gurney to the waiting medic van, the dead man's tubby belly jiggling under the sheet as the wheels crunched and rolled over the uneven gravel driveway.

Kesi walked around the small house. It was grey and could use a coat of paint. Several coats of paint.

She came to a door on the side of the kitchen that was open. Just inside, a pool of blood eddied over the tan colored tiled floor.

One of the town's few CSI's who was also a volunteer firefighter and a dental hygienist, was crouched beside the blood. She dipped a swab in it then tucked the swab in a plastic baggie. The friendly smile in the woman's dark face was broad as she looked up at Kesi.

"Hey, Agent Jasmari," she greeted her, "how's things doin'?"

"I'm good, Justine, and you?"

"Better than poor Mr. Francks," she said with a wry half smile.

"Yeah," Kesi nodded in commiseration. "Has Officer Dempsey been by?"

"Huh," Justine cut a dour snort. "Yeah, that fat ol' boy stopped by, spent two seconds writing notes. Didn't even look at the body, just blanched at the pool of blood and split."

"Hmm. So, what do we have?" Kesi asked.

21

Slipping the baggie into an open case, Justine wiped at her forehead and pushed back fuzzy tendrils that wisped around her round face with the back of a gloved hand.

"We think that apparently the victim answered this side door out of view of the street and the killer shot him point blank, he died instantly."

Pushing her hat back off her forehead, Kesi pulled out a notebook and pen from her pocket. She could make faster notes with ink than on her cell. "About what time do you estimate, Justine?"

The middle-aged woman glanced back out front where the body was being loaded into the medic van. "I'd say he was killed around 12:30 in the afternoon, 'bout an hour or so ago."

"Home for lunch maybe?"

"Nah," Janine said with a brief grin and shake of her brown ponytail. "They say he was injured in the mines and hasn't worked for months. Just, um, drinks beer and watches the telly."

Kesi glanced around. Other than Justine's rusted relic, there were no other cars in the driveway. There were no sounds emanating from the house, no one peered at them from around a corner. "Do you know where Mrs. Francks is? I assume she isn't in the house?"

"No. Luci Francks came by shortly after I arrived. I saw her get off the trans-bus right down there," she motioned with her head down the street. "She spoke briefly with the paramedics and scurried right off. Hasn't been back."

"Hmm. I suppose no one reported witnessing anything?" Kesi asked, making notes.

Shaking her head with a sarcastic smirk, the forensic tech replied, "Heavens no, we would be so lucky, huh?

Everyone around here works during the day, so there aren't many people at home at this time."

Kesi scanned up and down and then across the street. She only saw one other vehicle in the neighborhood and that was up on blocks.

Then she noticed next door a garage door was open and a car was visible inside. She asked the crime scene tech, "Anything else you can tell me?"

"Wish I did." Justine reached into her case for a black light to look for more blood.

"Okay, thanks." Kesi added to her notes that no witnesses had been reported then stuffed the pen and book in her pocket. "Let me know if you come up with anything."

She left to go around to the front door to avoid corrupting the direct crime scene.

"Will do," Janine called after her and bent back down to her work.

Cautiously, to make sure she didn't contaminate anything, Kesi pulled on paper booties and gloves and entered the house.

Removing her tinted glasses, she checked out the messy living room, two bedrooms, bathroom, and moved carefully past the kitchen where the murder had occurred.

There was a small family room or den, where a card table was set up and cards were tossed haphazardly on it not in formation of any kind of game. Scattered around the table and on the floor were articles of clothing.

Using her pen, Kesi lifted a few of them. Bras and panties. Different sized bras and underwear. She shook one, dust flittered off it. "Hmm, looks like Mr. Francks wasn't too injured to not enjoy the ladies. A variety of ladies. Good motive for the wife."

Pondering the clothes, she mused, "Perhaps Mrs. Francks came home early and caught Mr. Francks with his pants," the corner of her lips pulled in, "and everyone else's down. There were no witnesses noted, so maybe Mr. Francks heard her arriving and shooed the others out. Then, seeing the underwear left behind, Mrs. Francks shot her husband in a jealous rage."

Then again, Kesi told her herself, the CSI has said she was there when Mrs. Francks came home. And, it doesn't explain the dust. Darn, she really needed some witnesses to dig up.

She went back to the master bedroom and opened a few dresser drawers until she found the one that contained Luci Francks' underwear.

Gingerly, with her pen, she lifted a bra out and checked the size. It was the same size as one of the ones in the card-room, and the same style.

"Hmm," Kesi mused, "can you say ménage à trois? It appears that the wife was the third part of the triangle, or quadrangle judging by the other clothes in the living room."

Finding nothing else out of the ordinary, she removed the booties and gloves and tucked them in her pocket to dispose of later and went outside.

Sliding the glasses back on, she stood in the driveway and observed that the Francks weren't great with lawn maintenance either. The grass had grown past ankle length. Wandering around the house, she noticed the uncut grass was mushed near the side door to the kitchen but nowhere else.

Traipsing over to the flattened grass, she studied the area. It looked like someone had stood to the side of the door not visible from the window, to lie in wait.

A tall hedge lined halfway down the driveway blocked views from the neighbors. But Oswald Francks had opened the door anyway.

"Ouch-" Kesi jerked her arm back and looked down. She'd been pricked by a thorny bush. Red hives instantly sprung up.

Scratching her itchy arm, Kesi was leaving the house when she saw a neighbor out in her yard next door where she had noticed the car was, dressed in jeans and a flowery shirt, raking leaves. She strolled over to the woman.

"Hi," she said with a soft smile, prepared as always for the person's uncontrolled gasp of revulsion at Kesi's damaged appearance. But the woman smiled back.

Kesi introduced herself, "I'm Agent Kesindra Jasmari. I'm investigating the murder of your neighbor, there," she nodded to the grey house. "Oswald Francks."

Now the woman who appeared to be in her late thirties did regard her with an odd expression. "Seriously? You're just a child, dear, you can't possibly be a policewoman." She eyed Kesi with friendly doubt. She spoke English but with a heavy accent.

"Um, yes, well," Kesi replied, inelegantly pushing the slipping glasses back up her nose. "I am an FBI agent actually, not a police officer. May I ask your name?"

Still regarding her with mild disbelief, the woman answered, "I'm Malinda Maundoo. I live in that house," she pointed to the neatly trimmed, white house she was standing in front of.

"Uh huh. Nice to meet you, Ms. Maundoo. Do you mind if I ask you a couple of questions about the Francks?"

"You can call me Mali." She shrugged. "Sure, go ahead, but I didn't see anything or anyone. I arrived home just now from the store and saw the activity there and asked one of the fellas what had happened."

"Okay. Uh, Mali, can you tell me how you perceived the Francks as a couple? Did they seem to get along? Did you ever notice any fights or anything out of the ordinary?"

Mali's skin was a satiny, dark coffee colored. Long wild hair waved around her shoulders, her eyes were dark and cheerful. Leaning an arm on the rake, she laughed drily. "Oh yes, for sure. They fought all the time. About money, his laziness, and each constantly accused the other of cheating."

Kesi made a note, nodded, smiled politely up at Mali. "Have you ever seen them with anyone else?"

The wild dark waves swept the air with the shake of her head. "Nope. He sat around drinking beer all day long and she hung with her girlfriends. They were always over drinking tea or booze, playing cards or something."

Noting that, Kesi asked, "Can you think of anyone who would want to hurt Mr. Francks?"

"No. He was fairly harmless, just a useless lump of a drunk." She tilted her head to the side with a mild smile.

"What about Mrs. Francks? Do you think she was capable of…murdering her husband?"

Mali's head tipped to the side, her lids lowered as she considered the question. Then she shrugged. "I couldn't say. Luci's pretty, but mousy. Really, who could ever determine that kind of thing? People don't generally have 'I'm a killer' tattooed across their forehead, right? Anyway, her mother just moved back to the Caribbean, I really knew her better."

"Uh huh. What about strangers in the area? Have you noticed anyone acting suspicious? Unfamiliar cars driving by? Perhaps someone you've never seen before knocking on their door, peering in their windows? Things like that?"

She shook her head with a shoulder bump. "Nope. Nothing of the sort. This is a quiet, family type of neighborhood. I haven't even heard of a burglary or a purse snatching for years. Neighbors generally get along, we have street parties and things like that. The kids play in the street on the weekends. Crime is not that common in these parts."

"Would you happen to know of any of Mrs. Francks' friends? Women friends she might have played cards with?"

Mali's lips pursed as she shook her head. "There were two young women I saw a couple of times come around but I heard they'd moved back to the big city a few weeks ago. Otherwise, I try to keep my nose out of people's business, you know?"

"Okay, well, thanks for your time. I appreciate your help. If you think of anything," Kesi pulled out her notebook and pen and wrote her name and number down. Tearing the page out of the book, she handed it to her and said, "Please call me."

Accepting the paper, Mali's wide mouth broadened into a big friendly smile, she replied, "Of course. Have a nice day."

Kesi returned her smile and gave a little wave as she took off down the lane.

She trod up and down the streets knocking on doors. As Mali had said, there were not many people home, they were either at work or school.

The few that answered gave pretty much the same information as Mali had. No one saw anything untoward, and no one thought the young Mrs. Francks capable of cold-blooded murder.

Kesi decided to go to a few local places in the village and ask around about the Francks. Their house was near the main section of town so she was able to walk there in twenty minutes.

The village had been carved out of the tangled, dense snarl of jungle for the miners to have their homes close by. Farms had sprung up out of necessity for self-sustainment.

Beyond the meadows and crop fields, a web of never ending, thick, green tropical forests, surrounded the town.

Within the impenetrable bush, there were deadly bogs, along with hidden dangers like wild animals and illegal hunters, and steep mountains with undetectable cliffs.

The streets were part tar, part gravel, and part dirt, and partially bordered with intermittent chunks of cobblestone.

After leaving the third establishment, Kesi noted everyone said about the same thing. The couple bickered and fought like cats and dogs.

There were rumors of affairs but the people she questioned said they had heard that Oswald was impotent from some drug he had to take for his liver.

Still weak from her recovery, Kesi was growing weary, she needed to rest. She entered a tiny country shop filled with local fair, jams, pastries, canned goods.

A few people were hanging around the small luncheonette inside. Kesi ordered a soda.

Paying for the soda, she asked the cashier, "Do you know the Francks?"

"Oh yes, word travels like wildfire here. One of the paramedics, Joey stopped by for a cold beer after they dropped Mr. Francks at the morgue and he filled us in on the sad news."

The young woman nodded, her face fell. "Mr. Francks was a nice man. That's Mrs. Francks over there, the blonde. I feel so bad for her."

Kesi turned to see where the woman pointed.

Two women were sitting next to each other on stools at the lunch counter. Pots of tea and filled cups steamed in front of them. The blonde was the smaller of the two; Kesi assumed she was Luci Francks. Luci was smiling and giggling with the woman next to her.

They were sitting very close to one another. The other woman had short dark hair and was much heavier and larger than Luci.

"They look quite, um, chummy. Who's the woman with her?" Kesi asked the cashier.

A sly smile turned the woman's lips up. Leaning in, she conspiratorially, "That's Pilar Gomez. The word is," she leaned over further and whispered, "Luci Francks and Pilar are...involved. You know what I mean?"

"Hmm." Kesi surreptitiously watched the two women. It was odd that Mrs. Francks wasn't at the police station or the morgue. Or home.

"Can you tell me anything about them? Like, was Mr. Francks friends with Pilar too?" She took out her notepad and pen and wrote down *Pilar Gomez*.

The woman smothered a laugh with her hand and a shake of her head. "Oh no. He never went out and Luci and Pilar are always out at the bars except when they have other girls over to the house to play cards. They fight a lot, but still stay real close."

Warming up to her gossip, she went on cheerfully, "Pilar is one tough, angry woman. She curses like a longshoreman, barks at anyone that comes near her. Except of course Luci. Pilar does lawn work. I think that's how they met. The general gossip says that Luci was visiting a friend and Pilar was there cutting grass or whatever and they hit it off."

"I see, thanks." Taking her soda, Kesi strolled over to the two women cocooned in their own little world.

"Hi there," she greeted them taking off her glasses; it was darker inside the building.

Luci looked up with a dazed smile.

Pilar scowled at Kesi, her gaze taking a quick trip down her body and back up.

"I'm Kesi Jasmari, an agent with the FBI. I am investigating your husband's murder, Mrs. Francks." Both women were now scowling.

"Can I ask you a few questions?" Setting her soda on the counter Kesi held her notebook and pen in her hand.

Mouth mutinous and shut, Luci Francks glanced quickly at Pilar then glared at Kesi.

Taking that as a yes, Kesi asked, "Mrs. Francks, can you tell me where you were all day today?" Keeping a polite smile pasted on, she regarded the woman.

Luci Francks was petite with short blond hair and big brown eyes.

Shooting a quick nervous glance at Pilar before she spoke, Luci's eyes lowered. "I guess."

Another glance at Pilar before she looked at Kesi, Luci answered, "I was out of town visiting my sister. I took the bus. Just got back and saw the emergency people at my house. They told me what happened. I, uh, was quite upset of course, so I, uh, came here to uh, get some support from my friend Pilar, here and, well," she frowned, then became more confident, pulled her chest up.

She announced firmly, "You can check the bus records. I only arrived barely thirty or forty minutes or so ago."

"Uh huh." Kesi made notes then turned her attention to Pilar Gomez. "Ms. Gomez, how about you, where were you in the last two hours?"

Scowling darkly, Pilar stuffed a few fingers into the front of her short dark hair and pushed it back. "I work," she snapped, "some of us have to make a living you know." Her high cheekbones sharpened.

"Of course." Kesi smiled with her mild reply, then asked, "What do you do?"

Proudly, Pilar told her, "Lawn service. I work for Mel's Mows."

Pilar watched Kesi taking notes, she said quickly, "We aren't hired for the Francks' neighborhood. We only do the ones that can afford to have their lawns done." She sniffed and ran a knuckle under her nose.

"My super can verify that I was not near the premises, and that I never left work today until I got a call a few minutes ago from Luci and I came right here to be with her, poor thing." She patted Luci's hand, then kept ahold of it while they looked into each other's eyes.

"Uh huh." The polite smile still plastered on, Kesi repeated Pilar's words as she wrote them, "You don't work in the neighborhood. Did you leave your work site at all today?"

"Ah, no," Pilar denied. "I had a sandwich. The fellas like the hot sun but I prefer the shade, so I hung around the other side of the house we were working at and took my break under a big shade tree."

Kesi asked, "When was the last time you were at the Francks' house?"

Pilar's dark eyes froze, then shifted as she thought. Clearing her voice, she replied, "Because Luci's been out of town, I haven't been near her house in a week or so."

Kesi switched back to Luci. "I see. Mrs. Francks, do you have any idea who would want to kill your husband?"

Lids lowered over the big brown eyes, Luci peeked at Pilar then shook her head. "No, of course not. Ozzie is, uh, was, well, harmless. Useless. A drunk who never moved his ass out of his chair in front of the tube all day."

Kesi jotted down a few notes. She looked up at Luci and asked, "Have you noticed any strangers lurking in your neighborhood lately, anyone who didn't belong? Anyone acting suspicious? Anything unusual going on?"

At Luci's shaking head she went on, "Has anyone threatened you or your husband? Did he have trouble with anyone, at home or at the mine when he was working? Barroom brawls? Arguing with his friends?"

Luci's shoulders rose in a bored shrug. "No. Nothing. It was probably just a- a robbery gone bad, you know? I guess the burglar thought no one was home and was surprised Ozzie was there and killed him out of panic." She glanced at Pilar who was nodding her head and smiling at Luci.

Kesi's gaze flicked from one woman to the other and back. "Okay, well, thanks ladies, I appreciate your cooperation. If you think of anything," she wrote her number down twice on two pieces of notepaper then tore off them off and handed one to each woman. "Please give me a call."

It embarrassed Kesi that the FBI did not provide her with business cards, and she'd been sent so soon after leaving the hospital she hadn't thought of it herself to have any made.

When Pilar held her hand out to take the number, Kesi noticed a rash on her arm, in the same place as Kesi's.

"You look like you had a reaction to something, Ms. Gomez," she commented.

Pilar frowned at her arm. "Yeah, I guess I ate something today I was allergic to or got into some kind of poison ivy at work. Whatever, it stopped itching."

Taking out her cell, Kesi pretended to take more notes on it but took a picture of the rash. Her smile ever polite and professional, she nodded and said, "That's good, well, see you around. Please don't hesitate to call me if you think of anything."

She spoke to a few more patrons then not taking the rest break she needed, left the shop and started back down the lane she came from.

Using her cell, she looked up the phone listings for the town, then she called the bus station and asked for the supervisor. The supervisor was in the bigger town, Milčent, 150 miles away where Luci had gone for her visit.

While she waited, the supervisor reviewed receipts and spoke with the driver who was on his way back. The supervisor was able to confirm Luci's alibi.

Jotting down a note, Kesi then called Mel of Mel's Mows.

"Yeah," Mel snarled into the phone, "we were working a few streets over from that neighborhood. The guys came back grousing that the bitch had taken a really long lunch hour and left the harder work cultivating the fields for them to do."

"Ms. Gomez indicated to me that she stayed under a big tree near the house for her lunch hour."

"Ha," Mel snorted. "They were working clearing a crop field, honey, there ain't no houses or big trees anywhere near the area. Unless she drove about a half a mile away to the residential area."

Thanking him, Kesi returned to the Francks' house and took a picture of the bush that scratched her.

After another quickly glance around to see if she missed anything, she wearily trod down the street and a mile away to the vegetable and seed nursery. Once there, she showed the picture of the bush to the owner.

Denim overalls covered a big belly and flannel shirt. Sweat dripped from his pudgy face. "Yeah, sure, that's a blooming thrush bush. It's an exotic, not local at all. Someone had to have brought it in from the tropics."

His bottom lip pushed out as he said, "I'm surprised it survived the cold winters but it looks like a young shrub, maybe it hasn't been through winter yet. Gotta be the only one in town."

He grinned showing one tooth. "It does have some nasty thorns though. If you get scratched you'll instantly get a rash that lasts for about a day."

Before going home, Kesi stopped by the local judge who was also the mailman. He presided mostly in Milčent and brought mail once a month to Brutálni. Fortunately he was in town today delivering mail.

Kesi got a warrant signed for Pilar Gomez.

Pilar and the deceased's wife were in a relationship, and the day of the murder she'd had an unusually long lunch hour where she didn't account honestly of her whereabouts. She'd told Kesi she stayed on site and had a sandwich, which her supervisor disputed.

Pilar's proximity to the crime scene gave her sufficient time to commit the murder and return to work. Additional to her and Luci's alleged affair giving her motive, Pilar had lied about being near the scene as she had the same rash as Kesi did from the rare thrush bush near the Francks' door.

An hour later, tossing down two pain pills, Kesi stood outside Pilar's house while Dalton Dempsey, one of the few policemen the town had, searched Pilar's home. It didn't take long before the officer came out grinning.

"Hey Miss Kesi," Officer Dempsey said cheerfully, "you called it." The thirtyish man wore a khaki shirt with a badge pinned to it. The shirt was pulled over his big stomach and tucked into worn blue jeans.

He held up two bags. One contained a blouse covered with blood spatter he'd found stashed in a hamper, the other contained a gun that he'd sniffed and announced it had been recently fired.

"We have to send the evidence to Milčent, but as soon as we get a ballistic match I'll arrest Pilar Gomez and probably Luci Francks too. We'll have to wait on the DNA on the blood to be sent out before full confirmation, and match prints on the gun, but, I'd say we got 'em."

Kesi kept her expression firm, but inside she was doing a happy dance.

"Dumb as a box of rocks, that Pilar, keeping the blouse and weapon, eh? I showed up within minutes of the report coming in of a gunshot. Pilar must not have had time to dispose of the evidence. Good job, girl!" He praised Kesi with a jowly grin.

Kesi dragged her weary feet home, only pulled off her jeans before falling into bed.

Chapter Four

Kesi didn't really take any days off. The busier she was the less time she had to think. The thing was, the town was so small, so rural, other than the Francks' murder, nothing so much as a bar fight happened.

She hadn't seen any aliens either. Of course she took all that stuff in with a grain of salt until she actually saw one herself.

A shiver of fright rolled across her slender shoulders at the thought. It gave her the heebie jeebies to think about coming in contact with the aliens. She'd probably faint dead away right on the spot. The entire idea terrified the hell out of her.

The day was bright with sun and a smooth breeze. She wore a ball cap with her hair tucked up inside, and it thankfully blocked some of the glare of the sun.

Tired of walking around, she was sitting on a bench near a splotch of mown green grass designated a park.

Through her tinted glasses, she saw a woman in her early twenties with five children between the ages of 2-3. Hearing them call her Miss Gina, Kesi assumed she was babysitting while their parents either worked the mines or the fields.

Sitting on the ground a distance from the toddlers, Miss Gina was looking at her phone, she hadn't once glanced at the children.

Taking the needed break from her continual canvassing of the town, Kesi idly watched the children play.

Several dilapidated sheds bordered one side of the park. Kesi noticed someone had left a bunch of tools lying around, they would be dangerous for the children. She would speak to someone about-

The banging spatter of gunfire and people shouting broke the tranquil day!

A woman ran across the grass screaming, "We are under attack! Run for your lives!" and she disappeared down the lane.

With a squeal of fright, the babysitter hopped up and without pause ran out of the park, leaving the children.

A man appeared from a line of trees.

Not sure what to do, Kesi jumped to her feet, her heart racing she warily regarded him.

He was not a local, they tended to be of average height and weight. He was definitely not indigenous as he was huge and heavily muscled.

He wore cargo pants and a camo shirt, and, Kesi's yellow brows arched to her hairline, he was eyeing the children. Then he smiled at her, and he had...fangs.

Oh no! The alarm struck her fast, this must be one of the varieties of aliens that were reported to be visiting Earth. The newscasters reported that they were harmless, but, her brows drew down, this male looked anything but harmless.

Black tousled hair, flinty dark eyes glowered from under a heavy bridged brow. Thick, well-formed lips in a slashing curve warned of violence, and he was coming straight at her with a harsh sneer on his fierce face.

The children were between the man and Kesi. She shouted, "Don't come any closer!"

A leering grin scarred his face, and he kept taking huge, lumbering, threatening steps towards her.

Glancing about frantically for a weapon, Kesi had not been given a gun when sent to Původně. Noticing a rusty machete lying on the ground with other tools by one of the sheds, she made a dash for it.

Grabbing it up, she ran over placing herself between him and the children. She shouted to the evil looking man, "I said stop, go away, leave us alone!"

The coiled grin sharpened on the enormous man's rough face as he studied Kesi's face and figure. He laughed outright at her attempt to wave the machete at him. His voice deep and oily, he said, "Aren't you a sweet little morsel."

As he spoke, he let his gaze travel over the children that Kesi was trying to gather behind her like loose ducklings. "So are the babies. I like babies, they're tender and tasty and can be gobbled up in one gulp. Like sliders."

His tongue slathered his thick lips, and he came closer. "You need to lose the hat and those tinted glasses so I can get a better look at you, human."

Waving the machete at him, she declared, "I am with the FBI! I am giving you a- an order, step back, move away, right now or- or-"

"Or what, sweetness? You'll arrest me? For what? I haven't wolfed down a child yet, or," his eyes snaked down her with a leer, "taken possession of that fine little body of yours. I'll tell you, once I do, you won't want to arrest me, you'll want more, of this," he palmed his crotch still leering, and moving closer.

"No! Stop!" Kesi frantically slashed the machete at him, but he just roared with laughter. He had to be well over 6'5" of rocky muscles.

"Sweetness, I'm hardly afraid of a slip of a girl waving a toothpick at me. C'mere, after I taste you I'm going to fuck you into tomorrow." Teasing her- he lunged at her then backed away and lunged again, grinning at her gasping shrieks.

"Come on woman, give it up and lie on the ground like a good fucking bitch and spread 'em. I'll show you what human broads are good for."

Pushing at the children with one hand, trying to keep them gathered behind her and brandishing the machete with the other, she shouted, "You are an animal talking like that in front of the children! Take your filthy mouth and go away now!"

She feared he could hear her heart hammering, beating right out of her chest. As bold as her words were, Kesi could hear the petrified tremors in her voice.

He lunged for her again with a barking laugh.

Kesi jumped out of the way and screamed at the toddlers, "Run, children! Run and find mommy and daddy!" She couldn't keep the strident terror out of her voice and the children heard it, every one of them burst into tears and started wailing.

The man made another snatch at Kesi then growled angrily when she sidestepped his big hand. "All right, human bitch, I'm done playing, now c'mere-"

The humor gone, he started for her when a voice commanded from behind him, "Soldier, cease. Now."

The alien didn't look, but Kesi did, and blanched as her stomach flipped. She thought the man in front of her was terrifying, this other man was- a- beast.

Bigger than the rock attacking her, this one had lean muscle on top of bulked muscle, a severely hard face with bronzed skin and a shock of golden blond hair.

He wore the same cargo pants but had on a shirt that showed the muscles flexing beneath it. Tattoos scrawled the side of his neck, and his ears were pointed. Holy shades of Spock! But his eyes, death gleamed in the midnight green depths. Kesi felt the ground spinning under her.

Looking to the top of his head, her stomach lurched. There were horns, thick, like a ram's growing out of his yellow hair, the pointed tips curving towards his back.

Swallowing the nauseous fright that climbed up from her gullet to her throat, Kesi struggled to lift the heavy machete. Threatening both men with it, she ordered, "G- get away from us!" Damn, her voice was weak and shaking, she could barely spit the words out. "Both of you. I won't let you near the children!"

The two men shared a mocking look then turned back to her.

His voice heavy and harsh, the blond said, "Bruglon, take the children to their parents, I will deal with the female."

Bruglon's face pulled into an intractable scowl. "No. She's mine. I found her first. You take the fucking children, I'm taking her. Spoils of war."

The blond hissed, exposing fearsome fangs. "I gave you an order, soldier. You have one second to follow it or your body will be without a head." The horns on the top of his head swelled bigger. Claws unsheathed from his raised hands in clear threat.

Fangs! Horns! Claws! Kesi froze with terror.

Bruglon's skin paled, he muttered, "Fucker," and glared at Kesi.

The horned blond beast suddenly lurched to the side of Kesi.

She screamed and lashed at him with the machete- While she was turned, Bruglon swooped behind her and in one move scooped up all five children and started to leave with them.

"No! You can't take them!" Kesi screamed and tried to go after him, but the strapping blond stepped directly in front of her.

Her body trembled from head to foot but she held the machete up in warning. "Get out of my way or- or I will have to kill you!"

A slow amused smile curved up his harsh face before straightening into a menacing line. "Okay, *rostia tím,* little girl, give me the machete before I take it from you and use it on you."

"Stay back!" Kesi demanded waving the blade at him. It took all her strength to wield and keep the knife raised.

Ordering, "Set it on the ground and I won't hurt you," he advanced on her without a worry on his hard angled face.

"No, I told you, get away or I will- kill you, I swear-"

He moved so fast she didn't even see the blur. Pulling her back against his chest he had his hand wrapped around her wrist that held the machete and he forced her hand to hold the blade at her own neck.

His deep cold voice whispered in her ear, "I warned you, *rostia,*" his other arm curled around her waist hugging her spine to his chest.

It felt like she was pressing against a granite wall. He was so hard with rippling muscles and he held her so tightly she couldn't draw a strong breath. Kesi was afraid to swallow lest the lump in her throat get sliced by the knife.

He squeezed her wrist and demanded, "Drop it." She couldn't, she had a death grip on it and was too frozen with fear to unwind her fingers and let the machete go.

He squeezed harder, her wrist numbed; the knife fell from her loose fingers. "Good girl." His one arm still circling her waist holding her against him, he released her wrist and reached for her cap.

"Don't!" she yelped, tugging it down more firmly, pulling the front over her face.

"Why do you wear the hat and glasses?" He reached for the glasses but she ducked her head.

Kesi shouted, "Take your hands off me!" and tugged the hat down further. Her shaking voice rueful she said, "Don't worry, I am protecting your sensibilities." She added in a pained mutter, "I can't bear to look at me either."

His dark blond brows rose in puzzlement. "What the fuck does that mean?" When she didn't answer him, he snatched her hat off and shoved it in his pocket.

"No!" Kesi cried, her hands went to hold her hair up, but long blonde curls lighter than the lightest part of sun tumbled around her shoulders and down her back. She cringed that he would see the damaged tresses.

Keeping her between his powerful legs, heavy boots planted on the ground, he moved his big arm down the front of her to ensnare her thin arms. Holding them down trapped at her sides, he stuck his hand in her hair and clutched a handful. Rubbing the strands together, he lifted them and held them under his nose.

"Soft, everything on you is soft, and smells," he inhaled deeply, "plush." Rubbing a lock across his face he asked, "Why didn't you run to save your life? You had plenty of time before Bruglon got close. I could see through the trees."

Kesi glowered at him before the fear took back over. "You think I should have run away and left the children alone to die?" She twisted her body to break his hold but he ignored her struggles. "L- let go of me!" she stuttered, trying to take big calming breaths. It didn't help.

"Ah, but why should I let you go? You feel so damned good, human female." The man, or whatever he was, dropped her hair and wound both huge arms around her, hugging her to him.

Remembering the other man referring to her as a morsel, and gobbling the children, she whispered, "Are- you going to- to eat me?"

His immense chest rumbled with his chuckle. Squeezing her, his voice silky sultry he said near her ear, "Aye, I would sure like to. I'd love a taste of you right now."

On my God! Kesi struggled but he held her with arms like bands of steel. Gathering up her courage, she pushed through the terror of being held captive by a human-eating beast ten times more powerful than her, took a deep breath and said, "Listen, demon, I am an agent of the FBI, I order you to let me go!"

His laugh barked out, "Oh yeah? A wee *rostia* like you? Tell me another story little girl." He moved his hands to circle her waist.

Her back still crushed against his chest, she put her hands on his brawny forearms, trying to remove them, but couldn't get her fingers around the big limbs, she pushed at them but they didn't budge.

"Release me, immediately!" she ordered, pushing at him and twisting about trying to break loose.

"But I like the way you feel, *rostia*." He turned her around to face him and slid a huge hand behind her to spread against her back, with the other he plucked her glasses off and studied them.

"Give them back!" She grabbed at them but he lifted the glasses up so she couldn't reach them.

He held the lenses up to his eyes, frowned. "They are but clear glass. Why would you wear a hat on a warm day and glasses you don't need?" He stuffed the glasses in with the hat he'd put in his pocket.

"Hey! Stop it, you let go of me right now!" Fearing her clothes would be next to go Kesi pushed at his steel arms, and tried to kick him but he laughed at her futile efforts to get free.

"Honey, you must see that you will do nothing but what I let you, so stop struggling, you are using up your energy. Which I see," he tucked a thick finger under her chin and turned her head towards him, lifting it. "There are shadows under those exquisite eyes, you are already weary. You have been ill?"

Drawing a deep breath, her anger overriding her fear, she snapped testily, "That is none of your business. I insist you release me. Now."

"Ah, unfortunately, I must do as you ask. I am in the middle of a mission and have already dawdled too long with you my beautiful girl." He put his hands on her arms, then quickly patted down her entire body.

"How dare you!" Kesi shrieked at his hands roaming all over her body. She thrust from him, but he held her back with a laugh pulling out her badge and ID, and phone from her pockets.

Perusing them, his lips pulled in. "Well, I'll be damned, by Zeus, you are an agent. Shit. Your Earth is hiring children now to fight their battles?" He read out loud, "Agent Kesindra Jasmari."

Struggling vainly, she shouted, "Get your filthy hands off of me you- you monster!"

He thrust the badge and ID into her hands, shoved the phone into his pocket and kept patting her down. "Honey, as an officer, you must know I have to check you for weapons. I am wondering why an FBI agent has no gun? What's this?" He pulled her bottle of pills from her pocket and held them up.

"Hey! Those are mine! Give them back!" She reached for them but he held them over her head.

Brows knitted in a quizzical clutch, he read the label. Curiosity in his deep voice, he said, "These are serious pain pills. What would a young thing like you need with heavy duty pain pills?" He looked at her waiting for her to answer.

"Again," she glared at him and snapped, "none of your business. Now, give them back," she held her palm out for them.

His scrutinizing gaze traveled her pale face from her cyan eyes to the tiny plump lips. His jaw worked as he stared at her with her hand still out. Letting out an irritated sigh, he handed her the pills.

She grabbed them and held the bottle to her chest as if it contained diamonds. Holding her other hand out Kesi demanded, "Give me my phone."

"Nay." his hand twined around her arm he started walking. "All right, *rostia tím,* little girl, let's go."

Digging her heels in, she gasped, "What? Unhand me, I am not going anywhere with you." Was he going to cook her first, or just devour her in the bushes? Would he kill her before cutting her up, or just bite into her?

His chuckle a soft contradiction to his hard face, he said, "Honey, you have no choice. I have taken over this town, and that includes you. You will come with me. If you don't walk, I will toss you over my shoulder and take you that way. Which," one shoulder bumped, "I really would not mind. I can rest my hand on that plump little ass of yours. You can't see it through those ugly baggy clothes, but I sure as hell felt it during my frisk."

Shocked, trying to pull out of his grip Kesi parroted him, "You took over the town? What does that mean?"

His smiled hardened then went away. "You will see. Now, over my shoulder, or do you walk on your own?"

Kesi stared up at him. So big, tall, and strong as an ox, if his face wasn't a harsh slate of sharp cheeks, square jaw with stubble darker than his thick blond hair, strong nose, he would almost be handsome in a dangerous beastly kind of way.

His hooded eyes gave him such a lethal, predatory look they triggered a mess of shivers all over Kesi's small body.

If she was going to die, she wouldn't do it hunched over and crying. Gathering her dignity, with her nose in the air, she started walking to her slaughter, ignoring his quietly smug chuckle as he fell in beside her.

Chapter Five

Kesi had to hustle to keep up with the alien, his long legs moved quickly. He held her arm tightly, she feared if she slowed he would just drag her.

Her stunned eyes widened at the sight as they reached the center of the small town. There were long lines of people in front of the main rec hall they used for parties and events. It looked like every single resident was being herded by aliens into the rec hall.

Still holding her arm, the demon strode past the lines and brought Kesi inside the building.

Shocked, she looked around, then murmured, "Are you going to eat us all?"

Chuckling he replied, "Ah, I only have the desire to eat you, little one."

If possible, her face paled further, but she decided she'd be damned if she was going to go peacefully, she tried to wrench her arm free.

He said, "All right sweetheart," smirking at her scowl at his use of the endearment, "you go mingle with your neighbors while we finish gathering everyone. Needless to say, I do not have to tell you that you cannot leave this building. Please don't try, they will not allow you to exit." He positioned her to face the building and gave her a pat on the butt.

Furious, she swung around to chew him out, but he had already turned from her. Spotting her team, she crossed the crowded room to join them.

Richard, Jersey and Chris were huddled in a corner, mumbling together while observing the takeover of the town. Kesi saw another familiar face. A brunette female was standing next to Jersey.

When Kesi joined them, Richard said maliciously, "Boy you work quickly, Kesi, I didn't realize what a little slut you were."

Stunned, she reacted without thinking. "Oh!" she cried out and slapped him. "How dare you!"

She was unaware the outlander who had captured her saw her hit Richard. The horned alien's brows drew down and his lips pushed out, but he stayed up front with his men.

Rubbing his face, Richard whined, "You fucking hit me you bitch, you do that again and I'll fucking slug you back." He poked at his thin mustache to neaten it

"Don't you dare disrespect me, Richard Valsaint. I've taken a lot from you guys, but enough is enough," she admonished him.

"Geesh, Kesi, what are we to think when you come strolling in with that- that creature hanging all over you, I mean, you know." Jersey Gerard wiped the back of his hand across his sweating brow.

Skin of cinnamon, Jersey always dressed to the nines, even out in the jungle. His slacks pressed, white button-down, spiffed shoes, his hair in numerous braids tight to his scalp scrolled down the back of his head. With a strong build, he was a good-looking gay man.

Standing next to Jersey, his chocolate eyes rudely studying her, Chris Carpenter said, "You wear all that shit covering yourself up all the time, loose clothes, hats, glasses, who knew how attractive you became after the...damage done to your face. You've lost the hat and glasses, we can finally see what you look like. Now you need to change the homely clothes."

His gaze rolled down her figure. His smile smarmy, he commented, "Something nice and tight, low-cut, that'd make a big improvement, and we can view the goods."

Sure, busting her chops when they were all in terrible danger, Kesi frowned at the men.

She retorted, "The alien took my hat and glasses. I'm sorry you have to look at me now, but that is hardly important in the dire scheme of things. You're talking about my stupid looks when we are under the control of- of deadly supernatural beings."

Giving the female a quizzical look, Kesi inquired, "Arianna? What are you doing here?"

The young woman with medium brown hair almost to her waist smiled broadly at Kesi. She had perfectly round brown eyes she lined to give them more of a doe-eyed appearance. She was almost pretty, but not quite.

Her face was a bit too rectangle. Her top lip was a lot thinner than her fuller bottom one, and she had a way of looking at people like she was measuring them up, it made people uncomfortable.

And, she smiled all the time, *all the time* regardless of the situation. As if she had learned to do it and had never learned any other expression.

The smile never wavered as she answered, "Hey, Kesi, how are you doing? The boss sent me out here to see if I could be of help to you agents. He was so impressed with you solving that murder he thought there might be more going on here than meets the eye."

She shrugged a narrow shoulder. "He said perhaps you guys could use me to type up notes, do research, you know, admin stuff." The support staffer was around six or seven years older than Kesi.

"Uh," Kesi murmured, her return smile was awkward. "Okay, I guess." Rubbing her palms together, she said, "I guess we're all wondering what on earth is going on," she slid a side-glance to the demon huddled off to the side with his crew.

Not appearing in the least afraid, Arianna nodded emphatically with a grin. "Oh yes, it's really quite exciting don't you think?" The doe-eyes glowed as they traveled the room. Taking in the more handsome of the crowd of male soldiers, her gaze landed on the horned demon that had accosted Kesi. Her pupils flared, she licked her lips.

"I must say," she said with a heavy sigh, "they do make those exotics amazing. That big blond," her moan sounded like an orgasm, "damn he's hot. I wouldn't mind taking a go at him."

While Arianna was gawking at him, an extremely voluptuous woman with frozen blonde hair and golden brown eyes tripped over to stand next to the powerful alien male. Her blatant ogle was lewd and inviting, he ignored her.

"You have competition, hon," Jersey informed Arianna.

Arianna's smile diminished, but it was still there.

Kesi whispered harshly, "Okay, enough of this crap. It looks like these creatures have taken over the entire town, we need to do something!"

"Shh," Chris whispered. "You want them to hear you? We're better off if they don't know we're agents." He clawed his fingers nervously through the thick chestnut hair that waved over his head.

Chris Carpenter was an exceptionally good-looking man, and he knew it. He was usually successful when hitting on anything pretty in a skirt.

Appalled, Kesi remonstrated in a low voice, "Are you kidding? We are the only law enforcement here right now except for Dempsey who is less than useless. It is our job, our duty to do the best we can to protect the people. I mean," she cringed, "they said they were going to eat us."

Richard's already pasty skin turned to cloudy grey; his thin mouth dropped open lengthening his already long chin. Arrow-straight light brown hair slipped from its side part to cover one small round brown eye.

Nervously shoving the offending lock away, he scraped at his thin mustache and whined, "Are you freaking serious? We're going to be alien chow? Fuck me."

Jersey told them, "They already know we are agents, remember? They saw our badges and ID's, and took our cells and weapons."

Kesi resisted glaring at him mentioning that the men had been allowed to bring their firearms to the country but Kesi was not. Dukes told her she'd let the kidnapper get her gun and that caused the deaths of innocent people. He said that his superiors felt it was safer to not arm her.

Nodding, Richard added, "They took everyone's phones and weapons."

Arianna's eyes turned dreamy. "I wouldn't mind being eaten by the blond," she snickered, "if you know what I mean!" Her hands on cocked hips, with a coquette's smile, she peered at the foreign males over her shoulder, through a partial curtain of hair.

"Damn, aren't you the crass one," Richard sniped.

Jersey's lip curled at the brunette.

After the last human had been ushered inside, one of the aliens closed the double main doors to the building. Then he and some other creatures, including the one that had taken Kesi moved to the front of the room.

The blond terrestrial that had brought her there stood as if king of the realm until everyone quieted down.

"All right everyone, I will introduce myself." His deep voice dark and low, he told them, "I am Captain Martier Lucien Dravidian. As you can tell, I am not from the Earth."

He spoke over the murmurings flowing through the room, "This is what is happening; we have taken over this town, that means we are in charge. That means you all will do as we say or suffer unpleasant consequences."

Amongst the crowd's louder, anxious chattering, a brave soul called out, "Why have you done this?"

A small smile lifted the alien's full but hard mouth. "Ah, you do not need to know why we are doing this, only that you are to obey our directives without balking or attempting escape."

Another person asked with a trembling voice, "A- are you going to kill us?"

Dravidian shook his head with a crooked smile. "Not at the present time."

"What about…will we be eaten alive or will we be cooked first?" Someone with a strident, shaking voice spoke up.

The people next to him tried to shush him saying, "Shut up, don't put ideas into their heads."

He whispered back, "They already have an agenda, I wanna know what's gonna happen to me!" He looked cautiously to Dravidian, and with the fear heavy in his shaking voice, he asked, "Well? What are we to expect?"

The blond's midnight green eyes searched over the crowd until they landed with mirth on Kesi. He deliberately smiled at her, but said to the crowd, "Nay, we will not be eating you just now."

His gaze lingered on Kesi, apparently enjoying her uneasiness at the attention, and his amusement earlier at letting her believe he was going to eat her. He'd like to, just not with a knife and fork. He looked around the room and queried, "Any other questions?"

"Um," a man in farmer's clothing asked, "how long, uh, how long will we be...prisoners?"

The demon shrugged one huge shoulder. "I don't know." He glanced around but no one else had mustered up the nerve to ask anything else.

His humor suddenly shucked, he glanced around at the people with narrowed eyes, then he informed the crowd with all seriousness, "We have troops stationed completely around the perimeter of the town. You will be free to go about your business as usual. However, no one is allowed to go past the first line of trees that encircles the village.

"You may run your shops and bars, work the fields, the mines that are inside the perimeter, but you cannot leave the town. Is that clear?" He paused as people digested his words.

Planting his boots in a broad stance, he crossed his arms over the hulking chest and continued, "We have taken your phones and will disconnect the landlines and block satellite for computers. No one is to contact anyone outside of this town, especially law enforcement. Everyone is to attend to dinner here in this building every night so we can see that no one is attempting escape."

He paused, his face grim indicating he meant his directives. Then he said, "Does anyone have any questions?"

A murmur ran through the crowd, faces looked less anxious now that they were told they weren't to die, at least not right away.

They looked to one another. A few people nodded, no one asked another question. Their lives were safe, for the moment anyway. Unless the alien was lying. They could only wait and see.

Maybe they were all to be suddenly slaughtered, or taken away one-by-one to be disposed of. Only time will tell what their agenda is.

"Fine then, you are all free to leave and continue on as normal. Just remember, as I said, do not leave the perimeter or there will be grave repercussions." Dravidian's gaze returned to Kesi.

Seeing her discreetly take a pill, his jaw twitched. He started in her direction when a woman put her hand on his arm. His eyes fell to it, the green darkened with his frown.

"Sir, Captain," the woman with the hourglass figure with *big* emphasis on the chest and hips that had parked herself next to him, tipped her head up to catch his attention.

Tossing stiff blonde hair off her shoulders her grin sly and amber eyes inviting, she introduced herself, "I'm Tawny Chery." The lime green shift she wore clung tightly to her big curves and cut quite low in the front offering a generous view of her ample breasts.

Muttering, "Pleasure. If you will excuse me," keeping Kesi in his sights, she was nearing the exit, Martier Dravidian pushed Tawny's hand off his arm.

"Wait." She clutched at his burly arm again, aiming a pout up at him. "Honey, Martier Lucien," she purred his name with a low sexy drawl accentuating and drawing out the sounds of his name- *Mah-tee-aa Loo-see-ahn,* while rubbing her voluminous chest on his bulky arm.

"I've never seen your kind before. There are only a few of your species there amongst those soldiers. You," she murmured, rubbing so hard her breasts rolled, flopping obscenely back and forth over his big arm.

"I have heard about your kind though, warlords from the planet Nasitar. Rumored to be the most violent and vicious assassins, felon hunters, in the galaxy, and," the purr deepened, "in the bed."

She slid her hands up his buffed chest to link around his neck meshing their bodies. "Martier, with the long *a* sound for the tier- it sounds French, sexy, I like it. I would sure love a sample of that. Of you. What do you say we go to-"

His eyes still on Kesi, she happened to turn around and see the woman rubbing all over him, Tawny's lips seeking his.

Kesi made a face of disgust, turned with her little nose in the air and headed for the exit. Martier grabbed Tawny's arms and gave her a harsh shove.

"Hey," she squawked, stumbling backwards on steep heels.

"I like to do my own choosing, and I am very particular," Martier growled, and strode across the room. Before he reached the door, Kesi was already out.

Stepping out into the bright sunlight, Martier looked through the crowd milling around the grounds. Some were heading to their homes or businesses, but the majority wanted to hang around and talk about their bizarre seizure.

Kesi's brilliant blonde hair, the long curls a rival to the deepest, whitest center of the sun was easily noticeable. She walked with the three men and a woman she had been hanging with inside. Martier strode directly to her.

Richard saw him coming and every ounce of color shed from his long face. He mumbled, "Guys."

The others followed his train of vision and all stiffened with nerves at Martier's approach.

Except Arianna who smiled at him.

The others stood with wary, wide-eyes tracing the strange looking tattoo that curled on his neck.

"Agent Jasmari," the alien's voice, rough and deep caused the three male agents to take a step back. "I will speak with you."

Kesi's flaxen brows drew down. "Why?"

Not used to being questioned, his brows, a contrasting dark brown to his golden hair slashed down harder than hers. "I said I will speak with you. You others," he glanced dismissively at the other four as if they were bugs and announced, "may leave."

Arianna stared at the muscular man. Noticing his horns, she about drooled. Batting her doe eyes at him, arching her back to push her small breasts up high, she set her hands on thin hips and smiled with brazen invitation. "Hi there, I'm Arianna, I-"

Martier ignored her. "Kesindra, come," his directive icy, hard face implacable.

"Uh," Jersey coughed. His eyes twitching nervously back and forth, he said, "Maybe we should wait for Kesi-"

"Take off, *now*." Dravidian's threatening voice came from the cold depths of his powerful chest. The dark green eyes narrowed at the men.

Without looking again at Kesi, they left as quickly as they could. Arianna trailed reluctantly after them with continuous sexually inviting peeks back at Martier.

His gaze following them as they hurried away, Martier said with scorn to Kesi, "Those cowards are your fellow agents?"

Her eyes a light cyan blue, glared up at the big man with a rebuke, "It is not necessary to disparage them like that."

Lids levering down to hood his own enigmatic orbs, the edge of his mouth ticked up. "They would leave you alone with me, knowing I am a danger to you."

She blinked at his insinuation that he was dangerous to her then retorted with irritation, "You told them to leave, didn't you expect them to follow your orders, Mr. Demon Captain?" Her tone tinged with sarcasm.

Now his full, hard carved lips rose. "Ah, tis true, *rostia tím*, but if they were real men they would have insisted on staying with you, to protect you."

"Huh," she scoffed. "I do not need protecting, especially from men. From you."

"Hmm, I see. Why did you slap that one with the long face and thin mustache?"

Color flooded her round cheeks. She hesitated before answering. Then deciding to tell the truth, she said, "Because they saw you with me, touching my, um, you know, you smacked me on the butt. They assumed that you and I had…" her eyes lowered in embarrassment. "Richard called me a slut."

The angles of his stony cheeks sharpened, dark color rose up his neck. His jaw flexed but he didn't say anything.

Bringing him back to the subject, she asked, "Why did you want to speak to me?"

His gaze flicked down her body and back up. "You will tell me why you take those pills. I can see the haze in your eyes from them. Tis treacherous out here in this raw land, you should have all of your faculties alert. Tell me about them."

Surprise lifted her brows. Her lips parted then firmed, her eyes narrowed. "I've told you before, it is none of your business."

Hands clasped behind his back, legs spread shoulder-width, boots firm on the ground. His smile at her was not pleasant. "Kesindra, I do not like it when my questions are not answered. You-"

"You need to get over yourself, fire dweller." Kesi spun on her heel to leave; he snagged her arm holding her back.

A growl of jungle animal sounded from his depths, the green in his eyes darkened to almost black. "You will not walk away from me, Kesindra, until I give you leave to do so. You will answer my questions."

"Or what?" Scared, but also annoyed, Kesi stood her ground. "I am not one of your soldiers to command."

"Hmm." Letting go of her, he crossed his arms. The huge biceps flexed under his shirt, he cocked his head at her in contemplation.

"I am thinking you are in the frame of mind that you don't care if I harm you. I don't know why, but you do not, so," he sighed. "I will be forced to injure another if you fail to obey me and not answer my questions."

Her mouth dropped. "You're kidding!"

The stiff closed lips and hooded eyes indicated he was not jesting. Martier looked around the yard and settled on an elderly man. His lids lowered further but he said nothing, just stared at the old man.

Kesi got his point. The air slid out of her body in resignation. Lowering her shoulders, she said quietly, "I was…injured on the job. It was why we were banished to this…place," she waved her arm in a small arc.

"Injured in what respect? How?"

"Really, Captain, uh, sorry, I don't remember your name, how is this relevant to anything, and again, any of your business?"

The bronze in his face darkened further, eyes tapered at her. "Everything is my business. You don't need to question what I do or say, just respond. Now," his gaze drifted around her face, "tell me, how you were injured and why you were banished from your home." He took in the lines that suddenly pinched around her eyes, the tremor in her lips.

Seeing her lips thin and staying closed, he said casually, "When you are home later tonight, safe in your bed, remember when last you saw that man over there," he motioned with his head to the frail elderly man, "and he was still standing. Still breathing."

Her lips parted. Eyes lowered to the ground, she drew in a deep breath then told him, "I, we, bungled a mission. I was, uh, shot, beaten, burned a bit, and that's it." The shame in the words she uttered came through her reluctant answer.

"Specifics," he barked.

Her gaze flashed angrily back up to his tyrannical face. "For Pete's-" Seeing his jaw harden, Kesi sighed, and explained how the green agents botched the job causing the victim's and Carswell's death.

She rattled quickly the part regarding her own almost lethal beating and gunshot, the long recovery in the hospital and subsequent exiling to this country. Her voice dropped to a shamed murmur when she admitted it was all her fault.

He studied her miserable face for a moment. "You still feel pain? That is why you take the pills?"

Scowling at him for keeping this humiliation going, she snapped, "Yes. I have only just recovered. Well, mostly."

"I think you take the pills to shut off your mind, dulling your memory of the incident, and your guilt. Even as a weak, fragile human your pain should have receded by now."

"Why you-" Appalled at his nerve telling her what she should or shouldn't feel, calling her weak, she snapped, "I thought you were a- a warlord, not a psychiatrist. Thank you for your interest, but I do not need a shrink, or another boss." She pivoted and strode away.

Martier stared thoughtfully after her but let her go.

Chapter Six

*T*he next few days passed quietly, without incident. The aliens patrolled but didn't hassle the humans as they went about their daily business.

The weekend arrived and the residents were used to partying on the weekends, so they did.

People drank and danced on the crumbled asphalt and boogied along cobblestone streets. Tables were scattered up and down the few main avenues for resting and eating in between heavy drinking and wild dancing.

Music blared from speakers on rickety shops, everyone was cheerful and tipsy.

Kesi stood off to the side observing the scene. The dreary little town finally gave up some color. The residents dressed in bright clothes, laughing, singing, twirling in the boisterous street party.

Even the soldiers joined in. They mingled easily with the humans.

Martier and his close team, Trae, Slade, Jamir and Cisco stayed in the shadows. Sometimes observing, sometimes huddled in secretive conference. Most of the time, they weren't visible, letting the other alien soldiers guard the people.

Sighing silently in relief, at the moment Kesi didn't see the demon captain hovering around. She had felt his eyes on her every time they were in the same vicinity. Finally, he was nowhere in sight and it was her chance.

She had tried to convince the other agents to go with her, but they refused. Told her they weren't in any danger and why rock the boat. She was disgusted with the cowardly lot of them.

Oh well, quickly glancing around one more time for the demon, he was easy to spot. So tall, broad heavy shoulders, weird horns and the golden blond hair with contrasting dark brows and scruff, he stood out in the crowd, even amongst his own equally brawny men.

Not seeing the captain, Kesi slipped behind a row of buildings and hurried down the tarred alley that she could follow to the woods. She needed to get to Milčent and tell the authorities what was going on in Brutální.

Aliens had taken over the entire village for heaven's sake, and the residents seemed totally unconcerned about it. It was up to her to advise the law what was going on. Aliens just didn't take a town captive without a nefarious plan being afoot.

At the end of the alley, Kesi trod out onto flowing green grass. She strode briskly, but didn't run in case someone saw her; she would look suspicious if she was seen running for the woods.

Entering the cover of forest she let out her held breath, and now she ran. It was going to take well over a week or two or longer for her to get to Milčent, the next nearest town.

Keeping her head down, she arrowed her eyes a few feet ahead on the dirt trail so she didn't trip over rocks or hidden holes.

She didn't see the bulk that had stepped out a couple of yards in front of her until the last second.

Seeing the heavy boots planted on the dirt, Kesi let out a scream and almost fell trying to stop from running into him. Dread struck her hard- *Oh no, it's him!*

Surprisingly, he didn't look angry, in fact, he was almost smiling. "Kesindra, fancy meeting you out here, past the perimeter."

She said nothing, her hands hung at her sides with fists clenched, she held her panting breath. She was proud of herself that she didn't scream or shrink back when he walked towards her, huge, daunting, dangerously foreign.

The waning sun poked through the tree limbs lighting his hair making it look almost as light as hers.

Stopping a foot from her, he put his hands on his lean hips and shook his head. "I distinctly recall telling the entire town, that included you, that no one was allowed to go beyond the first line of trees. And yet, here we are," he glanced around mockingly. "You did not take me seriously, I see."

Her slightly pointed chin rose defiantly even though her body quaked from inside out. She said arrogantly, "You have no right to keep us prisoner. I refuse to abide by your...declarations. By the way," she said scathingly, "you sound like a foreign robot, your English needs modernizing. There's these things called contractions, it's weird if you only use some of them. Now, if you will excuse me, I will be on my way," lowering her head, she started to move around him.

His hand snapped out snagging her arm. Twining his long fingers around her thin arm, he said, "I think not, my small mutinous earthling." With no effort he pulled her to him, so close she had to tilt her head back to look up at him.

The dark green glittered ominously down at her, his full yet hard lips ticked up at one corner. "Please, do tell me what a wee bit of a girl is doing out here alone, heading away from the village?"

She considered lying to him, telling him she wandered off accidentally while following some animal or something, but seeing the smug look on his face, he probably already knew what she was up to.

"I was doing my job, Captain. I was, am, going to the nearest town to, uh, tell them about you, your men taking this entire village captive."

His hand wrapped around her arm, Martier's thumb brushed over her skin under the short-sleeved blouse she wore. With a slight glare of irritated disbelief, he said, "I see. I thought you had better sense than that, *rostia tím,* little girl, to venture into this jungle alone with no weapon, no food, no water. You are a fool."

Her small lips firmed in anger. "I couldn't take food with me, it would have drawn suspicion, and you have all the weapons secured, I had no choice. It is necessary for me to advise the authorities of your...kidnapping us." She tugged at her arm. "I am a grown woman, stop calling me 'little girl,' you are deliberately taunting me."

The side of his mouth turned up. "You acted stupidly, recklessly like a child, you would not have made it alive to Milčent. Wild hungry animals, unlawful smugglers, precarious cliffs and flooding waters all lie in wait ready to take your life."

"I am sturdier than you give me credit for. Now, release me, damn you." Kesi jerked her arm, but he held her limb easily like it was just a twig.

"Nay, *rostia tim*. I am in charge of this mission, and I give the orders. Everyone else follows them, including you."

Grasping both her upper arms, squeezing her slender flesh he practically pulled her up on her toes. "I was clear that there would be repercussions for anyone attempting to escape, was I not?"

Kesi forced herself to return his harsh gaze, clamped her mouth to hold in the trembles. Her shoulders bunched from him holding her up.

He held her so close to his face she could see a few dark gold hairs sparkling amongst the deep brown in the 5 o'clock scruff on his strong jaw. The odd green eyes striped with black fluctuated as he gazed back at her.

His scent, aftershave, interesting, aliens shaved? Mingled with the hint of...strong male. She had heard that the aliens were quite human looking with a few differences.

Kesi noticed this alien was even different from the others. He was the only one with horns. Of course there weren't any female aliens around that she had noticed, so she didn't know if the females had horns.

The other males he hung closely with had fangs and claws and slightly pointed ears like he had, but the soldier aliens with them did not. The soldiers were human appearing except they were much taller, bigger, more muscular with larger bones, a few did have fangs but most did not.

The heat of the captain's powerful body swarmed her, as did the tight-banded feel of his rough hands with long hard fingers that wound around her slim arms. So strong she feared he could snap her arms like pencils if he desired to.

"Ah, earthling agent, cat got your tongue? You had a lot to say a second ago."

The fear of what he could possible do to punish her, including torture, maiming, death, quivered over Kesi's heart-shaped face.

But she wasn't going down without a fight. She sharply jerked her knee up to kick him in the balls, she assumed he had them, but he laughed and turned his hips making her miss by a mile.

"I have been warring for... let us say a few centuries, and you, a young, inexperienced, *human female*, cannot harm me. I know your moves before you even think them." Her scowl at his intended insult only made him laugh more, exposing his fangs.

Stomach clenching at the sight of them, Kesi tried for bravado. "You- you arrogant- outlaw beast, get your hands off of me!" It was difficult to be commanding when the man outweighed, and out-powered her, and was holding her up on her toes.

Martier let her down on her feet, his smile exacting. "We will now see to your punishment, my order-disobeying, recklessly fleeing human."

Sudden terror struck her eyes, tears welled. Forcing them to not fall, Kesi asked quietly, "What are you...going to do to me?" Her head straight, she raised her eyes and saw the strange tattoo around the side of his neck. It looked foreign, foreboding, dangerous.

He regarded her thoughtfully. "Hmm, what to do to a haughty, flaunting, rebellious, rule breaking captive, too beautiful for her own good. Ah, let me see..."

A lascivious glint roved over her eyes and down to her lips, then lower still to her breasts where they lingered. "You cover up your lush curves so carefully, Agent Kesindra Jasmari, if I had not vaguely felt them I would not even know they were there."

Recalling his quick frisk of her, catching his drift, Kesi shuddered and tried to twist from his grasp. "You must let me go, Captain, anything you do to me will incur even greater sentencing for you when you are- are caught," her voice shook regardless of her efforts to steady it.

The dark brows rose. "I do?" He shook his head. "Nay, I don't think so. Hmm, aye, I believe the punishment for your first offense should not be so severe. You did not know the breadth of my...command. I will give you just this one allowance. But next time, I will be quite severe. Now, this is your punishment," he slid one hand to her back, the other to net the back of her head with his long fingers, and brought her face to his.

"A kiss, which you will participate in to avoid a more serious punishment." Martier let the words sink in before he slanted his head and lowered his mouth to cover hers.

Shocked, Kesi's lips didn't move.

Murmuring against them, he purred, "I said, you will participate, open your mouth and accept me, my pet, or suffer worse consequences."

He pressed his thumb in the hollow of cheek to force her mouth open. Licking her top lip, he nipped the bottom, then licked between them, and when she parted them to shout in outrage he thrust his tongue inside taking control of her mouth.

Martier tasted, licking, nipping her lips and sucking her tongue. Angling his head for a closer fit, the kiss heated, his hands tightened, pulling her taut against him.

Her soft curves pressing hard against his solid chest, her hands on his abdomen, Kesi could not stop herself from drowning in his forceful scalding passion.

Finding herself responding against her will, she suddenly had no control of her body- he drew her with him in the blazing, mind-blowing kiss until she felt the long thick length of his rigid erection pressing against her.

He may be a demon, but he was anatomically a man, and apparently with the same sexual arousal. She shoved away from him. Of course it didn't budge him an inch.

Lids almost completely covered the greens sodden in desire, just the tips of his pointy ears were red, Martier's lips were still parted from the kiss. Breaths heavy and deep, his gaze dropped to her breasts wedged against the iron slabs of his chest, and back up to her mouth.

"Ah, even more intoxicating, more fucking insanely hot than I had expected." Licking his lips, he moved his hands to grip her arms, his thumbs again brushing across her goose-bumped skin, and lowered his head to continue the kiss.

But, feeling her trying to move her hips away from the pressure of his heavy erection, he smiled. "Is my little human afraid of sex with me? You fear that once we do it you will not be able to exist without it?"

Her chin dropped, forehead furrowed in confused anger. "Why you conceited- let go of me, right now!"

Martier held her just to show her he could, then he loosened his hands so she could step from his embrace.

His gaze on her plump and reddened lips, he said glibly, "We will return to the village, Kesindra, and you will remember, if you attempt escape again, you will not get away. Many of my men saw you sneaking down the alley then fleeing into the forest. They only did not stop you because I instructed them not to. I wanted that pleasure for

68

myself. Now, any further escape attempts and your discipline will be quite severe. You understand?"

Kesi's mouth clamped, she refused to answer him.

His hand clutched her chin before she even saw it coming. He lifted it, his grip hard, the smile was gone. "I am not playing here, Kesindra, you will do as I say, and you will answer me when I ask you a question. Do you understand me?"

When she said nothing, his voice so quiet it was chilled, more menacing than if he'd shouted, he demanded, "You will answer me, now." The fingers on her chin tightened until they hurt.

Kesi gritted, "Yes, demon." Stifling her fear, she stared evenly at him, her lips pulled in.

Hearing the slight mock in her tone, he glared a moment at her, making sure she knew he was not joking, then he dropped his hand. Red marks from his fingers marred her fair skin drawing his brows down in a frown.

He brushed the pad of a fingertip over them. "You are quite delicate, little earthling, more so than most of the female humans I have…dealt with…" he trailed off with a smile at the anger that flickered in her blue eyes.

"Come, don't fight me, *rostia tím,* let us go on." He held a hand out to her, which she stuck her nose up at and stalked off back through the woods.

A grin and shake of his head, Martier traipsed after her then walked beside her back to town.

Chapter Seven

The next evening, as instructed, everyone in the village gathered in the rec building for dinner. The soldiers had chosen a few of the captives to prepare food for the masses utilizing the cooks from the restaurants and diners in town.

The villagers that were the rudest to the soldiers were told they would be handling the cleaning up.

When some of them complained, Martier or one of his direct team, Trae, Slade, Jamir or Cisco expressed their displeasure with a view of their descended fangs and a warning hiss. There weren't any complaints after that.

People came in shifts. Families with young children, and the elderly or sick had the earliest assignment. The tables were long with plain wooden chairs for seats, the room was packed.

Now at the second seating, Kesi sat with her fellow agents, Chris, Richard and Jersey; Arianna was way down the end of the table flirting with a soldier.

Idly nibbling at a roll, Kesi was highly conscious of Martier's stare burning a hole in her. He was sitting across the same table but a few people down.

Chris said to her, "You know, Kes, honey, since the…uh, damage to your face has cleared, your whole face looks oddly different. The same, but different. Without the hiding hat and big dark glasses, you are really quite beautiful, breathtaking actually. Why on earth would you hide those stunning eyes? You always had creamy skin, but the beating must have shifted things around, bones and-"

"Really, Chris, can you talk about something else?" Kesi stabbed a fork in her pasta.

She wanted to keep the whole heinous incident in the past and never speak of it again. The guilt and shame overwhelmed her enough without having to be reminded of it time and time again.

Clearing his throat, Chris set his hand over hers on the table and said, "What I'm getting at, is you are pretty fuck-uh, darned gorgeous. And, I was thinking, that little club down on Tangrey Street, Deep Bottle, is still up and running. Maybe you and I could wander down there after dinner, have some drinks, dance a bit, what do you say?"

She almost said yes just to see the demon captain's expression. He had kissed her for crying out loud.

The demon had kissed her, and, her fingers were trailing over her lips until she realized he was watching her under those secretive hooded eyes. A smirk curved up one side of his mouth.

Oh, he knows I'm remembering, damn him. She picked up her soda and gulped too fast and started choking.

"Hey, take it easy, Kes." Chris patted her on the back.

The demon's lids lowered further, jaw set.

When she stopped coughing, Chris said, "So, you game? We can go as soon as we're done here."

Sitting beside the captain, that voluptuous woman that was always trying to hang on him was yammering in his pointed ear while sidling so close to him their arms touched. He didn't look at her or respond to any of her endless yakking.

Right now, the demon wasn't looking in Kesi's direction. But, his head was still, and Kesi had a feeling he was listening in on their conversation. Probably thought they were plotting another escape. Harrumph, he obviously didn't know the chickens she was working with.

Her smile stiff, she said to Chris, "Uh, sure, that sounds like fun," as soon as the words were out she could have kicked herself. She had no desire to spend the evening with lecherous Chris.

She snuck a sidelong discrete glance at the demon. Dark color seeped up the bronze skin, a vein at his temple started a heavy beat.

A big shadow fell over Kesi as she wiped her mouth and set her napkin on her plate.

"Agent," a swarthy swaggering voice drew her attention.

Kesi looked up, her lungs tightened. It was that first male, Bruglon, that had tried to take her and the children. His black hair was not as unruly as before, but the slate eyes still regarded her lewdly.

Bruglon smiled, if a superior snarl could be called a smile. "I see our esteemed captain did not dispatch you into dust as he indicated he was going to do."

The sneer twisted snidely, he said, "He just fucked you and set you free, eh? So, now it is my time with you. Get up."

No one moved. It grew quiet at their section of the table.

The smile slid from his thick lips now turned coarse, marring the nice shape of them. Heavy black brows drew down so low only the glint in his dark eyes was visible.

Voice dark with menace, Bruglon snarled, "I said, get up. You cooperate and you will not be injured here. You piss me off and I will not gently carry you out."

He wrapped his huge rough hands on the back of Kesi's chair and pulled it back for her to get out, then gripped her upper arm.

None of the agents breathed.

"Soldier."

All eyes turned to Martier standing calmly, the tips of his pointed ears red. His green eyes sieved to obsidian, the horns on his head were swelling, both were warnings that he was riled.

Rolling his eyes, Bruglon exhaled his annoyance. "Yes, Captain, problem?" He kept his fingers wound around Kesi's arm as he turned his attention to the hostile blond.

"There will be if you don't release the agent, right now."

The two tough, huskily muscled men seethed at each other like powerful bulls stamping the ground.

Except for the agents, the rest of the humans around them silently got to their feet and fled.

Still gripping Kesi's arm, his body rigid, preparing to fight, Bruglon glared heated aggression at Martier.

The captain's gaze sliced through the air pinning the soldier with his tacit threat of imminent death. His mouth opened slightly, a warning hissed through the fangs.

Without another word, Bruglon released Kesi, spun on his heel and stalked out of the building.

Kesi's colleagues let out a collective sigh of relief.

Mortified at being signaled out when she did everything she could to stay blended into the background, Kesi stood up on shaky legs.

"Hey, uh, Kes, now we really need that drink, huh?" Chris chuckled beside her. Adrenalin hurtled through his veins. As long as it didn't involve him, he would enjoy a cool fight between such huge strong males, and aliens to boot. If only he had his phone. A video of the battling brutes would make him a mint back in the States.

Without looking at Martier, Kesi let her held breath out, wishing she hadn't agreed to go with Chris. "Uh, yeah, sure, I need to use the restroom, I'll meet you out at your jeep."

Again, the male agents were given approval to rent vehicles whereas Kesi had been told by her still angry handler if she needed to get around she could ride with one of the men. The sexism just infuriated her beyond belief, but she had no recourse.

Martier stepped back to lean against the wall.

Before anyone could move, a short pudgy woman rushed in and hustled right to the agents. "Sirs," she huffed looking from Richard to Jersey to Chris. Smiling slightly at Chris, she announced, "There's been another murder!"

"You're joking," Richard derided, skepticism in his voice.

The woman gave him a dirty look then put all of her attention onto Chris. "Yes, it's insane, but they found that retired district attorney dead. He's been shot!"

Richard scoffed, "No fucking way, in this shitty little town there are more murders than in freakin' New York City."

Kesi faced the woman with the short curly hair and asked her, "Can you tell us more about it?"

Chris was watching Kesi instead of looking at the woman.

Twisting her fingers nervously together, the woman said fearfully to Kesi, "Yeah, it's Patric Efrem. They found him in his office. They said it was a gunshot to the head." She wrapped her arms around her plump body to contain her revolted shudder.

Kesi questioned, "If he's retired, why does he have an office?"

Her eyes darting from one agent to another, the woman replied to Kesi's question, "He moved here from the big city to get away from it all, so he said. He still did some per diem consultation by email."

"Still, he could do that at home," Kesi said.

Her shoulder bumped. "True, but," she gave Kesi a wink, "I think it was to get away from the wife."

"Can you tell me where his office is?" Kesi pulled out her notebook and pen.

"Shit, Kes, this is not our job, that's what the local cops are for," Chris snorted, "the two of them." There were actually more police officers but they were frequently referred to as rent-a-cops due to their ineptitude.

The woman rattled off the address, Kesi wrote it down and said, "I'll meet you at your jeep, Chris, you can drive us there." Before Chris could grumble, she hurried off to the restroom twisting the top off her pill bottle.

When she was done in the ladies room, she decided it would be more prudent to slide out the back door instead of having to see the demon if he was still there.

The sun had said its final farewell when Kesi stepped out into the cool evening. The stars were as plentiful as strewn salt, there were so many of them visible due to the lack of town lights.

Just as she reached Chris' jeep, the demon exited the building and headed straight to her. Of course Chris was not in the vehicle so they could have just driven off.

"Agent Jasmari, you are not really thinking of investigating that murder," he said when he reached her.

If she had been looking at him she would have seen his frown. She crossed her arms and didn't respond, her mouth set mulishly.

"You need to back off from this, *rostia tím*, you are not here for that kind of work, it could be dangerous. Don't get involved, leave it to the local authorities." Tucking his hands in the pockets of his black jeans, he hunched his big shoulders. Dark green eyes rolled down her body then back up to settle on her angry blues.

Face creasing in indignant humiliation, Kesi groused angrily, "What? You think I'll botch this up too and get someone else killed?"

Moving closer to her he retorted roughly, "I hacked the report of that incident. It was not your fault-"

Eyes popping at him in surprise that he would go to that trouble then she cut him off. "This *is* my job. I can't sit around like a lame duck. I will not allow you or anyone else tell me what I can and can't do. I told you to stop calling me 'little girl.' Go play with your over-sexed blow-up doll what's her name- Ginger, Amber, Cinnabun whatever- and leave me alone."

As she turned her back to him, he snared her jaw with a hard hand, holding her from moving and forced her face up to his.

He snorted, "Her name is Tawny, my little agent." Stroking his thumb over her mouth, he watched the plump lips flutter. The timbre sensuously dark in his voice, he said,

"I find petite FBI agents more interesting than the local whores."

Releasing her chin, Martier slid his fingers into her tresses. "You have beautiful hair, Kesindra," he fondled the locks, letting them sift through his fingers.

She jerked her head to make him let go and scowled. "It was burned in the…anyway, it's ugly, please don't touch it." Kesi was mortified to have attention drawn to her destroyed hair. The picture of it singed when she was first hospitalized had stayed hammered into her memory.

"Seriously?" Continuing to caress her hair he mumbled, "You have got to be kidding, my fair human, tis sunshine and buttercups." Leaning in, he inhaled deeply and said, "Ah, smells like spring flowers."

Combing his fingers through the bulk of the tresses, he let the curls roll down her back but kept handfuls that he sniffed again. "Kesindra, my small one, you know what an aphrodisiac is?"

Snapping, "Captain," she grabbed her hair and yanked it out of his clutches. Reproaching him, "You are inappropriate. Why do you keep bothering me? You find it fun to try to frighten me? Annoy me? That woman, Fawn, won't give you a hard time, please go find her to hassle."

He caught her chin again, lifting it as he lowered his mouth to hers. She turned her head; he hesitated, then let her go.

Stuffing his hands in his pockets, he said, "Those pills, Kesindra, they will dull your wits, your reactions to danger, you cannot-"

Chris exited the rec building. Heading towards them he saw Martier with his hands on Kesi before he moved them. Chris shot the captain a pissed glare. Turning his glare to Kesi he said shortly, "You ready to go?"

Smiling sweetly, Kesi opened the passenger door and climbed in. Closing the door she replied through the open window, "Yes, let's head out."

Chris trod around to the driver's side and got behind the wheel.

"Kesindra," Martier said loudly, "the matter is not your concern, you should not-"

"See you around, outlaw," she countered airily as Chris pulled the jeep out of the graveled parking area.

Ten minutes later, Chris parked at the crime scene.

Once inside, they both poked around but there wasn't anything to see. Same pool of blood on the carpet as Mr. Francks, same gunshot wound in the head, same no witnesses.

"Looks like a serial, this is the second murder," Chris commented, heading back to his vehicle. He snorted, "Dempsey finally has something to do."

As they got back into the jeep, Kesi said, "It has to be just a coincidence, or a copycat. Two murders so close together when according to Officer Dempsey there hasn't been a murder ever on record here other than a couple of barroom brawls. It can't be Pilar Gomez, she's been in custody."

"Yeah, yeah, whatever. You ready to hit the tavern now?" Chris griped, with no interest in the murder. He turned the key starting the engine.

Kesi resisted rolling her eyes in annoyance at him. She was about to tell him no, instead she gave in coolly, "Sure. Let's go."

His disgruntled expression lifting with a grin, Chris drove quickly out of the lot and headed to the street a dozen blocks over.

He parked in front of a grimy block of cement with blinking neon lights, the majority of the bulbs had long burned out.

They exited the jeep and went inside.

The loud music and boisterous conversation blared in their faces as soon as they entered. Chris went straight to the bar. When the bartender came over Chris asked her, "What do you want, Kes?"

"Oh, nothing for me, thanks." Kesi strode away before she could hear Chris' complaint.

She approached a barmaid at the end of the bar collecting drinks on a tray. "Hi," Kesi greeted her with a friendly grin.

A busy glance at Kesi, the barmaid said not unfriendly, "Just get a table honey, I'll be right there to take you order. What with all those soldiers running around we've just been swamped. Not that I mind a lot of extra cock, ya know," she added chasers to the cocktails, "but it's exhausting."

She wore jeans and a blue t-shirt with Deep Bottle blazed in gold over her left breast. A short black apron tied around angular hips contained a black server book, cash kitty and pens.

"Oh, uh, yes, I can understand that. But," Kesi followed the girl as she swirled around making her way through the crowded room. "I'm with the FBI, I'd like to ask you a few questions if you don't mind."

Popping gum, the girl smiled briefly. "Yeah, I know who you are, you hardly blend in with the natives you know, it is a small town after all. I gotta keep moving, you got questions, you need to walk with me."

"Okay." Kesi hustled after the barmaid who had very long legs, no butt and a chest that was flat as a plate. "So…"

"Carrie," the girl proclaimed with a flip of her head, tossing a single braid over her shoulder to spiral down her back like a brown garden snake.

"Oh, so Carrie, did you know Patric Efrem, the retired attorney?"

"Sure, he hung out here a lot. It's sad, word has already traveled of his...demise. Get news like that and people practically run up and down the streets announcing it with bull horns."

Carrie set down a row of drinks at a table of five men. They paid her, made some raunchy rude comments; one smacked her butt. Carrie just flashed him a saucy wink and flicked her hips as she sashayed to the next table.

Her brows darted down, Kesi asked, "Carrie, doesn't that bother you that they touch you like that?"

"Nah, it's money, hon. The more they think they get away with the bigger they tip. It's worth a sore ass at the end of the day, matches my sore dogs, ya know what I mean?" She threaded through the room to the next table where she deposited more drinks.

While Carrie collected their money and moved on to a vacated table, Kesi hurried after her, practically shouting over the din of music and drunken conversation, "Can you tell me anything about Mr. Efrem?"

Shrugging one shoulder, Carrie tossed the braid back again. She picked up empty glasses and set them on her tray.

Wiping the table with a cloth that she slung back over her belt, she answered, "Not much to tell. He was never any trouble, was very quiet, stayed to himself and drank a lot. Said he came to this small town to get away from noise and traffic of Milčent."

Snagging bills off the table, she stuffed a portion of them and the check into her server book and tucked a few other dollars into her bra.

At Kesi's look she said, "Bar takes a cut of all our earnings, so I put some aside they can't get their grubby little paws on. We have been making money hand over fist, maybe now I can go back and finish my college."

"Hmm. So, Mr. Efrem," Kesi prodded.

"Uh huh, well, he was married but his wife liked to go to Milčent a lot and stay there with her sister. She claims that this town is too gritty and bucolic for her."

"Can you think of any reason why someone would want him dead?"

Shaking her head, the braid flipped back and forth like a rope. "Nah, he was just a tired drunk. No reason for anyone to want him out of the picture. The wife, Elsa, was dumpy, no jealous boyfriend to do away with the lawyer."

"Okay, thanks for your trouble. If you hear anything or think of anything that can be of help," forgetting no one had phones now, she scribbled her name and number on a notepaper, tore if off and handed it to Carrie, "please don't hesitate to call."

Kesi wandered around asking other employees and some patrons the same questions and got the same answers.

Seeing Chris engaged in a dark corner with a young woman with dusky skin and straight dark hair to her shoulders that flipped up at the ends, Kesi slipped out the door and strode down the street in the dark back to her rented shack.

Chapter Eight

Gastov'rin Rom-nul from the planet, 2nd Sequester, leaned over the naked human bound to a gurney.

A mass of blood saturated what was left of the human's body, tubes stuck out of every crevasse and then some that weren't original holes.

Choking on his leaking blood the human made strangled, gurgling sounds, rasping, trying to scream but he had no voice left to beg for mercy. Not that he would have been given any.

Rom-nul's rank is syntagma, a title equal to an Earth's colonel. Rom-nul, studied the dying man impassively as if watching water boil.

Like most of the males from his own planet entering other worlds, Rom-nul chose to appear as human as possible. Yet he still had reptile soft skin the color of copper covering his body of well over 7'2".

His kind didn't have hair per se, so the long webbing that grew out of his head to past his shoulders was an unnatural looking blackish-brown.

Syntagma Rom-nul maintained himself and the others he'd brought with him with most of the same body parts as the humans, more so now that he had an endless bounty of bodies to take things from. However, he had his own additional alien parts as well.

The female humans he chose to fulfill his sexual needs with found out he had more than just his phallus to imbed in them.

He had quickly learned he needed to be particularly careful with the human females as his own species was preternaturally strong, and since he was unused to the more frail humans, he tended to break them before he was done with them. Which was damned annoying.

Already a tormenting itch was driving him mad and he needed a female to relieve it. Unfortunately, he couldn't touch the legionnaire females from V'Am that were with him, so he was forced to wait until more humans were brought to the fortress.

But there were a few servants they'd brought with them, he could use one of them to relieve himself until he could get his phalanges on a human.

Scientist-doctor, Renzza Blyn-nul wiped one of his white lab coat sleeves across his sweating forehead. "There are only a couple more after this one, Syntagma, this one didn't even last as long as the others. He'll breathe his last shortly."

Rom-nul's heavy sigh knit was with aggravation. "All right. When he's done, incinerate him with the others." The V'Am syntagma shrugged out of his lab coat tossing it over by the waste disposal and complained, "We ran through that last group of human natives quickly. Already we need a new crop."

Turning to one of the guards posted by the door, he instructed him, "Soldier, tell Quamo to get the troops ready, we need to replenish our specimens." He said to the doctor, "You sure we can't use the children?"

Blyn-nul shook his head. Fret lines crisscrossed his pale face. Silver flickered in his narrow chin and up his long neck expressing how stressful his job was. The agony the victims suffered through the torturous experiments affected him, aging him well past his chronological years.

He shook his head. "No. They are not developed enough for our experiments until at least the age of 18, and even then they really should be a few years older. Their skulls aren't fully sealed until almost 25 Earth years. It's unfortunate that the young people between 18 and 30 leave as soon as they can get away from this indigent jungle."

"Yes, making a living mining in a nothing town must be miserable. So," Rom-nul's grin nasty, he said, "we are actually humanitarians, taking these poor people from their wretched existence and letting them donate their bodies, lives, to the betterment of science. Albeit it's science to benefit our species, not theirs, but c'est la vie," he ended with an indifferent shrug.

Syntagma Rom-nul stared down in the brightly lit lab without compassion or pity at the man dying on the gurney.

Surroundings such as walls, floor and doors were white. Everything else, tables, chairs, cabinets, tools, sinks, machines, were made of an alloy brought from their planet.

He said to the guard he'd given the order to, "Quamo found a cruddy little village a day's march from here. As usual, send the children and elderly, all the sick out, let the jungle devour them. But first weed out a young female for me, make it a good-looking one. I like them fresh, don't bring me some used-up hag or diseased strumpet. And not a fat one either, I find them too…squishy.

"And the bony ones break too easily. Human females' sexual parts are softer and plumper than our females. I want a young one with plump assets yet of slender build, and easy on the eyes. Find me one like that. You got it?"

"Of course." The guard nodded sharply and left the room. Another guard came inside to take his place.

Looking down at the dying human, Rom-nul remarked with wonder, "It's amazing that with all those seizures, the jerking and grueling twitching tearing at the creature, that it doesn't come completely apart. I guess there's some strong sinew inside it holding it together."

The human rippling with spasms, choking and croaking on the gurney futilely tried another scream, silent air escaped instead, and then he moved no more.

Rom-nul made a face as if there was a bad smell. He ordered, "Get it out of here."

Guards hurried to follow his command. Using boards, they shoved the messy corpse into a bag and two guards carried it out.

Crossing his arms, the conscienceless syntagma stabbed the doctor with a hard look. "Do you think we will ever come up with the right amounts of integration of our stred'le and their DNA and body parts that we can finally exist on this planet and others longer than a few months at a time?"

With a laborious sigh, the doctor replied wearily, "We can't give up, Syntagma." More silver streaked over Blyn-nul's face and neck and seeped down his arms as he spoke.

He said to Rom-nul, "Our entire species depends on us finding a way to merge these humans with us without of course killing us in the process. Don't worry, we'll get it. I think I'm close, just get me more specimens. Quickly."

Chapter Nine

The day after Kesi questioned the bar staff regarding the murdered ADA, Assistant District Attorney, she hit up the same shops and other bars as she had before when investigating the Francks' murder.

She was positive the murders weren't related because when presented with the evidence, Oswald Francks' wife, Luci, and her girlfriend, Pilar Gomez broke and confessed.

They had been carrying on an affair as well as all-female orgies in the family room, right under his nose while in the living room, Oswald Francks drank beer and watched TV in a drunken stupor. Plus, they had the murder weapon and Oswald's blood on Pilar's clothes.

Pilar figured they could get some insurance money if they killed him and enjoy a nice trip somewhere, so they plotted his death.

Luci was careful to have an alibi, and neither of them thought anyone would suspect Pilar. Although they were as discrete as samurai wrestles in a mud puddle, they didn't think anyone was aware of their affair.

When confronted with the evidence, and a possible death sentence if she was found guilty at trial in the bigger city, Milčent, Pilar admitted she was working near the neighborhood and had snuck over during her lunch hour, killed Francks and slipped back to work.

Regarding the current murder, the only new information Kesi obtained was that Patric Efrem apparently had a woman on the side that he saw whenever his wife was out of town.

Kesi had spoken with Officer Dalton Dempsey, and he advised her the mistress had an alibi. She had been in the hospital having her appendix removed on the days before and during Oswald's murder.

With no other possible witnesses to dig up, Kesi walked to the only jail in town where the agents had been given some space to work.

She greeted Officer Dempsey, and a couple of the rent-a-cops, and the receptionist-dispatch, Nancy Marquart. The police had dug up some two-way radios and were able to use them to keep in contact when out in the field.

Dempsey looked up briefly from his magazine, nodded, then went right back to reading.

The aliens had blocked all phones and computers so the people were forced to read the old fashioned way. At least they had television.

Actually, not that many residents had phones or computers anyway. They didn't have the money for luxury items and there wasn't much in the way of satellites out there.

Gritting her teeth, Kesi made her way to the desk allotted for her and her coworkers to use. Aggravation burned in her gut that Dempsey had made a cursory examination of the deceased attorney and his office, but other than looking into the mistress' alibi he wasn't actively investigating. Worse, her own fellow agents were nowhere to be seen.

Just as she sat with a thump in the office chair, Arianna Loomis strolled in the front door.

Waving blithely at the cops and the receptionist, she went straight over to Kesi. Plopping in the other chair at the desk, Arianna gave her a cheerful greeting, "Good morning, how's it going, Kes?"

Her brows arched, Kesi glanced at the wall clock and remarked drily, "Actually that would almost be good afternoon, it's 10:30. What are you doing here?"

"I saw Richard at the café, he said he thought you would be here. I came to see if I could help you with anything. Maybe type up notes, or do some research. Okay?"

Arianna seemed to be eager to help so Kesi politely acquiesced, "Uh, sure."

Settling back with a smile, Arianna said, "Great. What have you gotten so far?"

Her laugh short, Kesi fired up the ancient computer, stuck in a flash-drive, and replied, "Not much. Patric Efrem was retired, and the reports are that he had been a sucky ADA. He couldn't handle the busyness and chaos of the bigger cities so he came here. He did a bit of consulting for other attorneys by email."

She glanced down at her notepad. "He, uh, was married, and apparently ran around on her."

Arianna snorted. "I can relate to his poor wife. My husband cheated like crazy before I dumped his ass. So, it could have been a jealous husband, or his own wife, or the girlfriend who was mad that he wouldn't leave his wife for her."

Kesi said, "I went around and asked people who knew him the most about it. They said the women he went after were drunks like him with no partners, and his wife is handicapped and was at the doctor's office during the murder. His latest mistress has a concrete alibi."

She couldn't access the internet, but through Dempsey, Kesi had been able to get access to the county clerk's records in Milčent where Efrem had practiced law, and could retrieve it offline from the flash-drive.

He was an ADA so all of his records were with the county courthouse. Reviewing the password in her notebook Dempsey had given her, Kesi typed it into the computer.

Arianna left the room and made some coffee then brought it back with cream and sugar while Kesi poked around the deceased attorney's most recent cases.

Setting a mug in front of Kesi, Arianna went to the back of the building and borrowed another computer, brought it to the table and powered it up. "Give me that other drive and the password and I can help you research."

Kesi rummaged in the desk drawer and handed her the drive. She told Arianna the password then stirred in cream and sugar and took a sip of the hot brew. Setting the mug down, she scrolled through Efrem's cases. As a courthouse attorney, there were hundreds, maybe thousands.

The two young women searched for hours for some indication of someone being mad enough at the attorney to want to murder him.

Sitting back, twisting the kinks out of her neck, Kesi said, "I don't see anything worth killing over. A few DUI cases that he lost, and a couple of prostitution charges, there's nothing spectacular here. He hadn't done felonies in years. He only handled misdemeanors the past five years."

Yawning, Arianna rubbed her eyes. "I didn't find anything that stands out that someone would be angry enough to kill over."

Kesi refreshed their coffee and sat back down. Blowing the steam over the heavily sugared brew, she said, "So, you're not married now, Arianna?"

"No, I've sworn off men for a while. Just relationships that is, the other stuff," she gave Kesi a randy wink. "I'm not off sex. The more the merrier." She added with a leer, "As they say, variety is the spice of life."

"Oh." Stirring more sugar and another dollop of milk in her coffee until it was cream colored, Kesi took a sip, it was fine, she some drank more. "So, tell me about your family, are your parents still alive?"

Arianna doctored her own mug, one shoulder rose slightly. "Oh, there's really not much to tell. Both parents are deceased." She stuck her nose back into the monitor, long brown hair waved down her back.

"Oh, I'm sorry, Arianna."

Her lips pulled in. With a tiny shrug, Arianna said, "Thanks. It was a long time ago."

Kesi wanted to at least be liked by this support staff. The male agents could hardly stand her, except Chris, who didn't like her either but wanted to get in her pants. Although for the life of her, she couldn't figure out why. In the states he hadn't given her the time of day, and he only dated model types.

Trying to be friendly, she asked Arianna, "Where are you from? You have a slight accent, like California Valley or something?"

Her laugh spurted out, Arianna said, "No, I'm from a tiny place in um, Nebraska, you would have never heard of it." She smiled at Kesi. "So, you dating anyone?"

Kesi snorted rudely, making a face. "Trust me, you see this face, no one has any interest in me. Besides, who would I date in this one-horse dive?"

"I don't know, those, um, outlaws, those alien guys, they are pretty hot. Especially the one in charge. Oozing pure masculine arrogance, that dark blond alpha male has so many muscles he looks like he could lift the Empire State building!"

"That's silly." Kesi giggled, the girls laughed together.

"We worked through lunch and I'm starving. Let's go get something to eat." Arianna shut down her computer and gathered up their empty mugs.

****

Two days later there was another murder. Kesi had to walk to the crime scene as none of the other agents were around to give her a ride.

Clear on the other side of the town it took her over an hour to walk there. The only busses running in the village were few and unpredictable, and more often than not, broken down.

Her head hurt, the area on her back where she had been shot ached, the heat was oppressive today and she had to swat her way through giant mosquitoes.

Kesi hated feeling sorry for herself, but sometimes she just wanted to give up. She'd tried the best she could that day chasing the kidnapper, and now she has to spend eternity in hell for messing up.

Sure, she wasn't obligated to investigate the murders, but she felt it was her duty. Especially since local law enforcement tended to be very lackadaisical. It was appearing that there was a serial killer in the village, and

Kesi would be damned if she didn't step in and try to help capture the felon and save lives.

She tossed a pain pill in her mouth and strode up the walk to the deceased's house.

Officer Dempsey was there with a big frown on his doughy face. His shirt today was a light brown uniform top tucked into jeans, not what Kesi would call professional attire for a police officer.

Kesi wore pressed black slacks and a white blouse. When she reached him she asked, "Who is the victim?"

His sigh beleaguered like he had been pulled away from his favorite TV show, Dempsey scratched his head. "It's Daisy Hernandez. She's 68 years old, and, a retired judge."

Ignoring Kesi's perceptive brows like crescents raised over her blue eyes, he continued, "Appears to have been shot in her garage."

He nodded to a weeping woman with grey hair standing off to the side with her arms wrapped around her skinny body. "Mrs. Murdock said the judge was supposed to be on her way to play bridge. When she didn't show after an hour, Mrs. Murdock volunteered to go and check on her and, well, there ya go."

Dempsey and Kesi walked up to the garage, the overhead door was up. They could see the body spilling blood circling the dead judge like the chalk line police draw around victims.

Justine Gambles knelt over the body. Off to the side were the duo paramedics.

"Hey, Justine, you get called away from your other job?" Dempsey asked with a chuckle. The CSI was in her pale blue dental scrubs.

Justine angled her head sideways to give him and Kesi a grin. "Yep. No rest for the wicked as they say."

"Anything to tell us?" Dempsey asked.

"Same as the attorney. Shot in the head. Looks like it could be the same caliber. Bullet is still inside. They can dig it out at autopsy. Gwanas Pagano is going to be pissed. She just finished Efrem Patric."

The two medics nodded in unison. One of them commented, "Yeah, seriously, we're having a freakin' crime wave here, don't ya know?"

The medic that had hit on Kesi at the Francks' scene blatantly gawped at her. "Hey, Agent, you lost the glasses and hat, you are one hot babe."

He inched over to Kesi. "You still got those baggy clothes on, but shit, I'll take you out. We can get-"

"No thanks." Kesi mouth tightened.

What was in the water here? Was it pick on the plain girl week? Set her up to crash and burn with humiliation? Have her say yes to a date, then he stands back and they all have a snarky laugh fest, all a big joke on her?

Chapter Ten

After interviewing family members and friends of the Judge, Kesi changed into a short sleeved, thin, dark green sweater, and black jeans and headed to the saloon she knew the other agents hung at to get feedback from them.

She saw Chris, Richard and Jersey sitting at a round table with a couple of local girls. She trod over to them, dragged a chair over and sat down.

"Hey, Kes, what's happening?" Chris said as she joined them. "You want a drink? I'll buy it. I still owe you one after you snuck out on me the other day."

"No, thanks, Chris. I came by to talk about the latest murder. A judge was killed earlier today. Did you hear about it?"

Chris smiled ruefully at the girl next to him. She was cute but a bit overweight. "This is our partner we were telling you about, Kesi Jasmari. She thinks she needs to nose into the police's business." He turned back to Kesi. "I don't really care about some retired judge and washed up lawyer."

"How about giving the investigating a rest, Kesi," Richard grated, bored with the conversation. He wanted the girl sitting next to Chris but she only had eyes for Chris.

Kesi couldn't believe the laziness of these men. "Come on guys, for crying out loud. Dempsey is not capable of investigating this alone, I mean these two deaths are definitely the acts of a serial. We need to assist him. That's what we were sent here to do."

Chris opened his mouth to protest but Kesi persisted.

"I think undoubtedly the judge and attorney were involved in a case together at some point in time, and the suspect they put away might be out for revenge. There could be more victims, we need to-"

"No, *we* don't," Chris interjected in irritation. He bent and put his face an inch from hers. Dark brown eyes boring into her blues he said, "You want to go somewhere and fuck, I'm game, otherwise," he tossed back his beer, "I'm not interested."

"Ditto," Richard said.

Shocked at the way Chris spoke to her, Kesi looked to Jersey.

Jersey had a hand high up on the thigh of the man sitting next to him. He raised his other palm and smiled weakly shaking his head. They weren't interested in anything but partying.

Kesi narrowed her eyes at her colleagues. The people they were with had to be in their late thirties, maybe even forties, and the male agents were all mid-twenties.

"Great," she ground out standing up. "You guys are the suckiest agents in the world."

She started for the door when she spotted the demon outlaw.

He was lounging, his boots up on a chair, ankles crossed, sitting with two of his men, he wasn't drinking. The deep forest green eyes were drilled across the room at her.

Swallowing her nerves, she marched over to him.

Seeing her coming, Martier dropped his feet to the floor and stood up. "Agent Jasmari," he greeted her with a tentative nod. "This is Trae," he gestured to one of the men.

Trae wore a plaid driver's cap over spiked brown hair. He had a definite mischievous twinkle in his brown eyes, a deck of cards shuffled in and out of his hands. He half-stood respectfully and smiled at Kesi.

His voice friendly he said, "Heard about you, Agent. Nice to meet you," then sat back down.

Martier motioned to the other man. "That is Slade."

Slade's jet-black hair slicked straight back, it curled just below his ears. His goatee was black, and he had an earring in one ear. He also did a half-bow, mumbled, "Agent," but he didn't smile.

Face hard as rock, with his callous expression, he reminded Kesi of a warring Viking that traveled storm-tossed seas to pillage and plunder faraway lands. All three men wore dark cargo pants and long sleeved thermals.

Martier moved to stand in front of her. "What can I do for you, Kesindra?"

Kesi had avoided him whenever he was around, and would quickly leave if he tried to approach her. Looking up at him, she couldn't prevent the gulp over the knot in her throat.

The man was huge and broad-chested with arms the size of tree trunks. And a hard face that bespoke years, make that eons of fighting, and killing.

Normally she thought of blond men as being, well, less masculine, weaker. But this demon with his dark golden hair looked 100% male.

Her eyes rose to the horns and quickly dropped. Maybe it was them that put the edge there. Or the stalwart body. It could be the midnight green eyes under manly dark brows that made Kesi feel like he could look right through her, and turn her to ash if he had the urge.

Or the way the green eyes strayed over her body. She wasn't sure if he was even aware of the surge of lust that radiated from them when he looked at her.

Not lust, she corrected herself for being ridiculous. It was hunger, the hunger of one vicious animal desiring to devour another smaller helpless animal.

The rumors still abounded that at some point, when the aliens were done with whatever mission they had going on here, they would be eliminating the humans. And, possibly eating them.

Someone in the village had said the native inhabitants would be a high protein food source for the extra-terrestrials. Kesi recalled SAC Dukes had told her about several small villages where the natives strangely, completely, disappeared.

When several families called police when they couldn't get a hold of a loved one, authorities came out and investigated each incident, but claimed they'd found no evidence of foul play.

It was assumed perhaps a deadly storm had ravaged the area, or an illness had wiped out most of the people with a few survivors assimilating into other areas.

The police couldn't fathom why they kept quiet about whatever catastrophe had happened. The investigations were shoddy and brief, offering zero explanations as to how entire villages had vanished. And with no celebrities, politicians or wealthy residents residing there, no one seemed to care enough to find out.

Because no bodies had been recovered, it was presumed that wild animals had devoured the meat then toted off the bones, burying them where they'd never be found. Of course that didn't explain why there were no clothes or shoes, jewelry etc. left behind.

They were all extraordinary mysterious, and Brutální could be next on the list.

Kesi hoped maybe if the intruders got to know the people they may take pity on them, do their business and leave the humans behind unharmed.

But, for today, she needed them.

Stammering slightly, she said, "There has been another murder. A judge."

Martier didn't so much as twitch, he already knew. He knew everything that happened in the village.

Kesi told him, "I think it's connected to the lawyer who was killed. I would like more, deeper, access to the cases in Milčent where they both worked. I," she paused.

He stared at her so intently she had that same feeling when he had first accosted her that he wanted to fry her up and take a knife and fork to her.

Huh, by the looks of him, he'd just grab her and gnaw right into her, feast on her neck, tear off a limb and chow down. A terrible shiver of gross fear ripped up her arms.

"Yes?" he prompted her to continue. As if he was aware his fierce eyes made her nervous, he lowered his lids to hood them making them less obtrusive. However, it only made him appear so much more the predator hungrily eyeing a tasty treat.

Blinking away her sick thoughts, Kesi said, "Um, uh, you have taken our phones and blocked Internet access. I would like to borrow your phone to call the Milčent Clerk's Office for them to provide deeper access to the cases the judge and lawyer had in common."

He cocked his head, a brow arched.

Clearing her throat, she continued, "They can siphon the access for what I need through your phone then I can get it entered into my computer and still be able to work offline."

His dark brows rose then lowered in a hard ridge over his hooded eyes. "Nay."

She expected it but was still taken aback. "But, mister, uh, Captain, there could be more killings, I need to-"

"I said no. Leave it alone, young earthling. It is too dangerous for you to stick your nose into. You are too inexperienced to do an investigation like this. Remember what happened in the States, why you were sent here? It was because you were too-"

With a sharp gasp, Kesi swung around and stalked away from him.

Halfway across the bar she took out her pills and shook one into her hand then slid the bottle back in her pocket.

Suddenly, the demon was there. He snatched up her hand, forced the pill out of it and stuck it in the pocket of his jeans.

"Hey! You can't-"

He gripped her arms to hold her still for a second. "I cannot let you phone anyone, little spitfire. I cannot risk you getting a message to the authorities that we are here." He started walking with her, holding her arm, forcing her to move with him.

"Listen you big bossy brute, let go of me and give me back my pill!" Realizing she had yelled that out and half the intoxicated people roaming the bar looked at her, her cheeks turned as pink as bubble gum.

Wordless, Martier hauled her out of the saloon. Ignoring her protests, he dragged her around back to a barn behind the bar.

Hustling her inside, he stopped beside a wooden worktable. Straw littered the wood-planked floors, the walls were half rotted, the musty pungent smell of hay permeated.

"You let go of me you- you monster!" Kesi jerked from his hand, he let her go.

"Honey," he said, crossing his arms over his thick chest, "someone needs to save you from yourself. You are addicted to that medication, and you are thrusting yourself into what could be a deadly situation. You don't know what this killer is capable of, or who it is."

She opened her mouth, he spoke over her.

"It could be one of the most innocuous people in this dingy little town and take you completely unaware and make you their next victim for sticking your nose in."

Seething with anger and humiliation, Kesi grated, "What I do is none of your business. I've told you that before. I will do as I please. I do not need a- a watchdog or lecturer." She made to push past him, but he grabbed her around the waist, lifted her and set her on top of the workbench.

He thrust his hips between her knees, forcing them to spread apart and making it impossible for her to get away or get down.

"What do you think you're doing?" she screeched furiously. "You let me down right now!" Kicking at him, she pummeled her fists at his chest.

He caught her wrists and drew them behind her back. Scared now that he would kill her or hurt her, Kesi struggled, shrieking, "Let go of me!"

While her mouth was open, Martier bent and covered it with his. Holding her wrists back, he leaned his chest in to press against her breasts and moved his hips closer, forcing her legs to widen.

His besieging mouth took Kesi over, the soaring kiss scorching her from her lips straight down to her toes. She felt searing heat blaze out from her center core.

He bit her lips, licked them, stuck his tongue inside to chase after hers. Catching it, he sucked it then shoved his own tongue down her throat in his intensity.

In a daze, a frightened, sensuous daze, Kesi still struggled against him not realizing she was rubbing her breasts in the light sweater harder over his chest in her attempts to get free.

He held her wrists with one hand, and clamped the other on her butt. Pulling her closer to the edge of table, he pushed his bulging erection against her core.

At the shock of feeling his manhood erect and rock-hard pressing against her as if demanding admittance, Kesi tore her mouth from his with a gasp, "Oh my God, Captain, stop!"

Arching away from him, her breathless panting from his fiery kiss pushed her chest even firmer against his.

Half dizzy with the heady sensations racking her body, she'd never felt such surging heat and masculine power, such strength and male hardness up close and personal in her short sheltered lifetime.

Heavy-lidded, dark green eyes glinted into her startled blues. Still holding her wrists behind her, he moved his hand from her bottom to grasp her face. His voice husky, he murmured, *"Kesindra,"* and hammered his mouth back on hers, sealing their lips with molten fire.

Against her will, Kesi was being drawn under. Her mind glazed over. Losing contact with the rest of her surroundings, she was becoming aware of nothing but his mouth torturing hers, and his huge, thick erection rammed up against her as if he could shove it right through her jeans and into her. He wedged it straight into the cleft of her sex.

His rocking hips between her thighs made it impossible for Kesi to close them to his rampaging organ, along with manacling her arms, she was powerless to push him away.

Martier nipped at her lower lip then railed kisses down her cheek, behind her ear, lower to her neck where he sucked so hard she whimpered. Rugged growls rumbled in his chest, deep in his throat a moan stirred.

Moving back to her lips, he lathed the tenderness inside her mouth, then outside. Licking her skin, he kissed from her collarbone down to her breast where he bit a nipple through her sweater.

"Oh!" Kesi broke from him with a squawk. The surprise of him doing that cleared her head. She tried to tug out of his grasp but he had an iron grip. She coldly demanded in a quiet voice, "Let go of me right now."

Releasing her wrists, Martier shoved his hands up under her sweater wrapping his fingers around her waist. His voice a dusky rasp, "Ah, little agent, you have the damned tiniest waist I have ever had my hands on, the softest skin. Zeus," he murmured through a deep breath.

Eyes closed, he moved his mouth to capture hers again but she turned her head.

"Sweet human," his growl whispered against her ear. "Kesindra, come to my bed, come with me now." Squeezing her waist, he brushed her skin with his thumbs and fingertips and squeezed again spasmodically, forcing his erection harder at her, rubbing roughly against her center.

She shoved him with both hands. He didn't budge but he did look at her. Kesi was afraid her own eyes mirrored his; insanely lust filled, white-hot fire under lids heavy with passion.

The green in his irises was almost pure black, the horns swelled on his head. When he spoke, she could see his fangs, she shuddered. Her gaze followed the tattoo that scrolled up the side of his neck.

Her words tumbled out in a tremble, "I am not going to sleep with you, outlaw."

"Ah, Kesindra," he murmured, "why not?" His hands tightened on her body, fingers stretching up towards her breasts. His growl rough, a plea, "Let me take you, *rostia tím,* I need to take you-"

Turning her face from him she gasped, "My God, Captain, but you're an alien!"

His low sensual chuckle burned her ears. "Ah, do I complain that you are a human goddess?" He moved his hands to the under swell of her breasts. "Come with me, I will please you. I promise I will take care of you, care for you."

Under his lowered lids he watched her, the dark eyes glittered his desire for her as if they were stroking her skin. "You are beautiful little human, and so fucking soft, I have never felt anything like it in all the universes." He leaned in to sniff her hair, she pulled back.

"Stop it. You are insane. You can't just drag me off the street and accost me, hold me, kiss me against my will. I don't get this. Even if I thought you were doing all this for real, I certainly would not have sex with someone I hadn't even dated. That would be your friend Cinnamon."

His chuckle rumbled in his chest. "If I did not know better, Kesindra, I would think you were jealous of Tawny. Don't worry, I don't do tawdry. I have told you; pretty little FBI agents are all I am interested in."

The smile turned serious. The playfulness leaving his tone, he said, "I have tried to get to know you, Kesindra, but you avoid me or give me dagger glares as you flee from my presence. There is not much to do in this grubby little town, but how about you let me take you to dine at the Glass House. Tis rustic but adequate-"

"No, I-" she broke off when his hands moved.

His fingertips brushed against the silk of her bra. The sensation sizzled down her body spiking her sex, drawing heat between her legs, she could feel her panties dampen. His palms cupping just the underneath of her breasts, thumbs caressing her skin shocked her nipples into hard peaks.

Martier lowered his mouth to her neck, his hair bristled under her chin. Licking her fragrant flesh, he murmured, "If you don't want to be so public with me, I can get a basket of food and a bottle of wine," his fangs drew smooth lines in her soft skin, she shivered at the strange feeling of them.

"We can go up to the rise and watch the sunset, we can get to know one another. I promise I will not pounce on you, beautiful Kesindra, just enjoy your company. We will just talk."

Everyone was expected to show for dinner at the rec center, however, as the meal was mass produced and only one main dish prepared without option, many people reported in but then either ate their real meal at home or chose to go to a restaurant.

From the lull of his soft, deep murmurs, whispered breath with his fangs stroking her neck, Kesi's head fell back. His rough hands on her tender skin just barely brushing her breasts. Her nipples so hard, when he pulled her close, pressed into his chest like hard little points.

He edged his hips closer, spreading her thighs wide. His raging shaft nestled, thrusting against her cleft, throbbing like a runaway train. Her panties were getting wetter-

"No." She pushed at him, demanded, "Stop."

He stopped moving but didn't remove his hands from under the sweater, or halt his fingers from caressing her skin.

She was at his mercy. He could kill her, rape her, there would be nothing she could do to stop him, no one she could complain to.

Her voice strained, she said with emotional pain, "No, I am no good for anyone, not even an outlaw. Let me down." She tried to move from him but he didn't budge.

Exhaling his frustration, Martier's head hung, the thick golden hair brushed the top of her head. His sigh heavy, he stepped back and set his palms on the table beside her hips. "Kesindra, give me, us, a chance, listen-"

"No." She shook her head, murmured quietly, "Let me down."

He raised his head linking their eyes. His black pupils covered the green of his irises, white flames flickered in them. The horns had grown and swelled along with his erection. He moved his hands to loosely hold her arms. "Kesindra, just-"

"No."

Their eyes riveted in their connection, his blazing his desire, hers steady and unyielding yet still misted with the arousal he had skillfully, seductively built. His mouth pulled in.

With a heavy sigh, he put his hands on her waist, lifted her and set her on her feet. He trickled a few fingers under the side of her jaw to have her look at him. "Can we talk about this? I don't mean the sex, I mean-"

"Hey! Look who's here! I guess we aren't the only ones looking for a place for a quick fuck." Arianna toddled in the door hanging all over a man. Her completely unbuttoned blouse revealed she wasn't wearing a bra.

Kesi stepped from Martier's reach. Turning her head to hide her blush, she disclaimed what they were doing, "No, we were just…talking. I need to go." She hurried from Martier and out the door before he could stop her.

"No worries." Blocking the doorway, Arianna slinked forward, the shirt shifting, exposing her nipples. She grinned a huge leer. "I can take care of two lusty boys. Come, Captain."

"Hey," the man with her complained. Scowling, he clapped a hand over a bare breast. Fingering the small globe, he slurred, "I get firsts."

Without a word, Martier muscled past them. Outside he glanced around but there was no sign of Kesi.

"Goddammit," he cursed and started back for the saloon.

Chapter Eleven

*B*ack in the bar, his gaze hard on the floor, hands dug deep in his pockets and shoulders hunched, Martier returned to sit with his friends. Cisco had joined them.

A snicker came from Trae. Taking in Martier's mussed hair, the still visible bulge in his jeans and the way he threw himself in his chair with a scowl, Trae said, "You have a nice visit with the agent?"

"Fuck off," Martier growled.

"Seriously, *má bráthair*, I can't believe you thought she could reconcile having...relations, with what she considers a criminal. As well as a temporary resident. A very *foreign* temporary resident. She is way too rigid about laws and is completely by the book. She takes her job ultra serious."

"Huh," Martier grunted, slumping in his seat. His hands on his thighs, he dropped his head, his eyes darted back and forth as if debating what to say. Exhaling heavily, he said quietly, "Tis the Monmaret."

Devil's Seed

Trae's dark brown brows arched with skepticism. Chocolate eyes narrowed at his friend. "Your mate? You feel...she's your Monmaret Mate?"

Leaning forward, Martier nodded, his thick hair flopping slightly with the up and down motion.

Clasping his hands, he peered up through a loose blond lock. "Aye. I could feel it from the trees as I approached her and Bruglon that first day. When I...smelled her, touched her, I knew, aye," he nodded, "tis her. It takes everything I have to let her out of my sight, keep my hands off her. Well, mostly."

The men were quiet for a moment.

Slade disputed, "How can she be your Monmaret? You are from Nasitar, light years from here. We know who your...let's say *grandfather* is, and the agent is human. There is no way-"

"You would think, but tis true. Must have been eons ago that our ancestors met and mated, when the gods and goddesses still ruled." Martier sat back, dragged his fingers through his hair, pushing it back.

"Believe me, there is no mistake. I become an irrational, barely restrained letch when I am anywhere near her. My thoughts are consumed with her. Another man just looks at her and I want to snap his head off."

"Ha," Cisco snickered, "that's called being a male. She's a beautiful sexy woman, and even more irresistible because she has no awareness of it."

"Nay, tis more than that. Even if she was not so damned sexy and gorgeous, sweet as hell, and so brave," he said with a shake of his head and a crooked grin. "I can feel it, smell it, the Monmaret is there, tis real. Kesindra will only be mine. Every time she leaves me it feels as if half of me is ripping away. I want to- to tie her to me, literally, so she

109

cannot flee. The urge to mark her as mine is unbearably overpowering. But," he sighed morosely, "she denies me."

"So, just take her already. Who cares if she doesn't want to, what, the piddly human cops are going to chase you clear back to Nasitar?" Slade snorted.

Martier cast his eyes sideways to him with a frown. "I want a life with her. You think it would be a pleasant one if I abducted her, raped her, forced her to live with me?"

Slade muttered, "She'd get over it, eventually." He reached for a bowl of nuts on the table and scooped out a handful. "You've got the strength and the wherewithal to do with her as you please, she can't fight you forever. Ultimately she'd give in. Women need a firm hand, and you my friend, have one of the firmest in the universes."

He tossed a few cashews in his mouth and crunched loudly. "Just show her who's the boss, she'll grow tired of fighting you and get over her resistance."

Martier's scowl at his friend came with a dismal growl.

The men were silent again. Twisting his bottle of beer between his palms, Cisco asked, "So, what are you going to do? Does she know? Have you explained…who, and what you are and what the mating means?"

Shaking his head, Martier needed a drink, he looked for the barmaid. "She will not let me near her, will not listen to me, will not even give us a chance to get to know each other. And the fucking pills, they make her feel even worse about herself, they are dangerous for fucks sake. I cannot get her to see reason about them either."

Trae leaned closer to him. "Listen, she's had a rough time of it and now she's addicted to those pills. You can't force her to stop taking them."

"Wanna bet?" Martier waved down the barmaid and ordered a drink.

He waited until she returned and took the glass of dark amber liquor from her. Tilting his head back, he took a long healthy swig, his Adam's apple bobbing with his swallows. Circling the glass with his fingers, watching the liquid swirl, he said to Cisco, "You get the kids gone?"

Cisco nodded, holding his longneck between two fingers. He lifted it and took a few pulls. "Not entirely, but in the process."

"What about your agent, bro? You want her gone too?" Slade asked.

Martier sat quiet so long Slade almost repeated his question.

Then with a shake of his head, Martier said, "Nay. I mean, aye, I would like to get her the fuck out of here before shit starts to happen, but she would run straight to the authorities and blab."

Slade nodded his agreement.

Martier said, "Plus, knowing the stubborn wench that she is, she would just come back and try to figure out what we are doing and interfere, thinking she was rescuing the villagers. I think she will be safer with me."

Trae laughed. "You just don't want her out of your sight, my man, with other males sniffing after her until you can get your mark on her and ward them off."

"The mission is more important than a bitch," Slade reminded him.

Martier's head swung angrily at his friend he barked, "She is not a bitch, fuck off."

"Shit, fine, okay, whatever, you in?" Peeved himself now, Slade was dealing cards.

Martier didn't answer him; his eyes were latched onto the little blonde that had rejoined her friends who were now playing pool. Slade tossed a card in front of him anyway.

111

Chris smiled broadly as Kesi joined their group at the billiards table. "Hey, Kes, you're back. The way the fucking ogre dragged you out, I thought we might have seen the last of you."

Her smile sardonic, Kesi chided him with bitter dryness, "Oh, well, thanks for coming to see if I was okay or to help me."

"Aw Kes, come on. You know there's nothing we can do about those freaks. Here, let me buy you a drink; you still owe me some time. Okay?"

She opened her mouth to decline, but then peripherally caught the demon's gaze on her. She needed to show him she was not interested in him. Kesi still couldn't figure out why a dynamic male like the captain was chasing after her skirts, it just made no sense.

"Sure, why not. I'll have a…" she didn't really drink, but, whatever, she shrugged. "I'll have," she pointed at Jersey's pink glass with fizz and red cherry in it, "one of those."

Chris' brows rose. Jersey said, "Are you sure, Kes? It looks sissy but it's really-"

"Delicious. You'll love it. I'll be right back." Chris shot Jersey a glare to be quiet. Jersey glared back at him then turned his attention to the man he was with who was about to break the rack of balls.

The cute but slightly chubby girl was now cozied up with a smirking Richard, but Chris didn't appear to mind that he had been replaced. Chris didn't do less than perfect. The other girl was standing near the table with a cue stick in her hand waiting her turn.

Hurrying back before she changed her mind, Chris handed the frothy drink to Kesi. "Here ya go, don't worry, I'll see you get home safely."

Kesi sucked on the straw, her lips puckered. "Oh, it's sweet, but kinda strong, I guess it's okay, thanks."

"Cool. You want to take a turn at the table, Kes?" Chris sidled close to her, nodding at the pool table.

Her lips on the straw, she shook her head. "No, I've never played."

"Oh yeah?" Chris set a hand on her shoulder. "I'll teach you."

"Um, that would be…nice. Some other time, thanks."

"Sure." Chris drank some of his cocktail keeping his hand on her shoulder. The alien captain across the room caught his eye. The captain's seething glower was clear even in the lowly lit room. Chris stared smugly back at him.

People laughed and drank and wandered around the crowded room, music blared from an ancient jukebox. Sliding his arm around her shoulder, Chris subtly turned Kesi so she wasn't facing the big blond, horned bastard.

Kesi finished the sweet drink swiftly. Sucking the glass dry, she giggled when the straw gurgled.

"Here, Kes, I'll get you another, hang loose." Chris rushed off before she could stop him.

"Uh, wait, I don't think, uh," already Kesi's words slurred slightly and she swayed. Afraid she might drop it, she set the empty glass on a table.

"Kesindra."

The rough voice brought chills down her spine. Kesi ignored Martier.

When she didn't look at him, he clasped her shoulder and turned her to face him.

Glassy blue eyes and bright red cheeks told him she was already tipsy. "Shit, Kesindra, you are taking strong drugs, you cannot mix those with alcohol."

Her lips bunched, brows lowered. She slurred, "Stop telling me wah to do. I am an adult, I do's sas I chose."

"Huh," he snorted. "You sure you are an adult? By my reckoning you are not yet of a majority age."

"Leave me s'alone. This bar doesn't care, there are no laws out here and you know that. I can do's wah I want."

Still holding one arm, he cursed, "Dammit, Kesindra." Scowling, he whispered harshly, "Tis just stupid to mix pills and booze. I have a mind to take you the fuck out of here and bring you to a place I know where you can get help, get this addiction under control." He didn't mention it wasn't on Earth.

If he had a ship available here, he would just grab her and send her. It would solve two problems, get her safely out of the mission, and get her help for her addiction under a physician's care.

Kesi yanked from his hold. "You can't take me anywhere without my permission. I said leave me 'lone. I'ma lost cause. I don't care, don't you get it, Demon?"

Chris arrived with her drink. With a look at Martier, he took her hand and drew her away from the steaming captain.

Chris decided it would be good for Kesi to have a billiards lesson. He encouraged her to down her fresh drink.

At her hand raised to deny the cocktail, he said, "It doesn't have as much alcohol as the first one, hon. Don't worry, you can take it, it's mild, it's basically just fruit juice."

Shoving the drink in her hands, he waited for her to take a few gulps then he showed her how to chalk the cue and move it through her fingers.

She missed the ball entirely and broke into giggles. Handing the stick out to him, she laughed. "Here, Chris, I told you I can't do this."

Laughing, he held his hands up. "Naw, come on, I said I'd show ya how. Now, do this," he put his hands on her shoulders turning her to face the table and reached around her with both arms to hold the stick with her.

His mouth against her hair, he said with a sexy rasp, "Just feel me, I mean it, feel how I thrust the stick through your fingers, Kes." Maneuvering her and the cue, Chris pulled her in and leaned his chest against her back and framed his hips against hers.

"Hey, Kes." Richard sat on a stool holding his stick waiting his turn. "That bad-ass captain is just freaking glowering like the fierce man in the moon over there." He motioned with his head to Martier who was leaning his shoulder against a wall a few yards from them.

"Iss okay," she slurred, "he likes to control stuff. Show me again, Chris, I think I almost have it."

"You bet." Chris snuggled against her and helped her shoot. When she knocked the ball in the pocket she squealed with delight clapping her hands.

"You did great, hon," Chris praised her taking the stick. "Let me run the table and then I'll take you to the Seafood Hut. They've got great coconut shrimp and we can down a bottle of wine."

At her shaking her head, Chris handed his cue to another guy standing by watching, and said, "Come on, I know you didn't eat, let's go right now. You'll dig some plump fried shrimp, coleslaw, and maybe onion rings, whadya say?"

Trying to focus her wobbly eyes, Kesi could feel the heat radiating off Martier nearby, his face dark, green eyes shooting angry lightning. She turned to Chris and mumbled, "Sure, why not."

"Great, let's go." Chris picked her drink up, stuck it in her hand.

Pushing off the wall, Martier trod a few steps to them, and said angrily, "Kesindra, you are drunk, you don't know what you are doing." He glared at Chris, "You are taking advantage of her, you asshole." Back to Kesi he suggested quietly, "Let me take you home."

"Sure," she mumbled, trying to focus on his hard face, but her eyes wobbled and slid all over his harsh features. "An' you're so much safer than Chris. At least he didn't take an entire town hostage and he doesn't try to boss me around. Come on, Chris, less go."

"Because he does not care, Kesindra, he only wants to get in your pants. Listen to me-"

She stumbled backwards. Tossing her mop of blonde curls out of her eyes, she slurred, "An' you care? You saying you don't wanna to have sex with me?"

His lips bunched. He said brusquely, "Kesindra, I do care." But he couldn't deny he wanted her, bad.

"Uh huh," she took a step away. "Chrissssh," his name slid long on her loose tongue, "lesss go…"

Before she changed her mind, Chris grabbed her wrist and took off with her.

Kesi allowed Chris to drag her out the door, but by the time he bundled her into his jeep, she was having second thoughts. "L-listen, Chris, I, uh, I'm not sure, I feel…" her eyes fluttered, "uh, a little dizzy. I think I should go back inside."

Chris threw the gear in drive, pulled out and headed quickly down the street. "You're okay," he said, squeezing her knee, "didn't I tell you I'd take care of you? Relax, let's have a good time."

Martier watched her leave then went back to his table. Dropping down on a chair he mumbled, "I don't get it, why would she leave with that sleaze and not me?"

A mocking chuckle, Trae said to his friend, "Because you're an alien outlaw that is holding an entire town prisoner?"

Martier grunted still staring at the door.

"Listen, *má bráthair*, she's strung out on those pills trying to stick her head in the sand and kill the pain of what happened. Believing what happened was her doing, that people were killed because of her, she doesn't think she deserves anything good, you can see she doesn't care about herself. The guilt is strangling her confidence."

"Aye. But, shit, she is such a sweet, brave person, Trae, I hate like hell to see her like this. If only she would let me help."

Slade dealt another hand. Rubbing his black goatee with the back of his hand, his grunt short, harsh, he said with flippant disinterest, "Let it go, she'll figure it out on her own, or croak."

Martier opened his mouth with an angry retort, Trae cut him off, "Okay, just play cards. This is exactly why you've always avoided having relationships with broads, *bráthair*, they are too hard to control much less understand."

Cisco and Slade nodded, muttered together, "Yeah."

Slade offered a suggestion, "You need to tie 'em down sometimes, show them who's in charge. They don't obey you, then-" he shrugged.

"Then what?" Trae asked with interest.

"Hey, you can't beat them, they're chicks, but you can...spank them," Cisco suggested with a devilish smile.

Trae laughed. "I know quite a few babes that like that stuff, I can dig it myself. Smacking a jiggling bare butt, oh yeah, can lead to great sex."

Shrugging his shoulders again, Slade tossed a card on the table. "So, you give them a good stiff paddling then keep them locked up until they see the error of their ways and do as you tell them without balking."

"Ha!" Trae's chortle came with a shaking head. "What, are you living in the dark ages, son? Try that and the second you let them out of your sight they will run. You can't hold them against their will," he tsked his tongue and tossed in two cards and took two, "it pisses them the fuck off."

Slade's lips pursed to the side as he contemplated his cards, his black eyes flit to the hand Trae held but only saw the other man's smug grin.

Discarding then picking up two cards, Slade muttered, "Any woman of mine will do as I tell her. She doesn't, her ass meets my hand and she stays locked up until she gets with the program, learns who is boss."

Cisco and Trae laughed at his medieval ideas, then frowned when Slade set down a full house.

Martier glared into his drink and said nothing.

They played numerous hands of poker, drinking and watching sports rerun on a vid-cam on the wall over the bar.

Grumbling like an idling engine, Martier grew edgier and edgier.

Finally he couldn't take it anymore. Dropping his cards, he stood up and fished his keys out of his pocket.

"Going after her? Fuck Martier." Slade tried to reason with him, "You need to stay out of it, bro. Your little human chose to go on a date with another dude, also a human, and a fellow agent, let it go, man. Forget all about that Monmaret shit, there's plenty of other tail in this town, easy tail." He gestured with a slight nod at Tawny who sat with a group of people.

A man sitting next to her intermittently plastered wet kisses on her large lips. She allowed him the occasional grope of her assets, but Tawny's eyes never left Martier, hoping she was making him jealous seeing another man fondling her.

Martier didn't bother looking, he shook his head. "I cannot ignore it, Slade. That fucking chickenshit agent is taking advantage of her feeling bad about herself and drinking. I think she is…uh, sexually naïve, hell, and I don't think she has ever even had alcohol before."

"Yeah," Cisco snickered, "then the way that guy was pouring it down her throat she's more than likely to puke all over him, that should solve the problem. I recommend you let nature take its course. She's small, shouldn't take long."

Not responding, Martier strode away with his friends' snickers in his ears. Hopping in his jeep, he drove to the Seafood Hut.

The place was small enough he could see at a glance Chris' jeep was not there.

He drove to Kesi's place. "Motherfucker," he grumbled. Chris' car was parked out front.

Martier sat in his vehicle stewing. He just knew that piece of shit agent was taking advantage of her. She was so young, obviously inexperienced, he had felt it in her kiss.

His face warmed at the remembrance. Zeus, it was hot. Feeling her tentative strokes on his tongue with hers, damn she just sent him over the bend.

He knew he was getting her turned on, but her inexperience and fear kept her in her head. He should have moved slower. But, hell, she wouldn't ever let him near her; he had to do what he could when he could.

He felt a pang of guilt recalling he had basically kept her trapped on that wooden table, restrained her hands behind her back while he forced his kisses on her. If another man had done that to her, he'd have killed him. But, he'd hoped to get her fired up and she'd relax, let him love her.

Shit- he sat up, the crap that was floating through his brain was crazy. He needed her badly; it was affecting his thoughts, screwing with them. Another woman wouldn't take the edge off his lust, even the thought of another female left him feeling hollow.

Martier rolled down the windows in the jeep and stared at her house. Her windows were open. A sound wailed from the window.

He sat up straighter, was that a scream- It came again.

"Oh fuck-" It was a scream. Kesi was screaming.

Martier bolted out of the jeep and ran to the tiny house. He tried the door, it was locked. He started to call out her name when she screamed again.

"Fuck it-" he cursed. One kick with his heavy boot and the cheap door crashed open. Martier darted inside.

Kesi was on the couch trying to crawl off it. Half on top of her, Chris was tearing at her clothes, when she fought him he slapped her so hard he knocked her to the floor.

"Dammit Kesi, just fucking give it up!" Chris shouted as he jumped down and straddled her then grabbed her blouse and wrenched it apart.

She punched at him, he raised his hand to strike her again, it paused in midair when the door crashing open belatedly registered.

Bellowing a string of curses in a foreign language, Martier vaulted across the room.

Seeing him coming, Chris rolled off Kesi and tried to stand up.

Martier grabbed the front of his shirt with one hand and slammed his fist into his face with the other. Chris howled as blood spurted from his broken nose.

Throwing his own wild punches, Chris' fists did little damage on Martier as the alien wailed away on him- even when the agent was pummeled to the floor and now no longer moving.

"Stop, Captain, stop, don't kill him!" Kesi begged. Grabbing at his huge arms, she tried to hold him back from hitting Chris any more, shouting, "Please, stop!"

Martier pushed her away. On one knee, his other foot planted on the floor, he gripped Chris' shirt and jerked him halfway off the floor. Chris' face was a bloody mess, he gagged and gasped, choking, he spit out blood.

Kesi clutched at Martier's big brawny arms. "Please Captain, stop," she pleaded.

Chris' head lulled, Martier released his shirt, letting him thump on the floor.

Still half kneeling over the agent, panting with exertion and fury, Martier dragged a hand across his brow, wiping at the sweat with his bloody knuckles. His face a granite mask dark with rage and threatening death, he turned to Kesi with a fanged hiss.

She had stepped back when Martier let go of Chris. Her arms wrapped around her body shaking so hard her hair swished back and forth. The big blue eyes were wide and wet with teeming tears of horror, her tiny lips pulled in tight to control her trembling.

Martier stood up. Realizing he was frightening her with his violence and ferocious expression, clearing the rage from his face, he said softly, "You okay, baby?"

He didn't move to her right away, she was in shock. In the process of being sexually assaulted and knocked around, she had watched Martier crash her door in and almost beat her colleague to death.

And he would have if she hadn't stopped him. Martier had been in a blind rage and wasn't going to stop until Christopher Carpenter had become as flat as the rug.

Still trembling all over, Kesi pressed both hands over her mouth, the blues popped from Martier to Chris to Martier.

Moving very slowly, Martier trod the few steps to her, and catching her gently he pulled her to his chest. The tears finally fell as Kesi sobbed, burying her face in his shirt.

Martier stroked her hair with a shaking hand, murmuring lightly, "Shh, Kesindra, *několika,* everything is okay, you are all right now." He whispered soft foreign words of comfort she didn't understand but his deep soothing voice helped to calm her.

An arm around Kesi, Martier slipped his cell out, mumbled something in his own language into it then slid it back in his pocket. Wrapping both arms around her, he let Kesi cry her fright and shock out.

A few minutes and Trae peered inside the open broken door. Stepping inside, he glanced pointedly at Chris lying out cold on the floor and said to Martier, "Your work, I assume."

Slade stepped in behind him, the porch light glinted off his slick black hair.

Martier said quietly to Kesi, "Why don't you go wash your face, honey, okay?"

Wild tangles of blonde curls veiling her embarrassed face, Kesi nodded. Without looking at any of the men, she hurried off to her bathroom.

When she was gone, Martier said in a low voice, "There is no hospital here, take that piece of shit to the clinic. Drop him off and split."

Nodding silently, Trae and Slade crouched to pick up the unconscious man.

As they lifted him, Martier ordered in a cold dark voice, "Then give him a visit tomorrow. I don't dare go near him myself. When he comes to, tell him, he fucking touches her again, nothing will stop me from taking him out. You make sure he understands."

His normal cheerfulness dimmed, Trae said, "No prob, *má bráthair.* Assaulting a defenseless woman half his size," his lips straightened in an unforgiving line, "motherfucker is lucky he still breathes."

Slade roughly jerked Chris up to support him under his arms. "A spanking is one thing, but beating and brutally assaulting women," he shook his head with undisguised wrath. "I hear about him putting his hands violently on another female I'll take him out myself." The two burly men carried Chris out the open door.

Martier went around picking up tossed pillows and righting a table apparently Chris had knocked over while attacking Kesi. He straightened a couch cushion then paused seeing a stack of books on an end table.

He picked one up, his lip quirked as he read, "Learn Self Defense, hmm." He picked up another. "All About Firearms."

With a wry chuckle he lifted another and read out loud, "Martial Arts for Beginners, aye," he set the books down with a shake of his head, "the little girl sure needs some lessons. The Fibbers should be shot for yanking her out of basic training and sending her on that first job."

Chapter Twelve

Martier stood in front of the hall leading off the living room so if Kesi came back she wouldn't see his men picking Chris up and leaving with him.

By the time she came out, Trae and Slade were gone, and Martier was sitting on the sofa. He rose to his feet when she showed.

Kesi stood in the entrance of the hall, her bewildered eyes wide looking around the room. The coffee table had been knocked over, a chair, pillows shoved off the couch during Chris' attack on her.

She looked surprised to see it all back in order. "Where…is he?" Suddenly thinking he could be behind her, Kesi spun with a small shriek.

"Hey, baby," Martier murmured, striding to her, he pulled her into his arms. "He is gone. Trae and Slade took him to the clinic. You are safe." He bent, cupped her chin, lifted it gently. "You okay?"

Her white face was slightly damp from throwing water on it as was the hair at her temples. The blue eyes were huge and unblinking with shocked disbelief.

"Do you want me to take you to a doctor? Did he hurt you?" He ran his big hard hands down her slender arms feeling for broken bones. His stomach turned at the ugly purple bruises rising on her skin, fingerprints.

"Ah, the animal," he growled with suppressed fury, then gently touched the red marks on her face from Chris' slaps.

"I- I can't believe he- he did that, I don't understand," small choppy hiccups jigged against his chest.

"I," Kesi drew a deep shaky breath. "I was dizzy, I told him I wanted to go home. He was fine with it, said he would walk me in, make sure I was okay, then, I mean, he tried to kiss me, I said no, he became insistent, he," she took long breaths to calm her jitters.

"He pushed me down on the couch. I tried to get up, he- he hit me and shoved me down, climbed on top of me started ripping my-" she looked down in horror at her open blouse. Her breasts exposed in the lacey peach, mounded over the demi-bra.

Not what Martier needed to see right now, he grasped her blouse and pulled it together. He attempted to button it but when Chris tore it apart the buttons had flown off.

Quelling his own reaction to her tempting flesh, he pulled her back into his arms pressing her against his chest then strung his bulky arms around her.

Stroking Kesi's hair, he nuzzled his face into the locks scented with her natural fragrance. "Tis okay, little baby, *několika,* tis over now. Here, you sit down and chill a bit, I will fix your door." He helped her sit on the couch. "You have a hammer, some nails?"

She nodded, got back up and went into the kitchen.

125

When she returned she handed him a ball-peen and a handful of mismatched nails, all different sizes.

He smiled at the obvious fact that she wasn't oriented to doing construction.

It took only a few minutes for him to nail the door shut. "Sorry about that, but I heard you scream and the door was locked."

Seeing her face pale again, and her eyes lowered to the floor in shame, he lightened his tone. "Just use the side door until I can get someone here to repair it properly."

Setting the hammer and leftover nails on the table by the door, he trod over to where she stood awkwardly watching him.

"Yes, um," mumbling, the sigh slumped Kesi's thin shoulders. "Thank you for...helping me."

"Kesindra, I can stay here tonight to help you feel safe, I will sleep on the couch, there will not-"

"No," she said. Shaking her head she moved towards the side door. "I'm fine. Thank you."

He moved with her, put out a hand to hold her arm. "Honey, I can see your eyes are wobbly, you are still a bit intoxicated. If it makes you feel better I can take you to my place. I promise, swear, there will be no issues, I will keep my hands to myself. I just want you safe, let-"

Opening the door, Kesi didn't meet his eyes. "Thank you for...everything, I'll be fine. Good night."

Martier sifted a hand softly through her tangled curls. "Kesindra, let me help you."

Mortified at being in the position of her co-agent assaulting her and another man having to come to her rescue brought a tinge of anger in her voice. "I've told you, Captain, I am not worthy. My SAC told me that I deserve what I get, and I need to accept it. He says I'll…learn my hard lessons. Please, just, leave me alone."

"Nay, Kesindra, this fucking was not your fault. None of anything that has happened to you is your fault. That asshole agent, hell, Kesindra, just let me stay, I will-"

"No. Please leave." Choking back a sob, her head stayed lowered. "Thanks for…what you did, now, please, I want to be alone."

He sighed a reluctant growl. "If you would just-"

"Thank you, Captain, you are…" she looked up at him in wonder. "Uh, so sweet." Her sad eyes flicked up to his then dropped. "Good night."

He stared at her. Seeing she was adamant, he gave in with a resigned sigh. "All right. I will check on you tomorrow."

At her head shake, he said gruffly, "Yes, I will. Lock this door." He pulled it closed, waited to hear the lock click then went to his jeep that was parked behind Chris' truck.

Frowning with pursed lips, he needed to call Trae to get the keys to the truck and get it the fuck moved away from Kesindra's property. He didn't want her seeing it, and he sure as hell didn't want that bastard coming back here to get it.

Sitting inside his jeep, Martier watched her house. The lights stayed on. Damn, if she'd only lean on him, let him console, comfort, protect her. She's so pig-headed.

Naturally, he understood they'd known each other only a short time, and really didn't know each other very well.

Nonetheless, he had been instantly attracted to her the first moment he saw her. He didn't need any time or learning personal history to know she was the one for him. Kesi was the one that needed the convincing. They were soul mates, she just didn't realize it. Yet.

The more he knew her, spent even a small amount of time with her, the more he admired the feisty little thing. But that didn't mean he condoned her constant desire to immerse herself in freaking murder investigations. And alone at that. Those poor excuses for fellow agents were useless sacks of skin as far as Martier was concerned.

After a few minutes, he cranked up the engine, backed out of the drive and drove slowly down the narrow, tree-shaded street.

Tiny houses like the one Kesi rented lined the road in hodge-podge clusters. The neighborhoods tended to be built in an uneven way, no pattern to their development as homes sprung up here and there as the mines progressed.

Martier drove around for a while; he just didn't feel like going back to his own place. He actually felt like half of his body was missing.

Recalling how pale and shaken Kesi had been, he grew more and more disturbed. Exiled in humiliation and shame to a shitty country, accused of causing a disaster that was in no way her fault.

Now, tonight, she had been drinking and taking strong medication and had been assaulted by a man she had considered a coworker and a friend. She was undoubtedly devastated and likely feeling even more shame.

A bad feeling chiseled at the inside of his gut. "Fuck it." He knew Kesi wasn't in her straight mind.

Swinging the wheel, he turned the jeep around and headed back to her house. Chris' vehicle was still there.

Parking, Martier hopped out and jogged up to the side door. He didn't give a shit if she was pissed he was there, screw it. What could she do if he camped out on her couch? Physically throw him out?

The thought brought a slight curve to the side of his mouth. If she called the cops, the second they saw him they'd trip over themselves running away.

He moved to peek in a window before knocking on the door. Picturing petite Kesi on the skinny side trying to lift his bulk and drag him out the door, there was no way-

"Fuck! *Sonofabitch-*"

Kesi was lying on the floor.

He slammed his fist through the window in the door, reached in to unlock it and opened the door.

Racing inside, he slid to his knees beside her.

"Kesindra!" he called out. Setting his palm on her forehead, he felt it was clammy, cold. Laying his head on her chest he couldn't tell if she was breathing. He tried for a pulse at her neck, there was a faint thready movement.

Her bottle of pills lay on the floor near her hand. The lid was off, pills sprayed across the tile, a glass off to the side was in fragments, a pool of water around it.

"Fuck, Kesindra, can you hear me?" Keeping the panic from suffocating him, Martier hunched over her and lightly patted her face. She didn't move.

He cupped her chin, brushed her hair off her damp cheek, spoke urgently, "Honey, Kesindra, can you hear me?" Nothing.

Grabbing the bottle, he dumped it in his pocket then slid his hands under her, lifting her as he stood up.

He carried her to his jeep, opened the door and slipped her in the backseat then ran around to the driver's side, jumped in and raced to the clinic.

Tearing down the gravel and dirt roadway, he called Gwanas Pagano telling her to meet him there.

At the clinic, a one-story building of crumbling cement and peeling paint, by the time he reached it, the door opened.

"Captain Dravidian," calmly, the doctor greeted him, holding the door as he carried Kesi inside.

Gwanas Pagano, in her forties, taupe colored twists swung around her round head to her collar. The white lab coat covered a flowered dress that fit snuggly over her slightly lumpy body. Average height, sturdy legs and sensible shoes, with mahogany hued skin, the doctor was serious but amiable,

Gwanas gestured. "Second room on the right."

His boots tromping down the slate floor, Martier held Kesi high and tight to his chest.

Gwanas hurried after him.

In the small white room, he crossed to the bed and carefully laid Kesi down.

"Okay, step back, big boy, stay out of my way," Gwanas instructed Martier as she snapped on clear plastic gloves. "Do you know what she took?"

Fishing the bottle out of his pocket, he handed it to her with a shaky hand.

Two fingers on Kesi's pulse at her neck, Gwanas read the bottle. "Do you know how many she took?"

He shook his head. "Nay. There were four or five scattered on the floor. She had also been drinking. I don't think she has ever had alcohol before. She had some earlier…trauma. She was," he sighed, his eyes on the pale young woman lying so still on the bed, "despondent."

Her pleasant face set gravely, Gwanas took Kesi's blood pressure. Then she moved across the room, grabbed a machine and rolled it to the bedside.

Pulling a metal stand over, she retrieved plasma. Hooking the plasma up on the stand, she picked up a tube, pierced the back of Kesi's hand and stuck the tube with a needle in and taped it securing it to her hand.

While working, she said placidly, "I know, your men brought in Christopher Carpenter a short while ago. He's down the hall in another room. They refused to tell the nurse on shift what happened, but she overheard something about the guy won't be assaulting another woman anytime soon."

She removed the stethoscope from around her neck and set the diaphragm on Kesi's chest and the earpieces in her ears.

Her lips twisted with anger seeing the girl's blouse had been ripped open and there were bruises on her chest, arms, neck and face. "I can put two and two together."

"Aye," Martier let out a harsh breath. "The fucker is lucky he still lives. That is only because she," his voice softened looking down at Kesi, "begged for me to stop."

His fierce face gentled as he watched Kesi, so pallid, unmoving. "She has had it hard, Dr. Pagano."

The doctor moved the stethoscope around Kesi's chest, listened, nodded. "I know. We've talked, she didn't want to elaborate, the shame just engulfs her, but she gave me some idea of what happened back in the US."

She lifted the stethoscope tube and said sadly, "Poor baby. As crappy as she has been treated, she still perseveres. Tries to help here in town when she doesn't have to, treats everyone the same, always with kindness and compassion. Never complaining or trying to convince people she hadn't done anything wrong, or make excuses. Just silently bears it."

She smiled at Martier. "Please call me Gwanas, we're pretty laid back in the rustic corner of the world."

His brows rose in mild surprise. "You speak to me without rancor, Gwanas, when I have taken over the town and am holding the citizens hostage?"

One shoulder bumped. "I'm a good judge of character. You brought this sick young woman in when you didn't have to. I have a feeling there's more to this than just taking over a village. You have harmed no one," her lip nicked up, "except of course the male agent."

Seeing Martier's face darken, she said, "Don't worry. I have no intentions of reporting you for his beating. Not that Dempsey could, or would do anything about it anyway," she smiled wryly. "All I care about is seeing that this young lady is okay."

"And?" Martier's midnight green eyes set fearfully on Kesi's stillness. "How is she? Will she be...all right?"

Gwanas studied the machine hummed an affirmative, "Hmm." bending over Kesi, she lifted one then the other eyelid. "She'll be fine. I don't think she took an overdose. She probably took more than she should have in her distress to shut the world out for the night."

Her mouth pulled in at one corner, dark eyes roving over Kesi, she said, "And likely on an empty stomach along with the alcohol, combined with her lack of experience with booze, and her slight weight, she obviously overdid it. But she will be okay. A good night's rest, she'll be right as rain in the morning. Maybe groggy with an upset tummy or a headache, but all in all, she's fine."

Martier nodded with relief. Then he said, "Ah, the pills, can we take them from her?"

Gwanas' taupe brows tapered between her round, dark brown eyes as she looked from Kesi to the powerful alien with his concern clear on his taut face.

"No. She's taken them too long, too high a dosage, she would have to wean. I'll discuss it with her in the morning. I can't force her to stop, you know. She has a prescription."

"Aye." Martier grew silent, his gaze unwavering from the unconscious girl. The angles of his face hardened.

"That fucker, sorry Doc, that asshole, Carpenter, I don't want him near her. I will stay here tonight-"

"No." Firm, unarguable, she said, "You will leave. This is not a hotel, you are not kin. Mr. Carpenter is at the end of the hall on the other side of the building, I have a nurse staying the night, he won't even know Kesi is in the clinic. Not that he can even move a finger at the moment."

At Martier's stiff frown, Gwanas sighed. "All right. I can have one of the volunteer paramedics come in and stay."

"I preferably want someone who is gay. Or a tough female."

A loud laugh barked out of the doctor's mouth. Her voice buoyant with mirth, she relented, "Okay, I will take care of it. You have two minutes with her and then you leave. Clear?"

The smile lingered, but the brown eyes trained on the hard-muscled big blond, flickered up at the horns and pointed ears before settling back on his dark green eyes, were stern.

He didn't answer, just picked up Kesi's hand without tubes in it.

Gwanas knew if the alien wanted to stay there would be no way she could prevent it. But, he clearly didn't want to further upset the patient so he was behaving himself. With an amused smile, the doctor left them alone.

Holding her hand, his voice low, Martier said, "*Několika,* when you feel better, you and I are having a talk about those bullshit pills and your reckless behavior. Until then," he leaned over and gave her a soft kiss on her forehead, "sleep well, little agent."

He pulled the blanket up to cover her exposed chest, and stood over her, gazing at her sweet, sad face.

After a few moments, he left the clinic.

On the way home, he called Trae to see if he got Carpenter's jeep out of Kesi's driveway.

Chapter Thirteen

Syntagma Gastov'rin Rom-nul's number #1 officer stood at rigid attention.

Mags Nim-nul, a du roi, or rank equal to captain, to Rom-nul's syntagma or colonel rank. Mags stood almost as tall as Rom-nul's 7'2" but not quite.

He had the same reptilian coppery skin but his was laced with chartreuse green stippling, and his webbing of sandy colored hair were long, thin strips fluttering like fronds on a palm tree. Amber eyes stared blankly at his superior.

"*Polemarchos*, I mean, Warlord Rom-nul, uh, Syntagma, sir," Nim-nul advised, "we have settled on that small mining town to the north of here. There are more than enough people for the experiments. However, I fear it will draw a great deal of attention if all the people suddenly disappear for no reason once again.

"I suggest after we take them that you have the village burned to the ground. Leave the children and elderly to burn, that way when they find the remains they will just assume that any survivors had fled, scattered and assimilated somewhere else, and the animals took the carcasses of those that perished. We are just waiting on the rest of the troops to fly in and we can go take them."

"Sounds good." Rom-nul bent at the waist, moving his tall, sword-straight, hard as steel frame under the lower door, the breadth of his shoulders brushed the sides.

The incandescent lighting mottled Rom-nul's coppery skin and glinted off the black-brown webbed hair. He moved to a window to gaze out over the dense jungle saturated with wild creatures, wilder criminals and treacherous landscape.

Setting long, thorny, pencil-thin fingers like a grasshopper's on the sill, he said, "I wish we could fly through this wretched jungle, it would be so much easier and quicker, but we can't chop the trees down it would draw too much notice."

Thick lids lowered over silvery eyes, Rom-nul said to a guard standing rigidly near the door, "We preserved a few of the natives too young to be experimented on, but too old to be let loose in the jungle. They might have made it to civilization and told where we are and what we're doing."

The guard and Captain Mags remained rigid and silent.

The silver eyes glowing with psychopathic evil, Rom-nul's large mouth curved up exposing a litany of razor sharp teeth. The canines extra-long and curved to scimitar points, gleamed with saliva.

"That young girl, the teenager from the last group that was too young for experiments, she wasn't too bad looking. Nineteen or so, not quite as homely or unshapely as the rest of these indigenous people. Have her brought to my chambers."

The girl was chained to the wall in the lab. Her eyes wild with blind terror, she had been there day after day as the people she once knew were butchered in the most agonizing, torturous way-

Already her brain was shutting down with the abject horror of everything she'd seen. When the soldiers came for her, her mind scrambling with confusion and fear, hovered on the precipice of insanity.

The soldiers unlinked her chains from the wall and brought her to Rom-nul's chambers.

He was there waiting for her. He didn't care she hadn't bathed, or eaten in days. The soldiers stripped her and tied her belly down over a barrel.

Muttering in a language she didn't understand, a few took the opportunity to feel her up, quickly squeezing her tender breasts.

One slapped her bare butt with a stinging hard smack, another pinched her virgin nether lips and started to insert his finger into her anus but Rom-nul approached.

The men all stood back and at attention.

Moving in behind the captive girl, Rom-nul snagged a handful of her knotted hair, and lifted her head. He twisted it to the side to enjoy the mindless fright reverberating from her bugged-out terrified eyes. The fear was such an aphrodisiac. He was already hard and throbbing.

"All right, girl, you're going to love this. You ready?" He dropped her head letting her chin bang on the barrel. To the guards, he said, "Move her further over the barrel, I want her ass up so high her vagina is almost facing the ceiling."

The guards obliged. She was too weak and scared to fight back. The men moved the female around on her belly like she was a ragdoll, tipping her until the top of her head tapped the floor.

They tied her hands to a bolt in the floor in front of her. Then took her ankles, spread them apart and tied them down. At Rom-nul's nod, they stepped back.

Rom-nul picked up an apparatus like a lever and brought it to her spread legs. He put it against her vagina.

"Now, hold still sweetness, I like to look way up inside my…females, before plunging my sex organ inside. And, I need to, uh, widen you, to make you ready to be able to take me. I don't want to hurt myself tearing you apart with my breadth."

Handing the lever to Mags, he moved to stand in front of her, unfastened his pants and grasped her hair to raise her head to look at him. He pulled out his phallus. It was seriously as big as a baseball bat, a horse would be jealous. He smiled at her slack mouth dropping open, horrified eyes pinned wide in terror.

Enjoying her palpitating fear, he grinned, the sharp teeth glistening with drool. "You see, young human? My species is somewhat…let's be honest, our genitals are a tremendous amount larger than your human males' huh? That's why I need to open you up."

Dropping her head, he maneuvered back around behind her. Muttering, "I just hope I don't break you like I did the last one before I can finish. It's unfortunate you human females are only good for one shot."

Gripping her rounded bottom with his grasshopper fingers, he mused, "Maybe if I could, ah, control myself a little, I could get more than one or two intercourses out of you, but," his black webbing sifted back and forth with a sigh, "I simply don't like holding back."

The 7'2" syntagma spread her buttocks apart and said over his shoulder to the du roi, "Put the lever here."

Captain Mags, like a moving statue held the lever to the girl's private parts.

"Crank it." Silver eyes emanating pure tortuous lust, Rom-nul leaned in and peered inside the girl as Mags worked the lever, opening her, breaking her pelvic bones- It happened so suddenly, and was so agonizing, a scream couldn't make its way out of her throat.

Mags stepped back as blood gushed out of her body. Rom-nul put his engorged, gigantic phallus against her opening, his drool splatting on her quaking bare back.

The guards and Captain Mags Nim-nul lined against a wall, at rigid attention. Some eyes on the naked, petrified girl splayed open for Rom-nul to penetrate, others turning slightly green, looked away.

Rom-nul plunged, and her screams raced through the building, down the halls, through the rooms, bouncing off deaf ears.

Chapter Fourteen

At the crack of dawn, Gwanas drove Kesi home.

She waited as Kesi wearily climbed out of the passenger side. "Agent Jasmari, Kesi," the doctor said softly, kindly, "get some rest. I'll stop by later this evening to check on you."

Kesi tried to smile, but couldn't. She trod into her tiny house and stayed in bed for two days.

As promised, Martier sent people over to fix the door. He had gone to the clinic to see her but was surprised to learn she was gone.

He drove to her house. When he tried to talk to her, she thanked him for the door repair, offered to pay him, of course he refused, and then she shut him down.

The third day, she got up, showered, dressed, swallowed a pill and headed out. She went to the police station to see if there was any update on the murders.

Richard was there, he gave her a squinty, guilty look. "Hey, Kes. Haven't seen you around lately. You hear Chris

had a fall, slipped down a hill or something, he said."
Richard had seen the black eyes, those couldn't have
happened from a tumble down a hill. The damage done to
Chris had occurred the night Chris and Kesi had left to go to
dinner.

Chris didn't return to their rooms and Kesi was out of
sight for almost three days. Even an inexperienced agent like
himself could connect the dots.

"Uh huh." Not making eye contact with him, Kesi
walked in slowly looking around.

As usual, not much was going on. The dispatch operator
was sitting at a table leafing through a magazine. Since the
phones were out, unless a deputy came across a crime or
someone in need, people had to show up in person to report
an offense.

With the aliens that had taken over the town patrolling
everywhere, crime and even accidents were at a historical
low.

Kesi asked Richard, "Anything new on the killings?"

"That's right, you weren't here yesterday." His wan,
narrow face brightening, Richard pushed the thin straight
hair off to the side out of his small eyes. "There's been
another one."

"Another murder?"

"Yeah." He scratched at his thin moustache with some
exuberance.

"Well? Who? What happened, where, when-"

"Geeze, slow down, will ya? It was a woman. Same as
before, shot in the head. She was found yesterday in her yard
by her neighbor. Gwanas has already worked on her, said it
was the same caliber bullet as the others. No witnesses, half
the town was at the first dinner seating, the other half on their
way there."

"Give me the address."

"Aw, come on, Kes, you can't-"

"Give me all the information, Richard, now."

"Ah, fuck it." He stomped to a desk and lifted a sheaf of papers and photographs, stuffed them in a file folder and handed it to her. "The neighbor said she kept to herself, had no friends, seldom went out, only one ever visited her was her mother. Mother's info's in there too."

"Where's Dempsey?"

"Dunno."

"He look into this at all?"

"He doesn't care, Kes, no one does. There's no law here other than Dempsey, and we are all being held hostage. By goddamned aliens for crying out loud. I think we need to worry a little more about them boiling us all up in caldrons before chowing down on us or wearing our skins as jackets than some killer with a vendetta against particular people. The deaths have nothing to do with us, why should we get involved?"

"But, the town, aren't the people scared that they could be next?"

"You would think, but no. Like ostriches, they think it won't happen to them."

"Oh for the love of-"

"Whatever. I got a date I'm meeting at the saloon, you need anything else?"

"Great. No. Thanks a bunch." Kesi snatched the folder from his hands.

"Knock yourself out." He ambled out the door; the dispatch didn't even look up.

Kesi took a few minutes to peruse the file. She discovered there wasn't much. The deceased was thirty-six year old Lia Gallo. Like the attorney and the judge, she had moved to Brutální from Milčent about ten years ago.

Her only relative was her mother, Mary Gallo, a widow. Lia lived on an insurance pension, she'd been married when she was just twenty-two and her husband died in a mining accident. Her mother Mary worked at one of the clothing stores in town.

Kesi started out like she had before, canvassing the shops, bars, the few restaurants. She hitched rides, crisscrossing the town. As usual, no one knew anything.

Mary Gallo wasn't at work.

Kesi went home, ate lunch, cleaned up, changed out of her jeans and shirt into a skirt and blouse. She made her way to Mrs. Gallo's house.

The small white house was adorned with a border of shiny green bushes, the yard filled with leafy trees and clusters of bright flowers. Pretty as a cottage in a fairytale.

Kesi followed the stone walk up to the front door. She would have liked to call ahead, but, she had no phone. But then again, the aliens had blocked all service anyway.

She knocked on the door.

It wasn't long before the front door opened and a woman in her 60's peered out. Her pale blue eyes behind glasses were rimmed with red; she held a tissue to her nose.

"Hello Mrs. Gallo." Kesi pulled out her ID and badge and held them out for her to see. "I'm Kesindra Jasmari with the FBI. I'd like to ask you some questions, about your daughter, if you feel you are able to. Um, do you mind if I come in?"

The older woman took in the young agent standing on her steps. Kesi's long curly blonde hair was tied back in a ponytail, her white ruffled blouse was neatly tucked into a navy blue skirt that floated a few inches above her knees. The big, altruistic blue eyes were earnest and sincere.

Sniffing back her tears, Mary Gallo pushed her screen door open. Gesturing to Kesi, she said, "Please, come in."

Stepping carefully inside, Kesi looked around the living room. Prim and tidy, the powder blue room matched Mrs. Gallo's sodden eyes. White walls, white and blue comfy furniture was warm and welcoming.

"Please," Mary motioned to the blue flowered sofa, "have a seat."

Smoothing her skirt under her thighs, Kesi gracefully sat down on the couch.

Twisting her fingers in agitation, the eyes behind the glasses welled with tears. With a hitch in her soft voice, Mrs. Gallo asked, "Can I get you some tea? I have some already prepared."

Observing her sad smile, Kesi could see the loneliness behind it. "Oh, uh sure. That'd be great."

The older woman smiled weakly and left the room. She was right back with a tray of teacups, teapot, cream, sugar cubes, spoons, and a plate of sugar cookies. She set the tray down on the coffee table.

After pouring two cups of steaming tea, she offered, "Please Miss, uh, Agent, help yourself."

Sitting in the blue chair kitty-corner to the sofa, Mary smoothed the long pendulum skirt down over her legs, it covered almost to her ankles. She waited while Kesi picked up a teacup, mixed in cream and one sugar cube and set a cookie on her saucer before she got some for herself.

"How can I help you, uh, Agent?" She eyed Kesi warily. Kesi was used to it. Everyone commented on how young, how delicate she was; no one believed at first that she really was an FBI agent.

"Please call me, Kesi." Kesi stirred gently then set the spoon on the other side of the saucer and took a careful sip.

"Oh, of course. Please call me Mary. How can I help you about my…" her weak voice trickled off. She set her cup down to dab the tissue up under her glasses.

She had pinned up just the sides of her curly hair, only a few tinsels of grey knit through the brown, the rest of the curls swirled around the middle of her neck.

"I don't want to repeat what Officer Dempsey has already asked you, but I don't have any of his notes."

"Oh," swallowing tea, Mary shook her head, crossed her ankles and tucked them to the side of the cushioned chair. "He hasn't been by. I guess he's out interrogating suspects."

Kesi bit back her snort, interrogating his television more likely. Taking a few sips of the sugary creamy beverage, she set the teacup on its saucer and placed them on the coffee table and glanced around the soft room.

What appeared to be family pictures in frames lined the mantel of a fireplace, a few paintings of flowers and religious aspects hung on the walls.

White lacy doilies dotted under several lush African violets setting on a few tables, and under a vase in front of the front window.

There were all sizes and designs of crucifixes scattered around, the sickly sweet but mild aroma of a scent infuser wafted throughout the room.

Taking out her notebook and pen, Kesi set them on the table and got to her feet. She wandered over to the mantel and picked up a framed picture. "Is this Lia? She looks like you."

The picture showed a small boned young woman with dark hair and light blue eyes smiling shyly at the camera.

"Yes, that's my Lia. She was 24 then." Setting her cup down, Mary pulled her glasses off and wiped her eyes.

Kesi set the picture down and picked up another. It was of an elderly couple. "Mary, I am trying to figure out why someone would kill a lovely young woman such as your daughter." She already knew but as an icebreaker she asked, "Did she work?"

"No. I've been ill and haven't been able to work for a while, Lia spent most of her time with me. She hardly ever went out anywhere. My deceased husband's insurance pays the bills."

"Can you think of why anyone would want her dead? Did she have problems with anyone? A neighbor perhaps?"

The brown curls ruffled with the negative shake of her head. "No, Lia is…was, so quiet, shy, she never offended anyone. As I said, she hardly ever left the house, didn't even go to church with me."

Returning to the couch, Kesi sat back down and picked up her teacup and took a sip. "Hmm. Was she in a relationship? Or have recent past relationships? Perhaps there was a jealous ex or a stalker?"

Again Mary shook her head. "No. Ever since…" She took a deep shuddering breath and started again, "After that *time*, she only goes from her house to mine, and never in the dark. Her father, before he died," her lips stiffened with a little anger, "strongly insisted she have her own place."

Kesi smiled with kind sadness. "I'm sorry for your losses, Mrs. Gallo."

"Mary, please, I don't stand on formalities." Dabbing at new falling tears, she took a few more long deep breaths before going on.

"Lia was so torn up over…it. But Bran, her father, wanted her to be strong and felt if she lived with us she would become too dependent. He thought she would never get past the...incident if we coddled her. And now," tears slipped down her pale cheeks.

"What, uh, incident? Did something happen to Lia?" Kesi picked up her notebook, flipped a few pages.

The teacup clinked in the saucer in Mary's shaking hands. She took a sip then bent towards the coffee table, the china made a clunk when she awkwardly set it down.

The pale blue eyes clouded, mouth trembled slightly. Her glasses clutched in her hand, she leaned over and set them on an end table. Wiping at her eyes with the sodden tissue, already distraught, Mary became even more visibly disturbed.

Kesi sat silent, patient. Her heart bled for the poor woman, a widow losing her only child.

Mary stood up and went to a table where violets bloomed and plucked up a bunch of tissues from a box that matched the purple flowers.

As if needing the close companionship of another person, she went to the couch beside Kesi and sat down heavily on the cushion. The tears spilled, she wiped them up, patted her eyes then sighed wearily.

Taking a deep breath, Mary let it out with a frayed exhale. She fiddled with the long skirt of her dress rearranging it over her knees and smoothing it down her legs.

Finally, her voice quivering, the words squeaked out. She cleared her throat and the words came out with a waver, "I'm surprised you don't know." She covered her face with her hands.

"Mary, take your time," Kesi said softly.

It took another minute for the older woman to get control of her overwrought emotions. "Um, twelve years ago Lia was...assaulted," her throat closed with a choke.

147

A sob hiccupped from the woman, her voice very quiet, she whispered, "Uh, Lia was raped. Brutally. Viciously. He snatched her right off the street as she was getting into her car after work. The sun had long set, he'd hidden in the shadows waiting to pounce on her." Mary had to pause again to calm herself.

"Ah, anyway, after the rape, h- he half strangled her then beat her almost to death, she became blind in one eye." Mary took a breath, exhaled it with a sob. "He left her for dead. He thought he'd killed her.

"Thank God a couple was driving to a bar nearby and saw her lying alongside a dark road. He'd tossed her out of his car like she was trash."

With a sneer, Mary said, "My Lia had remembered him. She worked at Daffy's Diner and he'd been in for dinner. He'd taken a cotton to her right away and asked her out. She was so shy, she declined. He apparently refused to take no for an answer. She was in the hospital for months afterwards."

"Oh my gosh, Mary," Kesi cried, moved closer to her. "I'm so sorry. Was the person caught? Prosecuted?"

Mary sighed out her pain. She gazed blankly towards the front window, the sun was beginning its descent.

"Yes. The police pulled in every male in the area of his description with a record of assault or violence to women. Lia pointed him out first in photos then in a line-up thing. She had scratched him. He still had the gouges on his face, they matched his blood and skin under Lia's nails."

"What happened next?" Kesi jotted in her notebook.

"He went to trial and was found guilty of rape and attempted murder. He got 20 years in prison. Not enough as far as I'm concerned," she ground bitterly through clenched teeth. "God, he hurt my baby," the wail came from the bottom of her broken heart.

It took her a few long moments to again regain her composure.

Wiping her eyes, she let out a heavy huff. "She was never the same after that. Refused to leave the house, get a job. She had a small inheritance her grandma left her to support her. She was terrified of every sound and shadow and she wanted to live with us, I wanted to take care of her."

Mary gave Kesi the saddest smile Kesi had ever seen in her life.

"But," she went on with a bit of anger, "Brant, my husband, thought she would get stronger if she didn't live under our shelter. He forced her to move out." The bitterness oozed from every wrinkle on her face.

Kesi waited for her to collect herself. "I am so sorry, Mary, for your pain, for Lia's pain. Is he still in prison?"

A sorrowful twitch to her quivering lips, a vengeful smile steadied them. "No. He was murdered in prison five years ago. Good riddance to bad rubbish. He deserved it. Actually, I would have hoped he'd suffer first, the way my Lia did." She sighed.

"At least he was punished for his deeds. And now," the tears welled and rolled down her cheeks, "my poor baby has been mu- murdered," her shoulder racked with sobs. Kesi moved closer to her, and settled an arm around the older woman's shoulders.

When Mary calmed, Kesi asked, "Do you remember the offender's name?"

"Huh," a sputter of contempt burst from her sad lips. "I could never forget. Alain Montblanc."

Patting her shoulder gently, Kesi moved to perch on the edge of the cushion and wrote the name down.

She asked a few more questions about Lia's movements, people she knew, but there was little for Mary to offer. Lia seldom left the house and then it was to only go to her mother's house.

Kesi rose. She said softly, "Well, I think that's all for now, Mary. I appreciate your time, and the tea and cookies. If anything else comes to you," she tore a paper out of her notebook and handed it to the older woman, "do not hesitate to call me...or, uh," she remembered their phones were blocked.

"Miss Kesi," Mary said quietly while walking her to the door, "if I thought of something that might help, believe me, I would get to you to tell you. I have friends with cars."

It was late, Kesi walked home.

The next day she rose before dawn and went to the station. She greeted the dispatcher. "Hi Nancy, I'm going to do some research." She headed for the desk her computer was locked in.

"Sure, I'm going to breakfast. A long breakfast, lock up behind yourself when you're done, okay?" Nancy opened a drawer and took out her purse. Iron-straight black hair brushed her shoulders, her skin the color of burnt umber, big freckles smattered over her broad face that widened with her smile.

"See ya." She swept out the door.

Kesi set up her computer, set her notebook beside it and went to freshen up in the bathroom. She grabbed a glass of water on the way back and sat down and started pressing buttons.

The floor creaked behind her. Turning her head, she said, "Who-"

The world went dark.

Chapter Fifteen

Her moan made her head ache more. The short breath she drew hurt like she was breathing through raw skin.

Kesi wriggled slightly then peered out from under fluttering lashes.

Her bleary eyes flickered around the room. She was in the clinic. Again. But she wasn't alone.

Martier was sitting in a chair with his feet up on a box, his big fingers twined together rested in his lap. Dark green eyes blazed at her.

"Kesindra." His boots hit the floor. He stood up and moved to sit on the side of the bed, the mattress sinking with his weight.

Kesi's eyes swelled with fright, she struggled to sit up, frantically searching for the door to escape him.

"Ah shit, Kesindra, stop it. It was not me that hurt you. Would I not have finished the job? Would I be here now?" He didn't mention he would have just snapped her neck, not smash her head in with an ashtray then fumble at strangling her.

Scraping breaths rapid, shallow, and painful, the curl of her lashes lowered to brush her cheeks, she still tried to wriggle upright.

Getting to his feet, he said, "Here, let me help you." Martier grabbed pillows stacking them against the wall, then put his hands under her arms and gently lifted her to recline into their firm softness.

He sat back down on the bed facing her and waited for her to calm down.

Her breaths still anxious and fast, with a wince Kesi shoved her hair off her shoulders and rasped, "What happened? Why am I here? Did I faint?"

Her eyes flit to the door and back to him. "Why are you here?" Her hand settled against the front of her neck, she swallowed and winced.

"Ah." Facing her, he curled one leg on the mattress, the other over the side of the bed, his foot flat on the floor. Leaning back on his palm, he studied her for any signs of serious physical distress.

Then he cleared his throat, voice dropped deep and husky, he said, "You," he took a short breath before continuing. "You were found in the police station, on the floor, unconscious." Dark brows struck down with his anger. "You did not pass out, Kesindra, you were hit in the head."

Aghast yellow brows shot up in incredulity. Her hand moved up to cover her mouth, then she whispered against her fingers, "What? Are you sure? On purpose?"

She was so naïve, his thought was clear in his grim expression. Lowering his eyes so she wouldn't see his rage and become fearful of him again, he nodded. Quietly, he said, "Tell me what you remember, *několika*."

He reached out and took her hand, holding it gently, but tight enough she couldn't tug it away.

She stared unblinking at their hands. Then slowly raised her eyes to his.

The deep forest green glinted in the orbs leveled at her, his pupils dilated. Her gaze lifted to his head. Seeing where she looked, Martier smoothed a self-conscious palm over his horns. They were like ram's horns and curved towards his back.

Gently swallowing several times relieving the raw scraping she felt in her throat, she said. "I, uh," closing her eyes she thought back. "Yesterday I had interviewed the latest murder victim's mother, Mary Gallo. I went home right after. This morning…"

She pulled at her hand, he let it go. Rubbing her eyes, she missed his frown at her breaking their contact.

He prompted, "Where did you go this morning?"

She put a hand to the back of her head with a wince and closed her eyes again to remember. "I went to- to…" her lids lifted slightly, a hint of blue flickered back and forth. "Oh," she looked directly at Martier as she remembered.

"I went to the station. Oh my gosh, Captain, I found the connection between the murders. I think. Anyway, I went to research this, uh, rape that happened to Lia Gallo 12 years ago. I," her lids lowered as she ran this morning's events through her aching brain.

"I remember I turned the power on the computer. It's ancient, takes forever to come up, so I went to get a glass of water. There was no one there but me. Nancy had gone to breakfast. She knew I'd answer the walkie-talkie radio if there were any calls. I came back with the water, and, sat down, I think."

The strain of trying to recall what happened pulled the color from her fair complexion, drew lines around her eyes. Aggrieved, she gasped with a hic of alarm, "I can't remember anything past that." She leaned forward in her panic.

Martier gently pushed her shoulder, nudging her back against the pillows. "Kesindra, take a deep breath. You need to rest." He took her hand again.

Air whooshed in exhale from her lungs as she calmed down. "I'm fine. Just a slight headache. My throat," her hand went to her throat, "it's kind of sore," she massaged it with her fingers.

Eyes tapered to slits, his skin darkened, it was a struggle to keep the rage out of his voice. "You were found, *několika,* unconscious on the floor. Gwanas says it looks like someone clocked you in the back of the head with Dempsey's heavy glass ashtray; it was on the floor near you.

"Nancy must have scared them off. She had forgotten her keys and came back. She found you out cold, with," his lips bunched, pulled in, his thumb brushed the top of her hand, "a rope around your neck."

"What!" The curly lashes flapped over shocked blue, her hand went back to her neck.

Martier gently squeezed the hand he still held. "Shh, tis okay. Gwanas said Nancy must have scared the person off before the rope was…" his gaze dropped, picturing Kesi lying helpless, unconscious while some fucker put a rope around her neck and was going to murder her.

He stretched his neck side-to-side as he worked to unclench his jaw. He needed to do something to hide his rage from her, and squash the terror and panic that rioted through his system.

He got up and poured a glass of water from a pitcher and handed it to her then sat back down.

Not fully comprehending what he was saying, she sipped the water slowly, grimacing when she swallowed. She murmured vaguely, "It doesn't really hurt, just feels, rough."

Martier swallowed hard, coughed, his voice sounding rusty, he murmured quietly, "Aye. Gwanas says there was no permanent damage."

"To her neck, her head I don't know," the doctor said from the doorway as she entered the room.

"You think she might have a concussion?" Martier asked.

"I checked her pupils earlier, they were fine. She doesn't appear to be-"

"She can be talked to directly, Doctor. Contrary to popular belief, she is an adult." Kesi served her frown from Gwanas to Martier.

Gwanas' grin was huge. "Sorry, sweetie. It's just you're so young, so delicate, that we forget you are not a child, that you are an adult."

"Barely," Martier muttered, ignoring Kesi's dirty look.

"Anyway," Gwanas said, as she checked Kesi's pulse, looked at her eyes, "how many fingers?" She held her hand up.

"Three. I feel fine, Doctor."

"Dizzy? Light-headed? Blurred vision, any nausea?"

"No, no, no, and no. Just a bit of a headache and a raspy throat. I'm fine, I can go home." She started to move but Martier put a hand on her midriff and pushed her back. "Hey," she glared at his hand, "you-"

"Just sit for a minute, Kesindra. You were bashed over the head for fucks sake." He commanded with a low growl, leaving his hand on her lower ribs, "Give it fucking minute."

"He's right, honey, he has a filthy mouth, but he's right." Gwanas smiled, hanging her stethoscope back around her neck. "I need to go out on a call, when I come back I'll check you to clear you to go home. Okay?"

"But I can go now-"

"Stay put until I come back. Doctor's orders." Gwanas grinned at Martier and slipped from the room.

"This is ridiculous." Kesi pushed his hand off and rolled to the edge of the bed and stood up slowly. "See. I'm fine. No dizziness." She looked down at her skirt ruefully. "I am pretty wrinkled though."

"Pretty yes, wrinkled, no." Martier stood up beside her. Then his face sharpened, the planes hardened. His mouth a harsh line, he dictated, "Enough now, Kesindra, enough of this investigating bullshit. I told you it was too dangerous."

"Don't be obtuse," she objected, trying to push past him but he stood in her way like a towering blond redwood. "I am obviously getting close, I made someone nervous. This is the time to press it, push them out of the woodwork-"

"Nay!" he thundered, dark brows like hard ridges lowered over his furious eyes.

Jumping at his loud eruption, Kesi stepped back from him.

He pointed a long finger at her. "I said, enough. You are done. You are not a cop; you never even went through the fucking academy for Zeus' sake. You have no weapon, you are way too vulnerable, too fragile, nay," crossing his burly arms over his thick chest, he shook his head vehemently, "there will be no more investigating."

Her forehead creased, brows twitched with anger. "What? Who the hell do you think you are telling me what I can and can't do? You tried before, I told you what I do is none of your business. You can't make me-"

"Yeah, I can. I can make you do anything. You are at my mercy, little human. I own the town, I own you, and you are not strong enough to fight me."

An infuriated snarl rose up her throat, her eyes went squinty at him. "You do not own me, you do not control me, get out of my way."

She went to shove past him; he grabbed her around the waist and pushed her back at the bed, snapping, "I repeat, I own this town right now, and that includes you, *nĕkolika.*"

Kesi wrenched from him, he hauled her back, gripped her jaw, held it tight and seized her mouth with his.

He tore over her, dominating the young agent, his mouth pillaged her small lips with rampaging passion, heated aggression. Forcing her lips apart, his tongue dove in to take possession of her in an all-out assault, abducting every one of her senses.

Her struggles were futile. Furious, Kesi resisted being drawn in, even as her nipples tightened into hard little buds, and heat and dampness pooled between her legs.

He released her to reach for the buttons on her blouse and she shoved him and ran.

"Dammit, Kesindra." Cursing, taking a mere two steps and Martier grabbed her, brought her back and pushed her face forward, her palms slammed on the mattress.

"Let me go you- you-"

"I said enough, *nĕkolika.* I will show you who your owner, your master, is." His growl thrummed in his heavy chest, voice a hard threatening hiss, he snarled, *"You will obey me."*

He bent her over the bed until she was braced on her forearms on the mattress then he shoved her blouse up and roughly cupped her breasts with his hard hands.

A groan rumbled out as he wove his long fingers over her plump flesh, groping her luscious curves, filling his rugged hands with her fullness. His ministrations were not painful, they were devoted, cherishing, savoring.

The harshness in his voice turned sultry soft. "You feel like heaven, my beautiful human."

Kesi froze at his touch. A man had never handled her that way before. Chris had wrangled his hands all over her body but not with passion. He just ruthlessly gripped, painfully squeezed her everywhere with horny anger, disregarding how he was hurting her.

Martier caressed her breasts, harshly yes, he was such a big strong man, but she felt thrilling sensations in the aggressive yet carefulness of his rough grasp.

His moans of delight in her ear misting her skin, expressing his quintessential feel of Kesi's feminine body, his heated breath blew tendrils of her hair over her face.

He pinched and tugged her nipples over the sheer silk bra and groaned again when they turned to stiff peaks in his fingers. "Ah, Kesindra," growling his pleasure, he kneaded her full globes.

"So soft, fucking soft, firm and soft, baby, cannot get enough of you," he rambled then slipped into a different language.

When Kesi stopped fighting him, he leaned his chest against her back and slid his palm down her side, down to her thigh. As he pushed his hand up under her skirt, he nudged her feet apart with his boot.

When she murmured a protest, he pushed her to half lie over the mattress, holding her down with a heavy palm on her back.

"Captain," she gasped as his hand stroked up her thigh to her panties.

"Martier," he panted in her ear, "my name is Martier, you know that." He squeezed her thigh with his big hand and moved it to slide down into the back of her panties.

"Ah, fuck, baby," he muttered with an elated groan. Palming her bare bottom, he squeezed her cheeks like they were firm, plush, balls.

Her face smushed into the sheets, Kesi whimpered, "Captain, please don't-" her voice hitched when he moved his other hand from her back to up her skirt and now gripped her butt with both hands.

He fervently kneaded her flesh like he'd never felt a woman's ass before.

Demanding, "Call me Martier, dammit, Kesindra," he squeezed more painfully, then suddenly pushed her panties down, jerked her one leg up to push them off then shoved her legs further apart with his knee.

"Wait!" Kesi cried. On her stomach, blouse and skirt pushed up, her bottom half totally bare, panic struck along in confliction with the hot flush that flashed between her legs radiating up her body.

"Hush, darlin'," he muttered. Forcing her flatter on the bed with his powerful chest pressing against her back, he moved his hand around the front of her.

When he cupped her womanhood, Kesi jumped with a sound of fear and surprise, and a shock of sizzling heat.

His cool, tough fingers gripping her, such an unfamiliar feeling of a man's heavy hand on her most private, most sensitive, most *bare* parts she tried to get free of him.

"Tis all right, I will not hurt you, my little *několika*. Zeus, my gods you are wet," a groan grated from his chest through his throat. He lowered his mouth to her neck, kissed then sucked her flesh, his hard fingers wriggled over her woman's flesh.

"Captain, you can't, please, you can't…" her whimpers disappeared into the sheets with her stunned gasp and shudder sliding into a moan as Martier drew his fingers over her bared slit.

"Satin, baby, pure satin, I cannot wait to taste you here." He stroked up and down then touched her swollen throbbing bud, and sucked harder on her neck.

"No," Kesi whined, squirming against his hand, not from it but into it. "You can't put your mouth, uhh," the groan ground with tremors.

Martier caressed her clit, drew her own silk and swirled it around her sensitive bud.

"God, Captain, please-" Her words chopped off in a gasp when he dipped the tip of his wide finger inside her sex.

"Please what, *několika*, tell me, you want me to stop?"

His rigid shaft pressing into her bottom, he slipped his other hand up her front to clutch her breast while he fingered her clit, and carefully slid more of his thick finger inside her tender woman's canal.

His whisper coarse, "I will stop if you say so, do you want me to?" Buttering more of her silk on his finger, he very slightly moved it out then back in, while pinching her nipple.

She must make him stop, but, Kesi couldn't think; his stroking, sucking, plucking, penetrating her body was inflaming, whipping slashes of fire everywhere he touched.

A groan rolled up from her chest, then, "Oh!" Another gasp burst out as he delved his finger deeper into her.

She tried to move her hips from his hand. "No, yes, stop no-" Gasping, unfamiliar with the tingling sensations, pressure building, pushing and deepening in her sex, Kesi panicked.

Holding her against him, her soft slender body curled into his hard roughness, he clutched her breast tightly and murmured softly, "Ah, okay, just wait, just a second, sweet little human."

He pulled his finger out, lathed it around her sex, lightly pinching then circling her nub until Kesi's hips moved with his motions.

When moans rippled from deep in her chest up to her throat, he gently pushed his finger back inside, deeper. "Zeus, little one, you are too small, too tight," he wanted inside her so badly, but this wasn't the time. She could never take his girth.

Licking her neck with a modicum of guilt, Martier realized he was taking advantage of her weakened situation. She was unnerved from the attack, and desperately vulnerable, and he was deliberately seducing her with his experienced skill.

He wasn't any better than that prick agent that tried to rape her. He should pull right now from her sweet body, all soft and curvy, and fragrant as hell, ahh, but he couldn't make himself let her go.

She was obviously a virgin, he couldn't take her. Not now, anyway. He needed to build her trust, and her passion, for him. He'd known the day he captured her, took her from Bruglon, that she was his.

Now she would never know another man's touch, kiss, penis. He could have killed, and almost did, Chris Carpenter for his attack on her, *his* woman. She was his, he just needed to convince her of it.

No longer protesting, she was clutching and murmuring incoherently into the sheets as he worked his fingers.

His raging hard-on pushing intensely at her perfect round bottom, Martier sucked on her neck. Rolling his hard fingers around her clit, he slipped his finger in and out, deeper, then faster each time until her slender hips were pushing back at him, meeting his thrusts.

Damn he wished like fuck he could slam his cock into her precious channel right now. Damn. So hot, so sweet, fresh, tender, and so receptive, he had easily turned her on. She was made for loving, with him.

Gusty moans and kinked whimpers gravitated from Kesi, she was mindless, only aware of the burning agony Martier was building between her legs.

His thick phallus rubbed and strained against her, swelling in his jeans and growing harder and harder, same as his horns. His big hand clutching, crushing her breast in his fevered intensity.

When she arched back into him with a charged hiss, her channel gripping his finger in paroxysms, he knew she was on the brink.

"Okay, sweetheart, let it go, let it come, honey, I have you." His fingers moved feverishly in and around her sex until her hips were bouncing, her uncontrolled breaths ragged and harsh, building, louder.

"Cap- Cap- Captain," her stutter edged out shaking her core. "Fire, I'm on fire, it…I'm, help me!" she cried, sucking in a deep shuddering breath.

"Martier, baby, say my name, know the man who is bringing you the stars and rockets. I have got you," his rough purr blew against her skin.

He sucked her flesh hard, squeezed her breast and thrust his finger and thumbed her bud until her body started wracking. Her sobs bubbled up her throat; her spasming channel clenched his finger.

"Mar...*tier!*" she cried as the world disappeared and she was all screams and sensation, fire and lightning.

When her body started convulsing, her frantic fingers clawing the bed and gasping screams muffled in the sheets, Martier pushed another finger in and bit her neck, sinking his fangs, just barely breaking the surface.

He wanted more, but she was nowhere near ready to take what he had to give.

She came hard against his hand, shaking and quivering, her rubber legs gave out.

He moved his hand from her breast, wrapped it around her waist holding her up and snug against his chest. His penis rubbing hard against her, he almost came right along with Kesi.

"There, that is it *několika*, I have you," he promised, his thrusts gentled as her body quivered around his fingers.

When there were only faint tremors, he removed his hand and turned her around to face him.

Her cheeks were flushed, eyes closed, lips parted in rapid pants, her tongue circling them.

Martier leaned in and sucked at her lips, licked them like she had. Plunging his tongue inside, he tasted the last of her orgasm, her mouth convulsively swallowing his tongue. He had to fight to keep from ripping his pants open and shoving himself inside her.

Her chest rose fast and shallow. The shirt shoved up, those tits he was dying to see almost falling out of the peach bra, nipples peaked, poking against the light material.

Next time, he told himself, she would be completely naked, and looking at him while she came screaming his name as he pounded into her.

He slipped his hands under her and lifted her to stand on trembling feet. While she gathered her wits and her body calmed, he fixed her panties, pulled down her skirt, straightened her blouse. When he was done, he helped her to sit, then he sat next to her on the bed.

Gwanas would kill him if she knew what he had just done to her vulnerable, injured patient.

Kesi glanced at him then quickly away, her face flushed with red. Lying down, she turned from him on her side, pulled her knees up, and covered her face.

"Oh fuck no, Kesindra, don't you fucking deny what we just did."

"You…need to go. Now. Please." She refused to look at him.

"Nay, dammit, woman, come on, don't-"

"Please, please, go." Her shoulders shook with silent sobs of shame, her hands over her face.

"Kesindra…"

"*Please*," it came out in a sob. Her breath hitched, belly sucked in with each sharp inhale.

He didn't move, just sat and stared at her.

She was ashamed of her body's reaction to his seductive ministrations. His loving caresses, strokes of passion. She was so fucking fragile; he had to make her understand she could trust him.

Berating himself, he had moved too fast. But he wouldn't take it back if he could. Zeus, the way she came apart in his hands, shit, he was so hard he was going to have to take care of his own relief later or he wouldn't be able to function.

Later, in the privacy of his home he would recall how she keened, convulsing from his touch, gasping his name, the feel of her soft lush body. The way she had sucked with wild abandon on his tongue, the feeling of his fangs sinking into her.

Suppressing the shivers the memory wrought, without another word, he reluctantly got up and quietly left.

He heard her sobs as he made his way down the hall, each cry a stab in his heart.

Chapter Sixteen

Gwanas came back, surprised that Martier was gone. "Where's the handsome captain? The way he was looking at you, came right in as soon as he heard what happened and stayed here until you woke, I didn't think he would leave without you." Her brown eyes narrowed at Kesi.

Her cheeks red and damp with tears, Kesi wouldn't make eye contact.

Hurrying to the bed, the doctor said urgently, "Honey, he didn't hurt you did he?"

Kesi was mortified that the captain had done what he did to her right there in the infirmary room. Her cheeks reddened like beets, gosh, anyone could have walked in and seen him leaning over her with his big, powerful body pressed against her, her blouse shoved up, his hands all over her...breasts.

Her cheeks heated remembering everything. He'd pushed down her panties, his hand on, *in* her, his fingers inside her stroking, *oh God*, and she had let him!

She was no better than that floozy Tazzy or Tammy, whatever that blowsy woman's name is that was always hanging all over him. Kesi could picture the voluptuous, larger, sturdier, more experienced woman with the blond captain. She would be able to equal and satisfy his rough, lusty needs.

Why on earth was he wasting his time with Kesi? Her lips twisted bitterly, he probably thinks it's funny to screw with the cop.

He and his friends are probably getting a huge laugh out of the naïve, inexperienced virgin that screamed as she came from his fingers- *oh*, her cheeks were burning; she covered them with her hands.

Of course, he was an outlaw, a villain, a kidnapper. If he'd really wanted her he would have just taken her whether she was willing or not, but it was funnier to make her beg for it.

"Kesindra?" Gwanas broke into her revelries. "Are you all right, honey?" She stood at the bedside smoothing the long blonde curls off Kesi's damp face.

Blinking rapidly to hide her humiliation, Kesi pushed to the side of the bed to get up. "No, I mean, yes, I'm fine. The captain had, uh, things to do. I need to go, do….something."

She slid to her feet and smoothed down her skirt. The image of the captain's huge hard hands up it, touching her private parts made the blood rush back to her head, and between her legs. She moved quickly to the door.

"Wait, Kesi, let me drive you. You live too far away to walk, and we still don't know if you have a concussion. I'll get my keys and meet you out front. Okay?"

"I don't want to put you out-"

167

"Don't be ridiculous, there are no other patients here right now. Go on now, I'll meet you at the back door." She scooted out before Kesi could argue.

Great. At least she didn't have to walk the hall of shame. No one would see her rumpled clothes, bedroom hair, passion-misted eyes- darn, she needed to get out of there.

She quickly used the restroom. Throwing water on her face, she finger-combed her long locks and when she exited out the back door, Gwanas was there waiting for her.

The women walked to the 20-year old Fiat and climbed in. Gwanas turned the key…a few times, before the engine fired up. The old car sounded like a cargo train chugging uphill.

As she pulled out, Kesi noticed a jeep a few yards down the street parked beside a building with the engine running.

Gwanas chuckled.

"What?" Kesi stared at the jeep as they passed it.

"Your captain obviously planted one of his men to follow you, make sure you were safe, and out of trouble."

"You're kidding!" Kesi whipped her head forward. More likely to ensure she didn't try to escape again and flee to the authorities. "Can you lose him?"

Gwanas glanced at the young woman filled with contradictions sitting beside her. "You really want me to?"

"Yes."

Smiling, the doctor said, "This town is small but vastly laid out with spidered streets and dilapidated shacks everywhere, plenty of places to ditch a tail." She pushed the gas pedal to the floor and the old car roared down the street.

She'd used the element of surprise. The driver of the jeep hadn't expected to be noticed much less ditched, at least that quickly.

By the time he pulled out, the ancient Fiat was nowhere in sight.

"Crap," Slade swore a string of non-English curse words. "Martier is going to fucking kill me." He drove around for a while, but the Fiat was nowhere to be found.

He headed back to the captain's place to prepare for a chewing out.

When they lost the tail, Gwanas slowed down.

Glancing all around, Kesi said, "Can you drop me at the police station?"

The doctor's lips pushed out in protest. "Um, I think it would be wiser for you to go home and rest."

"The tail will definitely go there to find me. Besides, there's some stuff I was going to research when I was…assaulted."

"Exactly, the station is not the safest place for you, Kesi."

"Oh, I'm sure there will be other people there now. It'll be all right."

Gwanas skewed several worried glances at her. Sighing in relent she said, "Okay. But I'm not leaving you if there is no one else there."

When she pulled up at the jail, Dempsey, Nancy, and Arianna's vehicles were there. Irritation burned a hole in Kesi's gut. Even Arianna was allowed a vehicle.

Apparently Agent Dukes had decided Kesi could not get in any trouble if she was forbidden to rent a jeep or carry a weapon. She'd been told every time she checked the local car rental places that there were no vehicles available. Clearly Dukes had told them to lie to her.

Her belly burned more when she realized if she had been carrying gun, it would have likely been taken from her after

169

she was knocked out, and the person would have just shot her with her own gun instead of trying to strangle her.

A cold chill quivered through her, and she would be dead. *Gah*, things just kept getting worse.

Still, she refused to admit that not giving her a gun had possibly saved her life, making Dukes right. But still, it was wrong. And sexist.

She quickly got out of the Fiat before Gwanas could lecture her further.

Leaning her head back in the window, Kesi said, "Thanks for everything, Doctor, the medical care and the ride. Please let me know what my bill is."

Ignoring the part about the bill, Gwanas said, "Sure, anytime, honey. You be careful now, you hear me? Take caution of who and what is behind you at all times."

Kesi grinned at her. "I will." She strode to the station and went inside.

It was cool and dry compared to the balmy outdoors. The light was not as bright as the full sun's exposure but it smelled as woodsy as the forest outside from the old paneling and wood planked floors and walls.

She saw Dempsey sitting in his chair with his feet up on his desk, sound asleep. She could hear his snores from the doorway.

Nancy looked up as she came in. Her face immediately melted in concern. "Hey, Kesi, you all right? You should be at the clinic-"

"I'm fine, Nancy. And I want to thank you for your quick assistance. Gwanas told me you ran next door to get Robbie to go for help."

Nancy stood up. "Geezus, you gave me such a fright. I came in and there you were, out like a light on the floor with a rope tied around your neck. I thought for sure you were dead. I was terrified!"

"Uh huh, but I'm okay now."

"I was so worried," Nancy's brow wrinkled in concern. "You sure you're okay?"

Arianna soared over to Kesi and threw her arms around her. "Oh, Kes, I was so worried when I heard! I was on my way just now to check on you at the clinic. Should you be out of bed?" Her permanent smile was shaded with concern.

Kesi found it hard to look the secretary in the eye. The last time she'd seen her was at the barn and she'd been dangling on a man and her blouse was wide open completely exposing her bare breasts.

That was of course after the captain had stood between Kesi's spread thighs and had thoroughly kissed her.

And she had that thought that was the epitome of embarrassing. That session had nothing on this morning! The word bed made heat waves rush through her body.

Feeling herself blushing, Kesi looked away. "I don't need to be in bed."

Dempsey's snores rattled then choked and he sat up blinking and sniffing. Seeing Kesi he smiled. With a wide yawn, he uttered, "Hey agent, you're all right then?"

"Yes, yes, everyone, please, I am fine. A little headache that's all. I came in to finish my research-" She glanced around. "Where's my computer?"

The three people stared at her.

Arianna cleared her throat then said, "Uh, it's gone. As the paramedic guys were taking you, I happened to show up. I was going to get it and put it in your drawer where you like to keep it locked, but," she shrugged with her palms up. "I couldn't find it anywhere. I assumed you had taken it home or something."

Kesi's mouth dropped. She cried with disbelief, "Oh no, someone stole it!"

"Must have been when I went for Robbie, I guess," Nancy said, not too worried. "It's no biggie, we can always get another computer."

"But the information I need to find what I learned this morning was in it."

Was it only a few hours ago that she had gotten vital information from Mary Gallo, got clocked in the head, and had her first orgasm...by an alien...she felt her body dampening her panties, *oh my gosh, she had to stop thinking about that.*

"Uh," she mumbled and went over to the desk she had been using. There was nothing but her pen lying on it. "Has anyone seen my notebook?"

They all stared blankly at her. "Nope," Dempsey said.

"I can get you another one," Nancy offered.

Arianna said hopefully, "Tell me what was in it and I can type your notes up for you."

Her lips pursed, Kesi stood uneasily. She said, "I must be closer to the killer than I had thought. Somehow he found out and knocked me out and took my computer and notebook so no one else could figure out who he was."

More determined than ever to solve the mystery and get a murderer off the streets, Kesi clenched her fists and her teeth grit. "He has another thing coming, I am not giving up." She looked over at Arianna's desk. It was empty. "Your computer, where is it?"

Arianna followed her trail of vision. "My computer? It's home. I was up late last night looking at cases."

"Good. Let's go get it." Kesi tried to remember the name Mrs. Gallo had given her of her daughter's attacker.

Allan, no, Alain, yes, Alain something and a pen? Montblanc, that's it.

"You look like shit, Kesi, peaked and weak. Have you eaten yet today?" Arianna said with a mother hen to her voice.

"Hmm, thanks," Kesi muttered. Shaking her head she frowned. "This is more important than eating." She didn't need another reminder of how homely she was.

At least Arianna's words brought her back to reality. The outlaw was clearly playing games with her. He could have any woman in the town, willing or not, he certainly wouldn't have any interest in poor, plain, addicted Kesi.

If he had truly was attracted to her, as a criminal who was clearly outside the long arm of the law, Dempsey for heaven's sake disappeared any time Martier was present, Martier undoubtedly would have just taken her by now, with or without her consent.

"Nothing is more important than your health," Arianna claimed. Linking their arms, she said, "Come on, let me buy you a burger next door and then we'll go get my computer and you can do research until your fingers fall off. I'm not taking no for an answer."

She tugged Kesi past Nancy and Dempsey who were smiling weakly like concerned parents, nodding their encouragement.

Deciding it might be a good idea after all. The captain's tail might come to the station looking for her, she could hide out for an hour in the diner. Kesi gave in. "Fine. Let's go, I'm starving!"

Surprisingly, she stopped at her desk and saw her purse in the open drawer where she'd left it. She gave it a quick search. Everything that was in it before was still there. Even the forty dollars in the zipped pocket. So, the thief only wanted her information on the murders, and the flash-drive of cases that was in it.

She allowed Arianna to drag her out the door. The sun hit with full force. It was hot and blinding after being in the coolness and dimmer ancient station. The diner was right next door.

They opened the door to conversational noise and activity even though the place was slow as it was after the regular lunch hour.

The girls slid into a booth.

After ordering a BLT and a soda with a small side of onion rings, Kesi settled back against the red vinyl that had seen much better days, a long, long time ago. If there was any more tape on the seats they would be called silver cushions instead of red. She had to be careful not to snag her skirt on the tape.

The girls took turns washing up in the restroom and holding their table.

When Kesi returned, her soda was waiting, wetting a circle on a cocktail napkin. She slid back in and sucked heartily on the straw. She hadn't realized how thirsty she was.

Arianna was drinking ice tea, she squeezed the lemon in the glass then added several cubes of sugar before stirring and tasting it.

"It's funny the little things that are different in this country, or at least in this town," Kesi mentioned. She rubbed the back of her head feeling the headache from her wound.

Stirring more with her straw, Arianna used it as a sword to break up the ice. "Oh, yeah? Like what?"

"Like, at home." A funny feeling of homesickness suddenly shimmered through her. It was odd for Kesi to have that feeling, she had no family and hadn't worked for long in the states. She really had nothing to miss.

"Um, like the sugar. At…home, every restaurant has packets, but here, they put real bowls of loose sugar or sugar cubes on the tables, and real tubs of butter, pitchers of cream. It's like living in the last century, more farm-like and family style."

"I guess. Kinda unsanitary." Arianna's eyes were on a couple of miners sitting at the counter on stools.

Taking a small sip of her soda, Kesi asked with interest, "So, what happened with your…date, the other night? Are you seeing each other? Is he a nice guy?"

"Hmm," Arianna muttered disinterested, and continued to check out the two men.

One had turned slightly and caught her staring.

She cocked her head with a flirty smile, and coiled a lock of hair around her finger.

He smiled, held up his hand and wiggled his ring finger that had a gold band encircling it. Arianna flicked her gaze to the other man. Maybe he wasn't married.

"Arianna?" Kesi prodded.

Forcing her gaze to return to Kesi, Arianna smiled indifferently with a shrug. "Nah. Honey, it was a one nighter, ya know?"

"Oh." Kesi didn't know how to respond to that. It was info out of her league. She'd been so sheltered the idea of one night of sex with a stranger totally freaked her out.

That brought her thoughts back to the captain and the night in the barn. He had tried to get her to go back to his place. Then, in the infirmary, she blushed again at the remembrance, her hand went to her neck, she'd seen the puncture wounds he'd left earlier, but they were almost gone.

He probably expected either incident to turn into a one-nighter, and he would have then moved on to the next available female in the village.

He was big and powerful, and good looking if you liked that violent, dangerous-alien kind of thing. He's probably already done every available woman in town and she's last on the list to screw, that would explain his attention to her.

He likely screwed all the women in residence every time he...took over a town?

Kesi wondered what his true work was, if there was one. Maybe he took over rural towns, ransomed off the residents for big bucks then flew away on his spaceship.

She also wondered again if he had actually made his rounds with all the single young women in Brutální. The thought drew her lips down, her blush faded.

She'd heard the women talking about how roughly attractive he was. Many claimed the desire to sleep with him, but from what she ascertained, no one announced success. It must have been so horrible and brutal and painful they didn't want to talk about it.

As if she read her mind, Arianna said with a foxy grin, "What about you and the captain? We obviously interrupted something that night. You looked upset and he looked really pissed."

Ignoring Kesi grim expression, Arianna proceeded with a lusty grin, "He's a man I'd love to fuck, but I sure as hell wouldn't want him mad at me. You have to tell me all about your fuck with him. I can see he lives with violence and aggression on a daily basis. He just exudes savagery and forcefulness and-"

"Geeze, stop it Arianna, you're embarrassing me!" Kesi cut her off, what if someone was listening; they'd think she'd had sex with the outlaw demon who took over the town.

Technically, she did sort of have sex with him if having his hands on her breasts and her bare female parts, and his fingers up inside her denoted having sex. Feeling her cheeks flaming, Kesi grabbed her soda and drank it almost all the way down.

"Well?"

They paused as the server brought their lunches. Arianna had chili and cheese with crackers and a side of onion rings.

"Well what?" Bent over with the straw in her mouth Kesi looked up in discomfiture at her friend. At least she thought maybe Arianna was her friend. The other agents from the States treated her with unconcealed contempt.

Arianna at least spoke to her without scathing words and loathing looks.

The secretary picked up her burger and took a bite and set it down on the plate. While chewing, she grabbed the ketchup and squeezed a glob over the fries and also made a pile of it to dunk in.

"Come on, give it, girl, did you fuck? I bet he gives it good and hard, really rough, and he's big, right? You can see he's big, that huge cock shows in those snug jeans he wears. What about those horns, does he do anything kinky with-"

"Arianna, shut up!" Kesi squealed almost spitting out her sandwich. "Stop. No, we did not have sex. Get off it, move on."

Swiping one of Kesi's onion rings, Arianna dragged it through the pile of ketchup before shoving the entire thing in her mouth.

Chomping in contemplation, she suddenly sobered. "You didn't let him fuck you? He didn't force himself on you?" Her head shook, the long brown hair swept back and forth across her back.

"I can't believe that. You can tell that demon takes what he wants. And he wants you, there's no doubt about it. I haven't seen him so much as look at another female. Tawny Varela has blatantly hounded him endlessly and he won't give her the time of day."

Taking another of Kesi's onion rings, she said, "Even I tried, but no dice. Trust me, girl, before this is over, he will be fucking you, whether or not you want it. For some reason he needs to get you out of his system before he moves on to one of the rest of us. He's not the kind to take a no, so, prepare yourself girl for a hardy ride."

"Arianna, I beg you, stop, please. I don't want to talk about that outlaw. He is holding us prisoners for some nefarious deed. We could all be sold or murdered or enslaved, who knows what he has in mind for us?"

"I don't think we have anything to worry about. None of us are dead or have been harmed yet."

Remembering the beating the captain gave Chris, Kesi knew that not to be entirely true. But she kept that incident to herself. She didn't need the squad or Keith Dukes or anyone else knowing her co-agent had tried to rape her. Talk about losing any credibility she might have left.

Taking another bite of her sandwich, after chewing and swallowing, she changed the subject. "So, why were you sent here, Arianna? There's not really anything for you to do. You hadn't done anything wrong at home in Ships Bay, and you weren't involved in the...our, mission, that...failed."

That made her again think of Chris, and that led to recalling his assault on her, and then his own subsequent beating, Kesi's appetite stalled, she set the BLT down.

"No, thank God," Arianna spoke while chewing.

"So, then, why were you banished with us? This is not a dream location for a transfer."

Shrugging one shoulder, the support admin swooped up a bunch of fries, saturated them in ketchup and forced them all in her mouth.

Her sly gaze slid back over to the miners at the counter. The other man had turned around and was checking the girls out.

Licking each finger slowly, one by one, Arianna tipped her head to the side and lowered her lids in a sultry invitation.

"Arianna?"

Her eyes on the man, she shrugged again. "Uh, oh, the boss just felt you guys could use some extra help. I told you when I came, to type up notes, do follow-up, make calls, help with research. You know, stuff."

"Did Keith Dukes send you?" Kesi was suddenly suspicious that Dukes sent her to spy on the agents, make sure they stayed out of trouble, report their actions back to him.

"Hmm?" Arianna stole another onion ring and was slowly sliding it into her mouth, and back out, then she licked it, her eyes on the man at the counter, his eyes were on the ring.

"I asked if Senior Agent Dukes sent you? Did you make him mad somehow?"

"Oh, it's not important, Kes, we might have been getting too…you know, close. He's married you know. So I was distanced from him. Listen, I think I'm getting a date."

"Ari-"

One of the paramedics, Tim, stopped at their table. His face screwed up in worry. "Hey girls, did you hear?"

"Hear what?" Arianna asked, stretching her neck to peer over his shoulder at the miner sitting at the counter.

"The terrestrials, that blond haired freak, you know, that big captain, he's taken the children."

"What?" the girls spouted in unison.

Nodding vigorously Tim told them, "Yeah, they're gone. Every child and their parents. Gone. Vanished. Zippo." Sighing with anxiety he said, "I guess we're next. I hope they kill us before they eat us."

He shivered. "I gotta go." He hurried from their table and went out the door.

"Wow, get a load of that? I can't believe it!" Arianna's eyes returned to the miner. "Well, if I'm going to be someone's dinner, I'm fucking every damned guy I can get until then!" Arianna slid out of the booth, snatched up her purse and stalked over to the miner.

"Wait- Arianna!" Kesi called, but it was a losing battle.

Humph. She pulled her wallet out of her purse, took out some money and set it on the table; Arianna had said she was buying Kesi lunch. Oh well. Darn, she just could not believe the captain would-

The second paramedic, Joey, popped up at her table. "Hey Agent, have you heard?"

"About the children? Yes. Does anyone know where he's keeping them?"

"No. I heard that he's pissed because some bitch he wanted to fuck shut him down and he's taken the kids in retribution."

Kesi's skin chilled, her blood ran cold, stopping in her veins. "What? Who said that?"

"I'm not sure, it might have been Tawny Varela, maybe. She hangs around those queer demon fuckers, she hears a lot. What's the diff anyway? If that bitch he wants just goes and spreads them for the captain maybe he'll give the children back before they eat them all. I have to go, see you around, I hope." He took off leaving a stunned Kesi.

Her mind spun, heart drummed against her ribcage, Kesi felt sick to her stomach. She had turned the captain away and he had retaliated by taking the poor children.

Oh God, she needed to get to him, give him whatever he wanted, make him give the children back.

She shoved out of the booth and fled out the door.

Chapter Seventeen

*K*esi rushed home, took a shower, changed into a blouse and pink jeans, dried her hair and went to look for Captain Martier Lucien Dravidian.

She looked everywhere he usually hung out, the rec center, the saloon, but she couldn't find him.

She went home, tried to rest, but she couldn't still her mind. Images of tiny children being held over boiling caldrons and dropped in. Their screams of agony, their parents' shrieks of anguish as the babies were boiled alive and plucked out with a pitchfork like human fondue kept her awake.

Finally, hours later the sun was setting and she decided to go look for him again.

Her kind neighbor gave her a ride to the saloon and Kesi was thankful, and horribly apprehensive. Her stomach twisted when she saw his jeep out front.

With dreaded trepidation, she pushed the door open and slowly walked inside. She was instantly assailed by the smell of alcohol, cigarette smoke, loud chatter and louder music.

Kesi saw him right away.

He and his demon mates stood out like giant muscular sore thumbs in the crowd. They were playing cards over in a corner table. Interesting. Extra-terrestrials played cards. She wondered if they cheated, and what they bet with, or on.

She beelined to them.

Slade spotted her, nudged Martier and nodded at her.

His face implacable, dark green eyes almost black in the low lights gleamed unnaturally, lancing through the smoky crowd at her.

When he rose to his feet, Kesi's legs stalled and she halted. Her courage had fizzed like air out of a balloon.

He made his way towards her.

As he neared, his expression revealed nothing. The hard face all sharp planes and harsh angles, fearsome, so tough and rugged he was a warrior through and through. A frightening, strange, alien warrior.

Kesi realized every time she came in sight of him, he got to his feet, odd, did he do it to be respectful? He also always approached her whenever she was in view. She never noticed him do that with anyone else, male or female.

She just could not figure what his game was. But, whatever it was he wanted, she was going to give it to him. Go along with whatever he said, even if it was damage or torture, or death to her, as long as he saved the children.

A thought sifted into her frightened brain as she recalled how he had come to her rescue when Chris was assaulting her. How he paid for her door to be repaired, how he rushed her to the clinic when she overdosed, and he stayed by her bedside while she recovered from the knock on the head. It was almost as if he...cared about her.

But no, that was being fantastical on her part. He had an agenda and somehow it involved her. And it couldn't possibly be anything good.

Maybe he thought he could buy himself some protection down the road if he was caught for imprisoning the village and he had an FBI agent under his thumb.

Stopping close enough so they could hear each other, he towered over her. She had to tilt her head to look up at him.

He waited for her to speak, but Kesi's lips were frozen shut. Visions of his hands on her when she'd been in the clinic blew red up her face, she couldn't meet his eyes.

"Let us step outside," his voice dark and tough, quiet, he took her arm and ushered her back out the door.

The evening air was not as hot as the day's sweltering; the night sky wasn't yet completely black. A few stars sprinkled between clouds.

They stood just outside the door. People left the saloon and walked around them with curious notice, their hushed chattering and the loose gravel crunching underfoot as they passed by.

"Here," he spoke, took her arm again and brought her to stand more in the shadows out of the way, near a wall. And waited. Still she said nothing.

"Kesindra, why are you here?" He chuckled dryly. "You threw me out of your room and ditched my tail, and now it seems you have come looking for me?"

Her lips parted, she looked up at him. Big and bold, blond and brutally dominant, with horns and fangs. So foreign from her it defied her belief system.

Violent and cold, sensual and gentle, she was terrified of him, and inexplicably drawn to him. But the fear far outweighed the attraction. He had taken over an entire town, for Pete's sake.

She stepped back from him and her spine hit a brick wall.

He put a palm up on the wall next to her shoulder, half boxing her in. His sleeves were rolled up to the elbows revealing brawny arms covered with dark hair. It was so peculiar, the hair on his head was blond but everywhere else was dark.

Her attention moved to the tattoo on his neck. It too was foreign, she'd never seen anything like it.

Seeing her gaze latch onto his tat, he explained, "Tis my warlord sign. Defines my...heritage, and my...military background. Everyone from my land that is a warrior has one similar. My other...works," he smiled, "are ancestral. We have words and images imprinted on us as we grow."

He set his other hand on the other side of her.

"I...uh, see," she mumbled, pulling her eyes from it. Of course, it represented war, violence, death, and it was wrapped around his neck. Lovely. Totally not daunting. Right. A shiver raced up her spine

"Kesindra, why did you come to me?"

Before her courage completely ran out, on tiptoes, Kesi slid her hands up the starched shirt to his broad shoulders and around his thick neck, and she set her lips softly on his in an almost childlike kiss.

Taken by total surprise, Martier didn't move.

She kept her hands around his neck, their faces scant inches apart. She could smell the slight trace of beer, faint cigar smoke, his aftershave, and his own masculine scent, his very maleness. He had obviously shaved that day, but a dark shadow lined his jaw.

His voice deeply low and husky, he asked again quietly, "Why did you come to find me, Kesindra?"

Moving her hands up, Kesi slid her fingers into his hair. She was amazed, the dark golden locks were as soft as could be. Thick, strong like the rest of him, but soft.

A growl deep in his chest barely audible, he threatened, "You cannot play with me, Kesindra, you cannot tease me. I want you too much to stop with a brief kiss, or a…touch."

He still didn't move, his palms splayed on the concrete wall beside her head. His fingers flexed hard, as if gripping the rough wall. He had her in an iron cradle, if he chose to hold her, she would not be able to break away.

Her big blues glimmered into his midnight green eyes. His lids lowered, hooding the dark emerald, inhuman, color.

Kesi lightly leaned into him, faintly pressing her breasts against his rocky chest. Moving her lips almost touching his, she whispered, "I want you to kiss me."

Martier's body may have been made of steel, but his control when it came to her wasn't. He stared for a brief second into her innocent eyes, felt her soft breasts wedge against his chest, looked down at those plump cherry lips, and lost it.

His hands dropped, slipped behind her. One stroked down to grip her bottom, the other moved up to clutch the back of her head and he brought his mouth down on hers, harder than he'd meant to, taking her lips with savage ferocity, railing pure animal hunger on her, tearing at her tender lips.

Bombarding her with his unleashed hunger, Martier took and took from her, ruling, reaping all that was Kesi, until her mind was a searing black hole of sheer sensation.

The sound frequency in her head turned up to super high; she could hear nothing but shrill buzzing in her head.

Martier was not unaffected. His horns grew along with his hardening manhood. He pulled her in tight to feel his rigid shaft implanted against her female parts. He pulled hard enough for his phallus to push through his black jeans and hers, to thrust, force it into her woman's cleft.

Already about to burst, to spew his seeds from a single kiss, he jerked back from her mouth, panting. Lids shaded down so far no color emerged, only black light.

He hadn't realized he had pushed her hard against the wall with his body. His fingers an iron net around the back of her head were so tight he feared he'd crush her tender skull in his hand. His nails digging into her lush ass, he forced himself to loosen his grip and catch his breath.

Dazed, Kesi could only stare up at him with unseeing glazed eyes, chest pumping with fitful breaths, her lips parted, damp from the erotic kiss. Her knees buckled as if he had sapped the strength from them.

His arm braced around her, he held her up and against him. Martier was lost in those passion-clouded blue eyes. His palm at the back of her head tilted it up, her lids lowered so sultry he nearly cried.

Moving his hand to cradle the side of her face, his throat rough, he asked with a soft rasp, "Baby, Kesindra, come to my place?" His other hand slid to splay across the small of her back.

He didn't know why she'd sought him out now, she'd been obviously devastated earlier at what they'd done and had thrown him out. But he didn't care the reason why she came to find him now; she was here, in his arms, willing. He was taking whatever she was offering.

Martier's harsh voice brought Kesi back to Earth. His big rough hands warm where he held her, his eyes so intense they charred. She could feel his powerful body pulsing against her soft femininity. His virile heat, his scent, strength, kiss, overwhelmed her. She wanted to run. Fast. Far.

But, she blinked hard, the children. She had to save the children. "Y- yes." Her tight exhale didn't take any of her fear, the tension, with it.

Martier's lashes flickered in surprise. "You mean it? I am warning you, Kesindra, I cannot be teased. At this point, if you go with me, you cannot refuse me. I will take what I want. And that," he slid a knuckle down her cheek, "is everything."

He waited a few beats, she said nothing.

Cursing inside, he could clearly see her fear, of him. It pissed him off like crazy. But he wasn't letting it stop them.

"Well? You coming with me, Kesindra? To my place?" Martier wanted her in his home where he could keep her there, not her place where she could throw him out again.

Eyes now wide in the night, above her the broken neon lights on the bar flashed green and blue over her light blonde curls.

She nodded, he could barely hear her faint, "Yes."

He gave her only a few heartbeats to change her mind, then he grabbed her hand and strode quickly to his jeep.

He opened the passenger door. "Let me help you, the step on this one is high." His hand shaking slightly with anticipation, and the fear of her changing her mind, Martier held it under her elbow and mostly lifted her inside the truck.

He closed her door, and ran around to climb in behind the wheel.

Sticking the key in the ignition, he looked over at her. Kesi's face was so pale it shone pearl white in the moonlight.

"Kesindra, you don't have to-"

"I said yes."

He turned the key, the engine rumbled on. Staring at her in the dark he said, "I would prefer if you said you wanted to be with me, not just, yes."

She didn't respond. Well, she hadn't said stop or no, he sighed and put the jeep in gear. Lifting the emergency brake, he drove out of the lot and down the main street.

Without many streetlights, it was almost pitch black. He glanced at Kesi. Her face a pale moon in the darkness, she stared unblinking out the front windshield.

Martier set a hand on her knee. "You okay?"

Her leg jumped from the unexpected contact. Kesi's, "Yes," came out in a hush.

Her responses chilled him. But he wanted her so badly he could hardly breathe, couldn't sleep at night for the want of her, she said yes, that was enough.

They traveled the entire way in silence.

It didn't take long for Martier to pull into the lot where he was staying. It was the only hotel in town. It actually wasn't too bad. It was where a random few wealthy people from the big cities came to stay while big game hunting in the area.

He parked, pulled the brake on, and turned the jeep off.

Kesi sat stiff as a board, eyes straight ahead. Like a lamb to slaughter. He leaned over, clasped her jaw and pulled her to him, kissing her softly.

Martier was already on fire, even a gentle chaste kiss fueled him. Inciting lusting flames licked scorching heat through his hard body, and made his hands tremble with the need of her.

Forcing himself to release her, Martier hopped out of the jeep and went around to help her out.

Kesi hadn't moved. He understood she still feared him, but he had been up front, he had warned her, all or nothing. She agreed, she was there. He would take his time warming her up, getting her peaked, ready, make her as hot as he was right now.

He opened her door, held out his hand for her to take, said gruffly, "Come."

She looked at his hand, then set her small one in it and he helped her out.

He slipped his heavy arm around her shoulders holding her near to him as they entered the hotel through a side door, not drawing undesired attention on Kesi. She was going to sleep with the enemy.

Without speaking, they went up the staff elevator to the third floor and down the carpeted hallway. He stopped at a door then stuck the old fashioned key in the lock and pushed the door open.

Martier stepped in first, his training instinctual that he check for danger before bringing a defenseless woman in.

He could tell with one look no one had entered the room. He'd left almost invisible traps around that someone would trip if anyone had intruded.

"Here we are," he murmured, drawing her into the room.

Stiffly, Kesi looked around.

It was decorated in creams and gold, old, but richly decorated and clean. It was a suite with a separate kitchen and bedroom.

Closing the door without taking his eyes off her, Martier set his hands on her shoulders and pulled her to him. Her movements were clearly stiff and reluctant.

He was starting to get angry. She was making him feel like a rapacious ogre.

With aloof sarcasm, he growled, "I don't chop up and cook little human girls, honey, only the big ones. You are safe. For now."

Martier needed to see that she was truly willing, he didn't want her feeling shame like earlier, or crying rape later. Not that it would matter, at the moment he was the law in town.

She had no one but him to complain to. Not wanting to get involved with the aliens, Dempsey would look the other way. But still, Martier didn't want her throwing it in his face at some point down the road that he'd forced her.

Knowing she was shy, self-conscious, even with that rocking body, Kesi had no idea how hot she was, Martier said quietly, "How about you go into the bedroom, get undressed, get in bed. I will get us something to drink. I am dying to see you nude, *několika,* hold you in my arms."

He watched her pupils flare with unease before her lids shuttered over them. "Go on," he turned her to face the hall. "Down that way. I will be right in."

He could ease her into things, have a drink sitting on the couch, chat a bit, be more civilized. But, she was clearly on the edge, ready to freak out and run. If he got her into bed right away he felt he could have her heated up before she had a chance to talk herself out of it.

She hesitated, then she made her legs work and she trod slowly down the hall, as if going to her execution.

Martier wasn't worried about her reluctance. He'd drawn fire in her before; he could easily do it again, as long as she stayed. He went into the kitchen to get a bottle of wine and glasses.

Making his way down the hall, he thought about what kind of music to play. Something romantic, soft, to relax her.

He was pleased when he stood in the doorway to the large bedroom that she had done as he said, mostly.

She stood in front of the big window staring out, wearing only a silky bra and tiny bikini, shorts-styled panties. Holy shit. The bottom swells of her butt cheeks were exposed. Perfect, round, lush. Already semi-hard, his cock now strained at his pants.

Setting the bottle, opener and glasses on a table, he moved behind her, wound his fingers around her arms and pulled her back against his chest.

He moved her hair to one side, wrapped his arms around the front of her holding her tight, and lowered his head so he could kiss her neck.

He licked her soft skin, running his tongue over the goose bumps that popped under it. He slid his descending fangs over her smooth flesh, the urge to stab the sharp incisors into her screamed inside him.

Resisting the compulsion to bite her, he sucked until a red mark rose, it was the beginning of how he would brand her, lay his claim on her. Every single sweet part of her.

His horns were swelling. During lovemaking, when they were in the beginning throes of orgasm, the horns would turn and face forward and curve over Kesi from her front to her back.

When they climaxed together, the horns would plunge just under her shoulder blades, into her flesh, and she would be his, totally, irrevocably and forever.

He paused. Sliding his palms up and down her arms, he said, "You are freezing. Kesindra, tis warm in here, and you are shaking like a leaf. What is going on?"

Kesi slightly cocked her head. She smiled weakly, but didn't turn around. "Nothing. I'm fine. Let's uh, just do it."

Dark brows arched. "Just...do it?" That sounded so...cold. He cupped her breasts in the silk bra. The lush flesh spilled out of his big hard fingers.

A shiver gripped her, Kesi's arms pulled in protectively over her chest. Martier moved his hands to clasp her upper arms, and turned her to face him. But she lowered her head, he couldn't see her face.

Frowning down at her, a prickling of frustration gathering in his low voice, he said, "Kesindra, I can tell when a woman in my arms is hot and turned on, or terrified, and completely shut down. You are terrified. What the hell is up?"

Her head lowered, she put her hands on his chest, palms flat then slightly gripping the thick cotton shirt she murmured, "Nothing, it's all good, we have to, uh, I mean, don't you want me?"

Her hands stroked up around his head, her breasts pressed against his chest, mounding up, almost out of the tiny bra, but her head stayed lowered.

He grasped her wrists, pulled them down. Then he gripped her arms and lifted her up almost on her toes and shoved his face into hers. "Kesindra, tell me what the fuck is going on, why are you doing this? You clearly don't want to."

He could feel the slight off balance in her stance; see the mist of the painkiller in her eyes before her lids dropped over them. She'd popped goddamned pills just to force herself to have sex with him.

Her delicate shoulders rose in an uneasy shrug, she fiddled with a button on his shirt. "They said I had to do anything you wanted or you would have the children killed. So," her head down, refusing to make eye contact, anxiously she twisted the button.

193

"What in Zeus' name are you talking about?"

She kept her head down, he barked, "Fucking look at me, Kesindra!" Catching her chin he jerked it up forcing her to look at him.

The frightened blues briefly glanced at his rich green eyes rapidly darkening to black with his growing anger, then her lashes lowered, covering her thoughts.

When she didn't answer, his ire flashed in impatience. He shook her demanding, "Talk to me, dammit. Fucking look me in the eye, Kesindra and tell me what the hell is going on? What are you rambling about the children? What children?"

Martier shook her hard enough her neck whipped, blonde curls flung around her back.

Holding her arms tight and together pushed her breasts up and out until there wasn't much of the full round globes still encased in the bra.

His eyes dropped to her breasts, glowing at them like they were dinner, his pupils expanded huge in the irises taking over all the color. His mouth opened in a hiss, the fangs flashed, claws at his fingertips unsheathed, digging into her skin.

Tearing his eyes away from her soft femaleness, at her silence he shook her again, demanding, "Look at me, answer me!"

Shiny hair tumbled over her face at his rough handling. Kesi hunched her shoulders and tossed her head to clear the locks. She watched his gaze flick down to her almost bare breasts jiggling with his shaking her, and up to her frightened eyes.

He looked as enraged and as lethally fierce as Satan himself with his fangs and horns, and the claws, *oh my God, what have I gotten myself into*?

Another hard shake rattled her teeth. She pushed the sputtering words out, "The- they, uh, he said it was your girl Taffy who said you had taken the children to- to cook them, eat them, in revenge because I wouldn't sleep with you. So...I," the gulp rolled jaggedly down her constricted throat, "thought, maybe, if I...did...that...you would release the children unharmed."

Thunderstruck, his face darkened in fury, eyes so black they looked like pools of oil ready to ignite. His fingers tightened like vices around her slim arms. "So that is why you said 'you had to' not because you were as hot for me as I am for you."

He shook his head in disbelief. "You think I-" he lowered his head and shook it with a cold laugh, the thick hair flopped over one brow with his shaking head.

He raised his gaze to glare with zero emotion at her. "You believed that I took little children, prepared them to be dropped into boiling kettles. Killing them because you would not sleep with me? Un-fucking-believable."

His fingers wound so tight around her arms, his claws drew blood. The red vivid against her alabaster skin caught his eye, he abruptly released her.

"If it was not so ludicrous, infuriating, it would be fucking hilarious." He stared hard at her for a silent moment, then commanded with icy quietness, "Get dressed."

Her gaze fell to the marks on her arms that trickled with blood then lifted to his empty black eyes. "But the children, you can't-"

"Fuck the children, get dressed," Martier snapped and turned to leave the room.

Kesi saw a weapon, a gun on the dresser. She reached for it, grabbed it and held it with both hands, the barrel aimed all over his back with her shaking. She ordered, "Stop!"

His back to her, he chuckled without mirth. "Really, Kesindra you are going to shoot me?" Turning around, seeing the wobbling gun, the side of his lip curled up, he said sarcastically, "You would have to know how it works first, sweetheart."

"I- I know how to shoot a gun, and yes, I will shoot you to save those innocent babies-"

He spun and grabbed the gun with one hand, yanking her face forward against his chest with the other. He'd deployed so fast she never saw him move.

He gazed down at her breasts bulging up, pressing against his steel caged chest. White-hot flames flared in his dark eyes.

Tucking the gun in the back of his pants, his sigh heavy with frustration, Martier growled, "I am on the edge here, Kesindra. I am about to force an unwilling woman to fuck. I can tell you will not go through with it willingly no matter what you say, you are too scared. And I want you bad, so we are talking rape here."

He watched whatever color was left in her fair skin fade. "I warned you, *několika,*" his voice brusque silk. "I told you at the bar if you said yes I would not stop if later you demurred."

Air sifted from his lungs, lowering his chest. "So, do us both a favor and get dressed. I will take you home."

Releasing her, he snatched his jacket off a chair and dropped it around her shoulders.

Closing the lapels, he held them together with his fists. "You are cold, scared, and I am way too fucking tempted. Put your clothes on, I will meet you out in the front." He let her go so abruptly she almost fell backwards.

Kesi stood shivering in the empty room. When he left, Martier took all the warmth and energy, vibrancy with him.

She glanced around. King-sized bed of course, he wouldn't fit in anything else. There was a divan that he'd dropped worn clothes on, he was a bit messier than she would have expected from such a rigidly military warrior guy. It made him seem more...human.

Recalling his claws digging into her arms, his fangs into her shoulder, okay, not so human. She shivered again and quickly dressed before he came back in.

When she returned to the living room he was standing like she had been, staring out the window, his hands clasped behind his back. The golden hair the lightest thing in the room, he had only switched on a small lamp.

Martier heard her enter the room. Actually, his hearing was so acute he could hear her down the hall in the bedroom getting dressed.

He could hear her jeans scrape up her bare legs, her blouse rustle as she pulled it on, the buttons as she fastened them over those magnificent breasts. Fuck.

He turned, didn't look directly at her. His voice cold, without inflection, he said, "You ready?"

Kesi nodded. She started towards him.

"Your shoelaces," he noted, sighing with an eye-roll. A fucking FBI agent and she couldn't remember to tie her fucking shoes.

She was a damned child, and he needed to remember that. Zeus. But she had the body of pure sin, built like a goddess. And her face ethereal, so artfully exquisite as an angel, his heart melted as his loins heated.

He watched her kneel and tie her shoes. The saffron hair as light as the sun swept forward spilling curls over her like a veil of sunshine. His fingers itched to shove into it and grab handfuls. He looked down at the top of her head. Again, she knelt as a child would to tie her shoes.

But she was not a child as she kept pointing out to him. Martier had to turn away, his groin ached, his dick wanted her and it had no morals, it didn't care whether she was willing or not.

Standing, her voice small, hushed, she whispered, "I'm ready."

He glanced at her. She looked as terrified as ever. Zeus, he hated that she feared him so much she shook when in his presence. A dark scowl hewn the sharpness of his cheeks, firmed his full lips to chiseled rock. He opened the door without a word.

They rode the elevator in silence.

It was all Martier could do not to shove her facing up against the wall, yank those jeans down, and those fucking wet dream of panties, hell, he'd never seen anything like them, bend her, unzip his pants and plow into her from behind until their throats were hoarse from screaming.

Recalling what she'd said earlier, he muttered crossly, "Taffy, ah, *Tawny* dammit, is not my girl. Quit saying that shit."

The doors dinged open.

They trod through the lot in the pitch black. He opened the passenger door to the jeep. He couldn't bear to touch her, but she was so petite, the step was high, he grasped her elbow to help her up, letting go as soon as she was inside.

They started down the street. Kesi glanced at Martier. His face was dark and hard and set.

She could see his jaw working, a vein at his temple beating. "Captain?"

His beleaguered sigh, "Martier."

"Um, Martier, the children. What are you going to do to the-"

"Goddammit Kesindra!" he exploded. Wrenching the wheel, he forced the jeep to the side of the rode. Jamming his foot on the brake, he slammed the shift into park then turned and glared at her.

And grew angrier when she pushed her back against the car door and reached for the handle- to run from him.

He dragged a furious hand through his hair, mussing the thick golden locks. His voice as rough and deep as the earth he said, "For fucks sake, Kesindra. I captured this entire town without incident. No one was harmed. No one has been harmed."

He saw her eyes flicker, he rolled his. "Except for that sonofabitch Carpenter. He hurt you, Kesindra, he did not stop when you said no," he sighed with facetious contempt, "like I did."

She burrowed further into the door, gripping the handle, inciting his wrath even more.

"I have never hurt you, and you have given me plenty of good reason to. How many times I have had to fight the urge to paddle your behind for foolishness, like now. The shit that comes out of your mouth makes me want to rip those jeans down and smack the hell out of-" He took a breath, forked his fingers scraping over his scalp.

"Are you going to kill me?"

"What! Where do you get this shit?" He felt like pulling his hair out. "I just told you that I have not harmed the children. I have not harmed anyone, other than that prick," he saw her gaze lower to her arms, and he blanched.

There were cuts on her skin from his claws. He could have blocked the pain, healed them, like during sex, when they would unsheathe and grip around her breasts-

She put her hands over the cuts on her arms.

Instantly contrite, he said softly, "Baby, I am sorry, here," reaching for her, but she shrank from him.

"Dammit, I will fix them." He grasped her hand and pulled her arm out even though she resisted. He bent and licked her wounds. In seconds they were gone. He took her other hand while she stared in incredulity at her completely healed arm.

When he was done, he slipped his fingers under her jaw, lifting her face to his. He said softly, "I was a bit too, intense, earlier and lost my control. I would never purposefully hurt you. Please believe me."

Their eyes linked for several seconds before hers lowered. He fought the unbearable desire to kiss her, it was a bitch of a trial, but he resisted.

He put the jeep in gear and took off again for her home. The rest of the drive was again, dead silent, each deep in their own thoughts.

Pebbles ground under the tires as he pulled into the driveway. Turning the jeep off, he held his hand out. "Give me your keys, you stay here. I will check it out first."

"Captain, I come here alone every night, it's fine. I'm an officer for heaven's sake." Her keys were already in her hand.

"Fucking *Martier*, Kesindra, will you fucking call me Martier." He snatched the keys from her, got out of the truck. Slamming the door he stomped off towards the house.

He traipsed around to the side and saw the board still there that he had hammered over the broken glass. His sigh went down to his boots.

She was so alone and helpless, and vulnerable in a dangerous country, and refused to see it, admit it. His head swung back towards the jeep. He should just take her back to his place and force her to stay there where he could ensure her safety. From everything, except from him.

He sighed again. He was wound so tight his balls ached. If he took her back to his suite he would have her on the floor and be all over and in her before he got the door closed.

Damn. He was the wild animal she thought him. He couldn't control himself around her.

When had that happened? When had she tied his balls up and curled that beautiful soul around his dick, his mind, his heart? He quickly unlocked the door and did a diligent search of her home.

He strode back to the jeep, opened the passenger door and stuck his hand inside. "Come on."

"Cap- Martier, I can take it from here. I know my way inside."

He grabbed her arm and hauled her out, setting her on her feet. "I am getting goddamned tired of fighting with you, Kesindra, arguing every little thing." He walked her up the side and into the small house.

Annoyed at his manhandling and treating her as if she was helpless, she snapped, "Fine then, leave. Go get your-your rocks off with Tweety, maybe you won't be so cranky."

Martier bit off a smile. Standing in the doorway, he handed her the keys. "Tawny, her name is Tawny."

"Whatever," she sniffed. "Men have, needs, and I'm sure you will go directly to her to work off your…uh, vigor that we, I, you…never mind. Go screw someone you really like."

Pissed off again, grabbing her arms, he pulled her to him and growled, "I really like you, Kesindra Jasmari, trust me, you are the only woman I want to screw." He kissed her hard then abruptly left.

Chapter Eighteen

$\mathcal{F}$or the tenth time Kesindra frowned at the mirror. What in heaven's name possessed her to listen to Arianna? All she wanted to do was hang out at her tiny shack and do research. But Arianna had basically blackmailed her. Said she needed a wing-woman for her date tonight.

A soft snort escaped as she stared at her reflection. Since when did Arianna, Kesi had to admit the girl was kind of a slut, need another woman for coverage?

When Kesi protested going out with her, Arianna had said her date, Barney, had a very shy friend, Errol, and that Barney refused to take Arianna out unless she provided a date for Errol.

And that is why Kesi was standing in Arianna's house, wearing Arianna's gold iridescent top that draped low in the front, and a min-skirt of silver sequins. So not what Kesi would wear. She felt like a disco ball.

Arianna had insisted Kesi wear something of hers. She had said she didn't want to be embarrassed by Kesi's normal, baggy, huckster outfits. So Kesi had let her talk her into wearing the boudoir atrocity. Heavens, she looked like she belonged on a strip stage.

And the shoes, how was she going to walk in these sky-high stilettoes that matched the silvery skirt? She tipped her head to look at her hair.

Lord, Arianna had taken Kesi's long blonde hair and styled it in big wavy, stiff curls that clouded around her head and down her back. Let's not even talk about the makeup-

"I'm ready!" Arianna sang as she flounced into the room.

Kesi didn't know whether to feel better or worse that Arianna was dressed even more risqué than she was in a body clinging, royal red jersey dress that, for God's sake, had a gold zipper that went to her stomach, and it was unzipped halfway there already.

Big gold hoops swung in her ears, and she had on gold heels and gold bangles on both wrists. She had done her own long brown hair in the same 80's style she'd done Kesi's, big, wild curls. Great. They looked like Bobbsey-sluts.

"Listen, Arianna, I don't think I want to-"

"Oh stuff it, grow some balls, Kes, we're going and that's that." Arianna scooped her arm through Kesi's and hauled her to the front door just as the bell rang.

"Goody, they're here! You can't back out now." She hurried them to the door and opened it.

Two men in their thirties stood grinning like jackals on the doorstep. They were both dressed in black slacks, cobalt blue shirts and navy blue jackets. Bobbsey-fraternity brothers meet Bobbsey-sluts. Their faces looked a mix of European and native.

Oh, God, Kesi sighed. At their age and the way they looked at the girls, there was no way either of them was shy.

She stood awkwardly as Barney immediately pulled Arianna to him and they sucked face for what seemed like hours. His hands went to her ass where he grabbed both cheeks and squeezed hard until Arianna squealed with giggles.

When his hands started creeping up under the micro-mini skirt, Arianna brushed them away with a laugh, chiding a tease, "Save something for the ride home, handsome."

Second thoughts drowning her, Kesi's mind swirled as Arianna introduced her to Barney Jaarston, and then to Errol Manzo, her date.

Gaze slowly skimming her body, his leer grew totally wolfy. He tried to take her hand, but Kesi tucked both behind her. She had zilch desire to let this creeper touch her.

He was good-looking, tall, built, with dimples and a square jaw. A lock of dark brown hair swooped down in a sexy curl over one brown eye.

It looked staged to Kesi. Too cutesy-boyish, and when he smoothed it back and let his gaze roll down her body again and back up to latch onto her breasts, she knew he was well practiced.

"Pleasure, ah, Cassandra is it?" His deep voice and definite bedroom eyes probably made a lot of girls' panties wet, but his voice wasn't harsh velvet, and his eyes weren't midnight green. He had no effect on her at all. Maybe if he had horns…

The ride to the restaurant was interminable. In the front seat, Arianna was more in Barney's lap than in her own seat.

Kesi heard the zipper on her dress move, a lot, with giggles attached to each zip, and sniggling scolds for naughty Barney to stop.

In the back, Kesi had to fight off Errol-the-octopus Manzo.

The rustic restaurant they went to, Kesi let a sigh seep out, was the Glass House where the captain had said he would take her. There were only two decent restaurants in town and this was one of them.

The customers fluctuated due to Martier's rule that everyone show up at one of the dinner shifts at the rec building to be accounted for.

Arianna had poo-pooed the rule for tonight. "What are they gonna do to us that they aren't already planning?" she had sneered dryly.

"But, just in case I asked a couple of people to call out 'present' when our names are called for roster. See, I'm way smarter than a few psycho-ET's, no worries."

For her shrewdness, Barney gave her a long, wet, loud kiss.

The restaurant was glass on three sides, hence the name Glass House. It was pretty with verdant plants and colorful flowers filling all the spaces. Tables were covered with white tablecloths and romantic candles oozing wax in crystal globes.

The lighting was low but lit enough for easy reading of the brief menu. Soft music played in the background of cutlery hitting plates and muffled conversation.

Patrons had made a showing at the rec seating to be accounted for, then came to the restaurant to eat.

Kesi disregarded the cocktail Errol had ordered for her even though she had declined one. She sipped ice water instead.

The men ordered manly beefy, blood-red steaks. Arianna went for spaghetti so she could play with it, slurping each pasta string into her mouth, dangling a noodle over her lips then sucking it in.

Kesi picked at her seafood salad. The group had consumed several cocktails and a bottle of wine during dinner. Every time Kesi lifted her fork, sitting on her right, Errol took the opportunity to set his hand on her thigh.

He had grabbed her so many times, starting in the car, that her leg was red. There would likely be bruises there tomorrow.

She pushed his hand away but he patted her leg, too hard in his irritation that she wasn't more…giving, like Arianna was, then he moved his hand back to the table.

He leaned over, whispered very loudly in her ear, "You need to lighten up, sugartits."

"Do not call me that disgust-"

"How 'bout them aliens, what do you gals think about all that shit?" Barney asked, chugging a glass of burgundy.

Errol pumped his chest up when they discussed the aliens. "Bah," he spat. "I got no fuckin' fear of them. I can take them on with one hand tied behind my back!" Bits of chewed steak flew out of his mouth with his ridiculous declaration.

Tugging her lips in tight so she wouldn't say something to incite him, Kesi grabbed her cocktail and took a big gulp. Big mistake. It hit her stomach like firewater, she was so unused to drinking.

The only time she'd ever had alcohol was that night with Chris. She should have learned her lesson from the hangover she'd suffered the next day.

The men discussed sports, and sex, and sex, a couple of times they talked about their jobs. They were both safety overseers at the mines.

They puffed up talking about it. "Yeah," Barney said with pride and arrogance, "we're too good to go into the mines. I mean deep anyway." He leered at Arianna, "Not deep in the mines, but deep elsewhere, right babe?"

Arianna giggled and kissed him for his sexy innuendo.

"Yep," Errol agreed slurring his grin. "We're in charge of mostly surface safety and just a few yards inside. We're echelon, not like those other schleps that actually *work* the mines. See babe, you're with ex-e-cu-tives," he drawled the word like it meant they were important."

"Hey," Barney said, "little Kesi there is a real life FBI agent from America, can you believe that?"

"S'at right sugartits?" Errol slurred looking at her with amazement. "What the hell are ya doin' in this hole-in-the wall shithole town?"

Shoving a huge bite of meatball in her mouth, Arianna snorted, "She fucked up a mission. Got a bunch of innocent people killed so they banished her out here. Unfortunately," she chewed away like she hadn't just ripped a hole in Kesi's soul, "she dragged her poor team with her. Oh well, such is life, huh?"

Speaking though her chewed meat, she said, "That's why I push her to do fun things like this. Get her mind off her fuck-up, ya know? That's what friends are for."

"Hell, I got somethin' fun for ya, sugartits," Errol cooed to Kesi.

Kesi's stomach roiled. She'd asked him to stop calling her that, she couldn't believe he said it in public, out loud, but he was drunk.

"How 'bout you bring those sweet plump lips over here and gimmie a kissie?" Errol stuck his chin out, lips pursed, reaching for her arm to pull her to him.

"So why are you out here?" Barney asked Arianna with really no interest. His interest was in her cleavage.

"Oh, you know, my boss thought they could use some help."

"Arianna," Kesi said with a frown, "I don't get who sent you here? Was it Keith Dukes or-"

"Oh come on," Arianna snarled with annoyance. "Let's not talk shop and bore these big fellas," her hand went to Barney's lap, her lips to his mouth.

"Yeah, let's talk about what happens after dinner." Errol slid his hand back on Kesi's thigh and moved it up under her skirt.

Kesi jumped up. "Uh, I need to um, freshen up, I'm going to the ladies room. Arianna? You want to come with me?" She wanted to speak with the support admin about cutting the night short, very short.

She wanted to go home. Out at this restaurant being pawed by lecherous Errol was not where she wanted to be.

Visions of lying on Martier's king-sized bed, watching him disrobe in the candlelight with his rich green eyes glowing at her flashed through her mind. Shaking her head to dispel the bizarre image, she waited.

As throughout the dinner, in between bites, Arianna and Barney were locking lips. Both had spaghetti sauce smeared around their mouths.

The zipper on her dress was down to her navel, every time she moved, a nipple flaunted. Under the table Barney's hand was up her skirt.

She barely turned her head from Barney's lips to say with an intoxicated slur, "Nah, hon, you go ahead," and clumsily shifted her saucy face and naked boobs back to Barney.

"I'll come with." Errol got unsteadily to his feet. The lewd gleam in his eyes under drunk heavy lids made it clear why he wanted to go with her.

"No." Kesi gave him a little shove. As trashed as he was he flopped right back down in his seat. She grabbed up the tiny sequined purse Arianna had made her take and hurried from the table as quickly as she could.

Of course, she didn't have to go to the restroom; she just wanted to get away from Arianna's shocking display of sex at a dining table, and Errol's hands.

Feeling like a walking sequin, moving as hastily as she could in the steep heels, Kesi rushed from the room and down the hall towards the restrooms.

Suddenly there was a body in front of her, she half-crashed into it with a huffed "*Oof*," and dropped her purse.

Getting to her knees, she mumbled, "Are you okay? I'm sor-" The person crouched down with her to get her purse.

Her eyes widened at the muscular legs. A big hard hand grabbed her purse, the other wound around her arm helping her back up.

Her, "Captain?" was breathy with surprise.

His face harsh, on the edge of furious, regarding her under hooded eyes, he growled, "Martier," he handed her the purse.

"What are you doing-" she was going to ask why he was there, but of course he must be on a date. For some reason her stomach twitched.

"I ask the same about you, Kesindra. You were not at any of the dinner seatings as instructed." He crossed his burly arms over the huge hard chest. His inscrutable gaze down at her gave her no clue as to what he was thinking.

The night he took her to his place and she couldn't go through with having sex with him slammed into her mind. The fate of the children.

His extreme differences from her had her petrified. She remembered how cold and angry he had been that night. Kesi

209

bit her lip, she also remembered how she felt thinking he was leaving her and going to go be with Tippy, or whatever her stupid stripper name was.

"Um, uh, yes, I mean, Arianna said one, um, missed night wouldn't matter, wouldn't be too big of a *oh-*"

He grasped her arms, gave her a shake then held her tight. His fingers clamped hard around her upper arms.

"You know the rules, Kesindra. I did not say when you villagers felt like it. I said every single fucking night," his voice ground the ending words out, the dark timbre ferocious.

She couldn't tell yet how angry he was. His mouth was sculpted with harsh strokes and he hid his enigmatic eyes under hooded lids. But the fingers wrapped around her arms were just short of painful.

"What the hell are you doing here?" he asked, although he already knew.

"I, um-"

"Don't lie, Kesindra. I have watched you all night let that man handle you, touch you all over. You going home with him to fuck?" Rage bubbled about to boil over into wrath, his face dark, eyes flashing jealous fury.

"No, I mean, of course not." Her brows lowered over suspicious eyes. "Were you spying on me?"

His fingers tight, his thumbs rubbed on her bare skin. "We are not talking about me. We are talking about you being out with another man."

Confused, her brow scrunched, she repeated, "Another man? You mean other than Chris?"

"I mean other than me."

"I don't under-"

"And dressed like a fucking whore. You are going to dress like a whore, act like a whore, tis going to be with me,

Kesindra, only me. The sooner you get that through your head, the sooner we can move past your insecurities and fearful walls."

His gaze swept with contempt down her outfit, hesitating at the low draping that exposed the top swell of her breasts. His eyes darkened with lust, mouth tightened with anger. The scathing gaze lowered to the tiny skirt that showed her legs, too thin but so goddamned pretty his breath caught. He flipped a group of her wild curls. "Arianna's doing, I suppose?"

She nodded, afraid to speak. He looked about to explode.

"Ah, the makeup too, no doubt." His gaze scoured her again. "And the dress, tis all Arianna, baby, not you." He squeezed her arms. "I don't expect to see you in something like that ever again, unless you are with me. You understand me?"

"What? Don't be ridiculous, I will wear what I want-"

He snatched her in close and slammed his mouth over hers, kissing her hard, too hard. He raided her lips, looted every bit of tenderness and sweetness inside, spiked and inundated her taste buds until her mouth and brain wept with abandoned desire.

Her panties were sopping in a blink. *How could she be so afraid of a man that turned her on so much?*

When he abruptly pulled from her, she was so punch-drunk dazed he had to hold her from collapsing. His own lungs burst in rapid, shallow huffs from the lurid kiss, the horns had swelled huge in his blond hair.

Haggard breaths, primitive snarls roiled deep inside his heavy chest. Low and coarse, he growled, "I am taking you home, Kesindra." Black orbs glittered dangerously, his mouth moved to plunder hers again, she wrenched from his hands.

"No-" she gasped, turning her head. "I- I came with Arianna, I leave with her. I…" She stepped from his reach. "I don't want to be alone with you when you're…like this."

"Oh? You would rather be with that bastard who has been feeling you up all night?"

Lips in a tight line, Kesi ground out, "He was not feeling me up, just, uh, my legs. Anyway," she moved further from the steaming giant. "I will not leave my group like an errant child dragged home by her- her seething father."

"I would have preferred you had said 'seething husband'" his smirk annoyed, fury tightened the edges of his mouth.

"Really?" Now she smirked, "And how many centuries old are you?"

His lips bunched, eyes narrowed. "Don't go there."

"It doesn't matter, I will leave with the people I came with."

"They are trashed, Kesindra, tis too dangerous for you to drive home with-"

Kesi cut him off with a derisive snort. "The town is so small with gravel and dirt roads, how fast can anyone go enough to cause damage? I am leaving with them. Stop stalking me."

She turned from him to go back to the dining room. Not sure turning her back on him was the best idea, her shoulders stiff, she resisted looking back to see if he was charging at her.

Only his voice cold, darkly low followed her, "Enjoy the rest of your date, *tím rostia*, it will be the last one you ever have."

A chill raced up her spine, was that a threat? Were they getting to the end of why the other-worlders had taken over the town and were now going to dispose of the humans?

Striding uneasily on the steep heels back to her table, she could feel his burning eyes, lasers on her back.

Kesi didn't see him again. She didn't know if he left, or just made himself invisible in the crowd and shadows.

She had to fight off lecherous Errol all the way home. Thank goodness he was so drunk he was easy enough to fight off. Sober, she would have had a problem.

When they reached her street, Kesi ignored all their arguments to go on for more drinks, dancing, partying.

"Come on," Arianna whined, hanging on Barney. She was barely intelligible she was so drunk, her dress was more off her than on. "Let's party. Barney has some good shit, we can get naked, get blasted, have a group party, come on, Kesi, don't be a party pooper."

Yeah. Sure. Kesi wanted to do illegal drugs and get into a naked orgy with these people. The trio persisted until Barney pulled up in front of her house.

Errol made to get out but Kesi leaped out and slammed the car door in his face. "Good night, everyone! Thanks for a great time," she said gaily, but wearily trod towards her little house.

"Wait, Kessyandera," Errol slurred, trying to fumble out of the car. "I'll walk you to your door, come in wit ya. I'ma s'pposed to get a good night kisser, sugartits, wait."

He got the door open, but Barney was already swinging the car around to leave. Errol was thrown back inside and Barney drove off with the door partially ajar.

"Oh my gosh," Kesi sighed, "what a night." She glanced around suspiciously looking for a lurking blond demon.

It was likely he had followed them. The look in his eyes when he was pulling her back in to kiss at the restaurant rippled shivers up her arms. He looked like a stalking jaguar about to devour its prey.

But, the air seeped out of her chest; neither he nor his jeep was anywhere to be seen. He undoubtedly was already naked at his home with his date.

Damn, she hated how that niggled at her, twisted her stomach. It was wrong of him to kiss Kesi when he had a date waiting for him at their table or the bar.

Picturing hourglass-figured Tabby with Martier's big hands all over her bigger naked breasts, his fangs on her neck, her hand gripping, his manhood, gah, Kesi felt ill.

Hurrying up the steps to the side door, she paused. The window was repaired. A slight smile snuck over her lips, Martier had sent someone to fix it.

Locking the door behind her, she took a quick shower to wash Errol's handprints off her body and went to bed.

But, sleep was unattainable. Kesi finally realized that Martier could have hurt her, raped her, killed her, any time he wanted to, and yet he hadn't so much as harmed a hair on her head. Maybe all he espoused about truly wanting her was...true.

As she dozed fitfully, blond hair and horns, and midnight green eyes, danced in her head.

Down the street in the shadows of draping trees, Martier settled back to sit in his jeep for the rest of the night. She got home safe and was fucking alone, lucky for her and that shithead she'd been with.

If she'd let that yahoo go inside with her, Martier would not have been able to hold back his possessive jealousy. He would have had to confront them, make the clown leave.

He shook his head with a grunt, he should leave. Yeah, what he was doing constituted stalking, but he couldn't sleep knowing she was alone in that house vulnerable to every Tom, Dick, Chris, blind date and asshole in town.

Chapter Nineteen

Kesi couldn't sleep. Between the all-consuming toe curling kiss Martier had given her at the restaurant, something about last night kept creeping into the back of her brain. What was bothering her?

She rolled over on her belly; arm out as if she could feel Martier beside her. Ha- he would never fit in her tiny bed.

As much as she shied away from his overtures, she lay there wondering what it would feel like to have his heavy body sprawled over her, his crude hands on every inch of her body, his mouth- damn, she needed to get up.

Why was she drawn to the outlaw demon that would probably have sex with her and be gone before the dawn rose? Her core tingled, her dripping channel clenched with thoughts of him.

How could she fear him and desire him at the same time? Each time she saw him the desire ate up a little bit more of the fear. Her fingers strayed to between her legs.

She stopped, there was no way she could reproduce what he had done with his magic fingers. Her thoughts were only making her grow tingly, her nipples hardened, her breasts ached, it was time to get up.

Another shower wouldn't hurt her. Passing her dresser her badge and ID caught her eye. She'd kept her transfer papers exiling her to the country of Původně on top of the dresser to remind her what devastation disastrous mistakes can cause.

She stared blankly at the papers. Her heart sunk into her gut like it did every time she thought of that life-changing night in the alley. The gunshot wound gnawed at her back, she automatically reached for her pills to kill the memories, *I mean the pain,* she corrected herself.

She hesitated. Was Martier right that she had phantom pain? That she was trying to shut off her feelings, the horrific memory of that night and the anchor of guilt she carried? She set the bottle down and went straight into the bathroom to shower.

Her hair now dry spiraling in ringlets down her back, Kesi buttoned the frilly while blouse smiling down at the lacey black bra.

She might wear baggy clothes, but she'd always worn sexy lingerie underneath where no one would see. It made her feel feminine just knowing they were there. The feel of silk and lace stroking her body as she moved gave her a light, pretty feeling, when she knew she wasn't.

But today, she felt like dressing a little more feminine. Instead of loose slacks and baggy shirts, she decided to wear the snugger, lighter blouse and amber colored shorts. The shorts reminded her of when she had worn the shorty panties. When he saw them, Martier's tongue had actually hung out with his cartoon popping eyes.

You'd think the how many, probably thousands, of women he'd slept with that a pair of panties wouldn't turn him on so much. Thousands. Yuk, that made her feel sick.

She'd barely kissed a boy or two and Martier had been with- darn, she needed to get going. It didn't, shouldn't, matter to her one whit how many women he had slept with over however many eons he'd lived.

While in the shower, she had remembered what was niggling at her.

She changed into turquoise jeans thinking they would be a safer choice. After locking the door, she trod down the pebbly driveway, so much easier in the ankle boots than in the stilettoes from last night. Her feet still hurt.

Kesi walked right up to the jeep parked down the street under the shadowed canopy of a huge kapok tree.

The windows were open. Slumped down in the seat, his back curved against the corner of the driver's seat and door, left leg bent at the knee beside the wheel, the other leg stretched out somewhat across the rest of the jeep. He was too tall to be comfortable in most vehicles, much less a jeep.

The light morning breeze blew in and ruffled his golden blond hair; his arms were crossed over his chest accentuating the huge biceps. He was sound asleep.

"Geeze, some kind of stalker you are-"

Before she could blink he had his hand at her throat and a gun at her temple. Then, he hissed, "Fuck, Kesindra, you trying to get yourself killed?"

Even with the gun at her head, she said calmly, "I didn't realize what a light sleeper you were. Um, can you like let me go now and holster that thing?"

Martier had reacted instinctually. Comprehending he had a death grip on her delicate neck and his weapon at her head, he instantly released his hand and did as she said and holstered the weapon.

Dragging his fingers through his mop of hair he squinted at her. "I was not stalking. I was making sure none of your lovers returned to visit you unexpectedly in the middle of the night. That fucker you went out with last night, Mr. Hands, loverboy is lucky he stayed in the car. If he had gone in the house with you, I would have removed those roaming hands from his arms."

"Huh," her elegant snort cut with a short laugh. "I have no lovers."

"Aye, you do. Only one. That is all there will ever be."

"Who-" She shook her head, was he going to keep throwing Chris at her? "Never mind. Why didn't you just knock on the door, you could have slept more comfortably on my couch?" Of course she wouldn't have been comfortable with the big demon in her house.

His eyes skewed sideways at her. "Please, you know better than that."

Face scrunched in puzzlement. "Whatever. I need to use your phone."

Yawning, he rolled his eyes. "Kesindra, we have been through this before. I have ordered you to stop with the detective work. Tis too-" He swung around as she jerked the passenger door open and slid inside.

"Kesindra, not a good idea." He dropped his foot to the floor moving it to the driver's side and shifting over to make room for her.

"Captain, this is terribly important. I really must use your phone."

He laid his arm around the back of the seat and swiveled to face her. "You know, every time you call me Captain I have a good mind to tear off whatever you are wearing and paddle the hell out of your behind. I think I have mentioned this before. You just love to disregard my orders. You are pushing it."

His gaze slipped to the pants she was wearing. "Those pretty jeans don't look like they would put up even a second of resistance to my shredding fingers. They are delicate, like you. I could just pull them apart, I would not even have to use my claws."

He was saying things deliberately to scare her, run her off, but she didn't move.

A slow smile curved up his hard face. "I do like those turquoise jeans though, nice and snug. Are you wearing those little panty shorts you wore-" He shook his head. "Kesindra," he said with a sigh, "you need to get out of this jeep while you can."

"Is that a threat?" Kesi sounded coy for the first time in her life.

He groaned, "*Kesindra*," turned to face the steering wheel and dropped his head back.

"You can threaten me all you want, I need to use your phone."

"I don't have it. I left it to charge last night when I went looking for you when you did not show up at the rec building for dinner. Which reminds me, I need to punish you for that." He partially turned towards her.

His leer gave her goose bumps. "Fine," she said, "now I have two punishments coming. Regardless, turn on the car. I will tell you why I need to make a call on the way to your place to get your phone."

"If you knew me, you would not make light of my threats."

"Whatever. Let's just go, I'll run inside, make the call quick and zip right back out."

His head bowed, he twined his fingers together in his lap. He was silent for a moment as if gathering his thoughts, or his control.

Then, he raised his head and stared out the front window not looking at her. He said in a harsh quiet voice, "Kesindra, I think I have made it clear that we cannot be alone together. Especially at my place, or your place. Until you are ready."

She plopped her elbow up on the back of her seat and half-turned towards him. "Really, Captain, come on, you're telling me a man who claims to be this big bad warlord that has lived for centuries, been with really I don't want to know how many women, can't control himself around me?"

A sarcastic chortle burbled out of her throat. "Let's get real. Tell me the real reason you don't want to be alone with me to-"

He shot a hand into her hair and clenched a handful. Roughly dragging her across the seat, he belted his mouth over hers and took her in a harrowing brutal kiss, viciously invading her mouth.

Before he released her, he smacked her hard on her ass and stated, "That is for calling me captain," then gave her a little push back in her seat.

Kesi sat stunned with the back of her hand over her mouth.

Martier turned from her and set his forearm heavily over the steering wheel while he caught his breath, garnered his fleeting self-control. He cast a quick glance at her.

Seeing the big blues trembling over her hand, he sucked in a deep breath, exhaled with a ragged grumble then scrubbed his fingers over his night's growth of dark scruff covering his jaw.

"I want you, Kesindra. So badly I can barely think of anything else but...taking you. I cannot make it any plainer, any clearer, I want you. But, you still fear me, and you are not ready to fu- ah, uh, make love with me yet, so until you are, tis best we are not alone together. I fully admit my restraints on my self-control are sliding down to zero with you."

He expected her to run like the wind, get far away from him as fast as she could. But she didn't move.

Staring straight ahead again, he said, "Kesindra, you don't understand who I am. I am not like those gentlemen, those human men you were raised with. You think Chris was a prick? I am a warlord from a violent world you could not even imagine, in a whole other universe.

"I chase down the worst of the worst deadly, dangerous criminals of the galaxies. I don't know how to romance a woman, never had to. They throw themselves at me."

"Humph," she grunted glaring at him now.

A lopsided grin made him look boyish for an instant. "That is not said with conceit, tis just the way it tis."

His tone turned serious again. "I have the most intense control when it comes to everything else, fighting, torturing, killing, commanding, women," he sighed.

"But not with you. Tis been different with you from the second I saw you through the trees before Bruglon even got to you. You have been right to call me a wild savage. I am primitive, barbaric. I have never had to stop myself from taking what I want, and I will not be able to stop myself from taking you. I cannot say pretty words and pretend otherwise. Sorry, but facts are facts." The huge shoulders flexed in a shrug.

"I hate to say this, Kesindra," he went on, his voice grew quiet and low, "but, I must warn you. I will be taking you, at some point, with or without your consent. I am trying to wait until you are ready, but, the tether on my control is unraveling at an alarming rate."

He didn't look at her; he didn't want to see the fear or repulsion of him on her lovely face. It would cut him to the craw. But he wouldn't negate what he said, he meant every word of it, good or bad.

Pondering his words, she looked at him, but he was still staring out the windshield. "I keep getting mixed signals, Captain." Her face whitened when he swiveled quickly at her with a ferocious growl.

"I mean, Martier. Um, one second you say you can't stop yourself from…having sex with me, and you make it sound like you're not going to stop, in the next breath you say we can't be alone together. Last night you threatened that I would never have another date again, I can only understand that to mean you will kill me before this…whatever this takeover is, is done."

His head fell forward with a groan. He rubbed his eyes in frustration, turned and glowered with a hiss through his fangs.

Ignoring her cringe, he ground out through clenched teeth, "For the last time, Kesindra, I am not going to kill you or anyone else in the village. Stop saying that, tis really pissing me off. What I meant was that *I* will be the only date you will have from now on. I am done with seeing you with other men."

Her lips pressed together at his irritated fury. She picked at some of the frills on her blouse. "So, are you saying you want to have sex with me, and then leave me? Go off to your own world as if we never happened?"

A shadow passed over his eyes darkening them. "I am not planning on that."

"On which, having sex with me, or leaving me?"

Which a chuckle, he meaningfully looked down. "What do you think?" The huge bulge of his erection was straining at his jeans. His voice so soft yet coarse with desire, his lids lowered exposing only glints of perilous flashing dark green. "You are mine, *nĕkolika*, tis only a matter of time before you realize it."

Her lips parted. "I...think we should just, uh, go and get your phone."

Looking to the heavens with exasperation, his groan harsh he claimed, "I have warned you, Kesindra, how I feel, my disturbing lack of control around you. Hell, right now I just want to rip the damned crotch out of those jeans, pull you under me and shove into you." He grunted at her shocked expression at his crudeness.

"But, little human agent, I could not do that even if you acquiesced. You are too small, tight, a fucking virgin, I would tear you apart. Your, *our* first time together, and assuredly more than a few times after, will need to be slow, careful and gentle, then...I would unleash my true self on you." He cast a leering glance at her to see her reaction.

Her gulp audible, she licked her lips then chewed on the lower one.

He taunted, "No comment, sweet *nĕkolika*?"

She cleared her throat, said sternly, "I think you are trying to scare me on purpose. For fun, because you're bored, for whatever the reason, but I really must use your cell." Kesi faced the demon behind the wheel and pleaded, "Please. Take me to it."

His face impassive, expression inscrutable, Martier studied her for a few seconds, her gaze didn't waver. He could see the ripple of fear, her uneasiness to be with him, but she stayed her ground. Without another word, he turned the key and pulled out into the narrow street to head across town to his hotel room.

Conversationally, she said, "Tell me, Captain, where is your world in conjunction to Earth? Why do you, and the other aliens I've seen on the news look so humanlike?"

Driving in the rustic town was easy, there were so few other vehicles on the road and no traffic lights and only an occasional handwritten stop sign. Many of the villagers walked or rode bikes to get around.

Martier glanced at Kesi, her blues were bright and inquisitive, focused with interest on him.

"Well," he answered her, "all of us sentient beings, including you humans, were created by the chemical components of our bodies forged in the nuclear fires of stars.

"The chemicals making up the stars, suns, through gravitation and internal and external composites led to the first creation of life. Not necessarily man, or woman," he glanced at her, "but the very first etchings of living cells."

He glanced at her, Kesi was watching him with rapt interest.

He went on, "Differing climates, chemicals, make us unique to our planets, yet since we all started out basically the same, we are closely matched. After beings from all planets have been blending together, there are now many species of mixed blood. I will explain at another time...my...species. I am...ah, am a bit different from...the rest."

Her brow furrowed trying to take in what he explained. Getting the gist of it, she asked, "You don't believe in God? In a higher being that created all, us, everything?"

His lip ticked in. "Oh aye. On the contrary, I believe in my God. Yours is different."

At her raised brow he said, "Your own bible in Genesis states: I quote:

"**26:** Then God said, "Let **us** make mankind in **our** image, in **our** likeness, so that they may rule over the fish in the sea and the birds in the sky, over the livestock and all the wild animals,[a] and over all the creatures that move along the ground."

27: So God created mankind in his own image,

in the image of God he created them;

male and female he created them.

28: The Lord God made garments of skin for Adam and his wife and clothed them. And the Lord God said, "The man has now become **like one of us,** knowing good and evil. He must not be allowed to reach out his hand and take also from the tree of life and eat, and live forever."

Her mouth dropped open, and stayed there while she considered his words. "So, you're saying...what?"

Flashing a brief smile, he explained, "The Bible clearly states the use of the word *us* when God is speaking about the creation of man. There were more Gods, each chose their own...sections...like galaxies.

"That is why some of us can look alike, but then again depending on climate and the type of planet mixed with different evolutionary events, we can have vast differences like the wretched grizzly-dogs that thank Zeus, you know nothing about."

Kesi thought on his words. She would need to open her Bible tomorrow and check out what he said. This was the first she'd ever heard of God speaking plural about himself, or, herself.

"Um, okay. So how come you have come here but we haven't been to other...planets?"

"Actually, you have. Different aliens have brought humans back. There are even some other planets inhabited only by humans. But, basically, you don't know about us because we are so many billions of light years away that your detection devices, telescopes and such, are not powerful enough, not yet anyway, to discern our presence.

"Most Earth-sized planets- the exoplanets that your astrobiologists think are most likely to harbor life, are just too far away to study. You also don't have the technology, yet, to get to us."

"How did you find us...Earth?"

"Ah, dark matter's colossal gravitational influence on our differing universes permeates the cosmos. Dark matter tends to be concentrated in large halos around galaxies like giant bubbles, like black discs amidst the stars, planets, and gas clouds in the galaxies.

"We have advanced far beyond Earth's abilities to travel across and through this dark matter shaving off vast blocks of time."

It was hard for Kesi to comprehend all this; that aliens were trotting around on Earth and had been for some time. And that Earthlings have traveled, and actually live on other planets.

"Your accent, the way you speak English, where did it come from? You speak differently, a different cadence when you're talking in your own language. But when speaking English you sound a cross between the Irish and like, I don't know, Russian?" She laughed. "I see you learned all the curse words with no problem."

He glanced at her to see her friendly smile and returned it in kind. "Tis just from the first humans that we came in contact with. Many of them were criminals on Earth that other criminals from outside your galaxy came here and hooked up with; that we eventually captured and arrested."

When she was silent, his lip pulled in. "Tis a lot for you to understand, sweetheart. Later, when we have…time to…ourselves, I will explain in further depth, specifics."

He glanced over at her. "Now tis time for you to explain why tis so urgent for you to use my phone."

By the time Kesi explained her need for the phone, Martier was parking in the lot in the back of the hotel, still with the mind of preserving her reputation. For now. When he finally claims her, everyone will know of their union.

They strode up the back staircase together and then down the quiet hall to one of the rooms.

He unlocked the door, stepped inside first with a quick scan then let her enter.

"Make yourself comfortable," *said the tiger to the tasty bunny*. Hell, he had warned her again and again and still she came.

"I just need your phone, Cap- Martier."

His hands on his hips, he glared at her. Then his face cleared. "I have an idea, why don't you buy your time with my phone, without using money, I mean."

Taking a step back from him she uttered, "Uh, excuse me?"

With a smirk, he said, "Geeze, Agent Jasmari, get your mind out of the gutter. I assume neither of us has eaten."

His gaze an accusation down her body, he admonished, "You are too thin, and I slept in my jeep all night." He twisted his back to stretch it.

"Not great, but I have bunked down in a lot worse. Anyway, how about you rustle us up something for breakfast while I shower and change?"

Her face relaxed. "Oh. Sure. I can do that. What do you want, or probably should be what do you have that I can make?"

His mouth quirked. "I am a bachelor, obviously. At home and on my ship I have a majordomo. I did not bring him on this mission. He usually provides for me. I have eaten out most meals since being here, and the food here, I hate to say, sucks. So anything you prepare has got to be better. There are eggs, bread, stuff like that Trae and Slade brought over the other morning while we...met, for...business."

"Okay."

"I am kind of partial to egg and bacon sandwiches if you can do that." He took an awkward breath. "Anyway, the kitchen is right in through there," he nodded towards the other hall.

"I will be back in a few. Coffee would be great too if you can figure out the machine. I," he shrugged a shoulder, "have tried. But these ancient machines you humans still have, hell, I cannot figure them out. Coffee comes out too strong or too weak, or pours over."

"Hmm," she pondered him with a smile. "I have a feeling it's more likely someone's impatience with the machine that is at issue, not the machine.

He returned her smile. "Perhaps you are right. I have always known there are brains inside all that beauty." His eyes trailed down the frilly blouse, snug jeans and back up, then he turned on his heel and left the room.

Kesi got the eggs and bacon fried up and slapped between four toasted and buttered croissants with melted cheese gooeing out the sides, and was pouring the coffee when he came out.

She set the food and coffee mugs on the small dining table near the sliding glass door that opened to a miniscule balcony.

"Hey," he said softly, watching her working to prepare a meal for him. His stomach felt warm and fuzzy. First time he'd ever experienced that.

Kesi turned with a smile.

Barefoot, he'd pulled on faded worn jeans and was still buttoning up his shirt. His wet hair, now dark gold curled around his face and waved over the top and down the back, water dripped a little on his collar.

Contrasting, she saw a flash of dark brown hair on his chest before he got the last two buttons fastened. Some still showed under the top buttons he left undone. "Just as you ordered, Master," she quipped gesturing to the table.

He came forward with a smile. "Wow. Nice job Kesindra. Especially that master part. I believe I have mentioned to you before that is who I am. To you."

His smile broadened at her pursed lips. Then his eyes lit up. "Hey, fresh, noncommercial coffee, you rock, baby."

He grabbed up a mug and drank it down black. "Mmm," he sighed, licking his lips with a smack and loud swallow. "So good."

She stood back nearer to the living room area.

He pulled out a chair and motioned to it. "Come here and eat with me."

"Captain," she demurred shaking her head.

Brows drew down in hard slashes over his annoyed eyes. "Fucking Martier, Kesindra, do not make me say that again. Your ass will not thank you."

"I'm sorry. Martier, please, I must make that call, it's vitally important."

He sat down and picked up a sandwich, took a giant bite. Talking through the food that made a lump in the side of his jaw he scolded her, "You are frail as hell, Kesindra, come and eat." He washed the egg and bacon down with a swig of coffee.

He crowed with admiration, "Man, beautiful, sweet, smart as a whip and sexy as hell, and you can cook too. I have stumbled onto paradise."

Making fast work of one sandwich, he reached for a second of the four she had made and gobbled that one as quickly as the other. "The obstinacy and recklessness I can live without though."

"Please, Martier, someone else could die."

The look he shot her warned of his temper and that he was at the end of it. She glared back.

Cursing in English, stuffing a third sandwich in his mouth he got up and went into his bedroom and came back out cursing in a different language.

"If you don't take care of yourself you are going to get sick. You work my every last nerve, *několika*, you know that, right?" He had the phone in his hand. "I have never met a more stubborn, willful woman in all the solar systems, all the planets, all the-"

"Or for Pere's sake, stop whining and give me the phone," she groused and held her hand out for it.

A grin tugged at the corners of his mouth. He held the phone out for her to take. "You are so goddamned cute when you are in a snit."

"Ooo," she grated with a scowl, "give me the damned phone!" She reached for it.

He held it up over her head with a grin. "Ah, the lady agent curses. I like it. So sweet and refined with a potty mouth, what a turn on. I want you to talk dirty to me baby, you gonna do that? Whisper naughty things, in my ear while we are-"

"Martier Dravidian, I swear to God, if you don't give me that-" She jumped for it, he held it higher and wrapped his other hand around her waist jerking her against him. It was like hitting a brick wall.

"For a kiss," he teased lowering his mouth to hers.

"You making me pay for favors with sex?"

He froze. Glared at her. "That was shitty, Kesindra." He released her, grabbed her wrist and pulled her to the couch, gave her a slight push to sit down.

He plunked down next to her and asked coolly, "What is the number?"

She reached out to take the phone. "Here, just let me-"

His hand closed over it. "Nay. I dial." He cupped her chin holding it hard.

His expression no longer teasing, he instructed, "You say what you have to, no more no less. If I think you are giving him any kind of information at all about what is going on here you will never see the phone again and I will lock you up."

Her mouth dropped at his fierceness. She moistened her lips, their eyes connected, his furious black, hers frightened blue. Sometimes she forgot he was a demon from another world, until he acted like a cold-blooded ruthless warrior.

"Say you understand, Kesindra, or we are done here."

Her throat bobbed with constricted swallows. She tried to nod but he held her too tautly. She whispered, "I understand."

He glared hard at her for a minute deciding if he could trust her or not. Their mission was too important for one little screw up. But he knew she was an honorable woman. She had been honest that day he caught her trying to escape in the jungle, and she was very aware how much he was trusting her with this phone call. He held it in his palm and looked down at it. Releasing her chin he asked, "What is the number?"

Kesi let out her held breath, the numbers ticked off her tongue with a shaky exhale.

When Martier heard the male's voice answer, he pushed 'speaker' and held it to her with a severe warning in his eyes.

Taking it, again swallowing hard, Kesi started to speak but her voice was clogged with nerves.

She cleared her throat and started again. "Agent Dukes? This is Kesindra Jasmari."

Chapter Twenty

Martier got up briefly to snag the fourth sandwich then sank back down beside her. Making quick work of it, he licked his fingers.

Keith Dukes' voice boomed through loud and clear. "Agent Jasmari, finally! The satellite service must be shit out there, we've tried to get through for a couple of weeks but it's been no go. Richard Valsaint's mother is on our backs to get in touch with him. Who knew he was such a mama's boy, huh?"

"Um, yes, we've had satellite trouble. I-"

"So what's been going on out there in that shitass rural village in that crappy third world country? You kids must be bored outta your minds, huh?"

"Uh yes, no, I mean I called you for something important-"

"But I guess you get action with the natives, if you know what I mean," the leering innuendo came through. "That's where I got most of my action when I was a young buck and was out-"

"Agent Dukes, please," she cut him off. "I need you to look into something for me back there in Ships Bay. Don't question it, it's important, please trust me. I will explain if it pans out."

Sounding like he was only half listening, Dukes said, "Yeah, yeah, go ahead, what do you need?"

Martier leaned back against the cushion and pulled Kesi into the corner between his chest and arm. He did it so slowly and smoothly, she was so intent on the phone call she wasn't even aware of it. He settled his arm around her and listened carefully to every word she said.

First she gave the agent a brief rundown of all the murders that occurred.

Before Dukes could make a comment, Kesi said, "I have a question. Arianna Loomis, did you send her out here to be with us? Did you do the transfer?"

"Huh?" A grunt. "What the hell is going on in that shitbag of a loser country? Murders? I want to speak with Christopher Carpenter immediately! You need to send a report-"

"Yes, yes," Kesi said hurriedly, "as soon as I can. Now, Arianna Loomis, did you send her out here to work with us?"

"Fuck no, girl, why the hell would I?" He paused. "So that's where the hell she is. People have been looking for her. You tell her-"

"Agent, can you find out who signed the order for her to come out here?"

Silence. "What? What the hell? Who cares, she not pulling her weight? Write her up, tell her to get her ass on a plane and when you come back I'll-"

Kesi spoke slowly, calmly, enunciating her words, "I need to know who sent her here, who signed her transfer orders. How long will it take to get that information?"

A bit surprised at the young agent's calm commanding directive, Dukes cleared his throat. "Uh, shit, Jasmari, what happened to that sweet little girl that we sent out there?"

Iron gravel in her throat, Kesi said coldly, "You sent me out here." She spoke before he could, "Now, how long will it take for you to get that information?"

"Shit, Kesindra," he was thrown off. "Uh, let's say thirty minutes. Give me your number and I'll call you back when I have-"

Martier took the phone from her suddenly trembling hand and disconnected it. Looking at her pale face and shaking hands he said softly, "Let me get you a soda." He shifted her to sit back against the cushion and left for the kitchen.

Kesi pulled out her pills. They rattled in her trembling hands as she started to twist the lid off. Martier was behind the sofa, he reached over and took the bottle out of her hands.

"*Několika,* you are doing fine without these, you don't need them."

Voice pitched and high, Kesi said, "Martier, cut it out. This is none of your business. Give me my pills. I...I need them." Her voice shook along with her hands. Face pale as a sheet, sweat beaded at her temples.

"Baby, please, let me help you-"

"No!" she snapped. "I am beyond help, it's too late." She jumped up and demanded, "Give me my damned pills."

It wasn't a fight for now. She would need to be under medical care to stop without possible fatal danger to her system.

As soon as he got her the hell out of here, she was going whether she wanted to or not. With a heavy sigh, he handed them to her.

Shortly after she took a pill, her hands stopped shaking.

Martier subtly observed her. The entire morning he'd been with her, including while she was talking on the phone, she'd been calm, alert, confident. She didn't need the pills until she thought of them. "Here, sit down, baby. I ate all the sandwiches. I will make you one."

"No," she held up a weary hand. "I can't eat now. I'm too wound up." Her lip ticked up in guilt. "I'm sorry I snapped at you. I'm just, I haven't been sleeping well. This murder stuff is scary, I'm so afraid someone else will die and I can't prevent it."

A yawn took her words, "-Ah, hmm, then talking with Agent Dukes brought back all the horror that day I was shot." She dashed her palms at sudden tears that welled.

Martier responded, "And, my *několika,* you don't eat right, you let yourself get run down. You still blame yourself for something that was so out of your control, tis outrageous you carry the fucking guilt of it."

Gently forcing her to sit on the couch, he said, "Now, you stay here and take a break, I will make you something to eat."

A grin cut across his hard face. "It will not be as good as you did, it will be something a lot simpler." He cocked a brow at her. "But, seriously, for your own good you must eat."

He bent and cradled her chin. "I will not let you use the phone again unless you eat. That is not making you pay for favors, that is looking out for your health. Okay?"

Not having the energy to argue with him, Kesi nodded with a wan smile. "Okay." Her eyelids drooped.

"Good. I will be right back." He kissed the tip of her nose earning a sleepy smile from Kesi.

He was only gone as long as it took to make a ham and cheese sandwich and grab a soda on ice for her.

When he returned, she was curled up on the couch, asleep. Martier went back into the kitchen and put the plate and glass in the refrigerator then came back and knelt beside the sofa.

Smoothing her hair back from her face, he kissed her softly on her cheek. Carefully lifting her head, he tucked a small pillow under it, then removed her ankle boots and socks.

A smile tickled over his chiseled lips. Her tiny toes were painted fuchsia. She hid her taste for bright sexy things under wraps. At some point he will be kissing, licking, likely sucking each one of those cute little toes.

Geesh, his crooked grin was wry, when had he become a lovesick sap? The word cute had never been in his vocabulary; he couldn't even fathom where it had come from. The wee girl was wreaking havoc on his man card.

He sat in a chair and watched her sleep. His heart melted. She was so brave, so sweet, tried to be so strong, his little earthling.

A corner of his mouth lifted in affectionate ruefulness, he was wrapped around her little finger and he could never let her know that. This tiny human female had one of the most ruthless brutal warlords in the universe tied up in knots. He chuckled silently.

Trae had said he was pussy-whipped. He had spoken the truth. Martier had it bad now, when they had sex he knew he would truly be pussy-whipped.

Kesi didn't know it yet, but she would be the one and only pussy for him from now on. He just actually needed to get his hands back on it, and his dick in it. Hell, his pants were getting tight.

Kesi gave a little moan and stirred. Her lashes fluttered, then she opened her eyes. She sat up slowly, disoriented with her surroundings.

"Kesindra," he said softly from his chair.

She turned to him and blinked. Then she smiled, remembering how she got there. "I'm sorry, Martier, I didn't mean to fall asleep."

His smile tender he said, "That is not something that ever needs to be apologized for, unless we are having sex. In that case I wouldn't be doing my job properly, I'd have to work harder."

He was going to keep dropping sexual comments, letting her know he was serious about them being together and for her to get comfortable with the inevitable. That was going to happen today. He was done with waiting.

Besides, the shit was soon going to hit the fan and he wanted their relationship to be in cement before that transpired. Kesi would never learn to trust him until they became intimate and she understood they were going to be together forever.

Martier laughed at the moue her mouth made. "Sweetheart, you needed the sleep."

She swung her legs around to drop her feet off the couch. "Has it been thirty minutes?"

"Forty-five."

"Oh my gosh! I need to call Agent Dukes right away, he said thirty!" She jumped to her feet. "Can I use your phone, please?"

He stood up as well. "Now, don't get all pissy, Kesindra, but you are not using the phone until you eat something." He nodded at the ham and cheese he'd taken back out of the fridge a few minutes ago.

"What? Are you playing games with me, Captain? You said you would let me call!" Clenching her fists, she took an angry step towards him.

He stood impassive, a nonmoving tank. "Eat first."

"Of all the-" mouth pushed out, eyes narrowed, she looked at the pocket he had put his phone in.

He laughed out loud. "You are kidding, right? You think you can take it from me? Hell, girl, I wish you would try. Come on, come and get it, baby," he taunted with his arms open and inviting, fingers wagging, egging her on.

Fuming, Kesi crossed her arms. Obviously there was no way she would ever be able to take something from him he didn't want to give her.

"Eat and then no prob. As soon as I see half that sandwich gone, I will start dialing."

"You- you- demon outlaw, damn you." She glared at the sandwich before snatching it up and biting off a chunk. Chewing angrily she snarled, "Does this make you happy?"

"I can think of lots of things you can do, baby, that would make me happy." His gaze trailed down the front of her, lips drawing up in a lusty grin. Then his voice softened and his eyes warmed. "But aye, seeing you eat makes me happy."

Tears suddenly welled surprising them both. Kesi struggled to swallow the bread. No one had cared about her in a long, long time.

"Baby," Martier murmured. Moving to her, he helped her sit down. After handing her the soda, he sat beside her. "Take it easy, tis been a long hard haul for you."

His words sprung her tears. Wiping at her eyes, she took a sip of soda, choking while swallowing the sandwich.

Setting the glass down, a hiccup came out in a little cry as the tears fell.

"Aw honey, come here." He pulled her to his chest and wrapped his arms around her.

Kesi pushed from him. "I cry too much, I'm constantly breaking down. I can't keep doing this, I'm so weak."

"Ah Zeus, *několika,* you are one of the strongest people I know, stronger than most of my men." He drew her back against him and stroked her hair. "Those pills don't help, baby, we need to talk about them."

Kesi shoved from him, but he held her with steel arms and nestled her head on his chest.

"Martier," her voice was scratchy and quiet, "please, leave it alone. It's my problem."

"Uh huh." He stroked her, laid the side of his face in her hair. Inhaling her scent, he whispered, "Tis *our* problem now."

It took a few moments for her to compose herself. Kesi got up and went to wash her face.

When she came back into the room, Martier was sitting with the phone in his hand.

Her smile lifted pleased yet strained. All this breaking down and crying was driving her nuts, it wasn't who she was. It embarrassed her that this hard as nails, tough warlord captain saw her weak like this.

But he was smiling at her. Big, strong, an alien demon for heaven's sake, and he had comforted her in his arms, cared if she ate or not, and was smiling kindly at her. The world was awry, but if it contained a devastatingly handsome demon in it, heck, it might be okay with her.

She joined him on the sofa. He nodded at the phone. "I am going to dial. While you are talking, you finish that sandwich. Is that a deal?"

241

"Gee Captain," she bemoaned, "you treat me like I'm a child."

"Uh huh, and what happens to disobedient children? Ones who refuse to do as they are told?"

She looked at him confused.

"They get punished. And how do they get punished?"

Kesi blinked at him before it dawned on her she'd called him captain again. Her cheeks stained pink and she moved an inch from him. "I'm sorry, Martier, it's a habit."

He put his hand on her knee to keep her from moving. "Aye. One you are going to break. Now, what is that number again?" He remembered it, he had photographic memory, but he didn't let on. Besides, the number would be in his sent calls.

Eying him warily, she told him the number.

He dialed and handed the phone to her. When she took it, he wrapped his hand around hers, bent and kissed her hand before releasing her, then handed her the sandwich.

Her consternated gaze on him, Kesi took a bite and listened for the phone to ring.

"Agent Keith Dukes here."

Swallowing quickly, she cleared her throat and greeted, "Hi, Agent Dukes."

"Jasmari? Is that you? I tried to trace the number but it's blocked and is somehow untraceable. You hung up so abruptly I was worried-"

"Did you get the information I asked for?"

Martier maneuvered behind Kesi. Bending a knee, he could curl around her. He settled his back against the couch cushion, massaging her shoulders while she talked, and ate.

At first Kesi was rigid to his touch. However, she soon relaxed as his firm fingers rubbed and prodded the tension from her neck and shoulders.

"Yeah, yeah. Listen, Kesindra, are you all right? Are the guys all right? Something fishy is going on. Tell me what the hell is going on."

With a quick frown Martier set his hand over the phone and gave her a warning look.

Kesi said calmly, "Please, Agent Dukes, just give me the information." Licking her fingers she hadn't even realized she'd finished the sandwich. Martier handed her a napkin he'd stuffed in his pocket.

"All right, all right, don't get your panties in a twist. Wait a sec, let me get my notes." The phone sounded dead as he set it down.

As Dukes picked it back up and started to speak, Martier slipped his arms around Kesi and covered her breasts with his hands.

She jerked, turned beet red, but didn't push away.

"Okay," Dukes said.

"Huh?" Kesi started at his voice.

With a low rumble of appreciation in her ear, Martier's long fingers coiled around her full breasts, feeling the weight of them, squeezing their softness. Sitting behind her with her back at his chest, he started unbuttoning her blouse.

"You there, Jasmari?"

"Uh, yes, of course, uh, go on." She held the phone to her ear while Martier worked on her buttons while in between fondled her breasts like he couldn't leave them alone for even a second.

He set his chin on her shoulder, moved her hair to one side and put his mouth on her neck. Almost all the buttons undone, he moved both hands inside to cup her breasts, thumbing her nipples over the bra, he sucked on her neck, hard.

"Oh!"

"You sure you're all right, Agent?" Dukes asked.

"Um, yes. Go on." She tilted her head so Martier could reach her neck more easily.

"Okay, so, well, it's the damnedest thing. No one admits to signing the order for Loomis to go with you guys. I went all the way up to the colonel but no go."

"So, *ahh*," she couldn't stop the moan. Martier sucked her neck as he undid the last button and was pulling her blouse off her back while sucking harder on her neck.

Rubbing his fangs on her skin, he stroked his hands over her shoulders, drifting them part way down her arms. Her breasts mounded over the black lace bra, he trailed his fingertips over the exposed swells.

"You okay, Jasmari? You sound funny."

Kesi gulped hard. Martier was trying to push the cups of her bra down to get to her bare skin while his mouth trailed tiny kisses and licks to near her mouth.

He whispered in her ear, "I love this black bra, *několika,* tis sexy as hell." He dipped his fingers into the cups to touch her. "But I want bare flesh, baby." Feeling her shiver, he smiled against her cheek.

Kesi hacked out a small awkward cough. "Um, yes, there's a- a bad connection, I might have a cold. Anyway, can you find out for me who, ah," one hand kneading her breast, Martier lowered the other hand to cup her woman's mound over her jeans and went back to sucking her neck.

She was curled into him, his arms and a leg encircling her, holding her close while he felt as much of her body as he could get his hands on.

"What? I'm losing you, Kesindra!" Dukes yelled.

"I'm here, Agent, uh," she bit back a groan as Martier pinched her nipple through her bra and was pushing her thighs apart to rub her sex with his big hand over the denims.

Kesi struggled to close her legs without dropping the phone. Martier was too strong. His chuckle was a sexy rustle in her ear.

Kesi grabbled, "I uh, I need you to find the actual transfer order that got her on the private FBI plane that brought her here, see whose name is on it. I also need you to give me as much background information on Arianna as you can find. I'll call back in-"

"An hour," Martier murmured against her neck while tugging at her belt. "Make that two."

He got her belt buckle loose and cupped her breasts again, tugging at her peaked nipples, then tried to shove a hand down her pants.

She gasped, "H- hour- call you back in an hour-"

Martier snatched the phone from her, swiped it off and tossed it on the table.

Chapter Twenty-One

Martier reached for her.

Her blouse swinging open, Kesi held her hands up in a sudden panic. "No, no, I can't do this! You are a- a criminal, an outlaw, you kill and- and-" She pushed from him and jumped to her feet.

Following her, he grasped her arms and asked coolly, "Kesindra, was anyone killed when we took over the town? You accuse me of harming little children and murdering residents. Has any of that happened?" He pulled her to him.

"Uh, no, wait, the children, uh," her soft body coming up against his slate hard chest drew moans from both of them.

The ramrod length of his thick erection pressing into her made no mistake of her effect on him. Her unbuttoned blouse hung off one shoulder.

"The children are fine, they are safe and will stay that way, I promise." Dragging a hand down her back, he hugged her tight to his torso while cradling her head. Then he bent and kissed her, gently, slowly stoking the fires.

Their mouths glued together, when Kesi's body starting sinking into his and she purred like a wanton kitten, Martier leaned his head back from her.

His eyes heavy-lidded with desire, Martier growled, "Okay, Kesindra, I am only going to say this once. I have just a hair's breadth of control left to let you leave, let you go out to my jeep and I will bring the phone to you. Because once we join, that is it, forever baby. You stay another second and we will make love, regardless if you change your mind."

Setting her hands on his broad shoulders, she said softly with a hint of confusion, "I don't understand, Martier. Somehow you just," she clutched the stiff cotton with her fingers then smoothed her palms up his shirt, "drive me crazy, make me want you."

Her hands slid up behind his head to pull it down and she clamped her mouth to his.

Only startled for a heartbeat, he hauled her tight against his body, slanting his head to seal their mouths, then he let her have the lead.

Her sweet innocence came through in her kiss, and it was so extraordinarily different from anything he'd ever experienced, he was struck with a shattering wave of desire that shot a blast of hedonistic dizziness throughout his body.

He could feel her literally tasting him, his lips, his teeth, inside his mouth; she tentatively searched for his tongue. Finding it, she stroked it so lightly it was insanely erotic.

Martier fought to keep from coming in his jeans. Steaming hisses scraped up his throat like a radiator heater at boiling point. He thought he would pass out from the glory of her curious, inexperienced exploration of him.

Feeling her little teeth nip his lower lip, tug on it, when she sucked on it, Martier slapped his hand on her bottom and crammed her into his raging erection.

He couldn't stop himself from grinding all over her, shoving as much as he could through their clothes, into her female fissure. His dick throbbed in tandem with the blood rushing in his head.

Kesi's brain effervescing heat and passion, her private parts felt like they were scalding in a bubbling skillet they were so hot. She was wholly immersed in kissing Martier. She had never really kissed a man before.

They had kissed her, forced themselves on her, including Martier. But now he was letting her explore all she wanted, and judging by the enormous hard-on burrowing into her womanhood, he was liking it.

She marveled at the taste of him, so enticingly masculine. Heavens, he tasted so...*male* it made her head swim. Under her palms, his slight scruff scraped her skin, her thumbs brushed along his strong jaw. His virile scent pulled at her with invisible sensuous strings.

Breaking from her with a racing breath, he gasped, "I cannot take anymore, tis time, baby. Okay?" He couldn't stop now, and he wasn't going to, but he wanted her to feel it was her decision.

So hushed he could hardly hear her, her lashes lowered, she purred a shy, "*Yes*."

"Ah, beautiful *nĕkolika*," he praised, and lowered to his knees in front of her.

Lightheaded, fuzzy with a riot of carnal feelings, Kesi swayed. Martier spread his hand on her butt to hold her steady.

Her throat constricted with searing passion like molten lava oozing up from her core. She whispered, "What does that…what you call me, neco…something, mean?"

Martier undid the rest of her belt, unbuttoned her jeans and lowered the zipper. Spreading the zipper apart he put his mouth against her belly and thrilled at her shiver. "*Několika,* it means, 'precious one'."

"Oh." Swirling stupors of sensations mushrooming all through her body, Kesi didn't move when he leaned his shoulder into her and lifted her, draping her over his shoulder as he stood up.

Suddenly hanging upside down, she gasped, "Wha-what are you doing?" When he started walking she asked in a slight panic, "Cap- uh, Martier, where are we going?"

Chuckling, he pulled her jeans and panties down just enough to bare her bottom, his arm tight over her thighs to hold her against him.

"Uh, Martier…"

"I need for you to know I am a man of my word, of my threats, of my warnings. How many times did you call me captain after I told you not to?"

"What? I don't-"

Whack- He smacked her butt.

"Hey!" Kesi squealed, tried to squirm off his shoulder.

He kept walking and said, "That was one. How many times did I warn you not to call me that?" And he smacked her again.

At her shriek, he said, "I told you what the consequences would be. How many times did I say no more investigating? Huh? Did I say it was too dangerous and to stop? And did you?" *Wham-* another stinging slap with his big palm on her bare ass.

"Martier!"

"You flaunted my orders for everyone to have dinner in the rec building every night. Instead, you went out with another man for fucks sake and let him paw you. That deserves more punishment," he spanked her several times.

Kesi pounded at his back, struggling to break his grip on her shouting, "Stop it! Let me down!"

He splayed his hand on one bare cheek and squeezed gently. "I am not smacking you hard enough for it to really hurt, and I will kiss it and make it better, in a minute." He caressed her bottom, squeezing and rubbing.

"Damn, you feel round and soft, so hot, baby. You will see, along with punishment spanking can also be pleasurable." Heading down the hall he said, "Now, what else have you disobeyed me about?"

"No! Martier! Stop, please don't," the words choked, catching in her throat. He was right, it hurt just a bit and her bottom was…stinging in a way that made her lady parts burn even hotter.

Hanging over a man's shoulder with her pants half down and bare butt in the air while he smacked it, was…interesting.

He carried her into his room, trod over to the window and pulled the drapes just enough to let in soft illumination, then dropped her on the bottom of the bed on her back with her legs hanging off the edge.

He removed his boots and moved to stand between her knees. Her hands had fallen beside her head in an image of surrender, blouse spread open, yellow hair cascading in fat curls all around her on the blanket.

Bending over her, he grasped the front of her open jeans.

"Martier," balking, her face in a frown, Kesi went to sit up. Her palms braced behind her on the bed, shirt off one shoulder. "You can't just give me orders and spank me when I don't follow them. It's not right-"

He put a hand to her chest and pushed her to lie back down. "Where I come from, *několika,* tis a dangerous deadly land. The male warrior protects the female while she has the bairns. Tis the way it is. To do so properly, the female must obey him. You are not used to that way of life, so I have to teach you."

He leaned over to set his hands on either side of her and held his face inches from hers. Her big blues were layered with nervousness, anger, and heat.

Saffron brows slashed down hard, she claimed, "You will not teach me. I will not be ordered about and- and spanked when I don't do as you say. You can't make me. I'll leave!"

He dropped down to his elbows, she flinched. "Tis too late, *několika,* I gave you more than enough chances to say no, to leave. You did not. I told you there was no going back. In a few minutes I am making you mine, and then you will not leave my side." He licked her mouth

"And you will," he sucked her lips, "obey my every word. Tis for your safety, not for my arrogance."

His tongue and lips so fervid, her lids pulled down suddenly heavy with desire. Her distracted voice dreamy, she murmured, "What do you mean I won't leave your side?"

"That is enough talk for now, *několika,* I have already waited too long for you. I have to have you now or I swear to Zeus I will fucking explode." He tapped the tip of her nose with a finger then stood back, grabbed her jeans and jerked them down and off her legs, tossing them out of the way.

251

Alarmed at his sudden roughness, awkwardly yanking her panties up, Kesi stammered, "Mar- tier, I'm not sure-"

"Time for uncertainty is over, my sweet. Damn those are fucking sexy panties." His dark green eyes glowed at the black piece of lacey swath that barely covered her privates. His gaze rose to her blouse that was half off her shoulders.

He shoved a hand under her back, lifted her, and ripped the blouse off then stared at her plump breasts in the lace bra like a gator spotting ducklings floating in a pond.

"Fuck yeah," he muttered licking his chops and reached around her, unclasped the bra. When he went to remove it, Kesi brought her hands up to hold the lace against her breasts.

"You- you're moving so fast, Martier, and rough," she whined through chattering teeth.

"I will not hurt you, I promise, Kesindra, but I have been on fire for you for so long I am afraid I have to see you naked or I will fucking die."

He grasped her wrists, pulled them apart and tore the bra off and threw it to the side. Bending over her, he staked her hands to the bed beside her head, his gaze blazing at her jiggling breasts. If his eyes, dark emerald torches, were paintbrushes of fire, her skin would be burning.

"Ah, Zeus, I knew you would be beyond words, breathtaking. So round and perfect." He released a wrist to palm a breast. "*Fuck*," came out as a growl dug deep in his chest.

His eyes flit back and forth from a naked breast to the one he clenched with his big hand, watching his hard fingers knead and shape her lush pillow.

Kesi lay still on her back watching him.

He looked entirely enthralled with her bounty. She couldn't understand it, he has to have seen thousands of- she pushed the thought away and looked at him. His eyes just glowed staring at her bosom, his tongue circling his lips.

Still holding her one hand to the bed, bending over her, Martier squeezed the breast he held, plumping it up to his mouth and licked the nipple. A wave of tickling silk bristles fluttered inside Kesi, shimmying from the inside out. She sucked in a sharp inhale.

"Oh, hell yeah," he crowed, loving her reaction. He couldn't explain why her body turned him on so much more than any other woman's had, it just did. It was like he was seeing a nude woman for the very first time, a perfect goddess figurine. And she tasted succulent.

He gripped her nipple with his teeth and teased it with his tongue, moaning, "*Oh aye.*" At Kesindra's squirming, the loose breast jiggled enticingly. His jeans were becoming painfully tight.

Martier shifted to his knees and grabbed both breasts, thumbed her nipples then pinched them. At her soft moan he bit one then the other and Kesi was squirming like crazy.

"Your nipples are like miniature pink candy, baby, cute and sweet and hard." He bent and licked a nipple then sucked the entire areole into his mouth, swatting the nipple with his tongue while sucking hard on the breast, then did it to the other one. Kesi writhed all over the bed under him with mewing gasps.

Leaning forward, he grasped a breast hard and kissed her mouth, sucking her lips in before finding her tongue and biting it. Then he sucked it, sticking his tongue nearly down her throat until her tiny, breathless exclamations perforated the rushing buzzing in his ears.

He leaned back and looked at her. "Aye, tis true, you are a goddess, Kesindra. My goddess."

Her half closed eyes gleamed the intoxicated passion he was building in her. The little pink tongue whirled around her lips, moistening them and searching for his tongue he had taken away. Her bosom rose and fell with delicate rapid breaths. A fine sheen covered her body like a pearl veil.

Moving from her, Martier sat back on his heels and gripped the tiny panties, drew them down, slowly this time, removed them and dropped them.

"Zeus," he swore absently, his brain was turning to butter, he put his hands on her thighs and spread them apart. One finger slid light as a whisper down her slit.

Her body jolted, with a gasp, she shot up. Half sitting with glazed eyes wide, lips startled apart, Kesi tried to close her legs but his body was between them and he had his hands on her thighs again.

Even as she struggled for words to tell him…tell him what? She was sure she should make him stop…for some reason…she couldn't remember.

He pushed her legs wider. Fog permeated her searing brain. "Martier," she rasped, trying to talk but her tongue was heavy, too thick to speak.

"Aye, finally, you call me by my name. Now, lay back and relax, do not fight me. You have felt my hands here before, my sweet. But I did not have the luxury to see your beautiful womanhood laid out for me to enjoy looking at, and devour."

He put his hand on her chest and gently pushed her to lie back down.

When she was prone, he turned his attention to between her legs. "Glistening and tender pink, baby, so damned wet for me." He touched her core and smiled when she jumped again, but she stayed on her back.

When he had touched her there before, he had bent her over the infirmary bed and fingered her from behind. But now, Kesi blushed to her roots, no man had ever seen her nude before, not her breasts, especially not her private lady parts.

Now a man she barely knew, a demon, an alien, an outlaw, was kneeling between her spread legs and intimately studying her while touching her.

He drawled softly, "I cannot believe how perfect you are, Kesindra, like a tantalizing blossoming pink rose."

Stroking his fingers up then down her slit, he dipped a fingertip inside her to get her silk and slathered it on her clit, then circled it, tugged at it, and slid his finger inside her. He was rewarded with a gruff moan and spastic wriggle of her hips.

"Baby," he whispered while carefully moving his finger in then out, probing her on the way inside, learning her body, searching for her most sensitive erogenous areas. A smile spanned his harsh face at her every twitch and gasp knowing he had found them.

His voice growly with passion, he said huskily, "I am going to prepare you to take me."

No words left her mouth. Her hips lifting to his hand, grinding against it was her acquiescence.

His hands moved to hold her thighs as he bent and put his mouth over her entire core, and grinned at her startled gasp.

"Martier, I'm not sure that's, *uhh*," her protest sizzled to a sensuous whimper when he thrust his tongue inside her.

Licking her cleft, he carefully brushed her tender skin with his descending fangs and hissed between them, "Trust me, Kesindra, just trust me," and dove back in, tasting her, moaning at her fresh fragrant taste.

His tongue furled around her bud, then darted back inside her. He nibbled at her clit until Kesi's cries became incoherent, her body writhing so much against his mouth he had to hold her thighs to still her.

Her cream poured out. Martier moved his finger back inside her, thrusting with her moans, then he inserted a second finger and sucked on her bud. She was so small; he gently twisted his fingers to stretch her before inserting a third finger.

"Uh, Martier," her voice compressed, legs stiffened, "it-it's too- too-"

"Shh, I know, sweetheart, tis uncomfortable but I have to make you able to take me without causing you pain." He removed the third finger and quickened his thrusts with the other two while alternating thumbing and sucking her clit.

He murmured against her sex, "You taste as sweet and as fresh as a damned spring day, *několika*, tis like lapping sugar milk.*"* One of his claws unsheathed to stroke her sex, and that started her undoing.

Her breaths harsh and fast, Kesi grabbed Martier's hair. Tangling her fingers in the locks, she pulled them as her body rode up the rollercoaster almost to the top.

The edges of her hands butted his horns. In wonder she said, "I can feel them throbbing!"

His mouth on her, he rasped, "Aye baby, me too."

Then the breathlessness became rigid hitches. She cried, "Martier, it's, ahh, so much pressure, like lightning strikes! Uh," gasping, her body bucking. Martier firmed his grip on her thighs to hold her down.

Keening her wild sensations, Kesi was teetering at the top of the rollercoaster. Her fingers grasping his hair, she tugged so hard he laughed.

"Okay, Kesindra sweetheart, let yourself go, give me everything." His fingers rutted, sweeping inside her. Biting her nub, he then pressed his thumb and circled until a dark red flushed up her chest. Guttural squeaks raked from her as her spine and neck arched, curving her slender body up and off the mattress.

"*Martier*!" Jolting forward, Kesi wailed his name as her sex vibrated, convulsing around his fingers. She flew off the rollercoaster hurtling into the heavens. He shoved the third finger in during her wild climaxing throes, her entire body spazing.

Kesi's eyes widened at him but they were glassy, unseeing, fevered. Her spine still arched as she fell back on bed with a full body seizure.

He worked her until he'd milked every tremor, contraction. When she curled up forward with a wracking quake then fell back again, depleted, he removed his fingers.

Martier couldn't help kneeling there, drinking her in. So amazing, so beautiful. She was finally going to be under him and he was owning her.

Kesi sat up disordered. Her legs outstretched, palms behind her holding up her quivering body, hair wild, eyes crazed still hazy with her orgasm.

Through jagged breaths, she sputtered, "Martier," realizing he was staring at her naked sex wide open to him, she started to close her legs.

"Ah, nay, *několika,* never again will you close your legs to me, or hide your beauty from my eyes. You have become mine. Now, you will look me in the eye and scream my name while I fuck you into oblivion."

"Oh yeah?" Her energy surged back bolstering a mischievous glint in her shining blues. She maneuvered onto her knees and squirmed to the edge of the bed.

Fully nude and becoming less shy about it from his blatant admiring ogling, Kesi tossed her mussed hair behind her back, put her hands on her hips and thrust her breasts out.

His eyes zinged right on them. She laughed. "Come here," she wriggled a finger motioning him, "stand up."

Puzzled, Martier got to his feet.

"Thank you." Kneeling on the mattress she reached for a button near the top of his shirt. "It has come to my self-conscious attention that I am buck naked and you are fully dressed."

His mouth curled up in a wry grin. "Aye. If I'd had my pants off a few minutes ago we would be done now, and you would not be liking me too much."

"I see." Kesi unbuttoned one button after the other until his shirt was undone. Tugging the hem out of his jeans, she pushed the shirt lapels aside and blinked at his bare chest. "Mercy, Martier, you are a-maz-ing."

His chuckle rippled in his chest. "Feel free to touch anything you want, honey." Other women had gushed about his powerful chest but slyly, some were just performing.

Kesi was so guileless and spontaneous in her admiration, it made his heart tickle. He reached to unbutton his cuffs while Kesi put first one palm, then the other on his massive chest covered with dark hair.

"You are…furry, Martier," she commented. Sifting her fingers up through the thick hair and up to his shoulders then did it again.

"Aye. I know." He undid the other cuff.

Martier, you're so…manly, it's hot." Giggling at words she never thought would come out of her mouth, Kesi ran her palms over his chest, rolling over thickly hewn slabs of iron muscles, over his defined pecs, down to his abs of steel, so ridged they were like rock terraces.

Bringing her hands back up, she grazed his nipples and giggled again when he quivered.

"You think that tis funny, *tím rostia*?"

"You haven't called me a little girl for a while now. You think having sex with children is cool?" she teased him.

"Nay, sweet, you are not a child. But compared to me you are an infant in living years and experience. That is why I guide you. I have seen so many dangers and horrors that you could never fathom, and I hope you never will. Tis my duty to protect you from them."

"Okay Gloomy Gus, enough of that sexy talk," she chided. Her hands roamed up to his shoulders where she tried to push his shirt off. His shoulders were too broad, his chest too wide. "Martier, take your shirt off."

Grinning, he replied, "Anytime you want an article of my clothing off, you say and tis gone, baby." He quickly shrugged out of the shirt and tossed it. Crouching, he undid his boots and removed them and his socks. Then he stood straight and waited, letting her take the lead again.

Still on her knees, a look of concentration firming her softly sculpted face, Kesi tugged at his belt. It wasn't that easy but she got it undone.

She worked at the button on his jeans then unzipped the zipper and started to push them down but they barely moved. "You undressed me so easily, I need your big muscles to get your clothes off."

A chuckle at her consternation, he reached out and grasped her breasts. "You are small and slight, *několika*, let me help you."

"Uh huh, groping me is not helping me, is it?"

Kneading her chubby globes, he laughed. "Oh, sorry, I was helping myself to your body. Since it belongs to me now, or will in a minute, I can play with it whenever like."

To prove his point he pinched her nipples before pulling her close to rub her breasts on his bare chest.

"You make a lot of presumptions, Mr. Demon." Kesi tried to sound stern but couldn't help the moan of delight that escaped. Brushing her chest over his, she cooed, "Ah, that feels so good, like a bear on my bare skin."

He moved his hands behind her and grabbed her bottom with both hands, squeezed, digging his fingers into the crack between her cheeks.

"Oh!" she squawked jumping. "Enough of that!" Pushing back from him, Kesi gripped his jeans and struggled to push them down.

He stepped back from her, impatient now, shoved his jeans and boxers down in one movement and kicked them aside, his swollen manhood sprung up. Seeing her eyes pop at the size of him, he gripped his penis with his fist. "It will be okay, *několika,* trust me to take care of you."

Her eyes flicked up to his midnight greens with their odd shimmers of black light then back down to his fierce manhood. A nervous red flooded her cheeks; she pulled her lips in, biting them to still the sudden uneasiness.

Kesi looked at this huge hard demon, horns sprouting larger and a phallus that just, well she had mostly seen penises in pictures, this one seemed, very large.

Faltering, she whispered, "Uh, Martier," her hands dropped instinctively covering her sex.

Chapter Twenty-Two

Seeing her nerves overcoming her desire, Martier slid a hand behind her back and another under her thighs and lifted her.

Holding her briefly like a doll, his gaze rolled down her pearly body then up to her glossy lips and dewy eyes, he whispered, "Trust me, Kesindra," and bent his head and kissed her before holding her softness against his tough body. Then he laid her on her back on the bed.

He climbed on the mattress, knelt and moved between her legs. Nudging her knees apart, he gently smoothed her tussled curls off her anxious face. "I have you, baby, relax, enjoy our ride."

Kesi reached up and laid her palm on his face, he turned into it, kissed it. She moved her hand to touch his ear. "They are so different, Martier, your pointy ears. Kind of Spock-like only less pointy."

"Huh?"

"Never mind. They are really so cute."

"Humph," he grunted. "There is nothing cute about a warrior demon. Don't ever say that out loud in front of my men." He'd never live it down.

Lowering onto an elbow, he fisted his painfully hard erection and put it to her opening. Rubbing his phallus softly against her, getting her cream over it, he stroked her sex until moans like satin ribbons furled up from her core constricting her nipples into little points.

"Kesindra," his dark baritone spooled huskily, "I have to warn you, this will probably hurt a little. There is no way to avoid it, just stay with me, our joining will get better."

Martier cupped her face, kissed her with delicate finesse, gliding his tongue around her lips then fed deeper, capturing her tongue.

Like a flame licking pooled kerosene, his movements fueled, fired, inducing her response to equal his fevered pitch.

When he felt her go from anxious to writhing, Martier pushed against her feminine opening. It was as difficult as he thought it would be. Damn, he had to go and choose the most delicate petite woman he could find, throw in virgin, young and slight, his mouth lifted at the corner, but with lush killer curves.

He was a big male, all over, last thing he wanted was to hurt this beautiful dainty female. But, she'd gotten under his skin, he craved her too badly, no other woman would ever do again, he had to have her.

As he nudged in her, Martier kissed Kesindra, plundering her richness, driving them both blind and wild with crazed passion. She splayed her palms on his chest, stroked them up to his soldier's shoulders then dragged her fingers up his neck.

Slowly becoming impaled by him, she uttered a slightly pained, "*Martier*." A few fingers drifted over the curve of one of his horns.

"Shit Kesindra-" he barked, a jolting paroxysm bolted over his body causing him to thrust harder into her, forcing a pained grunt from her.

He lifted from her with a short smile and explanation, "My horns are as sensitive as my manhood, sweetheart when I am in...lust." He stopped moving so he could hold himself back; he was right on the edge.

Brow furrowing, she asked, "I shouldn't touch them?" Kesi awkwardly shifted her hips against his. He was big, filling her uncomfortably. It hurt, he hurt her inside, but there were tingles and delicious tremors everywhere he passed up her sheath.

"Ah, Zeus, *několika,* I love your touch on me, on my horns too. I have never allowed it with another, but I crave for your hands on all of me. Just be aware, caressing them is like stroking my shaft, both get bigger, harder, urging me to move...more aggressively."

"That's wonderful, Martier, I'm the first to touch them, *uhh*," he thrust another grunt out of her as he deepened his voyage inside her beautiful body. "Then you are sort of a virgin to me as well," she giggled, "in a way."

Her giggle contracted her sheath on his phallus causing him to gasp. "Damn, girl, don't do that or I will not make it to the end of you." He shoved harder to reach deep inside her as far as he could go, and stopped with a heavy sigh. He could feel her thrumming all around his cock.

"You okay, baby?" Martier leaned on an elbow to stroke her face, seeing the strain in it, he stopped moving to let her body adjust to his bulk. "I like that there is a part of me that is a virgin with you, a first with you."

He asked her again with a husky rasp, "You all right, Kesindra?"

Their warmth and scent radiated around and into each other, skin-to-skin, the world could blow up and they would be oblivious to nothing but themselves. So close their breaths met, so intimate they could feel nothing but the vibe of each other's body.

Her eyes closed, lips thinned, she nodded, "It's...I'm..." she took a deep breath and winced, "all right."

Petting her hair, his voice velvet textured, a low rough timbre he growled softly, "Give it a minute, baby." He reached down between them and gently then more vigorously abraded her clitoris. Releasing her woman's cream to lubricate her sheath, enticing her body to expand to accept his girth. Her hips moved now, begging him to continue.

"Kesindra," he groaned gruffly. "I will never forget this moment, this incredible feeling. We are one, this is for us and no one else to share, ever." His lips found hers again as he slowly drew out then thrust back in, relishing the feel of her silken sheath taking in his length.

As she adapted to his invasion into her tender body, the pain lessened, her hips met his more strongly. Sifting breaths hitched in her chest, her hands searched him out again, up into his hair. She raked her nails on the underside of the curve of his horns until Martier about howled from the blistering tormenting feel of it.

Blood pounded through his cock, he began plunging harder into Kesi. She gasped, "Martier, there's, *uh*," she grunted as he thrust deep. "I can feel bumps rising on your..." With each thrust, bumps on his penis pressed against every inch of her sheath, stroking her to unbearable pleasure.

"Aye," he said with a smile, sweat beaded at his temples. He looked down at her.

Her eyes were closed, tongue lathing her lips parted in little breathy grunts and gasps. He told her, "They are called pebble bins, only my kind have them."

Martier pushed her tongue aside with his mouth so he could lick her lips chastising, "That is my job, *několika.*" His hand reached for her breast, cradled it in his hard grip, molding it, squeezing, reveling in the luxurious feel of her.

Thrusting his manhood in her, turning as he went deep, he twisted so every bump rolled over every sensitive tissue inside her woman's channel.

His every plunge now shoved away every coherent thought, short-circuiting Kesi's clouding mind. Her breathing raced, chest pitching, hips bucked to meet his, tiny whimpers eked from her slack lips.

Martier thrust harder, so hard he had to put an arm around her shoulders to keep her from getting shoved from him. He grasped her legs, lifting them to wrap around his hips so he could penetrate deeper.

His fangs descended in tune with her cries. She was unaware his horns grew even bigger but were moving, turning to face Kesi and started curling over her to her back.

He looked between them watching her breasts bouncing with his thrusts to his heady delight; they were as perfect as the rest of her. He clenched her breast hard, pinched her nipple, a cry ripped from her throat inflaming him to thrust faster.

His gaze drew to her face. Perspiration gathered making her skin shine, yellow lashes fluttered on round cheeks giving flashes of delirious blue, her chest panted as the flush started to cover her.

Gruffly, he whispered, "Baby, I need you to look at me. I want to see your eyes, see you looking at me and shouting my name as you release."

As she struggled to force her lids up, Martier's claws descended and wrapped around her breast. Next time he'd put her on top so he could clinch both of her plush tits at the same time. The claws dug in, circling her plump flesh as his fangs descended and the horns still grew.

He drove into her lissome body. Both her legs wrapped around his lean pounding hips, she bucked to meet his thrusts. Moving his arm from around her shoulders, Martier shoved his hand under her butt to lift her up so he could pummel deeper.

Huffing squeals started deep in her lungs, her eyes were rolling back, her neck arching.

"Kesindra, look at me," he commanded. This was her first time, he wanted her to know who was making her a woman. See who owned her, who was bringing her this insane pleasure.

"Look at me," he urged louder, driving into her so hard her body shook from the impact.

Kesi raised her heavy lids; unfocused blue gleamed from under them at Martier. His face was strained from holding back. Brows low, forehead creased, lines cut around his eyes.

"Baby," he gasped, a vein beat at his temple, his head dropped. Dark blond hair swished over her face before he raised it again to see her lashes flickering. Her face in a pleasure-filled pained wince as he started pushing her over the edge.

She bucked so hard against him, Martier feared she'd be bruised. But she was wild, her eyes piercing at him, her fingers scraping lines in his shoulder.

His claws dug deeper, he moved his hand from her butt to her back and lifted her as his horns reached around aiming at just below her shoulder blades.

"*Ahh, Martier-*" A tight scream started deep inside Kesi as her body started convulsing, the faster he thrust the louder the scream grew.

Kesi wrapped her arms around his neck; her head fell back with the beginning shockwaves of her massive orgasm.

Martier stabbed his fangs into where her neck met her shoulder. Claws gripped her tender breast piercing deeper, his horns lanced into her back as he slammed into her going as deep and fast as he could.

Harvesting every ounce of Martier's voracious masculinity, Kesi levitated off the bed convulsing with a piercing cry.

Martier drew out his fangs to shove his tongue down her throat, devouring her climax while his hips drove into her faster and faster like a runaway train hurtling down a mountain.

Two galaxies colliding, sparking stars off in all directions, they bucked at each other.

Kesi's hands moved to fist into his thick chest hair, the pain of it set him off.

He flew as if with wings, soared, paused in midair, held aloft for a heartbeat, then bored into her again and again until he burst in a shock of blinding light and kinetic pleasure, so agonizing his mind and body blasted apart. His seeds surging into her with every grinding thrust of his hips.

Under him, Kesi's body undulated uncontrollably, hitting at him. Her hips, her breasts, her cries of his name ground down, unraveling until there was nothing left in her but hoarse gasps and bleating pants.

Martier collapsed on her with a saturated grunt, his body shuddering, twitching like a fish out of water.

His horns withdrew, claws and fangs sheathed, his sated animal growls rumbled in her ear as he shoved his face into her hair. His breathing so harsh and deep his chest slammed into hers with his heavy breaths.

Struggling to catch her breath and slow her racing heart, Kesi combed her hands into his thick hair, knotting his locks in her fingers, she held on.

With effort, Martier shifted his weight so he wasn't crushing her.

For a few minutes they lay still, silent, except for huffing breaths. Then Martier rolled on his side pulling her to turn with him, still imbedded inside her. His shaking hand skimmed over her face, smoothed her sweaty tendrils back.

"I cannot believe I survived that," he said gasping with a lopsided grin, shattered eyes twinkling under thick hooded lids. His hand stroked to her upper back. "Kesindra, I have never experienced anything as earthshaking as that before in my life."

Her faint laugh droll, she said, "Come on, Martier, not that I want to think about it, but you've had many...uh, trysts. You can't say-"

He put two fingers over her mouth. "Hush." With a slight frown, he said, "First of all, I never lie. I don't ever see the reason for it. I speak the truth, Kesindra."

He cupped the side of her face, kissed her. "That was mind-blowing, I cannot explain." He shivered, his cock twitched inside her still semi-hard.

"Trust me, I have never felt what I just did ever, *ever* before, sweetheart." He grinned. "Tis going to be a bitch to not throw you down and fuck you every second of every day."

"Martier, please," she murmured blushing, peering up at him shyly through lowered lashes

His face firmed. "And, second, can we not ever talk about me and other women again, it really takes the shine off us. I will add that to things you will be punished for."

"Hey," she playfully swatted him, "how about I punish you for your misdeeds, for your cursing, perhaps? How about I spank you?"

A laugh burst out. "Sure, sweet, you try, go ahead. Before you could get a tiny dainty palm near my ass you will already be lying across my lap and I would have your pants off before you could scream. Of course, afterwards, you will be screaming, but for me to go harder, faster."

"Martier! Stop that!"

"We will see, *tím rostia*, it will be a while before I can unleash my true sexual prowess on you."

Her dark yellow brows flew up. "What? You call what you just did holding back?"

Chuckling, he clutched a breast, fondled it, tweaked her nipple. "Baby, it was your first time, I had to be gentle. You ain't seen nothin' yet," he wriggled his brows at her.

She paled.

He rolled off the bed to his feet. "I am going to run a bath with Epsom salts in it for you. You will be sore, tender, I want you feeling perfect before we…" He leaned over the bed and kissed her, stood back up, "do it again."

Suddenly the color fell out of her face. "Martier, we didn't…I didn't even think of it, we didn't use protection," her hands went to cover her mouth. "What are we going to do?"

His smile softening his hard face, he combed his fingers through his thick blond hair. "No worries. My…species…does not carry disease, and I cannot get you pregnant until you," he broke off, there was a lot he hadn't told her.

Like who he really was and what he had just done to her without having her consent, without discussing prior to having intercourse with her, that what would happen would change her life forever.

He had known when he felt his horns turning what was happening, and he could have stopped it, but he didn't. His horns have never pierced another female; the fluid in them was for his life-mate only. His lids lowered over the dark green eyes to hide his guilt.

What he had done was wrong. But, his brother Devilos had done the same thing with his woman. He'd told Martier it was better to do it and then ask forgiveness later, rather than ask and she refuses.

Because at that point, both brothers knew they would take their women whether they acquiesced or not, and that would sure be an unpleasant way to forge a permanent relationship if the women said no, and the men fucked them and did it anyway. Because neither brother was willing to give up his female.

"Until I what?" she asked, puzzled.

"Ah, we will talk later, right now I want you to feel good."

He ran the bath. When he returned, she was standing by the window staring out, the sheet wrapped around her. Her head was lowered, from the door he could see a tear on her cheek glimmering in the moonlight. Martier strode to her.

"Hey, sweetheart, what is it?" He put his arm around her, turned her to face him, tucked his fingers under her chin and raised it. "Why are you crying? Did I hurt you? You should have said, I would have stopped. I did not mean to be such a brute."

Shaking her head, she lowered it to wipe at her eyes. "No, it was...unbelievable, more than I could have imagined, indescribable. I wish we could do it again."

Both his hands settled on her shoulders. Feeling his stomach dropping, Martier asked, "Why can we not? Why would we not?" His fingers crunched over her small shoulders.

She tried to step from him but he held her. "Nay, Kesindra, talk to me. What is wrong?"

Her gaze wavered from him, drifted to the floor. "Martier, you are an outlaw, I am an FBI agent. I could have stomached that, I had to, I couldn't resist you. But..."

"But what? What the hell?" Her words agitated him. His stomach churning, his fingers dug into her flesh, he sure as hell wasn't taking her only once then never again. That was not going to happen. "Why would you think to deny us?"

She hesitated, then looked up at him. "You are going to leave at some point. I can tell you and your men have come here for some kind of...mission, I can only pray it isn't unlawful or that anyone will be harmed."

"Kesindra, I am not-"

"As you've mentioned, you haven't hurt anyone yet, except Chris and that was...understandable, um, so I don't think you plan on hurting anyone." Her blue eyes filled with pain.

"But, you are going to leave, to I guess return to your own planet, and I will eventually be brought back to the states, and well," she shrugged. A tear strolled out and slipped down her cheek.

"We will never see each other again. There is no point in pursuing this when it will only make it harder in the end when we separate."

Chapter Twenty-Three

"Dammit, Kesindra, do you not ever listen to a goddamned thing I say?"

His bark startled her, her lips parted, eyes gaped. "I don't-"

Martier's fingers tightened so hard she winced. He loosened his grip but shook her. "I have told you, clearly told you, that you are mine. I own you. I said once we make love there would be no going back.

"By that I meant, you are with me, forever. I told you that you would not leave my side. I gave you the chance to leave, you did not. Now you are mine. Forever." She would have been anyway, but he knew he had to make her think it was her decision.

Her mouth dropped. "But, I live here, on...Earth, you live...not here." Plush lips curled ruefully. "Probably not even in this solar system." Her sigh heavy with anguish she said, "I got so carried away, Martier, I wanted you, I just couldn't resist you."

Dashing at a rolling tear, regret clouded her voice, "If I had known how…magical it would be, I never would have done it. It would have been better to have always wondered how it would be than have this time with you and then…it's gone. You're gone."

He just stood there staring aghast at her. Raising his eyes heavenward, he lamented, "Zeus, give me the strength to deal with this obtuse woman." Scooping her up in his arms, he stalked down the hall with her squawking to put her down.

Reaching the bathroom, the sheet got lost as Martier trod down the steps into the huge round tub with rushing spickets of whirling bubbling water. He sat on one of the steps and set her to stand a couple steps below in front of him.

So off balance with his sudden action, Kesi almost toppled over. "Martier, what are you-"

"Right now," he said, brow ridged low and hard, his order forbidding, "just be quiet before you say something else to piss me off more. I will tell you when you can talk again."

"What? What are you-"

He put a hand on her butt and the other over her mouth. "I said hush."

When he moved his hand, angry, Kesi snapped, "Stop telling me what to do. I need to call Agent Dukes, I said an hour, you promised we-"

"That is it." Martier lifted Kesi and dropped her into the deepest part of warm roiling water.

She came up sputtering, "How dare you!"

"More? Tell me when you have had enough, one more word and there will be punishment. I am warning you."

"You can't do this, you can't tell me to not talk, I won't-
"

He grabbed her, lifted her and dropped her again. Her head went underwater.

She sprang back up furious, opening her mouth, then saw the indomitable jaw clenched with determined ire, his huge biceps flexing as he reached for her, she shut her mouth.

He moved in the water back to the steps. "Come here, stand in front of me."

"You-"

A golden brown brow rose.

Her mouth snapped shut, brows slashed down over livid blue eyes. Shoving swags of wet hair out of her face, she slowly waded to him stopping a few feet away.

He sat on the step, elbows on his knees and wiggled a finger for her to come closer.

She hesitated, a leery eye on him, ready to run.

"Right here in front of me, Kesindra," he ordered.

Fearful he was going to hit her, she turned her head as she moved closer.

"Goddammit, Kesindra, you exasperate the fuck out of me. You know I am not going to beat you, now cut it out." He grabbed a bar of soap off a dish on the rim of the tub and rubbed it in his hands.

"How can you make such passionate love with a man that you think is going to beat you?" He put his soapy hands on her breasts.

She quivered then held still at the formidable glint in his eyes. "I," she paused; he was caressing her breasts with his soapy hands. It felt…amazingly sensual. "Um, Martier, I have no experience with males, and you are…unique. A- a demon from another world for heaven's sake, how am I supposed to take you? *Uhh*," she groaned, her body wriggled as he stroked and kneaded her breasts.

"Hmmm," he made a low rumbling sound in his throat. His face set hard, he kept washing her breasts periodically pulling on the budding nipples.

Seeing her body ease and her eyes droop rhapsodic, he lowered his hand to slide it between her legs and squeezed making her squirm. He drew his soapy fingers over the folds of her tender nether lips, smiling slightly at the little moans she huffed. He took her hands and set them on his shoulders for her to balance.

"Martier," Kesi whispered.

"Shh, no talking." He ran his hands down her back, up her thighs, around to wash the cleft between her butt cheeks. Discomfited, she tried to move from his hands but he held her firmly.

"Do not fight me, Kesindra," he warned, "you already have punishment coming. You need to learn to trust me, and to listen to what I say to you. We are together now, where I go, you go. Get that through your head."

Her face warmed. His threat of punishment, frightened, and titillated her. At least she thought it was titillating, of course he could have something else in mind. "Martier," she started.

"You are talking, does that mean you want your punishment now?"

Quickly shaking her head, her wet hair slapped back and forth. "I didn't mean to-"

He smacked her wet ass. "I said hush." His fingers roamed back between her legs to caress her slit. Prodding her swelling bud he slid a thick finger slide inside her. He nudged her feet to widen. She resisted.

"More punishment, Kesindra," he warned, pinching her bud hard enough to just spark a bit of pain, she squeaked.

He stood up, water and bubbles whooshed off splattering back into the tub. His manhood was hard as steel up against his taut belly. "Take it in your hands, Kesindra," he ordered.

Her eyes wide, she tentatively touched it, it jumped, she giggled.

"Hold it, *několika,* tight, with both hands." Martier looked down at the top of her head as she stared at his erection.

After a short pause, Kesi wound both small hands around his substantial girth. He wrapped a hand over her hands and showed her how to stroke him, down the hard steel and then up to the softer top. A drip of cream slipped out of the tip.

Remembering his mouth on her, Kesi bent and licked the cream, his cock flinched and he barked.

"Kesindra, shit-" He dragged in a deep calming breath. "You learn fast my sweet. You need to wait until later for that, I cannot take it right now."

Her wet hair draped yellow dripping ringlets hiding her nudity from his eyes. He reached to push the heavy locks behind her back and grasped her breasts, playing with them while she made herself familiar with his manhood.

Kesi stroked both hands down his length, squeezed, slid them back up and squeezed the head, smiling at his groan. She gingerly held his balls, they twitched in her palm, and he moaned again.

She toyed with him for a moment, then with a naughty gleam in her eye, she bent and took him in her mouth while skimming her hands hard down then scraping her nails lightly up his phallus.

His hips jerked back with a curse, "*Shit,*" He lifted her hands off him. "I said not now, damn it, I want more with you. I love it, but I will not last if you do that."

A rare flirty smile showed Kesi's pretty pearlies. She bent over to put her mouth on him again, but he stopped her. "That is it, you minx." He bent slightly and shoved her up and over his shoulder. "You have got to learn to obey me."

With a squeal, Kesi tried to cover her bare butt with her hands thinking he would spank her like before. But he marched back to the bed then set her on her feet.

"Do not move," he ordered and went back to the bathroom. He returned with soft towels, and a terry bathrobe, which he dropped near the bed. He rubbed her down with a towel then lifted her tossing her on the bed.

Bouncing on the mattress, she said with a sultry tilt of her head, "I can dry you too, Martier."

"Nay." He quickly dragged the other towel around his body. "You have already done enough, my sweet." He tossed the towel aside, set a knee on the bed and said, "Come here."

"Aye aye, Captain," she responded with a giggle but didn't move to him.

"Ah," he said, "you seek to mock me?" He put another knee on the bed, the side of his mouth curved up in a teasing menace. "You have a lot of punishment coming, sweetheart."

The gravel in his voice gave Kesi pause. She peered at him, he looked so…she couldn't tell what he looked like.

His skin was darkening, horns swelling; her gaze fell to that strapping chest covered with dark hair, pumping with deep breaths as he moved to her. The bed dipped and jostled under his weight as he reached for her, but she squealed and avoided his hand.

"Seriously?" His mouth turned up in a prowling grin. "A mistake for prey to run, the predator will only give eager chase, and relish the take down."

He threw out another hand, this time she screamed and tried to scramble off the bed. Martier snagged an ankle and pulled her to him.

Squealing louder, Kesi kicked at him and struggled to get away. He grabbed her other ankle and flipped her on her belly, then dragged her down the middle of the bed.

Holding her with a hand to her back, he reached over the end of the bed and picked up the robe, pulled the belt from it and let the robe fall to the floor.

"Uh, Martier, what are you doing?" She tried to push up to see but he pressed her down.

"Again, Kesindra, I need to teach you a lesson. I give you warnings, you ignore them, you then will suffer the consequences. I will show you who your master is, my sweet."

"Wait." Kesi trembled, she couldn't tell if he was teasing or serious.

"As before, honey, tis too late now." Martier straddled her butt, leaned over, grasped her hands pulling them over her head and together. He wrapped the robe belt around her wrists and was tying them to the railing at the headboard before she comprehended what he was doing.

Kesi lay on her belly with her hands tied above her head. Martier rolled off, moved further down the bed, grabbed each ankle and jerked her legs wide apart.

"Martier!" Kesi gasped. She couldn't move, couldn't even lift her head to look back to see what he was doing.

"Aye, sweetheart," he murmured with a velvety roughness, setting his palms on her calves. "This is where you learn who your master is."

He ran his palms very slowly up her legs, feeling every satin inch of her and smiling at her bottom twitching from both nerves and desire.

His hands reached her thighs and stopped. "You only tell me if I hurt you, or frighten you. Otherwise, I control your every sensation."

"You are not my master," she gruffed with muffled breathy huffs, "it is not your job to control me. Let me go."

"Ha, you are in no position to direct me, my sweet." To prove it, he pushed her ankles as far apart as they would go.

"Martier, don't hurt me," she whispered.

"Ah, *několika,* when will you stop thinking that I would ever hurt you? That makes me think you need more punishment," his chuckles filled with wicked intent.

Her murmur soft with worry, and heated with interest, she muttered, "Punishment sounds like pain."

"Hmm, pain and pleasure together can become blended, exquisite sensations." Gripping her thighs, he moved his palms up to lightly brush her sex with his thumbs.

"Oh!" Kesi's hips bounced at his touch, but with her wrists tied and his knees pressed against the insides of her legs keeping them spread apart, she couldn't budge an inch to get away from his nomadic hands.

Kneeling between her legs, Martier bent and licked the soft skin of her bottom while fingering her sex. Instantly her sweet cream cast onto his hand. His rumbled growl publicized his pleasure. "Ah, you want me again, my *tím rostia.*"

Her voice slightly muffled with her face in the sheets Kesi asked, "Why are my wrists tied? What are you going to do to me?"

His fingers suddenly enclosing her feminine folds shorted her question into a gasp. He clipped and twisted her folds.

With his adept digits scissoring the delicate lips so stimulating her, Kesi couldn't stop her hips from bucking and jolting at him to make his fingers work her harder.

Low and thick with lewdness, Martier's voice as deep as a bass drum thrummed, "You are tied so the only one who can touch you and make you come is me."

Puzzled she said, "I don't understand, we're the only ones here."

"Aye, only I will allow you to come. Trust me, I am going to make you insane with want to the point you will crave to relieve yourself, and I will not let you. That is your punishment for tonight. Not until you beg, and after I determine the sincerity of your pleading, will I let you climax. You will soon learn to understand who is in control, who is in charge."

He stopped moving his hands, just brushed his fingertips lightly up and then down the insides of her thighs. Close to her sex, whisper close, but not touching her.

His barely there touch was making Kesi squirm all over the bed. "Martier, I- I'm ready now," she told him. Tiny breathy puffs hitched out as her hips sought his hands but couldn't reach them.

"Oh, nay, sweeting." He smacked her on her bare butt making her squeak. "I think not. You don't sound ready to me." He kissed, then bit one round cheek, when she squawked again, he sucked on her firm flesh until red marks rose.

"Martier, please," she begged, twisting her hips. He allowed her pelvis to rub against his hand. Sitting back on his heels, he spanked her again, then put one big hand on a soft cheek and kneaded it while toying with her sex.

Kesi's moans and pleadings came in a muffled bumpy string. Her naked body writhing, her sex was in sweet torture needing release. Her swollen breasts rubbed on the sheets begging for Martier's big hands to clutch them.

He fingered her so lightly, she whined, pleading, "Martier, help me, *finish it*," her hips bucked trying to grind against his hand.

With skillful fingers, Martier drew her up to the top of the cliff, her cries wracking with her wriggling body, struggling to push at his fingers to make him let her go. But as soon as she was about to go over, he moved his hand to smack then grope her bottom.

"*Please*," her voice tinny with need.

Martier kept one leg crooked to keep her thighs apart and bent on his other knee outside of her hips so he could reach under her and grasp her breasts.

"*Uhh*, God, Martier," groaning, Kesi nestled her aching breasts into his hands.

His voice a rough murmur near her ear, "This what you want, *tím rostia,* my hands on your beautiful tits, fondling them?" He squeezed harder, she squirmed, thrashing atop the mattress.

Pinching her pebbled nipples, he crushed her breasts in his hands, grinning at her cries of rapture and pleas for him to give her release.

Kesi moved her hips trying to rub her throbbing swollen pussy on the sheets to force her own climax.

"Oh, nay precious, you do that again and we will start your punishment all over, and I will tie your ankles apart so you can't move."

282

Martier moved back between her legs shoving his knees against her thighs to spread them as wide as they could go to immobilize her. He gave her a couple of stinging slaps on her bottom, she shrieked and writhed.

His claws unsheathed and he circled each cheek with them, knifing into her soft flesh, stabbing harder with her wails of rapture, squirming, begging for relief.

Bending slightly towards her, he asked, "Does it hurt, Kesindra? Tell me, am I hurting you?"

Her head flopped back and forth in denial, a grunting groan and a wriggle of her butt told him she was on that threshold between pain and pleasure he had talked about, where they merged and one couldn't be felt without the impacting piercing injection of the other.

Sheathing his claws, Martier kneaded the pain from her bottom with both hands, then slid his hand down to get his fingers slick with her silk and probed inside her carefully, slowly.

Each stroke a tantalizing curse bringing her to the highest heights, but not far enough she could go over and find relief.

She tried to press down on his fingers to make them go deeper, move faster, but she was too secured. Naked, lying on her stomach with her arms stretched above her, and her legs splayed with a powerfully strong demon between them, so vulnerable, so hysterically turned on she could only scream in protest.

Then she did scream, "Martier, I am on fire, burning, *please*, help me!"

He skillfully moved two fingers inside her and thumbed her ultra-sensitive woman's scallop working her to a frenzied pitch. Her hips thrashed with incoherent gushes of pleading and moaning.

He spanked her with his fingers still inside her, she screamed and almost came from the intensity of it. But he pulled his hands away in time to prevent her release.

Then he slid his fingers back inside her, and when he worked the very tip of his finger into the opening in her bottom, she paused in her writhing and frantic sharp inhales.

Martier moved his fingers faster and deeper inside her channel, at the same time he just barely moved his fingertip inside her bottom.

Her body spastic on the bed, bucking against his fingers, wrenching at her ties, swollen breasts rubbing on the sheets, Kesi cried for him to let her come, "*Martier, please!*"

His fingers imbedded in her, Martier leaned over and asked, "Who is your master, Kesindra? Tell me and I will jam my big cock in your raging pussy and let you come. Tell me."

In a screeching fever, her mouth open into the sheets, eyes closed, sweat trickling down her face, Kesi muttered, "No, you are not my, uh," she gasped as he dove his fingers in hard, twisted them, and moved his other fingertip further inside her bottom.

"Uh, not my…" she rambled off as he worked her back up to the edge of the cliff.

Keeping her dangling over the precipice, Martier moved his hand from her bottom to brace beside her head while still finagling her clit, her hips bounced and trembled with her incoherent whimpers.

He whispered, "Say it, say I am your master and you will obey me, and mean it, and I will let you come. Go on, say it."

Pulling his fingers out, he pinched her tiny bud, ran his entire palm over her pussy palpating it, then slapped her ass twice before moving his fingers back inside.

Panting like she was in a race, almost totally fragmented, Kesi mumbled, "K...o...kay," gasp, "you are...my master...now, please-"

"Say you will obey me, Kesindra, say it, and no take backs," he demanded, swirling the pad of his finger around her clit, lightly tickling her bud.

Her body shaking with the burning desire he'd built in her, Kesi drew a ragged breath and cried with a whimper, "O...kay, I..." she took another deep breath, "will obey you."

"You swear on your word, Kesindra?"

Crying, "Martier, God, please you monster!" she grimaced, grinding her hips at his hand.

"Swear it."

"I swear I will kill you after this, that's what I swear," she snarled fiercely.

"Oh, okay, I guess we are done here." He moved his hands from her.

Kesi cried, "I swear damn you, I swear to obey you Martier." Hard little gulps rushed in her throat, grinding her words to bits. Her body stretched and strained, tingling like a taut piano wire.

"Ah, that is what I wanted to hear, *několika*. My job is to protect you. I don't want to lock you up to do that, so I need your cooperation. You will-"

"Shut up and do it, *Captain*," she growled.

With a big grin, Martier shoved a hand under her hip jerking her up and drove his cock straight into her, hard, but not to the end of her, she was too small and tight for him to do that, he would have hurt her.

But, he thrust inside her so hard her body moved a foot up the bed, her belted restraints were slightly loosened.

Her scream came out in a choke.

He stopped moving. "*Několika,* sweetheart, are you all right?"

She nodded, moved up on her elbows and knees, head down, long blonde curls swiping the sheets, a gasp spurted. "Yes, don't stop, Martier."

"Ah, I want to hear you say those words every damned day, baby." He yanked her hips higher forcing her face into the sheets, and pushed to the end of her, then drilled like a jackhammer, hard, fast, going deep.

Kesi screamed as her orgasm ripped through her, her body pendulating like a drowning person flailing in the water.

His fangs descended and plunged into her neck. In a frenzied rampage, Martier thrust faster, rougher, his balls slapping against her skin. In seconds she screamed his name as another powerful orgasm rocketed through her, tearing her up.

Fingers clinching her hip like a pronged vice, he held her immobile, driving so hard into her, Kesi was helpless to do anything but hang on and let him continue his rampaging assault on her body.

Martier pounded one more unbridled orgasm from her, then with her hoarse screams in his ears he let go. The fireball swelled in his balls, scorching every bit of flesh inside as it roared through his testicles up his cock and exploded out.

He drove maniacally into her until his seeds burst from him, his roar strained from unbelievable, excruciating, sensation.

Then he held suspended, rigid, as his own climax strummed and his seeds continued spilling with spasms. His body oscillating in convulsions with her name gushing from his lips, until he was utterly empty, and he dropped on her completely out of breath.

On the edge of blacking out from the extraordinary climax, Martier barely felt Kesi wriggling under him; he was crushing her with his dead weight.

With a sated exhausted grunt, he pitched to lie on his side bringing Kesi with her spine curled against his chest, still inside her, and curved his legs up under hers.

He reached up to untie the belt, then his hand possessively gripped her breast as he held her quivering, panting body against his equally palpitating, huffing form.

His breath still rough and rapid, he blew tendrils of her hair as he rasped in her ear, "Zeus, Kesindra, I have never experienced anything like that, like you, like us before. Gods, I feel like we were an exploding super nova, a damned star blasting into fragments hurtling through the galaxies."

Her giggles made her body wiggle in his arms; it brought a tender smile to his face. She murmured, "You sound like a poet, Demon Martier, your thoughts are quite fanciful."

His chuckle ticked her hair. "Aye, tis you that makes me feel that way. Don't you see, Kesindra," he drew his fingers through her hair, petting her. "It was just proven that we are destined mates. No couple experiences that kind of phenomenal sex that are not preordained mates. Tis why I was so compelled, so drawn to you. Tell me you have not felt the same about me?"

He pulled from her then turned her to face him, his large hand stroked down her back to grip her bottom.

She was quiet so long he was feeling disappointed, not dissuaded to let her go, but disappointed she didn't feel the same inexplicable, irresistible enamoring desire he felt for her.

287

But, he wasn't letting her go, so he would just need to teach her to want him with the same burning hunger that he wanted her.

He would again and again bring her to such intense unbearable heights that number one, she would never desire another man but him, and two, she would be thinking constantly of sex with Martier, like he already was of her, day and night.

"I..." her voice husky from screaming, her shyness returned. Kesi said quietly, "Yes, I have been attracted...had feelings for you that I just couldn't understand, couldn't explain, from the beginning. I fought them because, well, you are...alien from me, and, I thought you were a... although now I am doubting, that you are an outlaw."

His grin ear-to-ear, he sighed, "Zeus." Sliding his hand up to cup her chin, he looked into her blues misted with blurry passion and fulfilled desire for him.

"I am crazy about you, beautiful Kesindra, and gods, I do love punishing you." He kissed her giggling lips.

She said with a sleepy smile, "Do you now, Captain," and licked his lips with teasing strokes.

"Ah, don't do that, I don't have the strength right now, sweet, tempting *několika,* to punish you again. I need rest." Martier pulled her in close, into a tight embrace, and they slept.

Chapter Twenty-four

*P*oking his shoulder, Kesi said, "Martier, wake up."

"Huh." Grunting, bleary-eyed, he struggled to raise his heavy lids. Finally forcing them open, he smiled. Kesi was glaring at him, things were back to normal.

"What precious *několika,* after another salt bath and sex two more times, how can you have any energy left to even whisper?"

"Isn't that redundant saying precious *několika*? It's like saying precious precious one."

"Ah, you are too smart for your own good, baby." Rolling on his back he dropped his forearm over his eyes.

"You promised I could call Agent Dukes back, Martier. That was hours ago."

Squinting up at her, he groaned, "Now? You want to call him now? Can't you lay here peacefully naked in my arms and cuddle with me?"

"Ha," with an inelegant snort she slid off the bed and started to pull her clothes on. "A deadly demon warlord that

289

wants to cuddle, who woulda thought? Come on, you promised."

He watched her under golden lashes. "Okay, wait, Kesindra. I will get the phone if you don't get dressed."

Her hands plopped on her still naked hips. "Strings? You always have strings attached to your promises."

"Tis not asking that much, baby, just get back into bed and I will go get my phone." When she didn't move, cockling his head with a lopsided grin that gave him a rare boyish appeal, he said, "Please?"

"*Uhh*," Kesi groused, "you get out first. If I get in with you, I know you will be all over me and I won't get to make my call."

His eyes trailed hungrily up and down her body. "Aye, true that. I thought finally taking you would shave the edge off the blinding lust I have for you, but tis done the opposite. I only crave you more."

"Get up," she ordered.

"Fine." Sighing, he shuffled on the mattress towards her, but Kesi darted to the other side of the bed. His eyes cast to the side watching her beautiful body bounce and jiggle.

"The least you can do is move your hair so I can see those lush breasts." He leered with a wolfish grin like he wanted to take a bite out of them. "If I squint really hard," and he did, "I can just barely see a nipple through those flaxen strands."

Looking down to make sure her long curls were indeed covering her front, she shook her head. "Oh no you don't. I can see right in those green eyes your intent, demon. Go get the phone," she insisted and moved her hands to cover her sex from his wandering eyes.

"Hmm, you are pretty bossy for a tiny human female in the near clutches of a male demon warrior more than twice your size." He stood to his full height, scratched the dark hair on his muscled chest, the huge biceps flexing with his movements.

"That's right, Tarzan, now, phone please." She stayed on the other side of the bed where he couldn't reach her.

"Damn, you are tough." Shaking his head, he shot her a grin and traipsed out of the room.

When he left she hurried into the bathroom for a quick clean up then climbed back in the bed carefully wrapping the sheet around her nudity.

"Here," he said coming back into the room obviously pleased to see her back in the bed. "I will dial." Pulling back the blanket and sheet, he slid in and settled into the pillows stacked against the headboard. He dialed the number and handed it to Kesi.

Dukes answered on the second ring. "Jasmari? What the hell? You said an hour for fucks sake, where the hell have you-"

"Satellite disruption, Agent, can't be helped out here in no-where's land. What did you find out?" Kesi switched the phone from her right ear to her left to ward off Martier's hand creeping around her.

"Yeah, really fucking strange, Kesindra." She could almost hear him shaking his head through the phone, rubbing his hand back and forth over his short dark hair like he did when consternated.

"I found the transfer, it had Captain Stewart's name on it. The thing is, Stewart denied signing it, said he knew nothing about it. When I showed it to him, he said it wasn't his signature. It seems Miss Loomis forged his signature. Can you get a load of the balls-"

"Yes, yes, what can you tell me about Arianna? Where is she from? I think she's divorced, what were you able to dig up?" Kesi squirmed as Martier's hand crept from around her shoulder to take a hold of the sheet she had wrapped around her.

"Yeah, well, it gets stranger. She's from the same fucking country you're in, Původně, can you believe it? From a town called, uh, I don't know how to pronounce it properly, uh, Milčent. Not that you would know about it-"

"Her family?" Kesi asked anxiously, pushing at Martier's hands. His one hand was gripping the sheet trying to pull it down, the other was trying to slide in and touch her.

"Okay, Miss Patience, she is divorced, her maiden name was," his voice paused as if he were glancing at his notes for the history he'd dug up on Arianna. Then he said, "Montblanc."

Feeling rivers of chills raising goose bumps over her arms, Kesi whispered, "Her parents' names?"

"Uh," he hesitated. "Oh, here, mom was Elsa, father Alain. Kind of a fruity name if you ask me."

Kesi's eyes closed. Taking a deep breath she asked, "Anything else?"

"Nah, her mother lives in Boston, her father is dead. He died in a prison over there. That's all I have. Now, tell me what the fuck is this all about?"

Martier pushed his hand under her sheet to palm a bare breast. Kesi couldn't think when he was touching her, she squirmed a foot away from, frowning at his smirk.

"Jasmari, are you there?"

"Uh, yes, Agent Dukes. It seems that 12 years ago Arianna's father brutally raped a girl in another town out here, beat her literally blind. He was prosecuted and found guilty and was given a life sentence. But he was murdered in prison. That first murder here, Mr. Francks', I don't believe has any connection to the next ones."

"Really now, girl, your inexperience is showing."

His condescending voice roiled anger through Kesi. Ignoring him, she went on, "Regarding the other murders, and that old rape, both the judge and the district attorney on the rape case were murdered here, and now the victim of the rape has been killed. I think when Arianna heard we were being sent here, she managed to get a ride along so she could-"

"Avenge her father?" Dukes' heavy breathing came through the phone. "Are you fucking kidding me right now?" He was silent as he ruminated on the info.

At Kesi's inhale as she started to speak, he said, "It's so damned fantastical, so- so far-fetched, too unbelievable. Fuck, goddammit, Jasmari, but there is too much for it to be coincidences. Dammit." A string of vulgar invectives rolled through the wires.

His voice was muffled as he barked out some orders to someone. Then back to her, "I need to get you guys out of there and send in an experienced team to take care of this." He said, "What?" to someone there with him.

Mumbles were heard, then Dukes said to Kesi, "There's a fucking major storm burgeoning over half the country. We will not be able to get our people out there until it dissipates. Hopefully it isn't coming in the direction our jet needs to go to get there. Listen, Jasmari, stay away from Loomis. We will handle it on our end. Do you under-"

Martier took the phone from her numb hands and disconnected it. He tugged at the sheet. Okay, baby, I gave you yours, now you give me mine."

"Martier, no, wait, we have to get her, arrest her. She could hurt someone else."

"Uhh," he groaned, but had already speed-dialed Trae's number. As soon as his friend answered, he gave him a directive, "Tell Officer Dempsey to arrest Arianna Loomis on suspicion of murder."

Trae made a sound like a grunt. "Um, okay, sure, *má bráthair?* You gonna explain what it's about, what the hell is going on? You've been holed up in your suite, you got your hot little agent with you? Are you and Kesindra-"

"Later. Get Loomis. Keep your guard up, she has a weapon. I will call you back in a few." Clicking off the cell, Martier set it on the table beside the bed and turned towards Kesi. "Now, baby-"

Kesi shook her head. "No. I have a suspect and I need more information before proceeding. You know Dempsey won't ask the right questions, I need to do it." She turned to the side of the bed about to get up.

Martier sighed and forked his fingers through his hair in frustration. The gaze stroking down her body was hungry and angry. "It is pretty likely that it was Arianna that clocked you and tried to fucking strangle you. You will not go near her, or even do any more investigating on your own."

"Oh don't be ridiculous, I am an agent, not a baby. I can take care of myself. I'm aware now that she is the danger. I'm leaving-"

"Can you? Take care of yourself? You were pulled from the academy before you had any real training. You were almost killed by that guy in the alley that shot you. Then you were almost murdered here, and must I remind you of Carpenter?"

Her face black with a humiliated scowl she grated, "How dare you throw that stuff in my face! So, I was a bit green when I was chasing the uh, perp, that day, and I trusted Chris, he was my partner for heaven's sake. I should have been able to trust him with my life! And- and, Arianna, I mean, a horny exhibitionist secretary, who would have been suspicious of her as a killer?"

Martier crossed his big arms over his huge slabs of chest muscles. "My point exactly. You have already done the puzzle piecing together, the brainwork. You figured it out. You are absolutely brilliant but we will do the heavy lifting from now on. You will not leave this suite without me."

"You can't hold me captive, that's-"

His dark brows arched, then flattened. Saying it for her, "Kidnapping? Sorry, compounding the same offense that I did taking over this town is not going to give me more jail time. You try to leave without me and I will lock you up."

"You wouldn't dare!"

"Just try me."

"Oh for the love of-" Kesi thought about it. If she solved this serial murder she could go back to the states with her head high instead of with her tail between her legs or staying in the godforsaken jungle for the rest of her life.

Exhaling loudly, she sighed with graceless pique, "Fine."

"Fine what?"

"Martier." She rolled her eyes.

He just stared at her.

Kesi exploded, "You are the most infuriating stubborn person I've ever met!"

"Back at ya, honey. Tell me what you are not going to do."

With a huff, she snapped, "All right. I agree not to question anyone without you or one of your men with me. Satisfied?"

"Nay. You will agree not to do any investigating whatsoever."

"Martier, come on. Without my investigating, a murderer would still be unveiled and free to continue her killing spree."

Seeing his stubborn chin tilt up, she sighed. "All right. I won't do any investigating without you with me. Satisfied now?"

His frown ringed with exasperated annoyance. "That is not what I said."

"How about I just go with Dempsey to ask-"

"Nay." Martier reached for her. "I will not say it again, you are done with the interviewing people out there on your own. You go nowhere without me from now on. You get an idea you tell me and then we will decide how to proceed. Tis Dempsey's job, and your senior agents will take over when Dukes is able to get them here."

Changing the subject, his grin salivating, he said, "Okay, *tím rostia,* I gave you what you wanted, now I am taking what I want."

Her scowl darkening, Kesi crossed her arms over the sheet as Martier reached for the front of it. "You think you just told me that I am a virtually a prisoner and you block me from doing my job, that I want to do anything with you?"

"Ah, aye, I do." His smile a sexy promise, he leaned towards her, cradled her head and kissed her deeply. When she started unfreezing, he cupped her breast over the sheet, and she wriggled against his hand, their lips still locked.

Martier gripped the top of the sheet, pulled it down and leered at her naked torso. "Perfect. Come, I need to have more of you."

He peeled the sheet from her, laughing at her squeals and giggles and attempts to thwart him. In one second the sheet was gone and he was covering his hard body over her soft one.

They stayed in his suite for two days. Mostly in bed. Sometimes they ate and showered, christened other parts of the suite, then went back to the big bed. Then Trae called.

Without preamble Martier asked, "You get Loomis?"

"Nay, Mart, not yet. She hasn't returned to the office or the hotel. I think she's hiding out with some stud she picked up. Woman's a man-eater. I called because tis time, they're almost here."

"Damn. All right. Keep the guys after Loomis."

Martier reached for his jeans. "Got to get dressed, sweetness," he said to Kesi.

Kesi was nestled against a pile of pillows waiting for him to return to bed. "Why? Is something wrong?"

"Aye. Put on the biggest, baggiest, shittiest looking clothes you have and pin your hair up in a bun, real tight." He started opening drawers in the nightstand then the dresser, "Where the hell did I put your glasses?"

"Martier, what's going on?" She climbed to the end of bed on her knees and sat back on her heels watching him, her forehead wrinkled seeing him open and then slam drawers closed.

"Ah, here they are. Your hat," he muttered while rummaging around in the same drawer and pulled out the cap she had been wearing when they first met.

He turned to her with a frown seeing she hadn't moved. His voice cool and stern, "Kesindra, do as I said, we don't have a lot of time."

"But, what's going on? Tell me?" She didn't move.

He stomped over to her, grabbed her arm and lifted her off the bed to her feet. "This is serious, Kesindra, fucking do as I say right now. Get dressed and put these on." He thrust her hat and glasses into her hands and trod back across the room to get a shirt out of the dresser.

"Martier, tell me-"

He swiveled to her casting a scowl. "I cannot tell you, you have to trust me. Do as I said, we have to go, now." He stalked to the safe in the room, opened it and shoved his weapons and her badge and ID inside."

"Martier, what are you doing? Those are mine-"

Stalking over to her, he gripped her shoulders. "I cannot explain now. I will later. Do as I said. Right now. You will not like it if I have to dress you."

Eying him with wary puzzlement, Kesi did as he said.

When she started dressing, she watched him make a call, glancing over his shoulder at her he went into the other room so she couldn't hear what he was saying.

When she was dressed and had on her hat and glasses, Kesi entered the living room.

Martier didn't look angry, he looked concerned and determined. He went back into the bedroom and put his cell phone in the safe then came back out.

Her big eyes were trained nervously on him; he had so quickly changed from a sweet, lusting, cuddly man to a cold, sober demon.

For a second his face softened, he wound his long fingers around her arms and held her. "Baby, I cannot tell you. Why we were sent here is happening. Please, do not fight anything or anyone, you will only be hurt. I will watch over you, just believe that nothing will be as it seems.

"Do whatever...people tell you to without resistance. Keep your head and eyes down, and your hat as low over your face as you can get it. Do not let anyone see your face or your eyes. Okay?"

Blinking bewildered at him, she shook her head. "No, I don't understand."

"You have to trust me, Kesindra. Please." The humor and softness was gone, replaced by a chilling graveness.

She didn't answer him. Martier took her hand and they left the suite, went down the stairs, out the door and to the rec building.

They ate dinner like nothing was any different. But it was different. With Martier and his men.

His close team, Trae, Slade, Cisco and Jamir, and also the hired soldiers like Bruglon, were all stiff-faced and silent. The rest of the civilians were acting totally normal and going about their business.

What she did notice was that the room was packed to the gills. Every resident had been instructed to be present at the first seating.

Kesi's attention drew back to Martier and his team. They all wore hats too, pulled down to cover their pointed ears. Martier was the only one with horns. Some of the other soldiers had hats on too, but not all did.

They had finished dinner and were just sitting, hanging out at the tables. Kesi was just about to ask what was going to happen, when there was a commotion at the door.

Enormous beings marched through the door. They looked human but with differences, such as long webbing instead of hair, and silver streaked under coppery skin that appeared reptilian with leathered mottling.

They were armed with unusual looking weapons, and the weapons were aimed at the crowd in the building.

When the male that marched up to the front of the group spoke, he revealed exceptionally long, sharp canines along with a mouthful of smaller, razor sharp teeth like a crocodile.

At the sight of the teeth and the weapons trained on them, the crowd quickly grew silent.

As soon as he had everyone's attention, he announced, "I am Du roi Quamo from V'Am 2nd Sequester. We are taking all of you to our compound. Any resisters will be killed instantly. You will not speak, to us or each other, those that do, will die instantly. You will do as we order with no hesitation or fight. Now, line up and move outside."

He waited, no one moved. He pulled out some kind of space weapon and aimed it at the closest person, a man around 50, and shot him.

An orange blaze fired out and slammed into the man's stomach, he crumpled to the floor. The smell of sizzling flesh permeated the room with a hail of smoke whooshing from the dead man.

The new alien soldiers kept their firearms steady on the people.

Gasps of fright abounding, chairs scraped the wood floor as everyone hurried to their feet and hustled to get in line.

Martier and his team shared a look; they hadn't expected the being to kill outright to show he meant what he said.

It took some time for everyone to get outside. Too scared and shocked to speak, they followed directions. A few of the soldiers stood beside the door and drew a metal piece like a deck of cards down each person apparently to detect weapons as several were confiscated.

Martier caught Kesi's elbow, jerked the bill of her cap down over her face and guided her to the line exiting the building.

She shot him a confused look before following the others out the door. Martier and his soldiers were aliens as well. And they were…warriors. Why were they going along so peacefully without a fight?

She must do something. When she stiffened, thinking she would- Martier grabbed her hand and gave it a hard squeeze with a shake of his head and narrowed eyes.

Kesi stared at him, but he faced forward pulling her to follow behind him with Trae behind her.

Then it dawned on her, Martier and his men had expected this, that's why he left his weapons and her ID in the safe. This was part of their mission, their plan. But what on earth could be a good plan that got a man killed and the rest of them being abducted? Again.

She went along without a fight, Martier was right, there was nothing she could do. The creatures were well over seven feet tall and armed to the teeth.

Once outside, the beings were arranging the people into two groups, one of males, and the other females. Beside her, Kesi felt Martier tense.

Trae looked at him, hissed a whisper, "Don't abort the mission to save one girl. She will be all right." He thought he had spoken in his language, but when he saw the horror ride across Kesi's bewildered face he realized his mistake.

People were starting to murmur.

"Silence!" The du roi bellowed. He raised his weapon, "Next one speaks will die as will anyone near them."

A feather could be heard dropping in the grass it became so deathly quiet. As soon as he finished speaking, the other soldiers moved up the lines of people chaining them together. One hand was chained to the person in front of them, the other to the person behind.

As Kesi was dragged over and chained, she glanced up and saw Martier staring at her. His face completely blank, inscrutable, his body was as rigid as a bronze tower. He didn't struggle as his wrists were chained as well.

He shook his head slightly and lowered it, reminding her to keep her head down and not make eye contact with anyone.

Chapter Twenty-five

The du roi wandered down the line of females staring carefully at each one. When he neared Kesi, she kept her head down and her eyes on the ground, he passed her continuing on.

Arianna hadn't been in the rec room when the people were gathered, but she must have been grabbed just outside the building. She was chained along with the rest of the group, and looked just as frightened.

One of the aliens counted the prisoners and nodded to the du roi that all were present.

When the du roi reached Arianna, he nodded, then further down the line he nodded at Tawny and then looked disgusted.

He spoke with disdain, "Not a decent bitch amongst this entire village. All ugly as sin. Even those two aren't prime but they are the best out of the litter, ah," his face twisted in a fearful, foul grimace, "the syntagma will be very displeased."

Arianna and Tawny were unchained and re-chained at the front of the line.

Tawny sneered down her flat nose at the line of women, then directed her sexiest smile, her most alluring sultry gaze at the du roi. "Are we to be a present for your...king?" She not subtly shook her chest drawing the captain's attention to her inflated breasts.

Standing erect, without moving his head, Du Roi Quamo's smile was hideous. "Ah, actually, yes, but not our...king. The syntagma is in charge of this...expedition. Now, if there were any other decent replacements for you, I would kill you for speaking when I ordered silence, but, alas, the pickings are meager and repulsive. But, you speak again and I will fry you."

He pivoted on his heel and gave a motion with his hand; the soldiers prodded the people to start walking.

It was slow moving with an entire village, small, but still there were a lot of people trudging across the fields and then through the forests. Being chained made the moving slower.

They were allowed to stop once every two hours to relieve themselves. Several soldiers were tasked with observing the females while they peed in the bushes, the majority stayed with the men.

After a break, one of the soldiers was staring thoughtfully at Kesi.

Now understanding why Martier made her wear her hat and glasses, she kept her head down. Not that she needed to worry; she wouldn't be high on the list of attractive women in Brutální.

It was still beyond her why Martier had chosen plain old her. He hadn't been with another woman since they'd taken over the village. And not for want of trying on some women's side. Tawny chased him brazenly and relentlessly and there were others as well.

Tawny and Arianna were chosen to be given to the...whatever the creature had called their leader. Who knew if that was a good thing or bad?

She slid a low glance at Arianna. She was a murderer. For some reason, Dempsey hadn't arrested her. Then she saw the way the officer looked at Arianna, and her randy smile back.

Oh, Kesi understood. Arianna had sex with him as a bribe. Since there was no other law there, Dempsey could do as he pleased without repercussions, at least for a while.

Now, who knew what would happen to any of them?

Tawny and Arianna stuck their noses in the air and sneered smugly at the rest of the women.

Struggling to quell her fear, apprehension crawled all over Kesi, her skin popped with goose bumps.

If anyone stumbled, an alien would rush over, kick them, and then wrench them to their feet.

Quamo barked, "Anyone can't walk, their corpse will remain here," and trotted back up the line.

The people were relentlessly marched, fatigue and hunger ignored. Everyone was wide-eyed as they were led through an invisible cleft in the mountains that no one knew was there.

They were forced to travel over rock ensuring there would be no trace left of them. Kesi thought perhaps these aliens had carved the entrance through the rocky mountain themselves to stay hidden.

After a long day of hiking, one of the people made a sound of exclamation in their throat and everyone looked up.

Louise Furley

Ahead, about a half-mile, they could see the compound looming through the leafy forest like a daunting chunk of mountain.

The fortress they were being herded to, the whitish-grey, granular structure, probably limestone, had been concealed by a mountain overhang and the tangled canopy of thick jungle.

When Kesi looked up, the person behind her was looking up too and knocked into her causing Kesi to stumble and fall to her knees.

A soldier raced over to her with his fist raised. Under the brim of her hat, she saw Trae who was chained to Martier jab him hard with his elbow.

Martier's face strained with the effort to keep from reacting to Kesi about to be hit. The line of women stopped moving, then the men's did as well.

It was the same soldier who had looked at her funny after their last bathroom break. Instead of hitting her, he snatched her hat off. Her yellow hair was pinned tight on top of her head, but the creature dropped her hat and reached for the pins.

Her wrists manacled, Kesi was powerless to protect herself. He plucked out every pin and watched in amazement as the curls tumbled down.

Eyes like an insect's tapered in cunning scrutiny. He grabbed her glasses and ripped them off her face. Kesi couldn't stop the small cry at his roughness.

The soldier bent down to Kesi and gripped her chin yanking her face up. She tried to keep her eyes lowered to the ground.

"Look at me, human, or I will burn your eyes out of your head."

She slowly raised them, the terror in her cyan orbs reflected the gruesome creature glaring with sick delight at her. He jerked her to her feet and yanked at her jacket, pulling it down as far as it would go stopping at her chained wrists.

His eyes hard on her breasts, he reached behind her and pulled at her baggy shirt from the back so her chest would be outlined. The beastly eyes bulged, and his mouth curled up in leering glee.

Releasing her shirt, he again reached behind her and grabbed her ass with both hands.

He unchained her and moved her slightly away from the others. His repulsive chortle echoed in her ear as he bent over her. "Ah, thank the skeeves, we do have something the syntagma will want."

He glanced in relief at some of the other soldiers who were staring at Kesi with the same relieved, and lustful, pitiless looks on their faces.

Then he blocked view of her from the others with his giant body, and gripped her breasts over her thick loose blouse, squeezing them so hard tears came to her eyes. He couldn't let anyone see him touch her before the syntagma did or it would mean his instant fiery death.

He clinched her chin with tough fingers forcing her to look up at him.

Up close, Kesi could see the silver streaking under his coppery skin. Pure black eyes of an insect that had no light in them studied her.

"Oh, yes, you will do quite nicely, little female. The syntagma will be very pleased. I hope you last out the night with him, sometimes we get a shot at those that survive the first time." With harsh, inhumane moves, he clamped the chains back on her wrists and gave her a shove.

"Get going," he ordered them all. "The specimens we were able to snatch from a campsite have already expired. The syntagma will be eager to have fresh meat."

Kesi's stomach plummeted as he spoke. She was to be brought to their leader, and it sounded like she needed to prepare to be raped. Brutally. Or, the way he made it sound, gang raped. She took a chance to glance over at Martier.

His tanned face was white as a sheet; mouth a rigid line, his eyes burned across the grass at her. Trae and Slade were both holding onto him.

All three men's chests pumped, their biceps bulging. Taking the chance of getting caught, Trae was whispering in Martier's ear.

Hoping nothing more would happen to Kesi for now, Martier stopped struggling, but the strain of his rage, and desperate fear for her etched deep lines in his face, and despair burnt in his eyes.

The villagers were herded to the compound. The main structure, two stories and a block wide, was made of the off-white limestone. The top was painted dark green to blend in with the mountains and the jungle cover.

Only a few windows were visible making the building relatively impenetrable, that and the volume of beastly soldiers guarding the perimeter, as well as inside would make attacking it almost impossible.

On either side of the structure were a series of cells. The women were ushered to one side, the men to the other.

Seeing they were going to be separated, Martier became so agitated his horns grew under the hat, and his claws and canines descended, the wavering image of a creature like a beastly ghost moved over him.

Trae and Slade chained on either side of Martier moved slightly in front of him to hide his transformation and to hold him back.

"Not yet," Trae whispered, "she's safe until she's taken to the leader. A soldier told me the guards stand outside the opening of the dungeons, once they put the females in they do not access them."

"She is going to get hurt, fuck Trae, I have to go now-"

Slade pushed his back against Martier. "Not yet. We have to know who the leader is and where their ship is hidden, and take out the communications."

His teeth grinding together, dark green eyes projecting his impotent fury, Martier allowed them to stop him, for now. He watched as the long blonde curls disappeared into the limestone cells.

The chambers were built right into the side of the mountain the fortress butted against. The men were marched into the cells on the other side; groups of them were locked into individual cells.

Martier was in with Trae and Slade. Cisco and Jamir were housed down a few cells. All of the men locked away weren't witness to what happened next.

When Tawny and Arianna were about to be shepherded into the chambers, they protested. Seeing Kesi had been chosen over them and they were to be kept with the rest of the litter of females, they were infuriated, oozing feral resentment.

Refusing to enter the cell chambers, Arianna declared with an angry, haughty sniff, "I am not one of *them*," she said with a sneer. "I am not from this shithole of a country. I am better than them, I should not be penned in with those indigenous insignificants. I demand to be let go or brought to your king like you said. I will satisfy him, I am more than pretty, and," she glanced at Officer Dempsey, "I am *extremely* experienced. I will teach him things he never knew existed!"

One of the soldiers gave a short sharp whistle. In seconds, Quamo was there.

The soldier said to the du roi, "That one says she is not one of this country's females and therefore should be set free, or brought to the Syntagma. Says she is highly skilled in the sexual acts."

Hearing this, Tawny jumped in taking a step towards the captain. She declared haughtily, "And I am not homely and fat like the natives. I was the one who was supposed to be given to the leader as a gift, not that scrawny blonde bitch. I insist you take me to him. I hear he is a handsome, godlike male from a glorious galaxy rich with splendor and gold.

"Take me to him, I guarantee he will want me." The full-figured woman preened, a hand on a wide hip, she primped her hair then dangled a finger down her cleavage to show the soldiers what she had to offer.

The soldier and Quamo shared a smirk. "You heard about us, from whom, may I inquire?" Quamo asked Tawny, his lips contorted in a deviant smile.

Not to be ignored, Arianna moved up next to Tawny and said, "The soldiers. They were pretty handsy while chaining us, so we had some conversations while hiking here."

Tawny simpered, "Yes. So, we demand to be taken to your leader, your king." With the libidinous smile of a coquette, she brushed up against Quamo.

While seeing for himself what Tawny's big breasts felt like, he responded, "Syntagma Gastov'rin Rom-nul has been away on a conference with our scientists that perform the experiments at our planet V'Am 2nd Sequester. He is not due back for several days or a week. Nothing happens until he returns."

His exotic insect face frowned. He had pulled Tawny's blouse open and was handling her bare breasts, squeezing them in puzzlement. "They are unusually hard. That is strange," he said, "and not very...satisfying. Not like the other humans we...acquired."

"Huh," Arianna snorted, "they're fake, big boy. Mine are real, natural, you want to see if I meet muster to take to your leader?" She lifted her blouse up, but Quamo's nose curled at her small, slightly sagging breasts.

He said to Tawny as she buttoned only the bottom half of her blouse, "I can smell the scent of many men on you, too many to count. The vile stink is revolting."

He sneered at Arianna, "There is a pure evil essence that wafts around you, it makes me feel...queasy." He signaled a group of guards. Twelve of them came to him.

Quamo said, "It is nice that you females looked forward to being a treat for our syntagma. But, since you are in a hurry, and the syntagma will much prefer the small blonde," he pointed at seven of the soldiers, "you males, that one is yours," he gestured to Arianna whose mouth dropped open.

Quamo turned to Tawny and said to the remaining soldier, "This one is for you to share."

Tawny slapped her hands on her hips in irritation. "Hey," she complained, "why does she get seven and I only get five?"

His mouth turned up on one side as he watched the seven men grab Arianna. They were already tearing at her clothes. He had to speak over her screams, "Because, since I warned you about talking, and alas, here you are, mouth flapping, I saved the most vicious for you." He nodded at the remaining five guards who immediately approached Tawny.

"Oh, okay then." Tawny smiled at the men. "I do like it rough, come on boys, let's do it!" She opened her arms to the men.

One instantly grabbed the front of her blouse and tore it open. As the others converged on her, she giggled and put her hands up over her head in a 'take me I'm yours' gesture.

The men picked her up and followed Arianna's screams that were disappearing into the jungle. Quamo and the first soldier stood watching them go.

"That bigger one isn't going to last as long as the smaller one," the soldier commented, "you gave her to the cannibal tribe."

Quamo tucked his hands behind his back and grinned. "I know. She was irritating me." A shudder rolled over his long shoulders. "And she felt like *kantin*, like Earth's plastic, ick. Let's get going."

In the cells it was dark, dank, cold. The captives had to sit or lie on the ground. Buckets were deposited in the corners to use for their waste. It wasn't much because they weren't fed much.

Kesi shared a cell with ten other women. Those that weren't bawling were gnashing their teeth in dire dread.

At first the women discussed in quiet tones what they thought was going to happen to them. Their ideas ranged from rape to torture, dissection, to food for the aliens or other animals, to selling them to other aliens on other planets for a zoo or to study.

A tall, chubby woman wringing her hands, tears in her voice stammered, "They- the- things, said something like the other camp folks didn't last long…"

"Yeah." The woman beside her snuffled, wiped at her runny nose, wailed, "He referred to us as good meat," her shoulders hunched into back-wrenching sobs.

"*Fresh* meat," another woman's quivering voice joined in. "He called us fresh meat. Oh God, what's to become of us?"

Near the bars, a female tried to peer out. She said softly, "We don't know what our fate is to be, except," her sigh quaking with dread, "it doesn't look promising."

They were kept locked up for over a week.

The soldiers had taken Kesi's pills from her. Lying down with her arms wrapped around her body, even with a fever, her body shook uncontrollably, and her teeth chattered without cease. She struggled to not throw up, or scream, as she went through withdrawal.

The seventh day, she was feeling better. Hungry, but better.

The eighth day, they came for her.

The soldiers' boots clomped in time as they marched down the hard packed earth floor of the cell chambers.

Some of the braver women clung to the bars and peered out to see what was going on.

Other than food brought to them once a day, no alien soldier had been there. The women had zero idea of what was happening, and how the men were faring.

They wondered where the children under 18 and their parents were. The rumor buzz was that Martier Dravidian had them removed prior to these new aliens invading the village. But were they dead or alive was the question floating about.

The peering women pushed themselves back against the walls out of reach of the approaching alien soldiers.

They needn't have worried; the soldiers had only come for Kesi.

Chapter Twenty-Six

One of the soldiers unlocked the barred cell door. He stalked inside, grabbed Kesi's arm and hauled her out the door.

As she was dragged down the dirt aisle, Gwanas and a few other women called out prayers to her as she was marched past them.

Starving and still recovering from her withdrawal, Kesi was dizzy and could barely walk a steady line. The seven foot tall guard practically carried her by her arm.

Silently, he brought her inside the main structure and to a set of stairs.

At the grainy staircase, he bent and lifted her up in his arms as she was obviously too weak to go up them on her own.

He took her to a room. Inside it was all sterile white. Two elderly female aliens were standing at attention as if waiting for them.

The guard set Kesi on a small divan. His voice a bit metallic sounding, he said to her, "The syntagma will be back on this planet soon. You will be prepared for him. Our experiments on the captured humans will not begin until you have satisfied his appetite."

Every inch of Kesi's skin shriveled with terror.

The soldier spun on his heel and left the room. A distinct click alerted Kesi he had locked the door from the outside.

She turned to the two females. They looked mostly human to her, but had the same odd-webbed hair and silvery-copper reptilian skin as Quamo.

About to ask them what was going to happen, the women came right to her, jerked her to her feet, and started to strip her.

"Hey!" Kesi fought them, but even if she had been feeling her best they were much stronger than her. "Please, tell me what's going to happen?"

Speaking to each other in a language Kesi did not understand, they didn't respond to her questions, or even look directly at her. They just stripped her naked and hauled her to a room with a massive tub filled with warm bubbles and scented salt crystals.

After two days of bathing and eating, the women dressed Kesi and brought her to stand by the door.

Her hair had been washed and styled, and they dressed her in a gown. It was not a material she'd ever felt before. Soft as a cloud, it clung like a second skin. The front of the shimmery, honey colored dress dipped in the front to expose the tops rounds of her breasts.

Sparkling embroidery trimmed the bodice, and two strips of the embroidered material went across her upper arms as off-the-shoulder sleeves. The back was very low, draping to the indentations where her bottom started, revealing her tiny waist and perfect onion-shaped tush.

The gown pooled slightly at the back of her pumps. Her toes peeped out slightly under the front of the dress. A slit exposed part of one leg.

Kesi stood in high spiked heels, and the tiniest underwear she'd ever worn. Just ribbons of red sheer silk swept across her breasts and her private parts.

The women still did not speak to her, but now in smattered English they clucked to each other about how thin she was, and small.

Making tsking sounds, one snipped, "I do not ever understand the syntagma's, or any of the soldiers' interest in the human females, but," she shrugged, "regardless, this one is not going to last long."

Her cold eyes drew over Kesi in derision, there wasn't a shred of compassion in the buggy eyes. Arms like heavy lengths of rope crossed over her body. Built like a thick, ropey lamppost, flat on both sides like an iron, she just shook her head at Kesi.

The other woman's empty gaze swept Kesi with indifference, as if she was too insignificant for her to consider wasting her thoughts on.

She spoke through pursed thin lips, "Who knows about males, they have such...ludicrous cravings. How they could prefer this tiny, soft, shapely female to our stalwart iron-corded bodies is a mystery, eh?" Her mouth kinked in a sly smile to her friend.

Speaking in English, she wanted Kesi to understand her. "Whatever, Shaihlene, better her than us. At least we will see the sun rise tomorrow. We will not die after an eve's of," both women grinned metal teeth at Kesi, "ungodly torture."

The soldier that had brought Kesi there entered the room. His gaze poured down her figure. The only change in him was the dilating of each tiny section of his overlarge pupils.

"Ah," Shaihlene groused, "even Ketter there desires the small human."

Without a word, he wrapped long hard fingers around Kesi's slender arm and led her out of the room.

When he'd brought her there he had strode quickly practically dragging her behind, now, he held her lightly and moved at her speed which wasn't very fast in consideration to the dress and the spiked heels.

He didn't speak, and Kesi didn't think he would answer any of her questions so they trod in silence.

They traveled the length of the structure before he stopped at a large, wide, high-arched door with gold bordering and an elaborate gold handle. Guards stood posted on either side of it.

He knocked sharply three times then opened the door and ushered Kesi in.

The room was vast with cushioned chairs that appeared to be red velvet but not actually velvet material. Divans, tables, chandeliers, everything was opulent and ornate. It looked like an alien's idea of a harem's chamber.

But what held Kesi's attention was the male standing with his hands clasped behind his back staring at her.

The soldier pulled her to stand in front of him, then with a brief bow to the male, clicked his heels and moved to the side of the room.

The well over seven foot tall male was strikingly handsome in a fiercely menacing, chilling, foreign way. Through the waves of grisly violence and utter sociopathic sadism spewing from his dark eyes, lust roiled in layers up and down and over Kesi. He wore white pants, tunic, white boots; the webbing of black hair was slicked off to the side.

A smarmy, parasitic smile creased his coppery face. "Ah, they spoke the truth, you my dear, are quite extraordinary." He walked around her, checking her out from every angle. He noted with abstraction, "Stunning."

Kesi forced herself not to cower.

The syntagma drew his fingers through her hair. "Oh my, soft as the clouds of Sumpfleue region." A finger caressed her cheek, he cooed, "Silk." His gaze lit on her lips. "Damn, crimson drops I can't wait to taste."

He laughed. "Those amazing eyes, the way they glower at me shows spunk, gods I love a fiery female."

He leaned in, sniffed, "*Ah*," he hummed, eyes closed as he savored her scent. "I am going to just eat you up, you smell utterly divine, fresh, young, female." His fingers tunneled down her cleavage, she jerked from him.

Chuckling, he was instantly enamored. Delighted with his prize, he smiled. "Time enough for that later."

"You touch me and I will hurt you," Kesi uttered her silly threat. Her cheeks pinked at his mocking roar of laughter at her empty warning. He was enormous, and she had not a weapon, her threat was comical.

His big mouth turned way up at the edges in joy. "I've hit the jackpot. Gorgeous, fresh, tender," his gaze gobbled down her form. "Feisty, and the dulcet voice of the sweetest red-red roses of Sector Four. Your lovely screams will ring melodiously through the halls. We will get better acquainted my dear, shortly."

Without taking his eyes off of her, he waved a hand with one swoop to the guard and commanded, "Bring her to my chambers, prepare her. I have some things to see to, and then," he lifted a hand and slid a large bony finger across

Kesi's lips. He pushed the finger in her mouth, then pulled it out tugging her mouth up. He dragged his wet finger down her jaw.

"Gods, I hope you last. I would like to have you more than once. Hmmm." His eyes glowed preternaturally at her. "I will have to take care to not break you too soon. Perhaps if I am very, very careful I can bring you to my home planet and play with you there until you expire."

Then a frown wrinkled his forehead. "Although, I did promise you to my men if you survived a night with me. Well, we'll see how things go."

He stuck his finger in his mouth and licked it. His eyes closed in delight. "Yes, delicious. I can't wait." He motioned to Ketter. "Take her."

Kesi struggled, but the guard was enormous. Long and lean and strong as a bull, he walked her out the door, down the hall and into another room with no effort.

The room was sumptuous. Everything lavish in white and gold, plush chairs and a sofa decorated with fringed shiny pillows filled the outskirts of the room. Gilded mirrors and some unusual artwork decorated the walls.

On a glass table sat a crystal bowl of fruit as well as several carafes of different colored liquids, along with crystal flutes.

Kesi's eyes beelined to the huge bed. Covered with luxurious satin sheets and pillows, above it on the ceiling was another gilded mirror. It was one of the few chambers in the building that contained a window. Natural sunlight sifted through illuminating the golden cage.

Ketter hauled Kesi to the bed, easily lifted her and laid her on the huge mattress. She immediately tried to roll away to escape off the other side of the bed, but the male grabbed her wrist in an iron grip and snapped a restraint over it.

His uber-long arms reached over her and snagged her other wrist. Her struggles were futile; he had the strength of twenty human men. Next, he secured each of her ankles, tugged her dress down after pausing at a glimpse of her female parts then stood back and stared at her.

He was clearly thinking about how much he could get away with touching her, and more. His excessively long tongue swirled over his lips as if tasting her, like a frog swathing a fly.

Then, his webby brows darted down between his insect eyes. To touch anything that belonged to the syntagma meant a prolonged, agonizing death. His eyes hopped to Kesi's terrified and furious blues. Shaking his head, if he touched her she would no doubt blab.

Sounding like he spoke through a long drainpipe, the soldier said, "You are lucky, Chosen One, the syntagma is delaying his use of…torment devices in hopes that you might last longer than the others. Normally, the comfort of a bed is not part of his…fornicating."

He took one last hungry look at her, regretfully shook his head then turned and left her alone.

Kesi didn't dare call out for help; heaven knows it might only bring more of the hideous creatures. She tugged at her hands, the restraints were drilled into the wall. The ankle restraints were bound to the legs of the bed.

Her own fate up in the air, Kesi worried about the others, wondering how they were faring. About Martier.

He had covered his ears and head because he obviously didn't want these aliens to realize he was one too, but not one of them, which was why he stayed in disguise. Maybe he could get free and come and save her before-

Her chest hitched with a silent sob of hopeless despair. Martier was incarcerated in the impenetrable cell, he was as trapped as she. And that- king creature thing had every intention of hurting her, violating her, then if she survived, he would turn her over to his soldiers.

The truth struck her like a flat whip. If she survived until the aliens' time when they were done with their mission, the king alien said he planned to take her to some foreign planet where she would die after prolonged agonizing torture.

She wouldn't even have the blessing of being buried on her mother Earth. It was her punishment for daring to grasp at fleeting happiness with Martier. He, an outlaw and Kesi an officer of the law. Paybacks, she guessed it was for letting herself get involved with a criminal.

Deep anguish twisted her petrified gut, constricted her lungs, she strove to keep the tears in. She couldn't just lie there and let him come for her. She had to fight.

Kesi pulled, twisted, yanked, then wrenched at her restraints as hard as she could. They weren't going to come out of the walls, but, she could feel her hand sliding in the cuffs. She jerked, ripping at her own hands, tearing her skin off the outsides of them, until, one hand pulled free!

It took twice as long to get free of the other one. Scooting down on the bed, she realized if she took her shoes off, it was tight, but she was able to slide the cuffs off her feet, losing some more skin but it was worth it.

Kesi scrambled off the bed and quickly glanced around the room searching for an escape. She saw nothing viable, even the window was up too high for her to get out. "What now?"

Slipping the heels back on, she crept through the room and to the door. Amazingly there was no one else, no guards, inside the lux chamber. Tiptoeing to the door, she leaned her ear against the solid material. She thought she could hear rumblings of voices but wasn't sure.

"Well," she whispered to herself, "it's now or never. I wait for that creature to return and I'm dead meat. I can't stand here and hope someone will rescue me. No girl," she muttered, "you are on your own." And Martier thought Arianna was the fiend to fear. She had nothing on these horrendous monsters."

Kesi wondered what Martier knew about the murderous aliens. She assumed they were the reason he and his men had taken over the village in the first place.

But why? Why leave the defenseless villagers as well as themselves trapped as sitting ducks waiting for the aliens to come pluck them away without a fight?

Holding her breath, she lifted the handle to the door. *It was unlocked*! That stupid freak had been arrogantly sure of his restraints. Very slowly, Kesi pulled the door open. When it was open far enough, she carefully peeked out.

The corridor was wide and made of the limestone. Peering down the hall, she yanked her head back. There were three soldiers at the end. She waited, it didn't seem that they saw her.

She poked her head back out and observed them.

They were in a huddle and smoke rose through the center of them. Just like stoners on Earth, they were getting a buzz off who knows what. Their masculine giggles rambled down the otherwise empty hall.

She had to take the chance. Peeling the shoes off to prevent their noise on the gritted calcite, she slid the sling backs over her fingers and slipped out of the room in her bare feet, closing the door silently behind her.

Her eyes on the soldiers, she gathered up a handful of the gown and stealthily made her way in the opposite direction.

Breath held and heart hammering like pounding drums, Kesi made it to an open doorway. It was a staircase.

Listening carefully, hearing nothing, she slid into the opening, and hurried down the stairs. The steps led to another corridor with several wide doors. Sneaking quietly, Kesi moved as quickly as she dared along the hallway.

The doors she passed were closed.

She kept going, then, she heard cries, desperate cries, and blood-curdling screams. Her heart battering against the inside of her ribcage, she headed towards the cries.

At an open doorway, her hand pressed hard against her fluttering chest, Kesi peered inside, and about peed her pants.

Some of the villagers from Brutální were chained to gurneys. There were tubes sticking into most. A few were laying already flayed open and dead.

She glanced at those deceased, they were wraith thin, then she realized they weren't from Brutální. They must have been the victims from the camp the soldier had referred to. Moans, wheezing, gasping, weeping, every still alive person was in terrible physical distress.

Halfway in the doorway, Kesi could see an alien guard talking to a human man in a white lab coat. They hadn't noticed her. She considered running for help, but the people were in agony, some on death's last thread. Besides, where would she get help from?

Slipping into the room, she put her shoes on and spotted an iron bar leaning against a gurney. Kesi picked it up and carried it a few feet then set it down behind a table.

Then she sauntered only a couple of steps further into the room. Tugging the front of her dress lower to expose more cleavage, she cooed, "Hey boys."

The two males' heads shot up. They both gawked at her with mouths foolishly hanging open and eyes wide.

"You wanna have some fun?" Kesi invited, staying near the table.

"What the-" The man in the white coat froze, stamped across his face was, 'Where the hell had this female come from?'

The guard, letting his hanging tongue lead him, tramped right over to her. He was much smaller than the other soldier guards.

"Jawls Hell, yeah, wow," he blathered. His bugged out eyes traveled the length of her then settled on her breasts.

In her most wanton voice, Kesi tossed her curls back and said, "You like the front view? How about the back?" She turned around, looked back coyly over her shoulder at him, and shook her ass.

His eyes about tumbled out of his head. "Oh human…" He came right up to her, his hands stretched out to catch her around the waist.

Kesi quickly bent and grabbed the bar- putting her body weight into the turn she slung it as hard as could, slamming it into his unsuspecting head. Without a sound, he crumpled to the floor and Kesi hit him again.

Blinking the shock away, gathering his wits, the doctor rushed to her.

Kesi faked a half swing at him- He ducked, lifted his arm in defense and she bashed his arm breaking it. He let out a howl and fell to the ground.

Swiftly, she brought the bar down hard on his shins, breaking them both. The doctor writhed on the floor screaming.

Standing over him with the bar in one hand, she held out the other and said, "Give me the keys to the restraints or I will bash your head in."

When he just kept crying, she lifted the rod in threat.

Gasping in pain, he wailed, "All right, all right, they're right there on that hook." He motioned to the door with his head. Lying on his side, one arm and both legs broken, he sobbed.

Kesi hurried and grabbed up the keys then ran around unlocking everyone's, except the deceased, restraints.

Yanking out tubes and wires, and other things she didn't even want to think what they could be for, she helped them off the gurneys and to the door.

Sticking her head out to make sure it was clear, Kesi waved the prisoners on. She whispered, "Everyone, come with me, don't make a sound." Soft moans and sniffing quieted as they quickly shuffled behind her.

Not knowing where she was going in the labyrinth building, she just kept moving with the group trailing behind her helping one another stay upright, until she reached what appeared to be an exit door.

She pulled and pulled at the handle, it moved but she couldn't get the big heavy door open. Several of the men silently nudged her out of the way and managed to get it open.

Kesi urged, "Okay, everyone, hurry, run for the jungle, stay together and-"

A guard suddenly appeared out of nowhere.

The villagers fled through the open door.

With a snarling shout, the guard grabbed Kesi, slapped her in fury, and immediately tossed her over his shoulder. He looked out the door but the villagers were already scattering into the dense forest.

It was the same guard, Ketter, who had brought her to the head creature.

He carried her back upstairs. Kesi's torso flopped helplessly over his hard back, her body quaking with terror, there was no point in protesting or struggling.

He brought her back to the king's chambers and tossed her roughly on the bed.

"Thank the gods I came across you, human, it would have meant my life if the syntagma had returned to find you were gone. I've a good mind to-" He raised his hand to strike her again, but Kesi scuttled back from him.

Instead, he just grabbed her, pushed her down and tied her to the bed, ensuring the restraints were too tight to get out of again.

Standing back and glaring at her he said, "You are going to be so sorry when the syntagma hears what you've done, releasing those specimens. But don't worry," his ruthless sneer devoid of pity, "there are plenty more where they came from."

"You are a despicable animal!" Kesi shrieked at him fighting her restraints to no avail.

Blinking his insect eyes at her, he could care less what she thought of him. "Later you sneaky little *britvta*, that is bitch to you. After the syntagma is done with you, I'll be back to clean the blood off you.

"If you still live tomorrow, I might be splinting up your broken bones, eh? Anything else would be beyond repair. Then he may let me have my time with you. Ta ta," he sneered meanly and leered at her body.

The dress was shoved up exposing her slender shapely legs and the red silk panties. The guard had pulled the top down trying to get a look at her breasts as he was binding her. More, rather than less of her breasts were bared.

He'd had tastes of human females before and he couldn't wait to get his shot at this one. Stunning in looks, he also wanted to make her pay for almost putting his head on the block with her near escape and releasing the specimens. A breath of relief stuttered out Ketter's long reptilian throat.

But now, no one would know how the specimens got away and he had her back in this room where the syntagma had wanted her held.

The injured doctor would only be able to say that one of the human females had managed to get free and helped the others escape. They would assume it was one of the specimens.

The doctor had never seen this human before, he wouldn't know to tell the syntagma that it was she who got loose and set the others free.

Wiping the back of his hand to clear the drool out of the corner of his mouth, Ketter was again considering what he could get away with before the syntagma returned.

Chapter Twenty-Seven

The men were not only locked in the cells, they were also chained. The V'Am were taking no chances on anyone escaping and raising an alarm. If they were found out they would have to pull up stakes and hit another rural, sparsely inhabited area.

How many villages could they burn before they were more intensely investigated? Soon they would have to go to a different country.

His wrists cuffed, Martier paced the cell, it was all he'd been able to do for days. They couldn't make their move yet. All he could think about was Kesi. He didn't know if she was being fed, beaten, raped, killed.

They were fairly certain nothing would happen until the syntagma returned. The soldier aliens they'd managed to question said all of the women were still locked in their cells.

Trae and Slade sat on the ground with their backs against the gritty limestone wall. Their eyes closed, they conserved their energy.

Near the bars, Martier noticed a sudden influx of activity, excitement. The guards were rushing around and chattering. Moving nearer to listen, Martier picked up a conversation.

A soldier was saying, "Oh yes, she is as breathtaking as described. The syntagma is dumfounded with desire for her. He's had her dressed for him and brought to his rooms."

His snicker was laced with jealousy. "He has those, apparatus, toys, he likes to play with his females before fucking them every which way, you know?"

Another replied, "Uh huh. I've been in the room a few times when he's *played* with them. He gets insane with rage when he accidentally kills them before he's done. It is sick, true, but, still stimulating watching a nude female chained belly down over that horse apparatus and he gets those huge plier things-" the voices trailed away as they moved from the area.

Martier said to Trae, "Tis time. I will not wait any longer. Give the signal, *now*."

Standing up, Trae whistled, and he, Slade and Martier proceeded to break their chains.

A creature evolved like a ghostly vapor around Martier and he appeared to grow double the size of what he was. His teeth descended, sharpening and lengthening like a king cobra. The horns swelled knocking the hat off, and claws emerged from his thickening fingers.

At the same time Trae and Slade were developing somewhat the same but not exactly.

The three men pulled their wrists apart easily snapping the steel cuffs.

Martier stood at the iron bars, gripped one in each hand, and pulled them apart like they were made of butter.

Stepping through, Martier didn't waste words, he raced to the exit of the cells so fast he was a blur of color.

When he shot out of the dungeons, several stunned soldiers stared at him. He took that advantage and ran up to the closest one, grabbed his neck, twisted it, let the carcass fall and Martier took his dagger.

The soldiers drew their weapons, firearms, and knives, and attacked Martier.

An enormous beast had morphed into and over Martier so completely that his normal face and body were unrecognizable. He was gigantic and vicious, crazed and hideously fearsome. Flames of fire flashed and danced around his feet.

Almost invisible, in a whirlwind, he crossed the grounds to the main fortress, tearing around the area, fighting soldier after soldier, stabbing, punching, kicking, slashing necks with his claws, and stomping on heads, crushing skulls, ripping bodies asunder.

In only moments, he had shredded his way to the main building. Inside, more soldiers surged out like warrior ants, swarming and attacking him. Martier swirled around the room same as outside, slashing, stabbing, slaughtering anything in his way.

Trae raced in at his back taking out the perimeter soldiers circling the room.

Martier caught an alien soldier around the neck in a steel-clawed grip, lifted him off the ground by his neck and squeezed until the male turned blue then he released him slightly, and said, "Tell me where the blonde female is that they were taking to the syntagma."

The alien kicked out but held up in the air by his neck he had no leverage. His eyes bulged out of his head at the terrifying monster that gripped him.

Martier squeezed hard again, hissing through his lethal fangs, he promised with a growling voice, "You tell me quick and your death will be painless."

His tongue hanging out of his mouth, gasping for air, the alien stared into Martier's beastly eyes. The words scraped through his clenched throat, "Upstairs, fourth door on the right."

Martier gripped his head with his other hand and snapped his neck. Dropping the male, he glanced at Trae.

Still battling soldiers, Trae shouted, "I have this, *má bráthair*. Slade is releasing the people. Cisco searches for the ship, and Jamir the communications. Go."

Martier nodded and raced for the stairs.

He tore down the hall, his creature transforming back into his normal size and frame. Martier didn't bother with the door handle to the room he crashed through the door and jolted inside.

Syntagma Gastov'rin Rom-nul was on top of Kesi trying to get her dress off without removing her restraints. She was shrieking and struggling, but she was tightly bound.

With a roared war cry, "*Aragha!*" Martier ran across the room and launched himself at the alien leader. He smashed into Rom-nul so hard the two men hurled over the bed and crashed to the floor.

As soon as they hit the floor, Martier commenced thrashing the syntagma without pausing or taking a breath.

Rom-nul screamed, tried to fight back but was ineffective against Martier's superior strength and ability.

Martier just slammed him with his big fists again and again until the creature was unrecognizable, a bloody pulpy mess of reptilian skin and bones oozed on the bloodied floor. Green and silver goo spread around the body.

Trae entered the room. He nodded to Kesi lying on the bed with a crooked grin. "Hey sweetheart, nice to see you still breathing."

He reached Martier and said calmly, "Enough, *bráthair*, we need him alive." He reached down and gripped one of Martier's still swinging arms to stop him.

Martier stopped pummeling the syntagma and sat back on his heels, wiping sweat from his forehead and allowed Trae to drag the unconscious, virtually demolished Rom-nul by his webbed hair across the room and out the door.

Huffing and puffing, Martier's body was almost back to normal, the beast was fully mutated back in, his chest pumping quick shallow breaths, biceps strained from the fighting. He got to his feet and stumbled to the bed.

He grinned down at Kesi. "Aye, *nĕkolika*, this is how I like you, restrained and splayed out, ready for me."

Kesi was relieved to see Martier, that he was safe and well, and had rescued her just about in the nick of time.

But, she was lying there spread eagle with her dress up around her hips exposing the thread of red material over her privates, bodice torn open to reveal the tiny red silk bra that was barely containing her mounded breasts.

She growled at him, "Can you stop ogling me and get me out of here? And don't grope me while you're doing it…please," the last words slipped out weak, strained.

That drew a sharp look from him. "Have they-"

"Never mind," she said with a sigh, "it's over. Please, just get me loose."

Martier couldn't help it, needing to touch her, he set his palm on the side of her face, so grateful she was in one piece.

After hearing from the guards what Rom-nul did to his attractive female captives, his stomach had been tied up in knots in dreaded fear he wouldn't get to her in time. This is why he never got involved with anyone on a mission.

A tender smile softened his hard face as he slashed the binds on first one wrist with his claws then the other. Caring about someone on a mission, other than his men, could be death for her, as well as if anyone knew how important she was to him.

She could be captured and used to control him. But he had fallen too hard and too fast for her, and there sure weren't going to be any other females for him after this, missions or not.

"There you go, baby," he said, releasing the last ankle restraint then helped her to sit up with her legs hanging off the edge of the bed.

He sat down beside her and wrapped his arms around her. Kesi jammed her face in his chest and wept.

Martier stroked her hair, whispered soothing foreign words in her ear mixed with English, "Tis all over now, sweetheart, tis done."

He was fishing for her face so he could kiss her when Slade came into the room like a swashbuckling pirate.

Boots clomping across the floor, sword he took from someone in his hand, he said cheerfully, "Hey, Kesindra, good to see you are safe. This big lug was driving us bonkers with his worry for you."

To Martier, he said, "Your little honey is a hero," he grinned at Kesi in Martier's arms. "She had managed to get out of her restraints here earlier and escaped. Made her way downstairs and to the lab where they were committing atrocities on the humans. She took out a guard and a doctor with an iron bar, and liberated the captives being experimented on.

"She was helping them escape out the door when she was recaptured and brought back up here. A couple of villagers that escaped stayed back to see if they could help any others trapped inside and told us what Kesi had done."

Martier's smile was broad and proud. "Ah, I always said you were a brave woman with a heart the size of the sun, my precious," he nuzzled her nose then kissed her. The smile turned to a scolding frown.

"But you should have just run. Next time, don't think about others, think only of getting your own skin out of the fire. You hear me?" Sighing when she didn't answer him, he said, "Let us get the hell out of here, okay?"

"I'm ready." Kesi exhaled in relief.

Martier helped her off the bed. Her radiant complexion caught his eye. "You look, healthy, there are roses in you cheeks, your skin is not so drawn and wan, and your eyes are veritably sparkling."

Her lips pursed in a small moue of casualness. "When I was locked in the cell, they had taken my pills."

He grabbed her upper arms in concern. "Oh, baby, withdrawals, you could have died. Dammit, I never thought about it. I should have sent you out with the children. But I thought foolishly you would be safer with me, and we thought you might tell the authorities about us and all would be lost. I am so sorry."

She caressed his hard cheek. "Don't be. You were right, I was hiding behind them. Stuffing my guilt and shame and anguish instead of dealing with it. Yeah, it was rough," she shrugged calmly, "but I got through it and it's over."

He bent and kissed her gently, sweetly, said softly, "I am so proud of you, Kesindra, always was and always will be."

"Okay, kids, let's get a move on," Slade said, leading the way to the door. He told Martier, "We got the ship, the communications, and Trae has what's left of Rom-nul after you were done with him. You can say the mission was a success."

The three trod down the hall, Kesi asked, "What exactly was the mission?"

His arm wrapped tightly around her, Martier explained, "We were sent here to find Rom-nul. We knew he was taking entire villages captive and killing them after doing abominable things to them.

"They let the very young and elderly go because they were useless for their experiments. They did not want a mass of bodies to be found and set of questions, so they shoved them off to die in the belly of the jungle assuming the dangers of the jungle would quickly dispose of most of them.

"Although some of the youngsters made it, few outsiders believed their tale. The villages that were taken were so rural and so small, that when each town emptied and the law came checking, they all assumed the people had left on their own and assimilated into other villages. They ignored the few relatives that came to them asking for help in locating their missing kin."

"That is so outrageous," Kesi commented shaking her head.

"Aye. Lazy, incompetent police work, just like Dempsey. Anyway, word got to us through the communicators that are living here on Earth. So we flew here and started investigating. But, no one knew where his fortress was, we could not find it.

"The only way to locate Rom-nul was to let ourselves get captured along with the residents of Brutální. We have others of us placed around other towns because we were not sure which town would get hit next. Brutální was closest to the last village taken so we went there.

"We took over the town first to have control over who came and went. We put our guards around the borders, and sent the elderly and the children and their parents out to safety when we knew the V'Ams' arrival was imminent.

"The children are all in Milčent now. Our perimeter troops stayed hidden and then followed us to the fortress. If we had trouble, they would have been there to save everyone."

Listening to him, Kesi walked pensively with her head down.

When they got outside, Martier's soldiers were gathering the villagers to take them back home. It was noisy but not chaotic. Everyone was scared and relieved, and in shock. Martier's people had called in buses to take the villagers back to Brutální.

They reached one of the busses people were loading onto.

Martier said, "I have to stay until every bit of this shit here is cleaned up. Any soldiers still alive will be brought as prisoners to an air-station where they will then be transported to a planet where they will be...interrogated. I want you to go back now and wait for me in Brutální."

Staring in stiff contemplation at the ground, Kesi didn't answer him.

He asked her, "What is wrong?" As he spoke, he unbuttoned his bloodstained shirt, took it off leaving a T-shirt on under it, and dropped it over her.

The dress that freak had forced her to wear and with the bodice torn, was a neon sign telling men to feel free to grab at her. He'd rather she looked war-torn than available. No one but him needed to see those breasts.

She looked blankly down at the shirt then raised her eyes slowly, coldly to his. She stated flatly, "You never told me who you were. You could have told me, you knew I was on the side of the law."

"Kesindra," he started to answer her. But she kept moving. Then she stopped abruptly.

"Who, what are you, really? I saw the...thing...you transformed into, it was disappearing when you entered the room, but it was still there."

She wrapped her arms around her body and shivered recalling the sight of the gigantic beast surrounding Martier as he burst into the room.

"The other warriors with you, they don't have horns. But they do have...fangs, like that horrible creature, Bruglon."

Martier set his hands on his hips. How to explain this to her, there was no sugarcoating it. But he tried to think of a way anyway.

"Uh, I..." he turned his head, watched people boarding the buses. He looked back at her. "Kesindra, there is a...lot to tell you. This conversation would be better done privately and when we are both back in Brutální where we can-"

"Tell me right now."

His shoulders bunched, head lowered before he looked steadily at her and took a deep breath, let it out slow, ponderous. "Ah, we are a sort of inter-galactic private police. I am from Nasitar. My great-great-great etc. grandfather is, was, Lucifer. Uh, you know, Satan. The original one."

Yellow brows sprung into her hairline with disbelief. "What? How on Earth could that be?"

He chuckled. "Well, tis not exactly on Earth, honey. More like the...cosmos." It would take a minute or so for

Kesi to absorb and digest this information. Martier waited patiently, studying her to see if she was repulsed...or what?

Eyes wide with incredulity, she struggled to comprehend what he told her. Her gaze hard and direct, she watched him for a hint of joking, or lying.

But, he just stared steadfast at her, his expression profoundly serious. The horns, fangs, claws, the monster that encircled him, yes, he spoke the truth, he was...the Devil's grandson.

A quiver spiraled through her body. This was something that was going to take some time, a lot of time, to reconcile to. If she could at all. It was too much to fathom. Way too much. "You- should have told me, before...we...did it."

Tension cramped into his shoulders, his fingers dug into his hips. Her body stiffened, she leaned away from him, her eyes clouded with confusion, rejection. She was not taking the information well. Great. He might as well lay it all on her now.

"Um, Kesindra, I have something else to tell you."

She couldn't prevent herself from taking a step back from him, her arms raised to cross over her breasts. "What more could there be?"

Seeing there was going to be a battle, the bronze color seeped from his face leaving his cheeks unnerving red. He was going to have to win her all over again.

His chest swelled with a huge uncomfortable breath, letting it out, he told her, "When we made love the very first time, my horns pierced your back. At that time, fluid, with my, what you might call my DNA, was in it and it entered into you. It, uh, will, in about a year or so, turn you immortal."

"What!" Her head shook while she blinked rapidly trying to grasp all he was telling her. "How, I mean, is that true? Is there any way to undo it?"

He coughed, clearing the knot in his throat, shook his head slightly. "Nay."

Mouth dropping open in incomprehensible shock, her eyes so wide the whites were clear around the blue irises, Kesi stared horrorstruck at him.

The guilt of what he had done flushed crystal clear on his hard face, flooding it with dark color. He wrapped one arm around his waist, rested his elbow on it, and tapped the tips of his fingers on his mouth.

"How could you?" Her voice shrill and tight, Kesi dropped her hands, clenching her fists at her side. The two of them were completely oblivious to the crowd ebbing and flowing as the people continued boarding the busses. "How could you do something life-changing like that without asking me, telling me?"

Feet shuffling awkwardly, out of the corner of his eye he caught Trae across the grounds watching them with a grinning smirk.

"Baby, listen, I could not live through eternity without you. There was no way I was going to sit there and watch you slowly shrivel and die, or get a dreaded disease, or get killed. It took...eons, for me to find you. You are my eternal mate. I do not want an existence without you."

"But- but, you didn't ask me, then you didn't even *tell* me you did it! You can't do something like that, you just can't." Kesi covered her eyes with her hands as she struggled to take this all in.

He had known she would take it badly, but she was more horrified than he had expected at everything he'd told her.

He should have talked more with his brother, Devilos, about how he handled this with his mate.

Devilos had told him to just do it, like he had with his mate, and tell her about it later. She would be pissed, but she will, should, eventually accept it. He should have asked him how fucking long would that take?

"Uh," he stammered awkwardly, a lopsided grin ticked up the side of his mouth, "how about I let you spank me as punishment?"

Not amused, face white as a sheet, Kesi's eyes flashed angry blue lightning at him. "This isn't funny, Martier." She started to walk from him.

He grabbed her arm, holding her back. "Where are you going? We need to talk about this."

She turned furious at him, voice harsh, tone hurt, "We are done talking. I am getting on a bus. Right now. Let go of me."

They glowered at each other. Then he pulled her close to him. "Sweetheart, please, I know it was wrong, but if I had told you ahead of time and you said no, well," he shrugged, "I would have done it anyway and that would have been worse than not telling you. Right?" Now he wasn't so sure.

Tugging at her arm, she snapped, "You took away my choice, my rights. You stand there and tell me you- you're the- the devil, then you tell me you injected me without my consent with…stuff that's supposed to change me." Her lips pursed with repulsion, she asked fearfully, "Will I grow…horns…and things too?"

That drew his brows down. Piqued, he snapped angrily, "You did not seem to mind my *things* when they were sending you to the moon."

Her horror made his stomach twist. "Nay," he said quietly, "you will only have immortality, you will not age from the age you are right now. You will not get my *things*."

He tried to tell himself her disgust was really fear. In truth, his fangs, horns, claws, and other things had given an extraordinary side to their sex that sent them both into explosions of unnatural, yet insanely intense orgasms.

He rubbed both his hands up and down her arms and pleaded, "Kesindra, please, get back to what we had, have, together. Nothing has changed just because now you have…different knowledge."

She jerked her arms from his grasp and stalked to the closest bus.

When she reached it, he grabbed her again and pressed her up against the metal side of the vehicle. Ignoring the interested glances from people, he said, "When I return to Brutální we will sit down and discuss this. You will have a few days to let the…information settle by then."

His hands on her waist, thumbs rubbing her sides, he said with all due seriousness, "None of this changes a thing. You are mine. I will not let you go. So, make peace with it."

"You had sex with me without telling me you were a…the devil, then you injected me with…whatever," her head lowered, she stared at the ground shaking her head.

My God, she'd had sex with the devil. A real live, true freaking devil. It was way beyond comprehension, she just could not fathom it, take it in. Digest it. A quiver roiled through her body, she crossed her arms over her chest in a protective mode.

His sigh arduous, he cupped her chin, raised it, kissed her lightly.

When she didn't respond he let her go. "I will see you back in the village. We will talk it out. You will see, it will all be fine." It better be, or he'd be taking a livid, battling Kesindra to Nasitar. Because he was not going home without her.

Without looking at him, Kesi hurried to the steps and boarded the bus. She was the last one on.

The bus cranked up and headed down a dirt path, away from the fortress.

Martier stood and watched it until it passed into the canopy of green jungle blending in until it was out of sight.

Chapter Twenty-Eight

$\mathcal{T}$wo months had passed.

Back home in Ships Bay, after her debriefing, Kesi had been sent back to the academy to complete it.

The past thirty or so days she'd been submerged in studies, and had made a few friends there. Four of those new friends were sitting in her apartment waiting for her to get dressed.

"Come on, Supergirl, get a move on, it's time our celebrity goes out and celebrates," a young woman near Kesi's own age chided her as she sauntered into Kesi's bedroom.

Since she had solved the murder cases and rescued some of the villagers trapped in the fortress, Kesi had earned a new nickname that she abhorred.

Sure she received a commendation, however, due to that time when her team blew it and the kidnapped woman died, the black smirch in her record will prevent her from ever being promoted.

Clothes were strewn over the bed and on a chair as she hadn't been able to decide what to wear. All four girls had brought her outfits to try on so she wouldn't wear as they called them, 'crappy ass clothes' she normally donned to hide behind.

Kesi pulled her attention from her reflection and turned it to the girl with cheerful brown eyes and long brown hair that curled at the bottom of her shoulders.

"Val, really, I don't feel like celebrating. I really don't want to go out."

The sun had long set. Outside the window a cool silver moon softly outlined dark trees in the back yard. Kesi had pulled the white ruffled curtains back. Ever since that hideous time in the fortress, she wanted to be able to see the outdoors.

Val moved in front of Kesi to look into the mirror over the dresser. Using Kesi's brush, she brushed her own long hair and said, "It's a good thing I brought my little sister's clothes, the rest of us are too big in one way or another for you to fit in our clothes. You would look just as awful as you normally do."

"Gee, thanks," Kesi muttered.

"Oh, you know what I mean. You have the most amazing figure but you hide it under all that baggy stuff. Come on already, let's go."

She caught up Kesi's arm and pulled her from her bedroom to the living room where the other girls waited. Chattering and laughter wafted through the hall.

"Yeah," Val said, as they walked down the short hallway, "you haven't felt like doing anything except going to school since you returned."

Val stopped and brushed Kesi's curls off her shoulder letting them bounce down her back. "Kesi, honey, it's time you got over that…whatever he was, that alien creature, that Jersey told us about. Sure, I heard he was gorgeous, in a hard, fierce, warrior-scary kind of way, but he's gone, and you're here. You will never see him again."

Kesi's heart clenched, her throat hitched at Val's words. She swallowed back the tears that had threatened since she left Původně and returned home to Ships Bay.

She hadn't stayed and waited for Martier to return. She was so furious and indignant that he had taken her choice from her to decide whether or not to have…immortality, and whatever other biologicals he had deemed his decision to flood her body with.

Even now the idea was just preposterous. She didn't feel any different. Well, yeah, she did. Her heart ached with such a severe pain some days so much with missing him, that she thought she would keel over and die.

Yeah, she admitted, she missed Martier. Her body craved his. She missed his deep foreign drawl, sinister growl when he covered her body with his big, muscled- *ahh,* that wasn't helping things.

She needed to get over him. Move on. She couldn't be with a- a- devil anyway.

Even that idea struck her as absurd until she recalled his horns, fangs…sigh, those fangs that stabbed so deliciously into her flesh. And his claws that circled, gripped, and pierced her breasts while he drove deep and hard into her.

Darn, her panties were growing wet, she could feel them. Ultimately she owed her life to Martier. He had saved her just in time.

But, Val was right, she would never see Martier again. He was probably already in a totally different solar system much less planet than her. And she was probably not even a tiny faded memory in his mind. There were galaxies of women that he could have with barely a nod.

She blinked hard to dispel the memories of his tough face topped with wavy blond hair. That massive chest covered with thick masculine hair she loved curling against, soaking in his protective warmth, *sigh*. His way too hot, hard muscled body, and his kisses. Yeah, could that demon kiss-

"Kes!" Val shouted. "Stop thinking about him. Oh no, don't deny it, your flushed face is all sad and haunted and dreamy." She patted Kesi's shoulder.

"Listen, there are tons more fish in the sea. Fish of your own kind. You come with us tonight, drink, dance, you will undoubtedly find a dude to take your mind off…the…alien." Val shivered. Just the thought was eerie, scary, and somehow mysteriously titillating.

"Anyway, you're so gorgeous now that you don't wear those crazy hats and those horrible tinted glasses you used to wear. The men fall all over themselves to get your attention." She linked her arm with Kesi's and they entered the living room.

"Yeah girl, I wish I had the bait you were blessed with," Susanna, with long pretty blonde hair and hazel eyes, nice legs, but slightly chubby, trilled from her chair.

"You guys ready? I'm dying to hit the bars and drink drink drink!" Cathy got up from her chair pulling down her short skirt and fluffing wavy dark hair. "I got a hunkerin' for some sausage, I want me some man meat, girl. I need to break my dry spell."

"Sure, Cath, a week and half is a darned long dry spell," Val said dryly.

The fourth girl hopped up and trod to Kesi and Val.

"Honey," Lorelei said, grinning at Kesi. "You look so sizzling you're gonna burn up before you get to the bar!" She tucked her light brown, curly hair behind her ears but the ends still tickled the sides of her face.

She said to Kesi, "That skirt is so mini you're going to have to be careful when you bend over. But I think you should unbutton a couple more buttons on that lacy blouse, you have great titties unlike poor little me," she looked down sadly at her small breasts. Even in the pushup bra, she had very little cleavage in the low-cut blouse. "Show what you got, girl."

"Come *on*," Cathy whined, heading for the door, "let's freaking go already!"

The girls grabbed their purses and left the apartment. Outside they piled into Cathy's BMW and headed for the Star Bling Saloon.

"Great," Kesi muttered as Cathy parked the car, another reminder of Martier. Stars. Her throat closed as she tried to keep her despair from erupting from her stomach, up her throat and out her mouth.

She missed him with every fiber of her being. Her dreams flooded nightly with the huge alien. She allowed her friends to drag her out of the car and gaily giggling, thrust her into the bar.

They found a round table and ordered drinks right away. Returning from the ladies room, Kesi looked down at the glass filled with amber liquid and ice cubes in front of her seat. "What's this?"

"Since you might not be legal yet, and you won't tell us, I gave the order while you were washing your hands," Cathy informed her. "That sweet shit you drink won't loosen you up, so I got you something different." With a saucy wink, her grin wide, she said, "Drink up!"

Kesi rolled her eyes at her friend, but heck, she wasn't driving, she took a sip. "Whoa," making a face, she exclaimed, "that is strong." The heat rolled down her throat freeing the constriction in it, and burned into her belly warming her, then she felt it hit her head.

"Take another swallow, girl, you'll get used to it more quickly if you drink it fast," Cathy encouraged her while guzzling her own cocktail.

In less than forty minutes, the girls were laughing loudly and slurring their words. Each one had danced numerous times, except for Kesi who declined every offer.

After turning down the fifth guy that asked Kesi to dance, Val complained, "Come on for Pete's sake, Kes, you are out here to have fun, to forget what's-his-name, and find a new fuck-buddy. That's not going to happen if you sit there like a lump turning dudes away."

Shaking her head at another guy who had just approached the table, Kesi said, "I don't want a fuck-buddy, Val, I don't want any man. I'm never dating again." Just thinking of another man's hands on her made her sick to her stomach.

Rolling their eyes, the girls all shared a look. "Well, then," Val murmured, glancing around the busy bar, the room was stacked knee deep with people. The dance floor was crowded, the music loud.

"We are going to have to help you get out of your funk, honey." Val waited a second as another man approached. Kesi didn't see him. Val and Cathy jumped up, swiveled Kesi's chair and pushed her out of it into the guy's arms.

Both the man and Kesi were taken by surprise. The man grinned broadly and quickly clinched her wrist as if he thought she was about to flee.

Kesi scowled at her friends as he dragged her off. The girls all waved cheerfully at Kesi's sour face.

"Wow," the young man said when they reached the dance floor. He pulled Kesi hard into his arms and wrapped them tightly around her.

"I saw you shoot down guy after guy, I never thought I had a chance. But, you couldn't resist these hunk-o looks, huh?" He was handsome with Patrician features, dark hair spiked on his head and bedroom brown eyes which he was seriously trying to seduce her with.

Crushing her against his chest, inches from her face, he said warmly, "You are hot, sweetheart, you and I would make a really hot couple. I'm Chad, what's your name?"

"Uh, nice to meet you, Chad, can I have a little breathing room, please?" Kesi put her small hands against his chest and tried to push back from him.

"Aw, hell, come on, sweetness, you can see we're made for each other, at least for the night. Those damn fine tits fit just right propped on my big hard chest, we're perfect together. So, you didn't tell me your name, beautiful?"

He forcefully pushed her hands down then swung his arms around her holding her tightly and shifted her back and forth to make her front rub against him.

His gaze was now not on her face, it was on her breasts that were pushed up mounding out of the top of her blouse from the pressure of his arms holding her so tightly.

"Listen, Chester, I don't feel like dancing anymore, I'm going back to my table," Kesi announced and tried to lift her arms to push at him, but he held her from leaving.

"Naw babe, come on. That's Chad, not Chester." He was annoyed at her for not falling all over him like most girls did.

"You and I are making a night of it. I'll buy you a couple more drinks, loosen up that tight, little round ass, and then take you home. With me."

For emphasis, he put his hands on her butt and jerked her pelvis into his so she could feel his hard-on. "You'll love my place, babe. I have a king-sized bed and 56" flat screen."

Angry at being manhandled, Kesi vainly tried to shove him away. She ground out quietly, "Let go of me, get your hands off me, right now."

She was pissed, but mortified too that this asshole was groping her in public, and she didn't want to call attention to them and embarrass herself.

He strengthened his grip on her bottom, purred, "Relax babe, I got ya handled. Just rest those hot titties against my chest and I will-"

"You will get your motherfucking hands off her before I break your neck and toss your fucking head away," a fierce voice darkened with brute rage made the hair on top of Chad's head stand up more than it already was. And it made Kesi swoon.

Chad scowled at Martier. "She's mine, bro, go find yourself another one. Take a hike."

The visceral growl that rumbled in Martier's chest bridged with the lethal promise in his midnight green eyes got Chad's attention and he moved his hands from Kesi's ass to her arms.

Then Chad's unsettled gaze rose to the horns swelling in the thick blond hair.

Martier hissed his last warning through descending fangs, "*Go.*"

Chad's face struck white, he removed his hands from Kesi, his fingers still curled as they were around her arms. Stepping sideways from Martier, his eyes on the alien, he walked backwards for a few feet then he spun like a top and ran.

Martier wasn't even looking at Chad, he was staring at Kesi, drinking her in like she was a cold drink in the scorching desert.

Her gaze turned from the fleeing Chad, slowly, she was scared to death to make eye contact with Martier. When she did, his green orbs had turned to pure rich black, glowing with intense proprietary indignation, and passion.

"You left me, Kesindra." Seeing a hint of fear flash in her eyes, he scowled. "Dammit, I have never hurt you or another innocent, you drive me nuts with your fear of me."

The edges of her lips tucked in. Stuffing her nerves, she said wryly, "You can't see it from your point of view, but, I am not exactly a big tough person. You tower over me and have muscle on top of muscle.

"Heavens, you took over an entire village holding it hostage. Then, according to Richard, you easily broke out of your steel chains and iron bars of the cell. You have this- this beast that rises from you, around you and you become a killing machine. You are a warrior alien, a devil, from another planet, a violent planet. You inseminated me without my knowledge or permission."

She scraped her nails over a yellow brow then pushed her palm up her forehead shoving her hair back. "I am shocked and surprised to see you here, and you look madder than a wet hen."

Her lips ticked up. "Make that a wet bull looking for something to smash your horns into. And you wonder why I fear you?"

He listened silently, watching her. His horns swelled earlier from rage, grew bigger from being in her presence.

"I would never harm you, Kesindra. I have explained to you that tis my duty to protect you, with my life if necessary. And, do not doubt I would lay my life down for yours."

Her gaze flit around his hard face, still so unsure of him. But, gads, she had missed him so much.

"Come, Kesindra, let's go where we can discuss our issues in private. Like I had said before I left the compound, you were to wait for me in **Brutální** so we could hash this out when I returned.

"Give you some time and space away from me so things could settle in your mind. I could not fucking believe it when I returned in three days and you were gone." He crossly dragged his hand roughly through his hair.

"Why has it taken you two months to come…here?" Kesi edged closer to him to feel the warmth of his strong body radiating, possessively enveloping her.

He folded his arms over his chest. "When I returned to **Brutální**, I knew I would have to transport the surviving V'Ams to the penal station. That would take some time. My plan was to take you with me. Imagine my dismay, my…ire…when I got to the village and you were gone. I had to take the prisoners and only then could I come for you."

His infuriated gaze trolled hungrily up and down her body. He declared, "Trust me, Kesindra, I am not leaving this fucking planet without you. You have had time to get over things. You still have a problem then we can work on it, while on my airjet on our way to Nasitar, my home planet."

While talking quietly, Martier took her arm and walked her to her table. Her friends gawked wide-eyed and mouths dropping at the huge, dangerous looking male with actual horns on his head.

"Holy shit, Kes," Cathy gushed, waving her heated face, "does he have a brother?"

Martier grabbed Kesi's purse and handed it to her. She arched a brow at him. "How did you know that was mine?"

"Ah, *několika*, I have been watching you all night. I wanted to just…watch you, soak you in. And," he glanced at the girls, "I wanted you to have some time with your friends before I came and got you, and took you…home."

He saluted a few fingers to his forehead at the girls. "Nice to meet you all," he said exhibiting a slaying smile.

Seeing his fangs when he smiled, Val proclaimed, "Hell, I think my panties are wet." Beside her Lorelei moaned.

Suzanna sighed, "And a killer accent, with a foreign pet name for her. Kes, you have all the luck."

His attention on Kesi, Martier wrapped an arm around her and said, "Let us go home, baby."

"Oh, um, wait-" Kesi looked to her friends for help, but they were all gawking at Martier like he was a movie star.

"Say goodbye to your friends, Kesindra," he told her as he tugged her from the table.

"Uh, g- goodbye, I'll, write, or something," Kesi mumbled at the grinning women.

Martier drew her along with him, away from the girls to the front of the building.

All the women's envious eyes followed the couple cross the crowded saloon and disappear out the door.

Martier kept her moving until they reached his rental car. When he opened the passenger door for her to get in, Kesi refused. She asked warily, "Where are we going?"

"To your apartment. We will do our talking in private."

"Uh," Kesi demurred, knowing if they were alone they wouldn't be doing much talking. His eyes were already heavy with lust, they hadn't stopped roaming her body since he was on the dance floor running Chad off.

"Get in, Kesindra. Sorry, not taking no for an answer. You owe me that much after deserting me." He glared at her and waited, not patiently. Even if she balked, she was going whether she wanted to or not.

She could see the determination in the set of his jaw. He wasn't letting her just walk away. Not that she wanted to. Kesi slid onto the seat, hooked the seatbelt and clutched her fingers together over her purse to still their shaking.

Martier closed her door and strode around to the driver's side and got in.

He glanced at her. Saw her pale face, clenched hands, the strained anxiety in her beautiful blues. He craved to touch her, but, she was already on edge.

"Kesindra," he worked to keep his exasperation out of his voice, "I swear, I am not going to harm you. I never would. Stop being afraid of me."

She didn't respond, just stared out the window.

With a sigh, he turned the engine over and drove out of the lot and down the street.

They were at her apartment in a silent fifteen minutes. He parked in front.

She glanced at him. "You know where I live?"

"Aye, sweetheart, I know everything about the woman I love and plan to marry as soon as possible so she cannot flee me again." He exited the car then went around the hood to get her.

Opening her door, he wasn't giving her a chance to protest; he reached in, grabbed her arm and gently pulled her out. When he closed the door, she leaned against it.

"Martier, you love me? I-"

He cut her off with the sudden pressure of his mouth on hers. Cradling her jaw, he slanted his head and put a thumb on the tip of her chin, pushed it down to force her mouth open then buried his tongue inside with a shuddered groan.

His kiss was aggressive and greedy, hard and needy and he was unrelenting, making up for two months' worth of kisses, until she pushed back with a panted gasp.

"Martier, please, stop," she begged, setting the back of her hand over her mouth.

"Fine. We will go inside," he said, releasing her. His hair had grown since the beginning of the mission, now it flopped over one eye making him look unnaturally boyish. He impatiently shoved the lock back.

She put her hands up. "No, wait, I think it would be better for us to talk out here."

His dark green eyes narrowed at her, mouth firmed. "You had your opportunity to talk in Brutální, but you chose not to. So, we are done with talking. We are going inside, and you know damned well what is going to happen," he reached to catch her arm.

Chapter Twenty-Nine

Kesi turned her body to avoid his grasp. "No, wait, you can't keep taking my options away from me. I want to talk. Right here."

The smile that curved on his face was dangerously sly. "Sweetheart, we have nothing to talk about. In the morning, you will pack up your shit and get in this car and to my airjet. From there we will go to my planet where we will live. Together. As husband and wife, raising our family. End of story."

"Martier, I can't just- up and leave. I have a job, a home. I can't live on a totally different planet for heaven's sake! Going to Původně was the first time I'd ever even been out of Ships Bay. Even the academy and FBI satellite office is here. You can't expect me to- to go into space!"

"I do expect you to go where I go. I am going to Nasitar, and you are coming with me. No point in yakking about it. The only thing I plan on doing with my mouth tonight is shoving my tongue down your throat, biting those pretty little nipples of yours, licking those juicy nether lips, sucking your-"

Mortified she yelped, "Martier! Please! I have neighbors, stop!"

"I said let us take it inside, but nay, you wanted to stay out here, so," he shrugged, "okay." He threw his hand around her back pulling her to him and shoved his other hand under her blouse. Letting go of her back, he pushed both hands under her blouse, grabbing both breasts.

Clenching and squeezing with a ravenous growl, he ground in a rasp, "I missed these, baby, I missed all of you, but these sweet tits, ah, how could you take them from me?"

He kneaded her plump flesh so hard she couldn't move away from his fierce groping. Grunting moans escaped with his long fingers feeling and gripping each heavy breast.

Kesi's hands fell on his shoulders, her fingers curled over the broad width. She clung to him as his growls spooled silk from her sex.

"I warned you, *několika,* you will never close your legs to me again," a deeper growl came with his words as he moved his hands behind her. Pushing the back of her skirt up, he shoved his palms down inside her panties, and gripped her bottom.

Lowering his head to her breasts, he sucked at a nipple through the blouse while grumbling possessively, "Why are you wearing this slutty shit? You go out on the town for every fucking male around to ogle you, cop a feel?"

He moved his mouth to her other nipple, wetting it through the material and squeezed her butt until she whimpered from the roughness of his large hard hands.

"M- Martier, my friends said my clothes, uh," the breath oozed raggedly from her throat as he caressed her bare skin.

Pinching, kneading her rounded bottom, while he sucked at her nipples.

"Listen, Martier, stop, my neighbors," she cried through quivering moans.

He lifted his head, moved his hands to pluck at the buttons on her blouse ignoring Kesi's weak efforts to stop him. Spreading her blouse open, he gazed down at her breasts nestled in peach silk, the flesh mounding over the soft cups. "You want to go inside, *několika*?"

He pushed the blouse half off her shoulders. "Just say the word, I am amenable. Or, we can finish this right here. On the ground, on the car, in the car, against the wall," he bumped a shoulder, grabbing handfuls of her breasts, "wherever."

When she said nothing, just dug her fingers into his shoulders and writhed into his hands, he muttered, "I have waited too fucking long for you, Kesindra, we can do it standing right here if that is what you want. Better make your decision fast, I am at the end of my leash. Two months seemed like two years without you."

Kesi's neck arched, her head fell back with the sultry moans he was inciting in her. She felt his thigh move between her legs and nudge them apart to press his burgeoning erection against her core.

There was no doubt he was going to do exactly as he said and she was powerless to stop him. And she didn't want to stop him. "Okay."

"Inside?" he mumbled, his mouth sucking the swell of her breast that the bra exposed.

"Uhh," a gravely groan at his lips and teeth on her, biting and licking any bare skin he could reach. She nodded and gasped, "*Yes*."

Instantly, he stuffed his hands under her bottom and lifted her to wrap her legs around his hips, and plowed his mouth over hers, reaping her sweetness, her adorably hot daintiness.

Rolling a forearm under her bottom to hold her, he pushed her shirt further off her shoulders; down her back and cupped her fullness with his free hand.

Kesi kissed him back with burning need she had suppressed since she'd left him. Their lips stuck together, melding, welding with their heat. She started to unbutton his shirt and felt him smile against her mouth as his tongue continued besieging hers.

When they reached the door, he pulled his mouth from hers. Breathing heavy, his cheeks dark red, horns swelling huge, he rasped, "The key, where is your key, baby?"

Brushing her chest over his, Kesi said, vaguely, "My purse, car…" She pushed her fingers up to drag through his hair, grab his blond locks and tug hard on them. Her thumbs stroking over his cheeks, his temples, a curved horn.

"Fuck, cannot wait, too far," he muttered. "I will just kick it in-"

"No! Purse," she slurred, relishing the feel of her soft flesh on his rock hard pecs.

"Zeus," he growled, and pushed her up so she was draped over his shoulder, her head hanging down his back. Her giggle as her head flopped against this back made him smile.

Martier hurried back to the car, got her purse, took the key out and handed the purse to her.

He'd shoved her skirt back up and was feeling her ass over her panties. Sticking his fingers up under the silk trying to get them in the crease between them, ignoring her squealing protests, until he reached the building.

Unlocking the door, he stepped inside, slammed it shut, dropped her and shoved her against the door.

A small oomph burst from Kesi at the sudden impact.

Martier took her hands and pushed them up over her head holding them to the door, and settled his mouth back on hers with a soul ravaging kiss.

Letting go with one of his hands, he stroked down her body, over her breast, squeezed it then ran his palm down further. Her skirt was up around her thighs; he pushed under it and shoved his hand in her panties and harshly gripped her mound.

"Oh!" she squeaked.

Against her mouth he murmured, "Too rough, baby? I have missed every part of you too much to be gentle."

Her arms stretched over her head, Martier's tongue circling, licking her lips, his hand cupping her sex. He rubbed his palm over it before gripping it hard again. Her hips pushed into his hand.

"No, not too rough, more-" she gasped as his tongue found its way inside her mouth then down her throat.

A grunt was his response. Martier picked her up again, her legs around his hips, "Which way to your bedroom?"

Kesi was nipping at his mouth, his tongue, pushing aside the lapels of his shirt to feel his chest. Sifting her fingers through the thick hair, she mumbled hazy, "Down hall."

Only seeing one hall, Martier trod down it to her bedroom. He set her on her feet.

Lightheaded with passion, she swayed, he sat down on a chair and pulled her to stand between his legs.

Her head cloudy, Kesi went to put her hands on his shoulders but missed and fell forward her palms landing on his thighs.

His grin big. "Oh, nice, *několika,* you want to suck me? I am good with it, but I have to do something first."

Her face red at his words, she pushed off his thighs to stand straight.

Martier stuck his hand in her hair, pulled her in for a tight hard kiss until she was dazed again. Releasing her hair, he grasped her blouse and jerked in down her arms and off and tossed it.

He caught her legs with his knees to hold her still and reached behind her, unclasped her bra, pulled it off, dropped it, then bent over to pull her heels off.

"Martier," her protest was faint.

"Hush, just stand still." He cupped her breasts, kneading them. Bending his head, he kissed one then the other then reached for her skirt.

He worked his hands behind her to unlatch the skirt but couldn't figure how it was fastened. His forehead furrowing, he turned her around to look at the buttons and hooks. With no patience, he gripped the skirt and tore it open then shoved it down her legs.

"Martier! That's not my skirt!"

"Huh, slutty shit anyway. We will swing by her place on our way out and I will give her money for another. Now, hush." He stuck his big fingers in her tiny panties and pushed them down, lifted each foot to get them off.

She swiveled around to face him. His gaze went straight to her bare breasts, his hands followed. "Martier, I'm...naked and you...aren't."

"Aye. You have punishment coming."

"What! No! No Martier, don't you even think about-"

He clasped her waist, lifted her and set her belly down over his lap. One hand on her back, he caressed her bare butt with the other.

"Martier, come on, don't do this," her voice muffled, she tried to kick her legs but he pushed them down then slapped her bottom, hard.

She shrieked, "That hurt!"

"Aye. You left me, Kesindra, without a word, a note, you just disappeared." He smacked her, she shrieked again. "You know how I felt when I got there and you were gone?" Another sharp slap, her butt turning pink shook with the action.

Setting his palm on her skin, he leaned over near her head and whispered, "You ever leave me again, *několika,* you do not want to see my wrath."

Muffled, she cried through her hanging hair, "That's stalker talk, Martier, you said you would never hurt me, you're spanking me!"

"Ah, sweetheart," he stroked his palm from her shoulder, down the inner curve of her lower back to her bottom where he smacked her again. "You know I am not hurting you. Just a bit of stinging. If there is a next time though, I promise you will not be sitting for a week." He moved his hand to push her thighs apart.

"What- are you doing?"

"I am not done with your punishment, *několika.*" He moved his hand that was on her back to her thighs keeping them spread, and slipped his hand between them to cuddle her sex. She was already wet from their kissing and his fondling her.

When he drew his fingers over her folds, pinched them, with a tiny whimper her silk poured into his hand. He pushed her thighs apart as far as he could and dipped his thick finger inside her.

Moans trickled from her crunched throat, she wriggled on his strong thighs.

"You like that, *tím rostia*?"

When she didn't answer, his voice dark and low, rumbled, "Answer me, Kesindra, you like that?"

Her head upside down she said with a hitch in her voice, "*Y-es.*"

He grunted and slid two fingers inside her. Pushing her thighs hard open, he pulled his fingers out and slid them up her slit, then back inside her, curled them over her hot spots then back out and up her slit then he flicked her bud and she gasped, her legs loosened.

He did it again and again with little smacks in between until he heard her rapid breathing, her skin darkened, the moans bunching then fluidly rushed out of her throat. Her legs tightened, she was on the cusp of coming, he stopped and moved his hand.

"Martier! Let me come…" squirming to find his hands, her voice dribbled to a whine.

He did it several more times, brought her to the peak but wouldn't let her go over. He suddenly lifted her to stand on her shaking feet, she almost toppled over but he held her. Then he bent and removed his boots and socks.

Standing, he shuffled out of his shirt and tossed it then grabbed his belt, yanked it open, his button, the zipper went down and he shoved his pants down and off.

Kesi watched him, his steel rod flush up against his belly. So on fire, so hot, shudders rolled up and down her body from her feet to her head to strike back at her core. She moved her hands to his sex, but he grabbed them.

"Nay, sweet. We are going to talk first."

"Huh?" She tried to fight him, she was just on the edge, at the very curve ready to sail over. Tugging at her hands, she couldn't get free of him. "You want to talk *now*?" she wailed.

His chuckle a deep rumble, he said, "Actually, it will be a short conversation." He slipped his hand between her legs and played with her folds, pressing them together, rolling his thumb around her clit then lightly but sharply, slapped her sex.

Kesi bent back, her body jerking with a shock of violent heat at the sudden slap. Her legs shook, she almost came, but he stopped again.

"Martier, stop doing this to me. Stop controlling me. Let me come." Angry, she moved her free hand to her sex, but he laughed and captured it.

"Nay. You will come when you agree to what I say."

"And what is that?" her voice an irritated, unresolved, whine. "You can't do this every time you want me to say something or agree to something. You can't forcibly hold me down and work me up but not let me come until I do as you say."

"Aye, I can, as long as it works." His fingers went back to her tender moist nether lips and stroked her. "Say you will go with me, without argument or hesitation, to my galaxy, my planet, and there will be no regrets, no reneging."

Her head fell back with a shuddering moan, her legs spread apart so he could touch her, finger her, inside and out. Her hips palpitated to his ministrations, seeking a rhythm for relief.

When his hand clutched her breast and pinched her nipple, she almost cried at the pleasure of his hands.

"Kesindra. We are meant to be. Mates for eternity. There is nothing here for you. A job that although you proved yourself above and beyond, they will never raise you higher in rank because of that one regrettable episode, that was in no way your fault. You were as much a victim of that as anyone. You have no family, a shoddy little apartment, your friends are too new in your life to make a difference."

Her head flopped over forward, her hair covering her face, she leaned over and put her hands on his thighs, her legs were giving out.

"But, I want," she breathed deeply, "my job. A job where I can," she gasped at his wrestling fingers circling her pussy then penetrating it, "investigate, put away the bad guys."

"Baby, you can do that with me. Once you are immortal, not before then," he said firmly. "We will fight side-by-side. You can save worlds, universes, instead of one small planet of people." He brushed at her sex with his emerging claws, she jolted then shuddered, a scream lodged in her throat.

Gasping, Kesi could barely stand the inferno of her own body, she cried, "We are…different," her hips twitched as he worked his claws around her sensitive flesh.

Sheathing the claws, he moved his fingers harder inside her feeling her sex rock into them, striving to make him let her come.

"Are you going to say you don't want to be with me? That our slight differences, the fact that I gave you immortality so we can be together forever without asking you first, you are going to let that keep us apart?"

Her hips pushed and rolled at his fingers. When he crushed her breast in his hand and his mouth sank onto it, he bit at her nipple, flicked it with his tongue, she cried out in delirium of delight, and agony of no relief.

"Answer me, *několika,* answer me one way or the other and I will let you have your release. Tell me you don't want this, desire this, what we have, what I can make your body feel. You think you can get this from any other man?"

He forced her legs wider and was ruthless and unrelenting with his fingers moving harder inside her, thumbing her clit until her body was almost rotating with it.

"Answer me, do you want to be with me?" Pray Zeus she says yes because he loved her. Enough to let her go if that's what she chose?

No. He could never imagine his life without her. The past two months without her had torn him up. The fear that she was here alone doing all the reckless shit she normally did? Hell no.

Martier wondered if she said no, after he forced her onto his ship how long it would take for her to get over her anger and forgive him. Learn to love him. Because, hell or high water, he was not leaving without her.

"Ahh," guttural groans ratcheted from her chest to her throat. "Yes, Martier, I want to go with you, be with you."

Relief swelled his chest then emptied it with his held breath. "You sure, sweetheart, there will be no going back. I take you from here, you are mine, you will not come back here unless you want a brief visit at some point."

A soft smile, her lids heavy over shining blues, Kesi tipped her head back and peered at him with a nod. "I missed you so much, Martier, when I thought I was never going to see you again I couldn't bear it. I don't ever want to be away from you again. Where you go, I will go. No regrets, no complaining, no turn backs."

"Shit, Kesindra." He stood up, lifted her to the bed, laid her down and pushed her legs apart. Climbing between them on the mattress, he shoved violently into her with one hard thrust.

A guttural scream flew from her as her body shook uncontrollably; undulated so hard he had to hold her down.

Her back arched, head fell back with his name another scream on her lips and she came with rocket ships and gunfire. Convulsing so violently her sex crushed his phallus driving his growl into a harsh groan.

It was too much, he couldn't hold back. Martier drove into her with everything he had, so fast, so hard, deep as he could slam, so fast his fangs couldn't get out and get to her neck. He came like a nuclear bomb exploding, the shock of it shooting into the air with mushroom clouds, all sparks and fire.

He still thrust again and again, the veins in his neck straining.

Kesi convulsed another orgasm around him, it was the catalyst for the rest of his seeds to erupt from his balls hurtling inside of her.

Martier pounded a few more times, then spent, he collapsed. His breathing like the racing roar of a rampant lion, he slid slightly to the side but stayed on top of her, in her.

He lay panting until his pulse calmed and his breathing steadied, then he shifted slightly to the side of her but retained their connection.

In only seconds, both fell into a sated, happy doze.

Epilogue

Her drowsy eyelids lifted ten minutes later. She moved a hand to hold onto his bicep that still bulged from his vigorous straining, the other slid into his hair. She tugged gently then stroked the soft strands.

Smiling, Kesi thought it was like a raging grizzly had fucked her in a rampage and then died on top of her grunting and rumbling. The thought made her laugh.

Weak as a kitten, his face in her hair, he mumbled, "What is so funny, *tím rostia?* I am sorry I could not last, tis been too long. I needed you too badly. It was too fast for other things to participate." Referring to his fangs, claw crimping, and the pebble bins. His hand found her breast, he held onto it.

"Hmm, I'm just likening you to a bear."

He smiled into her hair, playing with her breast.

"Martier?"

The seriousness in her voice made him shrug off her. His arm rolled around her shoulders pulling her against him. "What is it baby, regrets already now that I let you come?"

He had let Kesi voice her choice, her decision. Regardless of her answer though, he was taking her with him anyway, but he didn't want her to accuse him of not giving her a choice. Luckily she chose the right one.

Shaking her head with a smile she replied, "No. Did you mean what you said about me fighting with you? By your side?"

Nodding, he answered, "Aye. After you are immortal, and after I have seen to your proper training, you will be with me. Except for the really dangerous felons. I cannot, will not, risk you going after them.

"You will have my immorality but you will not have my strength, and other...physical weapons I have. You can still be injured. I will not allow you to be captured or harmed. But you can do all the investigating you want."

Twirling a finger in his hair, she said, "Hmm. You aren't telling me tales to get me to agree, are you?"

His chest bumped with a grunt. "I have told you, *několika*, I do not lie. I may leave things out that I don't think you need to know about at the time, but I will not lie to you. You will be with me, until you have the babes. Then you will stay safely on Nasitar with my brothers and their families."

"What?" She went to sit up but he held her down. "Babies?"

"Aye, my babes. Our babes. Kesindra, I want a family. I mean after a while. For a long time I want it to be just you and me, for a very long time. Then I want children. What do you say?"

Her sigh safe, relaxed, well loved, and satiated for now. Kesi smiled at Martier beaming over her and murmured, "I say, my love, that is perfect."

The End.

www.ingramcontent.com/pod-product-compliance
Lightning Source LLC
Chambersburg PA
CBHW021432240626
47153CB00001B/115